Mastermind Malfred

by

Alexandria May Ausman

This book is a work of fiction. Any references to historical events, real people, or real places, are used fictitiously. Other names, characters, places, and events are products of the author's imagination, and any resemblance to actual events or persons, living or dead, is entirely coincidental.

Book cover design by Alexandria May Ausman
Editor: Jon M. Ausman

Library of Congress Control Number: 2023924308

ISBN: 978-1-963335-01-9 (ebook)
ISBN: 978-1-963335-00-2 (paperback)

Published By:
Ausman & Cousins, LLC
1700 North Monroe Street
Suite 11, Box 284
Tallahassee, Florida 32303-0501

For author interviews: ausman@embarqmail.com

Das Kaiser Haus Series

The Rise of the Priceless (Chapters 1 to 10)
Metal Illness (Chapters 11 to 19)
Jonas the Vampire (Chapters 20 to 29)
Prince of the Elders (Chapters 30 to 40)
Leo's Lamb (Chapters 41 to 50)
Mastermind Malfred (Chapters 51 to 58)
Priceless Lost (coming soon)
Felicity's Child (coming soon)
Broken Silver (coming soon)

The Collar King Series

Return to Das Kaiser Haus (coming soon)

The Psycho Series

Cemetery Kid (Chapters 1 to 20)
Stop Calling Me Psycho (Chapters 21 to 33)
Motor-Psycho (Chapters 34 to 44)
Delusion of the Collar and the Key (Chapters 45 to 53)
Brutality's Prisoner (Chapters 54 to 64)
Aesthetic Akathisia (Chapters 65 to 74)
Metallic Burden (Chapters 75 to 83)

27 Masters Series

Anita the Benevolent (Chapters 1 to 7)
The Beast and the Witch (Chapters 8 to 16)
High Priestess of Schizophrenia (coming soon)

Book 6 Characters: Mastermind Malfred

Agnete: mother of Christian
Anna: a Haus Femdom
Barnum: a deceased Elder of the Haus
Ben: a deceased Haus trainee
Bladrick: an Elder of the Haus
Casper the Ghost: another name for Malfred
Christian: the anger and lust shard
Christian Axel: a Haus submissive, the Priceless
Claus: an Elder of the Haus
Cora: a FemDom of the Haus, the Fur Queen
Debbie: Meine Liebe's sexual psychopathic and sadistic mother
Der Goldene Hund: the Voice or the Boss shard; the Conscious shard
Der Makellos: German Shepherd named "The Unblemished"
Drexel: a deceased Elder of the Haus
Edgar: a black collar boy
Egon: Haus seduction Master and trainer
Elsa: a Haus black collar
Evelynn: a kitchen black collar
Felix: deceased black collar door guard
Geraldine: deceased Haus trainee
Gerard: stepfather of Christian Axel
Grisham: a Haus Dominant
Gretta: a Haus Elder, the Silk Queen

Gunter: a black collar Torture Master
Gustov: a Haus Dominant
Heidi: deceased Dungeon Mistress; sister of Helga
Helga: deceased Dungeon Mistress; sister of Heidi
Hemmel: deceased Supreme Dungeon Master
Ivar: a black collar Torture Master
Jonas: an Elder of the Haus
Julius: a deceased Haus Dominant
Karl: a Haus Dominant, father of Ryker
Leo: a Haus Dominant
Mad Max: the sadistic shard of Maximillian, aka the Heart and Judgment
Mad Maxx: husband of Meine Liebe; a Haus Dominant
Mad Maxx: the masochistic shard, aka the Brain and Guilt
Malfred: a Haus Dominant
Max: the Soul shard
Maximillian: the submissive name given to Christian by Peter
Maximillian: the seductive shard, aka the Libido
Maxximillian: the submissive adopted by the Elders
Meine Liebe: submissive and spouse of Mad Maxx
Mila: a Haus FemDom
Olaf: Haus black collar door guard
Peter: a Dominant of Der Kaiser Haus; best trainer of submissives
Russell: spouse of Debbie, a switch
Ryker: deceased Haus trainee
Sofie: schizophrenic sister of Leo; known as Maus
Stefan: a deceased Haus Dominant

Tamina: Malfred's valuable silver
The Lambs: Abelard, Annette, Geraldine, Milo, Ryker
Vilber: Haus black collar door guard
Xavier: deceased Fur King of the Haus

Prologue

In book six of Das Kaiser Haus series, Mad Maxx finds himself the hostage of a new enemy. Through a brutal series of events, the Voter called Malfred the Mastermind has trapped the boy in his metal. As the Elders rush to save their Priceless collar, Mad Maxx's schizophrenic symptoms intensify.

The plot thickens while the leaders of Kaiser House prepare for an epic battle that refuses to take prisoners. The shards of Mad Maxx, always ready to serve their Masters, grants a perfect service return for those who put them into harm's way.

The five shards are left to fend for themselves when Der Hund is accidentally sent into the void. They find the task of discovering a path to escape their deadly situation far too complex to handle without their General's help. Maximillian "births" a brilliant solution that they all hope will ultimately set the boy Mad Maxx free. That is if Taube can manage to remember the reason he was created in the first place.

Madness and cruelty rein in the realm of Mastermind Malfred. Unless the shards can halt their strengthening psychosis, and deepening despair, all seems lost. They will need to do the unthinkable to accomplish the unbelievable. By seeking the aid of the man that they hate the most, Master Peter.

Language in italics is a conversation between the adult male Master Mad Maxx and his female submissive Meine Liebe.

Chapter 51: Pool Party

I wailed and screamed till I was hoarse from Master Grisham's brutal dry sodomy. When at last he moaned out loudly in his apex I was near despondent, and close to fainting. Master Malfred would not allow me to find mercy in unconsciousness. He ordered Master Gustov to get a cupful of pool water to rouse my fading alertness. I heard him speak, but it sounded far away. I thought he told the brutes I had to be awake during the blood bonding process or there could be questions of my compliance.

I wondered how the hell he could refer to rape as such a thing as willing in anyway. I sputtered and gasped as the water was thrown into my face. It managed to drag me back kicking and screaming to the harsh reality of that cold stone floor. I came back from the void just as Master Gustov was taking his place for his mount.

Master Malfred saw my look of terror as the Dominant Gustov cut his member as the others had done. I kicked at him with all my might and let out a long raspy screech of desperation. Master Malfred grabbed the top of my hair with his free hand then leaned into my ear.

He chuckled with much wickedness. "Calm down, just one more to go. This agony is almost over, meine taube (dove). Relax and endure what you must. When Gustov is finished, you are trapped in your metal. I will have you for my own for all your life. This was always your fate Christian Axel. You were created to serve me. I must say, you have done me proud. Who knew Peter and Agnette would create a true Priceless. I thought I would merely get a false one from that pair of nothings, but again you have habitually exceeded my wildest expectations, meine taube. A winning horse of legendary prowess from those two nags. Even with my genius I couldn't have predicted such a fruitful outcome. Now, brace yourself, Gustov is not very nice, but it is only this once. Never again will you have to tolerate his lust. He is owed this taste of the thing he can only dream of for the rest of his days. Gustov, move it. Cora is due any minute." He yelled out leaving me near mind blown at his words.

Master Malfred was correct. Master Gustov was rougher than either of them. He slammed into me with all his youthful strength. I cried out in agony while the bastard treated me like a punching bag with his cock. He was yelling out in pure thrill when a knocking began at the sealed doors of the pool room.

Master Gustov paid the noise no mind. He shouted out in orgasm while Master Malfred directed Master Grisham to let Mistress Cora in to witness this horror triple blood bonding. Well, gang rape to be brutally honest.

The newest Voting Council Member, he had replaced Julius when Master Malfred raised him in a rush, fell over on me panting and mumbling about his enjoyment of his taste of the Forbidden silver. I laid there weeping uncontrollably unable to find the strength to even bother struggling anymore.

There was no reason to fight any further. The deed was done, and Master Malfred had won. I was trapped in my collar, and "married" to four of the foulest motherfuckers in the whole Haus. Mistress Cora had arrived to seal my doom for all time.

She smiled while she stood over me. I couldn't escape her humored gaze. I was being pinned to the floor by Master Malfred and under the weight of the still coupled Master Gustov. I closed my eyes shuddering with despair. I wished I had been able to get that breath of the blue water to end my life. This fate was far worse than growing a tree in the yard.

Mistress Cora snorted. "Well, Malfred you are indeed a clever sonofabitch. I would have never thought of getting the job done this way. Bravo."

Master Malfred smiled with evil. "That is why I do all the thinking my love. Now, you witness, this collar is blood bonded times three this very night. There are no further bonds allowed by Haus law. The Priceless is now three-fourths the Voting Council's property. Jonas is the only Elder to have any rights. He has been effectively neutralized. He can no longer obtain his precious female Priceless now that the male is trapped in his collar."

Mistress Cora frowned. "Well, one slight problem there Malfred. This thing likely didn't bond to you brutes willingly. I find that hard to believe and I knew the plan.

Gretta will believe it when the thing says it was raped. Your bonds will be no good."

Master Malfred chuckled. "He won't dispute our claims to his silver, Cora. If he claims rape he will be put to the yard. You won't tell your Mistress Gretta you were raped now will you Mad Maxx?" The beast Dominant looked down into my weeping face.

I opened my eyes. "Ja, I will tell her the truth of this dishonor. I tell you now Mistress Cora, I never agreed to any of this. Call the fucking Guard. I wish to be killed. I will not fight the Russians, but I will scream rape till the Haus comes down," I wailed out in despair.

Mistress Cora stepped back with an expression of surprise. Master Grisham shot a look of terror at Master Malfred. Master Malfred merely smiled and shook his head, appearing unaffected that I was saying I would not comply with his plans.

Master Gustov uncoupled with me and stood up. "You never thought of that did you Malfred? The Priceless would rather die than be trapped in the collar of his. Everyone knows no Priceless lives long because of that. I for one am grateful I got my taste before the legend gets sent to feed the grass like all those before him." He began laughing, sounding quite humored at this grave situation.

Master Malfred scoffed. "I did think of all this, fools. Mad Maxx, you listen to me very closely, meine taube. You will tell Gretta and anyone else that you did agree to this triple blood bonding. If you dare to open your mouth otherwise in the next twenty-four hours, then you can kiss your beloved Leo goodbye. Are we clear?"

My eyes went wide as Peter hauled Master Leo, who was struggling but no match for my strong father, to stand with all the others staring down at me. I looked up at Leo's tear drenched face with fear making my heart speed to painful levels. I saw Peter pull out a knife and hold it to Leo's throat with a smile on his face daring me to say another word about rape.

Master Leo wailed out. "Meine hase (bunny), tell Gretta the truth. Don't worry about Leo. I am not scared of these brutes. We die together and I will be honored to travel to the river with you by my side." Master Grisham jumped forward and backhanded Master Leo with much violence.

Mistress Cora yelled out, "Enough, Grisham, what the fuck do you think you are doing? Leo is an Elder. You will not handle him like a common silver. Keep your fucking hands to yourself or find yourself out of this Haus." Master Grisham growled but stepped away from the bleeding Master Leo as Grisham had busted his lips with his cruel blow.

Peter sighed loudly. "Speak the fuck up, Maximillian. Will you comply or do I cut this sonofabitches throat and be done with it."

I shook my head. "I will comply, let Master Leo go. Don't hurt him I beg of you, Master."

Master Malfred smiled with glee. "You see Gustov, you need only to speak the boy's language. There now, meine taube. You dry those tears. Being my submissive is not so bad. I am most fair, and you will be treated well all your days. Cora, you can begin your witness of the blood bondings now that this is settled. Mad Maxx has agreed to our offer to marriage with all of us."

I began to weep louder as the man lifted my upper half. He then wrapped his arms around my chest hugging me tightly from behind and ordered Grisham to restrain my hands for the Mistress's examination. Mistress Cora pulled out a rubber glove and lubrication preparing herself for the seeking of blood and semen within the boy.

Maximillian pulled me around to look at him. "At that time, a woman could not bond with another female because only the seed with blood could be counted as the blood bond. That has been changed, but since you will never be bonding with a female, Meine Liebe, there is no reason to discuss the way that is done. I will only say yuck. Either way it is beyond humiliating and disgusting."

I nodded while shooting Maxmillian (Master Mad Maxx) a hateful look.

He smiled and shrugged. "Well, sorry about that nastiness, Meine Liebe, but it was the only way I could keep you. I hope you can forgive that in time."

I nodded again while sighing. He kissed my forehead then turned me back around in his lap. I snuggled back into his unit saying nothing.

There was no point complaining to him, or anyone, about it. What was done was done. The twenty-four hours had long since passed, and even if I could have argued I was raped, I no longer felt the need to undo his bond. I did love him with all my heart and was happy to call him my husband. Though I was too young to understand the seriousness of any of it yet.

Besides, I couldn't undo his blood bonding, and neither could he. Now that I had heard how many blood bondings, and the horror behind them, he had suffered, I sort of felt sheepish complaining about that one I had endured with him. Two, if you count the one he never told anyone about.

QUICK NOTE: His story has earned my respect (and awe) by this time. I no longer felt the need to interrupt. I wanted to hear how this horror show had somehow ended with him winning the game. I also had finally come to understand he was not being irrationally cruel in his treatment of me. I had learned the man I called Master was just like me in so many ways.

Master Mad Maxx, also known as Christian Axel, was and is a product of the torturous environment that held him hostage since childhood. He had endured many rapes, other unwanted sexual encounters, outrageous exploitation, beatings, isolation, torture, and betrayed by almost everyone he ever knew. He too was unloved by his parents, and even could claim incestuous abuse at the hands of his father.

Even at the tender age of nine, I realized he was telling me his own painful story to convince me that if he "the Priceless Mad Maxx" could make it to the top with so many aligned against him, then Meine Liebe could do it also.

For me, his tale was no longer entertainment; it was the secret to survival in my own brutal world. On with the story.

Master Leo yelled out just as the Head of the Haus approached me. "You may be able to keep Christian Axel from claiming he was assaulted and forced but you cannot keep Leo from telling on all you. They will not put me in the yard for that. They will end him, and I will happily follow him with my own hand, Malfred. So, you can check all you like Cora. It will do none of you any good."

Master Malfred shot a look of fear at Peter then back to Master Leo. "Nein. You will keep your mouth shut too, Leo. If you speak up during the twenty-four-hour annulment stage, then I will make sure that Gretta doesn't put the boy to the yard. I will get her to pass the sentence of confinement for life. Then the Council will lock him in a cell down in the dungeons. Then Grisham, Peter, Gustov will join me to attack him every day without any mercy. Peter here will drown you in that pool and make it look like an accident before you can get to the boy to aid him. You will die knowing your precious little silver is the tortured bitch without end nor hope. Do you want to test me? I dare you, Leo. I have my ways of making people disappear, even Elders."

Master Leo's eyes went wide. "Did you hear this, Cora. Malfred just threatened to kill an Elder. I demand to have him arrested and brought before the Head of the Council."

Mistress Cora rolled her eyes at that. "I heard nothing, Leo. You would do well to take his words to heart. No one would miss your backstabbing ass, especially me. Hell, I would come watch Peter teach you to breath under water for the thrill of it."

Master Leo stared at her with hate filling his expression. "You are one to call another a backstabber. You are a fucking Elder bitch. You side with these nothings and ignore your brothers."

She chuckled with much bitterness. "Schwuler brothers that hate the woman. Not my kind, Leo. I side with the winners fool. Are you going to shut that fucking mouth, or do we shut it for you? Make up that fickle mind of yours. I am tired of this arguing. I have a fucking blood bonding to witness, and the blood is congealing."

Master Leo shot me a look of pity then looked at the floor. "It seems I have no choice for now. I will keep my tongue still if you can promise Mad Maxx is treated with kindness and a loving touch. I do apologize, meine hase they will hurt you worse than they already have if I seek to aid you with reporting this crime."

I nodded. "I forgive you, Master. I understand that they have us. Best not to struggle, but I assure you, every fucking one of you, I will kill you the second I get my chance." I wailed out with fresh tears erupting from my eyes. *I didn't even know I could cry that much. The flesh is amazing stuff, you know? Hey, wait a second, you do know. I have seen you cry for hours. fucking Mad Max is the brute, ja? I nodded but said nothing.*

Master Malfred joined the others in there laughing at my threat. "Ah, Peter, a real fighter just like you said. Even now in his defeat he lays claim to future acts of violence. Such a pleasure to behold. I am going to enjoy this treasure. I never have officially thanked you for bringing him into my life. What more could a man want? Soon, Malfred will have it all. Now, Cora, can we hurry this up? I would like to get this beauty home before midnight, ja?"

I waited till Mistress Cora leaned down to go for my hindside with her finger. With all the strength I had I kicked that bitch right in her face. She went flying backward to her ass with a surprised wail of pain.

I began laughing wildly through my tears. "The horse face got kicked by the jackass for a change. Come back here and I will kick you again." I howled out in maniacal laugher losing my shit right there as Master Gustov rushed to aid the Mistress back to her legs.

Master Grisham let go of my arms and backhanded me with enough strength to break my bottom lip nearly in half. Master Malfred let out a roar of fury.

"I told you to keep your fucking hands off my Priceless, you Gott damned brute. Gustov, restrain his legs. Grisham, you hold his arms still or I will use that penknife of mine to cut more than your cock, you motherfucker."

Master Malfred squeezed my chest till I could barely breathe from him holding my lungs hostage.

Master Gustov rushed over and captured my flailing legs. I got a few good kicks on him, but the strong Dominant withstood my attempts to stop Mistress Cora from her task. She come forward again bitching that I had broken her jaw and wanted me whipped for such insolence. Master Malfred assured her I would be punished for my misdeed to her.

I yelled out insanely, "Jack and Jill went up the hill to fetch a pail of water. Jack fell down and broke his crown, but Jill will wish she stayed on the fucking ground.." I broke out in another round of crazy laugher with tears.

Mistress Cora hesitated and shot a nervous look at Master Malfred. "The boy is mad Malfred. Are you sure we shouldn't just call the Guard? I didn't know about any of this. He may attempt to kill all of us."

I nodded wildly. "There won't be any attempting horse face. The devil is waiting for my delivery. You will know many I will send ahead of you. So at least you will never be lonely, even as ugly as you are." I howled in laughter even louder and began to struggle with much strength despite the heavy hold on my flesh.

Master Malfred tensed as did Grisham. "Ignore him, Cora. He is mad. Mad Maxx is a true Priceless. We accidentally selected the Forbidden Metal for this plan. I am overjoyed at this stroke of luck. I have the skill to manage his beast. On with your examination. I will not fucking tell you again. I am really tired of this."

Mistress Cora nodded then dropped to her knees. She roughly examined the boy making damned sure to make it as uncomfortable as possible. When at last she had "dug out" enough of the evidence to convince her that the three men had climaxed in the boy she demanded to have them let her see their manhood.

She researched the smiling Master Gustov, then the growling Master Grisham. Her final patient the Mastermind Malfred let Master Grisham restrain me while he proudly allowed her to handle his mutilated penis.

Mistress Cora removed her glove with a smile. "I pronounce this boy blood bonded with all three of the honorable Council Members. You may count on my witness before the honorable Gretta for recording of these legally binding rights to this Priceless collar."

I laughed even louder. "I will blind them alright. You won't be witness to anything without any fucking eyes, bitch."

Master Malfred frowned at my giggling, insane threats then walked over to his jacket and removed a syringe. "Hold him still, Grisham. There has been too much stress for his troubled mind. I need to calm this collar before he says things he doesn't mean to the wrong people, ja?" He made sure the bubbles were out of the fluid.

Master Grisham nearly sat on me while Master Malfred shot me up with his drug. Within moments I felt I couldn't breathe, and my heart raced in my chest. I thought he had killed the boy for sure. Then suddenly the pain went away, and I was no longer upset. I couldn't recall why I had been in the first place.

Master Grisham got off me and Master Gustov let go of my legs. I laid there for a moment trying to figure out where the hell I was. Then Master Malfred came over and knelt next to me smiling.

"Do you remember me? I am Casper, your friend. This is where the dead go, Christian Axel. Come put on your clothes and we go speaking to Gott. You will get to live with me in my apartment in Heaven." He ran his hand along my cheek with tenderness.

I shook my head giggling at that bullshit. "Casper, there is no Gott, fool. There is no Heaven either. There is, however, a pool in the Haus. I do believe we are in that hell hole. You shouldn't lie to your friends. I suppose robbing banks makes you untrustworthy, ja? Hey, you have a face? I thought they blew it off. Ah, you are playing tricks on me. Can I go see my lambs now? I bet they miss me a lot. Did you know you look like that motherfucker Malfred? I hate that guy. Did you know he killed me?"

Master Malfred nodded with a smile. "Never mind all that. We can go see your lambs. First you get dressed though. It is cold outside, ja?"

I sat up and looked around at every one of those spirits staring at me. "Ha, I killed all you fuckers. You are dead too. Good, I hope whatever I did hurt bad. Especially you Peter. I am sorry to see you, Leo, but that is okay. Here they cannot keep us apart anymore, ja."

Master Leo nodded. "Ja, meine hase, they cannot hurt us anymore. Get dressed Christian Axel. We go to see the lambs."

I shook my head. "Prudes, we are dead. No one gives a shit if you are naked. They cannot even see us. I will not dress. Here none of you can tell me what to do. I am going swimming right now. I am tired of all the orders." I got up quickly ran and without hesitation jumped into the pool and immediately began to drown.

I awoke coughing up water and then vomited viciously. I was confused as towels came out of the thin air rubbing the flesh roughly. I shivered and babbled incoherently while hands without a head started forcing on my clothes. I tried to struggle to keep the materials off me, but other hands came from the void to hold me still. I whimpered and cried unsure why this was happening. I recalled at that point I was dead. This was not a good day for the Mad Maxx.

Strong arms pulled my weeping spirit to its feet. I stood there weaving and sobbing. I heard a voice telling me to follow. I assumed this was the Devil as my leash lifted into the air. I felt a tug on it, and I took a step staggering as if drunk.

All around me flashing lights and fast-moving shadows danced. I felt sick to my stomach and sleepy. I staggered along following my chain but within only moments my knees felt they were made of water. I fell, unable to hold my weight. The leash kept pulling tighter, but I laid down ignoring the discomfort. I needed a nap. This place was as good as any.

I closed my eyes listening to the sounds of angered souls shouting around my head. They were upset someone gave the boy too much of a sedative drug. I smiled at that news. The poor kind was likely dying from that overdose.

I thought maybe once I was rested, I would find this boy and make friends with him. I assumed he would be in the land of the dead by the time I awoke. I hoped he was a cool guy. I could really use someone to talk to. The darkness of unconsciousness overtook me, and I recalled nothing more.

I opened my eyes. The light was too bright. I groaned and went to shade my vision but found my arms were bound tightly behind me. I sat up with a startle. I looked wildly about but didn't recognize anything of my surroundings. I gasped in terror as I was leaning onto a black leather couch. Several matching armchairs and a fancy mahogany coffee table surrounded me.

I was sitting on a Persian rug in someone's apartment, but not one I ever had been in before. I struggled against my restraints, moaning out in agony as the flesh sent signals of distress from my backside. Shit, I remembered now. I was fucked, literally.

I had a terrible headache, and my stomach was rolling to add to my misery of the residual pain of the dry rapes. I realized this must be the home of one of the brutes that had assaulted me. I groaned out even louder when I was proven correct. Master Malfred come into the room from behind a door off to the left of me.

He smiled upon seeing me alert. "Ah, you have returned to us, meine taube. You were a tired young man. I can understand that. Big night you had, ja? I would expect fatigue when a man gets married three times in a single afternoon." He walked over and stood over me still grinning.

I looked at the floor. "So, it is done then I suppose. You trapped me in my fucking metal, you bastard."

Master Malfred frowned. "Christian Axel, you better watch that insolent speaking. I own that collar of yours now. I can have you sent to the chains for being insubordinate to your man."

I shot him a look of hatred. "Well, maybe I call one of my other spouses, ja? I do have three others to choose from if I recall correctly. Go ahead and take me to the chains. I don't care. You can go fuck yourself too while you are at it motherfucker. I will fight you until you kill me and end my pain."

Master Malfred shook his head and sighed. “Christian Axel, this is most unbecoming of one in your station. Now, you will mind me because if you don’t, I can do more than beat you till you cannot stand up. I can also hurt that horrible Leo you seem to love so much. Or did you forget that while you were napping?”

I grimaced. “You are a rat bastard. Leo says he doesn’t care if he dies. Good luck threatening one that has nothing to live for. You trapped me in my metal. I would rather be dead, and I don’t mind having my Leo on the other side. So, I repeat, go fuck yourself, Malfred.”

He chuckled then sat down in one of his leather chairs. “You are a true gem, meine taube. Well for your information I have trapped you in that collar of yours, but not for good.”

I narrowed my eyes in suspiciousness. “What is this bullshit you are trying to feed me? I say to you I am not hungry. I couldn’t stand to eat another bite. Try getting another to eat your lies. I am through with all of you. End this nightmare life of mine and I thank you for the fucking mercy of it.”

The shady Master shook his head. “You do surprise me, meine taube. I thought you would fight harder to survive than this. First of all, ja, I took all your blood bonding spaces. This does trap you in the collar if none of us with draw our claims to you.”

This made me scoff. "Oh, I do believe you all made it clear your intentions to lay your claims to me. Ask my backside about it motherfucker."

He chuckled at that. "Well, I am sorry for that brutality, meine taube. However, for my plan to work I needed to make sure the threat I make to your Elder Masters is real. There was no other way to assure that other than to do the dirty deeds. Now, are you listening to me closely? I will only say this to you this one time."

I rolled my eyes, then sarcastically snorted. "Do I have a fucking choice, Master? I seem to be a captivated audience to whatever bullshit acting job you are pulling. By all means, be my guest and continue this horror show. I am just dying to see how the play ends."

Master Malfred laughed out loud. "You are the comic. I admit I have enjoyed the dark humor over these last few hours with you meine taube. Never mind. Time grows short. I am taking you to a meeting of the Elders and the Voting Council in thirty minutes. I will present them with a choice. They give me what I want, or I will go to see Gretta and record the three blood bondings as legit."

I frowned. "What? Wait, if they do give in to your demands, then what?"

He smiled most diabolically. "Then Gustov and Grisham will withdraw their claims of blood bonding to you. They will let the twenty-four hours pass without recording the event. You, meine taube, will be in the race for breaking that metal once more. However, if you breathe a word of the rapes, or of my plan, I will bypass the whole thing and settle for my holding your collar with my brothers Grisham and Gustov."

I looked at the floor with a shiver and a gleam of hope. "May I ask what it is that you are going to demand in return to relinquish your threat, Master."

He smiled with much humor. "Why Christian Axel, I would have thought by now you know what I want."

I nodded feeling a deep aching in my chest. "You want Barnim's place as an Elder. You want me to kill Master Leo so you could bring Master Grisham with you. Then when Master Bladrick or Master Claus died, you two along with Mistress Cora would raise Master Gustov and Master Peter. You intended to take over the Haus. You are the one that is behind all of this, even my existence."

Master Malfred blew out his breath and laughed with a clap of glee. "You are indeed intelligent, meine taube. You are also correct. I have been using the Elders and others to move you to clear my path to the top all this time. Xavier, Barnum, Drexel, Hemmel, and that fucking Felix the betraying rat. The only one I couldn't get you to eliminate was that fucking Leo. Oh well, you did a marvelous job otherwise. I cannot complain. I will rise despite my age, or the Elders will lose their coveted Priceless collar. Those old perverts have tasted your pleasures too long to ever give that up now. Once I am elevated to Elder at the tender age of forty-one, not only will I be a legend, but I will have control of this Haus at last. Cora is my creature. She does what she is told. The Elder brotherhood will be in my pocket thanks to you, meine taube."

I shook my head. "You and Mistress Cora are still outvoted by four Masters. Your plan to control this Haus is worthless."

He grinned with pride. "Is it? Oh, meine taube, you don't know the truth of your powers, do you? The man that wields the Forbidden Silver wins. Your Master Jonas is the fool. He has never used a single bit of what is available to him thanks to the blood bonding. The idiot could have been the king of this Haus, but instead plans to use you to go hunting for the mythical female of your kind. Well, he can have you to fulfil his quest when I am done with you that is."

I groaned. "What the hell do you want with me? Seems you already got everything in the bag. You used me to gain your entry as the legendary Master Malfred. Why not let me go then? I beg you to withdraw your bond claim with the other two brutes the second you are elevated to Elder."

Master Malfred stood up and grabbed my chain leash. "Not on your fucking life, Christian Axel. I have watched you grow up all this time waiting for this glorious day. Now that you belong to me, I never intend to let you go. I sacrificed my beloved Tamina and all the other silvers to become the Elder. The only collar an Elder can hold is that of the Priceless collar I engineered with my own hands. You are the best silver this Haus has ever been blessed to hold. I am the best player of the game in the history of this place. The best deserves the best and now I have him at last." He hand-signaled for me to stand.

I moaned in agony from my rough treatment but minded his command. I could only pray he was telling me the truth. If Master Grisham and Master Gustov removed their claims I would still have a chance to break my collar. I realized this insane bastard was likely planning to trip me up before my collar selection in only seven months, but that bought me time to make his ass take the short way to the first floor from the fucking banister.

For now, I would have to play along like the perfect submissive I was trained to be. Christian would get his chance to add the X to the number one spot on our list of targets.

MASTERMIND MALFREDS PLOT AND THE CREATION OF CHRISTIAN AXEL:

You see Meine Liebe, Master Malfred was the reason I was born. We had been searching for him all our life. It had come to light at last the entire plot or at least a great deal of it, and how we fit into it. This shady fucker had decided more than fifteen years ago to make his mark on the history of the Haus.

In order to do that, he would have to do something never done before. He set his sights on becoming the youngest Elder ever seen. To accomplish this, he contacted his buddy Peter and his girlfriend Agnette. The two of them were promised a place on the Voting Council, then an eventual rise to Elder if they would make a kid to pass off as a Priceless.

Master Malfred had been trying for years to make one with his Tamina, but all attempts had failed. Thanks to that, he had to seek this outside aid. To the plotters joy, Agnetta became pregnant. She of course could not marry the father, or the plan would be discovered. She married Gerard to hide the identity of the High-Born Dominant she carried.

The three of them awaited the birth of their fake game piece praying for a male. If a female, she would have to try again. Only the males would be a believable Priceless thanks to the legends about them.

By the time of my birth, Peter and the volatile Agnette had become estranged. She decided to end her association with Peter and Master Malfred, taking off for her homeland of Denmark. I was left to rot in the hands of the abusive Gerard. Master Malfred and Peter could not allow this opportunity to pass. She had birthed the male kid they had been seeking. With much work, and two years of intense wooing, Peter managed to get Agnette to return to their side.

The rest was pretty much already explained. Master Malfred gave Peter the orders to have me hijacked, held in isolation, beaten, and eventually raped without mercy to make me near crazy from it. The two of them wanted to make sure I looked the part of the insane Forbidden silver. What neither of them expected was that I would turn out to be the real thing.

Master Malfred had also not expected that Master Jonas would slip under his radar. The Vampire had paid the doctor to tell Peter I was hopelessly hebephrenic and would never recover from my disease onset. The idiot believed it and Master Jonas slipped in and stole Master Malfred's prize.

Just as he never expected Gerard to cut up his "beautiful boy," he was forced to recalculate his ultimate goals thanks to Master Jonas's trick. The clever Master Malfred had used Olaf and Vilber to keep the information about the Elders flowing into him. He knew the vicious Barnum and twisted Drexel would seal dare own fates.

Master Malfred knew his Priceless creation had become violent and unforgiving thanks to his brutal treatment for all those years. He only had to sit back and watch his targets fall to their deaths from the sixth floor.

He made sure to whisper in the ears of Master Bladrick that Helga, Heidi, Hemmel and Leo needed to be eliminated or they would aid the newly risen Cora. Cora's rise was also a part of Malfred's plan.

Cora had been the fucking mole that Maximillian had missed during Peter's reign, not Felix. I had missed that bitch in my confusion. Felix was fated to be killed thanks to his betrayal of Master Malfred when he went to Gretta and had Ryker put to the lawn. You see Prince Ryker was Master Malfred's favorite nephew. Felix really fucked up when he forgot that little fact and helped get the boy killed.

Master Malfred had Geraldine come after me by using Cora to set the girl up. Geraldine was promised to belong to Cora if she would trap me in my metal and break my vows of monogamy to Peter. The hateful Mistress had let Felix in on the plot telling him where and when to catch the act happing.

Cora had led Felix to believe this was a plot to get rid of his rival Maximillian once and for all. Master Malfred knew I would take offense to Felix being involved in a plot to end me as that got people killed, ja? Felix found his peace for his part in the conspiracy and Cora walked away unscathed just as the Mastermind Malfred meant to happen.

Then there was the fall of Tamina to consider. It turned out Master Malfred told the girl to do everything possible to become impregnated by Olaf. She followed the commands and to the joy of Master Malfred she came up positive for the one thing day both had tried to accomplish for years.

Sadly, for the expensive silver, Olaf shot off his mouth and Master Leo heard the news of the father. He went to the Voting Council and reported that Tamina was forced into pregnancy by her uncaring Master Malfred. Master Leo thought he was aiding the girl since no pregnant silver could be punished by death.

Unfortunately, Master Malfred had his sights set on the boy he had been merely using as a game piece all that time. He had been so busy with his own plotting and happy with his Tamina he never bothered to even view the one he had ordered birthed only for his exploitation of him. He had spied me leaving Master Claus's apartment when he was going to see the man to beg him to help him untarnish his Tamina.

I had not noticed him passing me on the stairs thanks to Master Jonas's having just confronted me with the news that he knew of my birthright. I also was in a hurry to get back to Peter's apartment and clean up before he caught that indiscretion with Master Claus from our arrangement that I would be his lover on Thursdays at one.

To hear Master Malfred tell it, it was love at first sight. He said that he asked Master Jonas about the silver that had rushed by him and was told this was the Priceless Maximillian. This sudden interest in the forbidden silver changed Master Malfred's plans. He went to Master Claus and instead of demanding Tamina be spared, he stated he wanted a weekly leash with the Priceless to compensate for his loss.

Poor Tamina and all his other silvers were sold off to another Haus. Specifically, to his brother, so Tamina didn't fare badly just so you know. His brother was happy to gain the beautiful, talented silvers from Das Kaiser Haus. It was at this time when Master Claus denied him his desires, that Master Malfred decided the time had come to spring his trap.

To his astonishment, I had an onset of the disease schizophrenia. His plans were halted as his creature twisted and shattered in the bowels of the Haus. His fake diamond became the Priceless gem of legend. Then Peter tossed it all away.

Master Malfred was the man I wanted dead more than anyone on Earth. Not Agnette nor even Peter held a darker place in my heart. This man that had wealth, beauty, all the best that the world could give him, still had not been satisfied.

This greedy sonofabitch had reached out into the ether and snatched out my soul. He forced it into flesh then hijacked the boy he created. All this horror I had endured was for nothing more than his despotic desire for absolute power in a Haus of criminals, rapists, thieves, and degenerates.

Der Hund had sent me, Maximillian, to seek the one to which we owed a death for bringing us into this living hell. With our target identified at long last, Christian would stand ready to send this bastard to the fiery pit where he surely belonged. Master Malfred was the Mastermind, but Mad Maxx was the many minds. The battle for my survival had just gone into full bore. Killing this monster was not gonna be easy, but it sure would be my pleasure.

I followed Master Malfred out of his apartment on the fifth floor where the apartments of the Voting Council are located. There was nothing I could do for the moment. He held my leash tightly and my arms were bound behind me with strong leather cuffs attached by chain. Peter knew me well. This was one restraint I had yet to conquer.

I kept my eyes to the floor while Master Malfred halted and waited by the stairwell. I heard the sounds of Master Grisham, Master Gustov, and Master Peter come up behind me. I didn't have to turn around to know it was them. I was not so daft not to be aware that we were awaiting the rest of the voting Council and the two that could claim the right to my special services. This was all those bastards except Agnette and Gretta. They were waiting to see if the Elders went for the deal of course.

Master Grisham took the left flank and Master Gustov the right. Master Peter took up the rear as Master Malfred led me down the Elder staircase. I didn't look up doing my best to brace myself for whatever may come.

When we reached the bottom there was a scattering of every Dominant, silver, and black collar in our path. I noticed the light and realized I had been asleep all through the night. I assumed it had to be around nine or ten in the morning based on the amount of traffic in the hallways.

Our group of criminal brutes arrived in the large space that led to the main staircase and the front door. I gasped when I stole a look up those stairs and saw the Elders including Cora and Leo storming down them in a pack.

Master Claus was leading them. Master Bladrick and Master Jonas walked side by side behind the crossdressing Elder. Then came Mistress Cora and Master Leo holding up the rear. I saw the panic caused by the sight of seeing the members of the Voting Council and the Elders converging in mass.

All around us everyone was gasping, running, and some collars – both black and silver – screamed in terror. No one understood what was going on, but everyone knew a battle was about to begin. They didn't want to be the one accidently killed in any crossfire.

Master Malfred and his group of brutes stood there coolly awaiting their foe without any signs of fear. The Elders were storming our way with murderous expressions on their faces. I could tell even from a distance all my Masters wanted to beat these thieves into spots of blood on the Haus carpets.

Master Claus shouted when still at a bit of a distance, "Malfred, you beast, let Mad Maxx go this minute. You have no business holding him like this. That is the collar of the Elders, you sonofabitch."

Master Malfred shot a smile of arrogance at Master Grisham who smiled back. "Well, good morning to you Honorable Claus. I can see why you are so renowned for your fine manners," he yelled back causing the brutes to chuckle amongst themselves.

The group of Elders approached still packed together like ancient wolves. I saw my Leo staring at the floor and wiping his eyes. Mistress Cora shot him a look of caution, but he didn't bother to return her gaze. Master Jonas was looking me up and down seeking injury, while Master Bladrick glared in pure hatred at Master Malfred.

Master Claus held up his hand. “I will say it again Malfred, release our collar this minute or find yourself exiled, motherfucker.”

Master Malfred stopped chuckling with humor and frowned. “You will not speak to me this way Claus. I do have the right to this collar, as do Grisham and Gustov here. I believe Cora has given you the good news. We married your boy last night. You may own his collar, but we own the rights to his services.”

Master Jonas bellowed out, “Fucking rapists. I know damned well what you bastards did. We all do. You will withdraw your claims, or I will kill all of you with my bare hands.”

Master Claus put up his hand as the Voting Council backed up a bit, feigning fear. “Easy brother Jonas. There is no reason to become beasts like these criminals are. We agreed I would speak for us. Allow me to do what I was voted to do.”

Master Jonas scoffed, then spat on the floor “Then fucking get to doing the talking and get my man back, damn you.”

Master Malfred broke out in a fake smile. “Ah, your man, Jonas? You mean our man. Now Claus, if you can keep your honorable brothers under control, we can go into the Great Hall for the meeting I requested? I do believe it has been cleared for this.”

Master Bladrick snorted. “What need is there for a meeting? You raped our collar and claim a blood bonding. There is nothing more to discuss.”

Master Claus shot a look of anger at Master Bladrick while Master Malfred nodded. “Well, you can claim that if you wish. Go tell Gretta. This collar is as good as dead the second such a theft is found guilty. The way I see it, you can come speak to me like a gentleman, deal with the Voting Council blocking your rights to the Priceless, or you can call the Guard to end this argument right now. I will be happy to hand him over to them if he was indeed raped.”

The Elders all looked at the floor as Master Claus sighed. “You obviously have us at a disadvantage, motherfucker. What are you waiting for? Lead the way to the Great Hall. I for one would like to hear what the fuck you want from us so bad. I cannot believe you so stupid that you would dare to incite our deadly wrath with this egregious crime.”

Master Malfred chuckled. “Well, I must say the old saying if it its bad for you it is delicious for me. I never enjoyed anything as much as I have my taste of the forbidden silver. It was worth all the risk I took at setting off the fury of a bunch of neglectful old fools. If you wish to get a second chance to cuddle what you have stupidly lost, follow me boys. There is a way to clear all this up without hurting your feelings too badly. I would like to offer you a deal you be wise not to refuse.” He motioned the Elder pack to take the lead.

Master Claus scoffed but stormed off toward the Great Hall. The other Elders trailed behind him without breaking their ranks. Master Malfred shot his boys a look of victory then took off after the trailing Mistress Cora and Master Leo.

Once again the hallways cleared like the red sea for that Moses fellow. In every direction people fled heading for the safety of their apartments, auxiliary hallways, and a few even rushed to hide in closets. I heard Master Grisham and Master Gustov giggling at the sight of the fear this group of powerful men and Cora were causing.

Master Peter reached out and gently pushed the men when dare laughter got too loud. I kept my sights on the floor reminding myself that killing these sonsofbitches would make all my pain worth it. At least that is what I wanted to believe.

The attending black collar of the Great Hall nearly shit a brick when he saw this horror show of brutal men approaching him. I could see him trembling in terror as he asked if they needed him to seat them.

Master Claus informed the man no one was to enter the Hall and to close the room off behind all of us. The black collar nodded then waited patiently for the last man, Master Peter, to pass. I heard the slamming of the big wooden doors that to my knowledge had never been shut before.

Master Claus and Master Malfred took seats across from each other at a large table. The men and Cora surrounding each side stood around their leader. I stood next to Master Malfred until Master Grisham roughly put his hand on my shoulder and pushed me down into a kneel behind the shady Mastermind's chair. He glared down at me with an angry gaze at my lack of minding protocol. Well, *I didn't see any reason I should. He behaved like the baboon, so I treated him like one, ja*?

Master Claus began the bargaining. "Okay, we are here as you requested. Get to it. I would like to see you desexed before my lunchtime nap, you know."

Master Malfred scoffed. "Here now, Honorable Claus. There is no need for threats. I am a reasonable guy. I will get right to my demands. I want you and your brothers to give me the slot open on the Elders' floor. It is that simple."

The Elders all grumbled in anger except Leo and Cora who already knew what Malfred was going to demand.

Master Jonas spit on the floor then growled out, "This is bullshit. We don't reward thieves motherfucker, nor do we embrace them as our brother."

Master Malfred rolled his eyes. "That is my only interest in this situation. You meet my request and raise me to fill Barnum's apartment and Grisham plus Gustov will withdraw their claim to Mad Maxx's blood bonding."

Master Claus groaned. "You will too Malfred, or no deal."

Master Malfred sat back chuckling while he crossed his arms. "Hell no. You see the Elders hold this precious collar for their own. I happen to know that Jonas here was planning to go to Gretta this very week and end all of your rights to your own silver's special services. If I release my claim, then Jonas will block me too. Fuck that. Part of the thrill in being the Elder is having the Priceless's top level services. You will raise me, and I will file my blood bond. Otherwise, the voting Council here takes Mad Maxx home to the fifth floor. I will make sure that he is torn to pieces. Jonas you can have what is left of him when the three of us have had our fill."

Master Jonas came forward ready to grab Master Malfred from his chair for a thrashing. The Voting Council brutes, all three of dem, moved to halt his reaching the shady bastard with the speed of jungle cats.

A huge fight was about to break out when Master Claus yelled out. "Enough. Jonas, get your ass back in line. This shit is your fault, and we all know it. Your greed to take this boy from all of us gave these rat bastards the idea. They simply beat us to the punch in all. You back up or I will you whipped and thrown in the dungeon for this disruption, damn you."

Master Jonas's eyes lit with the fires of hell, but he backed away returning to his spot behind the now very irritated Master Claus.

Master Claus then focused on Master Malfred. "You have us at the disadvantage. I will have to take a fast vote with all the Elders regarding your offer. You will remove yourself from this Great Hall and we will call you back once the decision is made. You can leave the Priceless behind when you leave."

Master Malfred stood and motioned me to rise. "Good try, Honorable Claus. Mad Maxx comes with us. You take your time. We have only another eight hours before I must assume you don't take my threat seriously. You hurry this shit up or we go to see Gretta and make that record solid. Come meine taube. You walk with the real men this time." I was hauled out by chain and pushed along by Master Peter, a hostage to the Voting Council.

Master Malfred and his crew stood around laughing and joking. I was forced to a kneel by Master Peter then watched by my hateful father. I glared at him, and he returned the sentiment. Only about fifteen minutes passed before the Elder Bladrick came to the door and called the brutes back inside. They all packed up and dragged me back in with them.

Master Malfred sat back down while the others took their places. I knelt on my own this time. I didn't want fucking Grisham touching me anymore. Master Claus waited for all the men to settle then he took a deep breath and frowned.

"The vote was unanimous. We want our Mad Maxx back. We hereby raise you Malfred to Elder in the place of our late brother Barnum. We have called the Honorable Gretta to the Hall to record your blood bonding as honest. She will be here in a moment. I assume this meets your approval, ja?" He smiled with wickedness.

Master Malfred shot a pleased smile at his brutes then ruffled my hair which I jerked away from in anger. “Ah, see I knew you boys would be reasonable. I am most happy to call all of you brothers.”

Master Jonas smiled with evil. “Good, we are happy that you are happy Malfred. Now give us back our Priceless.”

Master Malfred frowned. “I am not done with him yet. I only had that single taste. I want to spend a little time getting to know my collar better before handing him over to those already well versed in his services. Besides, I am blood bonded to him. I can and will stop all of you from sharing my man. Jonas, I suppose will work out some deal with you soon. Otherwise, the rest of you can fuck off.” He leaned back, crossing his arms while the brutes chuckled with glee at that statement.

Master Leo smiled happily, which made me wonder what the hell was going on here, “Oh now brother Jonas, let the man have his time with the boy. He is right you know. Getting time with our Mad Maxx is truly to die for. An honor only an Elder, oh sorry blood bonded, has the rights to.”

The doors of the Great Hall opened up and the Guard rushed inside. I saw them and hit the floor screaming in terror. They came flying at Master Grisham and Master Gustov. The two men were confused as the armed and hairy as hell men took them by their arms.

Master Peter took off to the other side of the table as did Master Malfred, both of them were in complete shock. The Guard said nothing as they began to haul the two big brutes away.

Master Malfred wailed out, “What the fuck is this shit.”

Master Claus and the Elders, even Cora, smiled with fires in their eyes as Master Jonas bellowed out. “It is a crime to steal from the Elders, Malfred. These two have tasted our silver, which they had no rights to. That is theft. The punishment decided by us is death. Mad Maxx will also be punished right this very second for his stupidly allowing these idiots to take what didn’t belong to them. Claus, Leo, get to it brothers.”

Master Leo came over and snatched my chain from the surprised Master Malfred and dragged me to the table. Master Jonas pushed me to my face and told me to hold still for my punishment. I panted and begged for mercy assuming they were gonna whip the hell out of me for my indiscretion.

Master Claus came up behind me and told Master Jonas to hand him his lancet. The crossdressing Elder ripped my pants down and took a moment to cut his member. I let out a wail of agony as the Elder forced himself into me in a blood drawing dry mount. He began his rapid thrust just as the two rapists Master Grisham and Master Gustov were hauled out the Great Hall doors weeping and begging for their lives.

Mistress Gretta come in passing them with a smile on her face. She stopped and waved at them sarcastically, then walked over to the blood bonding of the Priceless with Master Claus already in progress.

Master Malfred yelled out in fury to her. “Sister, Claus is raping this collar. Have the Guard return and remove him at once. I happen to know Mad Maxx didn’t agree to this. They attempt to punish him with something that cannot be forced.”

She smiled sweetly. “Ah, Claus you bastard, are you raping this boy?”

Master Claus paused his agonizing thrusting. “Sister Gretta, this is my collar I seem to recall. I cannot rape my own property, can I?”

Mistress Gretta crossed her arms grinning like the cat that ate the canary. “Well, there you have it brother Malfred. You cannot rape your own collar silly.”

Master Malfred shook his head as Master Claus went back to engaging me in this horror. “The Priceless didn’t agree to the marriage. This is bullshit”

Mistress Gretta looked at my face that was twisted up from the terrible pain I was being forced to endure. “Uhm, excuse me Mad Maxx? Is your Master Claus forcing you to comply with his blood bonding you? Speak up boy, I need to hear you agree to this rite with your own words.”

I took a deep breath and wailed out, “If that is my Master’s pleasure than it is my own Mistress. I thank him for the mercy of it." I screamed in pure horror as Master Claus slammed into me reaching his climax amazingly fast given the fact that there was a fucking audience and no Gott damned lubrication. This was pure bullshit.

Master Claus was panting and leaning over my weeping flesh when a loud shot rang out, then a second one followed in moments.

Master Jonas smiled and wiped my tears away. "Looks like there will be a few open apartments on the fifth floor, ja?" The other Elders and Mistress Gretta giggled at that.

Master Malfred stared into my furious eyes with an expression of terror. "You cannot just kill half the Voting Council. Peter, get over here and speak to your Sister. Honorable Gretta what the fuck is going on here."

Master Peter shook his head. "You are on your own Malfred. I am going home. I have had enough of watching my treasure used like a whore." He began to move swiftly toward the doors.

Master Leo yelled out, smiling with much evil in his expression, "See you Peter, real soon."

Master Peter turned to look at him. He shivered then took off in a run back to his apartment without turning around again. I gasped and shuddered as I felt Master Claus uncouple. Mistress Cora quickly examined both me and the crossdresser then nodded to Mistress Gretta. She took a small book from her purse sat down and wrote down that Master Claus was successfully blood bonded.

Master Jonas frowned, then shot a look at Master Leo. "Okay brother, you're up. We cannot have even one bond floating around open. You got lucky as Master Bladrick cannot take your spot. If I had it my way, never mind. I agreed that we work together. Get to it. Time is wasting."

Master Leo came around and looked into my grieving face. "I do apologize for this, meine heart, but it is the only way to protect you from these plots. Forgive me for what I must do to hold you for my own."

I nodded then closed my eyes to brace for the pain. "I forgive you Master. Please show mercy and be quick." I sobbed hard at saying those words despite myself.

Mistress Gretta called out from her seat, "Mad Maxx, do you agree to this blood bonding with your Master Leo?"

I sucked in my breath as I felt Master Leo take his place behind me. "I agree to this bonding Mistress. I thank my Master for the mercy of it."

Mistress Gretta shot a look of triumph at the now horrified Master Malfred. He sat down in a chair appearing dumbfounded.

His best soldiers Mistress Cora and Mistress Gretta had betrayed him. He simply couldn't understand that the second the two FemDoms got what they were after, they didn't feel the need to answer to his nothing ass anymore.

He had managed to make it to Elder as he desired. He even managed to get his hooks into the rights to hold the Priceless collar, but he would have to share with four others. I saw him close his eyes appearing as if he felt it when I screamed out in agony at Master Leo's dry, brutal entry.

Master Leo called out for me to focus on the lambs and Der Makellos as he harshly assaulted me in his blood bonding intercourse. I gritted my teeth and did my best to do as he commanded. Master Jonas had to tightly hold me to the table. I couldn't help my urge to try and escape that agonizing thrusting of my beloved Leo.

He was able to reach his orgasm relatively quickly and mercifully. He would tell me later he closed his eyes and imaged we were in the pool alone together to rush his apex. I of course was more than a little grateful he did me that favor, even though I was now trapped in my metal for real. I had no more slots for blood bonding with my Frau unless one of my Elder Masters died. I bet you can't guess which one Christian and I were eyeing to open that slot, ha!

Mistress Cora again made short work of her examination and approval. Master Leo, Master Claus, Master Jonas, and Master Malfred had successfully been recorded as my blood bonded mates. Master Bladrick was not concerned. He knew his brother Master Claus would never deny him his rights to the London Bridge. *Well shit, nothing works in my favor you know.*

Master Leo gently pulled up my breeches as I was still bound with my arms behind me and let me lean on him. I shot a look of worry at Master Jonas and noticed he was grinning with hateful thrill at Master Malfred.

I turned to Master Leo in confusion. "I don't understand Master. Master Jonas is not jealous of you anymore?"

Master Leo chuckled, then whispered in my ear. "Meine Hase, you have to understand we have been trying to flush Malfred out for some time now. Only Peter knew the identity of the man behind all the intrigue around here. Jonas was pissed, there is no doubt, but you managed to give him a reasonable excuse. He thinks you see me as the Frau I do believe. I groaned that Master Jonas told him that. Anyway, when you came to me to tell me of his plans, I called Cora. She informed Claus and Jonas that this was the weakness that would bring our cockroach to the light. There he sits. Now that we have him in our sights we can gang up and put an end to his bullshit. Give it time, meine heart. You will have your revenge. You need to focus on finishing up that test of yours. Jonas agreed to our blood bonding with you without quarrel for the price of seeing you break that collar. We all voted unanimously to see that happen. Your sacrifice will be worth the freedom that is now almost assured you, my love."

I closed my eyes and began to weep harder than I had been, but this time with gratitude. My flesh was wrecked and my soul tired, but Master Leo said the words that I had given all I had to hear. Freedom was almost within my grasp. I could see the lights at the end of my dark tunnel at last.

The Elders stood around, minus Master Malfred still sitting in the chair flabbergasted, quietly talking amongst themselves. Master Leo helped me to a chair, but I told him I would rather stand. *I wasn't going to able to sit anywhere for a while. That horror of five blood bondings, after a violent rape from the Vampire and the London Bridge. I will just be crass and say it: I was all fucked out.*

Master Claus looked at my Master Leo. "So, it is decided you attend the injured Priceless for the next two days. I will take the two after you. Then Jonas, you hold him for two. Malfred, I am sorry to say but there is only the one day left in a seven-day cycle. You get Sundays only after Jonas finishes his interest's with him." He chuckled with much humor at their taking the majority of my services for themselves and placing him after the brutal Vampire.

Master Malfred growled out in irritation. "That is bullshit. Why do all of you get two and I only get the one? I have as much right as any of you do."

Master Leo chuckled. "Well, you see Jonas is the first man, so he gets preference. Claus is carrying Bladrick, so he gets two to cover his extra burden. I got two because, well this boy is my lover. That leaves you the youngest, weakest, and newest of the Elders, to take what is left of him after we have our fill. Oh, and he agreed with all of us in front of the Head of the Council. I do believe you were a lowly Council member when you wed him. That make you less than any of us, even Bladrick, motherfucker. You have a problem with our share schedule, take it up with Jonas. I am sure he would be thrilled to meet with you privately to discuss your taking advantage, oops, I mean your wishing to visit more often with his man."

He wiped my tears and I chuckled with Master Leo when Master Malfred stood up and stormed from the room. Master Bladrick shot me a look of mischief.

"Oh, hey Malfred, brother. You can move into Barnum's old place right away. Just watch out for that banister. That fucker is dangerous. One little slip and well, you will make history again I assure you." He cackled like a wicked crow as Master Malfred pushed out of the room never looking back.

Master Claus clapped his hands with glee, "I am fucking starving. Let's order some breakfast and party like there is no tomorrow. Sisters, feel free to join us old farts for a feast."

I leaned all my weight into Master Leo then felt the world tilting. "Master, I don't feel well, something is wrong."

The lightning flashed from the sky sending the boy into a spasm. I saw the Elders coming at me just as my eyes rolled back in my head and I crumbled to the floor. The madness had come for me at long last. A new shattering had begun due to too much stress, and I was already worn the hell out from it. There is a rule against a tired shard running the wheel, but I was the only choice Der Hund had, and we still had so far left to go.

Chapter 52: Taube

I have no memory of what happened for the rest of that day. When the Grand Mal seizure hit the boy, Master Malfred had left to lick his wounds. Master Peter ran from the scene to warn Agnette of the misfiring of the plot and of the death of their brothers Master Grisham and Master Gustov. I had been forced into a double blood bonding with Master Claus and Master Leo, which effectively had trapped me in my metal.

That was my punishment for being gang raped by the Voting members, a lifetime of servitude in my collar to my Elder Masters. Master Leo had told me that Master Jonas had agreed to allow for the double blood bonding with his man with the understanding all of the Elders, except Master Malfred, would see that I did become judged Dominant during the collar selection.

Normally, I would believe Master Leo. I wanted to have faith that the Elders wouldn't backstab Master Jonas nor me. I had granted them perfect service by enduring the gang rapes and flushing Master Malfred and his thugs out of hiding. It seemed only fair that for my sacrifice, and lack of being able to prevent the rapes, they would never betray me at the last minute.

However, Meine Liebe, I was no longer Mad Maxx the fool. No one in that fucking Haus is ever what they appear to be. Everyone in that place was liars, thieves, molesters, murderers, and criminals of the worst kinds. The only difference between one or another was the limit to how much debauchery they would feel comfortable width.

Even my beloved Master Leo had been in on the plot to discover the identity of Master Malfred. He knew I would be attacked in the pool room. That is why he sent me fifteen minutes ahead. Though he didn't know they would rape and blood bond me, he was aware I would be harmed. He still sent me convincing himself the results were worth the sacrifice. Easy for him to say. It wasn't his ass on the line. I mean that literally by the way.

With the horror of killing Julius, the violent rape by Grisham, closely followed by Master Jonas's foul alcohol driven sexual attack that night; you heap on the London Bridge, nasty molestations of the older Elders, then the brutal gang rape, followed with the harsh blood bonding in a crowd of watchers in the Great Hall, well I was in a hell of a stressed out state.

I suppose I was likely cracking at the seams long before all that shit. Then finding out every fucking terrible thing that ever happened to me was because some horse's ass wanted to be Elder at forty-one, yike. Worse still, I had done everything perfectly to make that happen for the dirty motherfucker that ordered my Gott damned birth and engineered all my nightmares.

It shook my foundations, collapsed my faith in myself, and sent me right to the hell of despair. I had seen the light at the end of the tunnel of my oppression, but I was almost certain it was a lie. I had to face the facts. Everything in my whole fucking world had been an illusion.

Nothing I did had been of my own design. I had been wielded like a fucking weapon by this sonofabitch Master Malfred through all of my Masters all the way back to Peter. Even the rage fueled killing of Julius had been in the favor of my creator Malfred.

The dark epiphany of my reason for being, extreme trauma from the many rapes, along with Master Malfred's overdosing me on his sedative set off a massive mind shut down. The resulting seizure was quite severe. I didn't regain consciousness for over eight hours even with aid offered by the Haus doctor. There was even some fear I had been brain damaged by this cataclysmic electrical misfiring inside my empty head.

In the hour before the boy awakened, I found myself on the floor behind the wheel. Christian was moaning and bitching about being thrown around during the fleshes bucking in his many spasms. There was a large seizure and a few smaller ones that rapidly followed. I felt sick to my stomach and my head ached.

"I feel awful brother. How are you fairing?" I called out to the anger/lust shard.

He growled back full of the fury. "Like a baby diaper, brother. What the fuck happened?"

I shook my head. “I am not sure, Christian, but I think may have gotten a little fatigued. I must have fallen asleep at the wheel.”

He stood up appearing shaky. “Sleeping on the job. I should report your laziness to Der Hund. Fuck, I was knocked out by all that gyration of the boy. That was pure bullshit. You ever do that again; I will shatter you myself.”

I winced and fell back to my knees feeling foulness in my middle. “Shut up. I am terribly ill, brother. Something is wrong with me. I cannot take this horror. I think I my vomit.”

Christian narrowed his eyes. “What the fuck is wrong with you Maximillian? You are a fucking shard fool. You can’t vomit. You don’t have a Gott damned stomach. Mad Max said you are the drama Queen. Damn, if he wasn’t truthful. Get the fuck off the mind’s floor and back to work. The flesh is trying to awaken. You need to do your job, fatherfucker.”

I groaned in agony. “Nein. I am going to be sick. This is not happening. What the fuck. Help me, brother,” I screamed out just as I opened my mouth and spewed out a nasty black substance onto the wheel ground.

Christian backed up with his eyes wide in horror. “Holy shit. You just blew chunks. How the fuck did you do that?”

I shook my head feeling immediately better but weakened somehow. I stood up staring at the gross pile of darkness. Christian walked over and joined me to gaze upon what neither of us thought possible. I saw the edges of that crap moving. I gasped as Christian backed up in fear almost knocking me over.

"It is moving brother. See it is getting larger too." I pointed at the mess as it began to twist and reach upward.

Christian screamed in horror, "I know what this is. You have shattered, brother. On, sonofabitch. That is a mirror shard. Gott damn, we are in trouble. Back up, there is no telling what this what this thing will do. Fuck, you should have called Der Hund before you let this get out of hand. We are doomed for sure." He fled to the wall as far as possible, never taking his terrified eyes off of the goo that was quickly forming into an exact copy of myself.

I stood there confused, frightened, and curious as the black substance began to solidify. The Mirror Maximillian had his eyes closed while the dark substance wriggled and took its places to create each part of the creature. When the last of his image was created, the movement settled, and the wet looking thing began to dry quickly. I almost let out a scream of terror when the Mirror Maximillian opened his glowing blue eyes.

An evil looking smile broke out across his lips. "Hello brother Maximillian. Are you ready to party like there is no tomorrow or what? Let's find sum trouble to get into, or maybe we can cause the ruckus ourselves, ja?" He straightened out his arms and stretched his neck as if he had just woken from a nap.

I backed up and joined Christian against the wall in complete fear of this Mirror shard. "You need to rejoin me, uhm, what are you called," I yelled out.

He chuckled so hard the wheel moved at the sound of it. "Taube (Dove) brother. Master Malfred called me to the surface. We must mind our Master, ja? Come now brothers, what are you all worried about? Did you think I would come to eat you for my dinner? Nein. I came to play the game. What shall we do first? Oh, I know, lets go swimming. We could go see the lambs or perhaps we can see if Master Malfred can teach us to fly?" He flashed a diabolical look at Christian.

"Oh, hell no, get back over here Taube. You cannot just break free and claim space," I shouted out in anger.

Christian put up his hand. "Wait a second brother. I like this guy. He has the right idea. Let him stay awhile. Let's see what he can do. You are far too fast to judge, you know. You are the schwuler freak so you have no right to do point any fingers."

Taube giggled wildly at that. "Well, he may be the schwuler, but I am the freak, brother Christian. Welcome to hell boys. Now, which shall it be? Dancing, romancing, swimming, or killing. I am up for anything."

I shook my head while Christian and Taube met up in a high five. "This will not do. I am calling Der Hund. This thing is not part of the mission. Playing? We have not time to play, brothers. Did you not witness the trouble the fucking boy is in? We are trapped in our metal, motherfuckers. The mission has failed."

Taube frowned then shot a playful look at Christian. "Nothing to lose brother. Even better, when all is lost, party till they throw the dirt on your grave fool. I see a game of Augen Auf (Hide and seek) is in order. Come on brother Christian. Are you in or out?"

Christian smiled with murderous glee. "I am with you brother. I will be happy to join forces on your team. We form the winning one. Them against us. I almost feel sorry for those losers."

Taube elbowed Christian smiling with cruel delight. "The only thing worse than a sorry loser is the arrogant winner, ja? That fool would think no one can steal his medal. Well, we shall prove to them that the dark horse can come up from last place."

I shook my head and crossed my arms. "Taube, if you plan to stay here then I warn you to avoid Christian. His goal is not one you will want to be involved in. You came from me. There is nothing about me in common with that fucker."

Taube smiled even larger. "Oh, you are so wrong there, brother. There is a little bit of Christian in all of us. You seem to forget once you ate him for your supper. You are what you eat brother. Now, you can call Der Hund all you like. He can do nothing about me. I refuse to go back in you. I like being free, and I plan to stay here for a very long time. Tell you what, if you leave this our secret, then I will help you both get the mission back on track. There is no reason to get the Core all stirred up, ja? Besides, you call him he will find out you motherfuckers screwed up so bad if something isn't done fast, we are toast."

Christian glared with anger at Taube. "Are you blackmailing us, you bastard?"

Taube nodded with a giggle. "Ja, sure am."

Christian broke out in wicked laughter. "Ah shit, let him stay Maximillian. I merely liked this guy, now I think I may love him. His style is one I can appreciate. Finally, there is a sneaky, conniving, backstabbing, dirty, sonofabitch of my own heart to hang with. Since old Mad Max went schwuler over that monster Max thing, I haven't enjoyed riding the flesh at all. Taube, you are welcome to hang with me anytime."

Taube nodded. "Oh, I intend to hang out with you brother. We have work to do. Here are the rules of the game. I set them up and you knock them down. Nein mercy." He laughed wildly while Christian nodded, his eyes glowing red as fire.

I groaned and covered my face. "Fuck, you are right Taube. If Der Hund finds out we are trapped in the metal he will shatter us and kill the boy. Okay, you have a deal if you can help us clean this shit up before that grouchy Core finds out. What the hell we got to lose anyway? I bet we will grow a fine tree."

Christian shouted in joy, "Now you are speaking my language. Wake the boy up, let's get this show started. We rested enough. Hell, ja." He high fived with Taube again, the two of them laughing till they fell on their asses.

I stood dare a moment watching them. I thought to myself briefly about that doctor saying we had the schizophrenia. For a second there I almost believed it. This was some crazy shit, and I was the only sane one in the boys head. I shook off that horrible thinking and took the wheel after taking a deep breath. It was time to awaken the flesh. Let the games begin.

I opened my eyes and found myself in Master Leo's bed. I had been stripped, bathed and all my wounds were treated. I groaned out in agony as I sat up. Master Leo had been sleeping next to me. He startled to alertness and sat up reaching out to pull me to my back.

"Meine Hase. You are awake. Lay down, you had quite a spill. The doctor has ordered rest and quiet for the next week. Tell me, how are you feeling?" Master Leo leaned down looking into my burning eyes.

I moaned out in pain. "What the hell happened, Master? My head is killing me. Did I break my arm? The right one won't move." I panicked a little at the poor condition the flesh was in.

Master Leo shook his head. "Nein, Christian Axel. Your spasms were violent. You hit your head many times before we could stop you. That arm of yours was the one you landed on. It is only pulled, not broken. You did bite your tongue before I got my quirt into your mouth. The doctor says the injuries are minor compared to how bad they could have been. He has increased your anticonvulsants to prevent this from continuing. I am very grateful to see you are alert. I was frightened you may never wake up." He pushed my hair away from my forehead and kissed it gently.

I scoffed. "I wish I hadn't Master. I am trapped in my metal. There is no reason to continue this bullshit. I am finished."

Master Leo shook his head and smiled with pleasantness. "Nein, meine heart. You are only trapped there on paper. You will be judged Dominant by the summer next year. I have no fear that you will pass the last two sections of the test. The rest is in the bag. Have a little faith, will you?"

I narrowed my eyes and glared at him. "In whom? You? The other Masters? Myself? The Gott that doesn't exist perhaps? Everyone is the liar, and I am a fool. You can go ahead and call the Guard, or I will make sure they have cause to come get me soon enough."

He frowned. "Christian Axel. What the hell has gotten into you? This is not the sure and strong boy I know speaking. This seizure has shaken you up, that is all."

I shook my head. "Nein. I am sick of this shit Master. I did everything the Masters want, and all I ever get is the sore ass from their constant screw jobs. I will not stay on my knees sucking wrinkled cocks for all my life. Call the fucking Guard, Leo."

I sat up and swung my legs over the side of the bed swooning from dizziness. Master Leo reached out and grabbed me around my arms and chest to restrain my leaving. I struggled against him, but he was stronger than me back den.

"Christian Axel, you lay the fuck down this minute. That is my directive," he yelled into my ear, making my head pound even harder.

I wriggled and fought his hold. "Or you do what, Leo? Call the Guard? Good, do it motherfucker. I double dog dare you."

The door of his room swung open, and Master Jonas came rushing in. I shouted out in anger as the Vampire came to aid his brother Elder to force me to my back.

"You called this sonofabitch. Leo, you snake. I hate you both. I hope you all burn in hell. Get the fuck off me, perverts. You make me sick. I want to die. Call the Gott damned Guard now, motherfuckers," I screamed at the two as they pinned my arms and yelled for Master Claus and Master Bladrick to bring the ropes.

It took all four of the old men to restrain me by bondage to Master Leo's bed. I pulled and cursed them. I even spit twice into Master Claus's face before they got me where my struggles were of no avail. I was stuck as usual while the four of them stood around staring at me while sweating and panting from their labors.

Master Jonas shot a look at the others. "Mad Maxx, you settle your ass down right now. I mean it."

I laughed loudly. "You don't mean that really do you? Gosh Master, how can you fuck me if I calm my ass? Does it turn you on to tie up a little boy? Bet you all got hard-ons right this minute from it. Well, what are you waiting for? I cannot stop any of you. Here I am. Go for it fellow. The Mad Maxx is open for business." I howled in laughter until tears come to my eyes from that crazy statement.

Master Claus came forward and backhanded me causing me to pause a moment of my mirth. "Enough, Mad Maxx. Be still."

I recovered from his blow and smiled at him with mischief. "Foreplay over? You know how to make it hurt, Master, I respect that. Did you learn that from your mother? I learned a lot from my own which is why I ask. She is the wormy apple of my eye, you know. Never mind, are we doing this thing? There are four of you so two will have to wait their turn unless you decide to free my hands. Batter up. A swing and a miss. Foul ball. It is okay, that was not a strike out," I howled out in maniacal laughter.

Master Leo wailed out, "Stop this, Christian Axel. You are only hurting yourself by acting the fool like this."

I giggled wildly at that. "I am hurting myself, he says. Ah, hard to do with my cock in a cage and a chain around my neck. Who-hoo, all aboard. This ship is headed right to hell boys. Better head for the poop deck, ha-ha. Life is so grant. I know I cannot get enough of it. Can someone call the police? I think there was a crime committed or maybe I should be committed." I couldn't stop laughing at that right there. *I admit I laughed my ass off at that too. Hey, I was nine. He said poop, cut me some slack.*

Master Leo's eyes went wide. "Jonas, we need to send Christian Axel to get professional help. His mental illness has gone acute. He is mad. We cannot leave him tied up in my bed forever."

Master Jonas scoffed. "Fine by me. We can move him to mine if you have an issue with him staying here."

I wailed with tears and laughter. "Ja, I go live with the Vampire and leave the snakes. Creepy crawly things abound. I am not scared of you Vampire man. Did you bring your lancet? The answer is in the blood, you know. The demons live there, Leo. I have seen them. They come in the dark but that is okay, I like the dark."

Master Bladrick put up his hand while I continued to scream in rambles. "Call the Haus doctor. Have the boy sedated and get him a heavy prescription of valium. We keep him quiet till this madness subsides. It always does. Mad Maxx is merely stressed. He will recover. I don't see anything that he has not done all along. It is only louder this time is all."

Master Leo's snapped his finger with his mouth open with in surprise. "Wake the fuck up Bladrick. The boy is gone. Sedatives? That is your fucking answer? I cannot believe this shit. He needs help, real help."

I smirked and wailed out. "Who are you talking to Leo? The walls? Who is the insane one now. They hear nothing but the sound of their own heated blood. Sedatives keep the flesh quiet. Hard to say nein with a cock in your mouth and drugs in your brain, ja? I laughed again and pulled hard on my ropes.

Master Jonas came over and backhanded me with much brutality. My teeth rattled in my jaw. I giggled as my head spun to the side then turned it and spat the blood from my mouth into the cocksucker's face.

"There's your dinner, Vampire. Lap it up, motherfucker. Don't you feel younger already? I give you whatever you want, whenever you want it, Master." I began to scream without stopping, my face turning red as the crimson on Master Jonas's face.

I was yelling like that because above me the vortex was spinning, and the webs of the tapestry were weaving. The shattering was coming for Mad Maxx. There was no escape either. Those stupid fuckers tied me up. I couldn't run or anything. I closed my eyes as the universe split into a million pieces. Time stood still and the emptiness of that world behind the real one filled the flesh.

Christian, Taube, and I huddled together screaming with terror as the light flashed and the world spun. The winds of delusions screeched through the boy like the lost banshee. Whispers, threats, gossip, fears, all the thoughts of the residents of the Haus rose to our ears. The noise was deafening. The boy couldn't even cover his head to drown out the sounds.

Then to our greatest horror, we saw Der Hund caught up in the spinning cyclone within. He was being ripped to pieces by the tempest. The three of us ran for him grabbing his legs holding him from with all our strength. I wailed out to Christian to find rope. We had no choice but to bond him to the wheel or all would be lost.

Der Hund heard me begging for ropes. He let out a blood curdling howl then kicked me in the face. I was knocked backward. Taube couldn't hold him alone, and Christian couldn't fight his way through the storm in time. I watched helplessly as our Core was pulled into the raging vortex and thrown from our sights to the other side of nowhere.

I covered my head sobbing in pure hopelessness. Taube sat there stunned, unsure what to do. Christian stared dumbfounded into the direction Der Hund had gone. We were on our own. Our Core had been tossed. Our mission was more than failed our fate was sealed. We lost.

Christian sat down trancing into the nothing. Taube babbled and I continued to cry. This was dishonor of the worst kind. I decided without Der Hund the second they untied the boy we were going over the banister. There was no reason to continue. Not like this, a shell of shards and no Master.

Da Haus doctor came and shot the flesh up with heavy sedation. We didn't care. The fast moving drug wasn't necessary any longer. The boy had gone silent, near catatonic with stillness. The Elders come each in their turn and kissed the forehead of our wheel. None of us bothered to respond as they left us tied up and turned off the lights, leaving the room.

Mad Max, Max and Mad Maxx came out of the shadows. They all had their heads down in grief. I looked up from my weeping, waiting for the brutes to say anything snotty. There was no reason to kick me anymore. The end was here at last.

Mad Max sighed. "Der Hund will find his way back Maximillian. He always does. He will be more disfigured, but he will come home. You must stop grieving. I for one think if we work together then maybe he can come back to find us on track once more." Max nodded but didn't look up from the floor.

Mad Maxx sniffed and wiped his tears, he was openly crying. "I agree with brother Mad Max. Der Hund is tough Maximillian. We can do this if we try. There will be a sunrise and if there is one that the boys eyes can see, there is always hope, ja?"

Christian finally spoke up. "I hate to agree with the pussies Maximillian, but they are correct. I have known Der Hund the longest. He always endures what he must. If you can stop wishing for death, this can still be fixed."

Taube stopped babbling and looked at me. “We play the game, Maximillian, till the boy is no more.”

Mad Max narrowed his eyes glaring at Traube. “Who the fuck is this crazy motherfucker? What the hell Maximillian? Did you get pregnant during one of your many trysts or something?”

Max giggled with a start. “Christ, Mad Max, really? You are supposed to be making Maximillian feel better. Not picking on him.”

Mad Max growled with irritation. “Shit. How can I help it? Look at that bastard. Hey whore do you even know who the father is?”

Taube smiled with mischief. “That would be Master Malfred brother. See I have his eyes, but soon I will have his throat…in my hands.”

Mad Max smiled with evil. “Ah, slap me and call me a fatherfucker. Maximillian, you brilliant cocksucker. I cannot believe what I am looking at. The answer to all our troubles sits there and you are weeping like the damned Frau. Get your schwuler ass up drama queen. We have work to do.” He pulled on his leash with a playful smile, nearly knocking Max to his ass.

Mad Maxx smiled too with wickedness in his gaze,. “This is indeed wonderful. Welcome to the show brother. Uhm, what is your name?”

Christian winked and proudly announced, “This is Taube, brothers. The solution to our X.”

The Maxes all nodded their heads and shot each other looks of victory. I shuddered and did my best to quell my tears.

"I see I am outvoted. I wish to end the boy, but you insane fuckers think this thing will bail us out. How the fuck can a mirror shard do that?" I stood up shivering from my crushing despair.

Taube smiled at me. "I am the perfect man for this job brother. I am the mirror to which the Master will see his own reflection. I am whatever he believes he can see in me. From you, our most talented shard, is birthed a game piece of Malfred's dreams. That man wants the perfect, seductive, submissive who will make all his dreams come to truth. He should beware what he wishes for. Those that climb too high fall to their deaths when pushed off the summit." He giggled into his hands with his blue eyes shining full of demons.

I shot a look at the Maxes. They all smiled with glee. I looked back at Taube and suddenly, I understood the plot. Der Hund had expected this to happen. He would come back. He always finds his way back. The boys were right. I had to stop worrying about everyone else betraying us. I needed only to have faith in me.

Mad Maxx let out a yell of victory. "We got this, brothers. I for one swear my allegiance to each of you for all our lives. I will never let any of you down. I am a man of my word."

Mad Max nodded. "I hate you Maximillian, but you have my respect and my word. You can count on me to back your ass, as long as there isn't some nasty cock coming at it." He choked on his words when Max kicked him hard.

Max shot him a look of caution, then looked at me with a friendly smile. "What my misguided brother means is the two of us give our word. We will be here for you brother. You have our word."

Christian snorted then laughed. "Ja, okay schwuler boy, you have my allegiance as well. Now pick up your pansy ass and drive this boy right to the fucking bolt cutters. You and Taube focus on getting the loose ends bound up, the rest of us will move those that try to block our play the fuck out of our way anyway we must. Finish line, here we come."

Taube smiled at that. "This is the way it is done. Now, I will handle Malfred. Claus and Bladrick, those cocksuckers are yours Maximillian. Mad Max, you handle Leo. Mad Maxx, the Vampire is all yours."

The shards all agreed this was a fair division of services so none of us would tire behind the wheel. Christian grumbled that he would like to handle all the Masters. We giggled that would be the easiest way but also the quickest way to the orchard.

Christian was calmed when we promised he could take Malfred's head. We sweetened the deal by assuring him he could eventually kill Jonas and Peter too. We still needed those two fuckers for the time being, like it or not. Getting the collar busted was only half the trouble. The bolt cutters would come in handy once our Dominance was completed.

None of us knew how long it would be before Der Hund returned to us. Until that time our symptoms of madness would be volatile, hard to control, and misfiring would happen. We braced ourselves for the coming instability and swore unwavering brotherhood no matter how bad things got in the future. At last, the shards had made peace, and the war within the boy's head had come to a truce.

That doctor's sedatives were the good ones. The boy slept for many hours. Master Leo and Master Jonas took turns making sure the flesh drank fluids and they cleaned him up when he soiled the sheets. There was nothing we could do until those nasty drugs wore off. Taube, Christian, and I kept each other entertained with stories of things we were going to do the first second we were free of the Haus.

Christian wanted to get a car and look for women to woo. Taube and I agreed this was certainly first on our list too. I wanted to run barefooted in the grass far from the fucking yard. Taube wanted to find a fancy club and dance till his feet were worn to nubs. We laughed and teased each other a great deal during those dark hours of our unconscious.

After nearly two years of constant squabbling, I have to say getting along with my brothers was one of the few nice things going on in our brutal world. I was almost sorry to let these quiet, calm moments go when the night became the next day. The medication holding the flesh in limbo began to lose hold.

I stretched then shot my brothers a smile as Master Leo walked into the room. They nodded back indicating they were ready. It was time to get back on the mission. We had rested enough. The Elder opened the curtains to let the early morning sunlight frighten away the darkness. He turned to check on the flesh and let out a yelp of surprise upon finding me looking at him with a grin.

"Christian Axel? How are you feeling, meine heart? Better I hope?" Master Leo came over and felt my forehead for signs of a fever that was not there.

I nodded. "I am fine, Master. Thank you for asking. Is there something I can do for you?" I grinned even wider at him.

He pulled back his hand from my face as if I bit him. "Huh? Nein, Meine Hase, you are many things but doing okay is not one of them, nor are you in the condition to do anything for me."

I chuckled at that. "Oh, I beg to differ, Master. If you are referring to these ropes, well give me a second. I will make them go away like magic. I have that power you know. I am Mad Maxx the Brutal. The one and only of legend." I watched him back away from the bed appearing startled by my answer for some reason.

Master Leo shook his head. “Meine Hase, you are delusional with much grandiosity. This is your disease speaking to me, not you.”

I scoffed. “You hear them too, I suppose. You must learn to never mind the others. I am capable of service Master. You untie me and I get right to it. No matter what you heard about me, they lie. I am the best of the best, ja?” I returned to smiling.

Master Leo shook his head. “I will not untie you, Christian Axel. You are full of the demons of your madness. You need to be in a hospital bed far from this fucking Haus.”

I turned my head and looked all around the room appearing stunned. “Nein, Master. I see this is your bed. I believe we are in Das Kaiser Haus. What is this you say about this being the hospital? Ah, you are funning with me, ja? You wish to play a game. Can you show mercy and give me the rules of it? There are no such things as demons. That is pure fantasy. I hope you are not foolishly scared of such mythical creatures. I would think you learned such things are false before your minority was through with you. Oops, that sounded insolent, ja? What the hell am I saying? This will never do. I must beg your forgiveness, Master. I will stop that unbecoming behavior at once. Now, are you hungry? I can get your breakfast if you want or run your bath for that service.” I returned my gaze to him after making sure I was not in a hospital bed nor mad with any disease like he tried to tell me I was.

Master Leo snorted then looked at the floor. "You are forgiven, Christian Axel. However, I already ate my breakfast, meine heart. I am clean enough as well. Are you willing to eat something for me? Let's play a game called finish our plate. That would please your Master Leo a great deal. You have not eaten in two days."

I smiled brightly. "Your pleasure is my own Master. I do whatever you want when you want and where you want. When you're satisfied with my service then can we go see the lambs? I must get back to my responsibilities. There is no time for all this sleeping on the job. How is Der Makellos?"

Master Leo took a deep breath. "Der Makellos grows strong. He will be coming to live in our home soon. You can see the lambs when you can behave yourself and mind your manner, meine heart. I am going to call the kitchen for a tray. You eat it all and mind your Master Leo, then maybe I will take you to the barn this afternoon as your reward, ja?"

I nodded wildly. "You are most generous to this unworthy boy, Master. I thank you for the mercy of it. Can you ask Master Jonas to turn down his radio? I know better than to bring it up to him. I will give him no quarrel if he wishes to blast it like he does. He is the Master after all, ja?"

Master Leo narrowed his eyes. "You hear a radio, meine Hase? This music you hear is loud?"

I giggled with much humor. "Ah, I see you try to trick Mad Maxx. Nein, I hear nothing Master. Your will is my own." He almost caught me with his attempts to get me to complain about the Vampire's loud stereo.

The door comes open. Master Claus walked into the room staring at my smiling face staring at him. He flashed a quizzical expression to Master Leo then looked back at me.

"Mad Maxx? You are awake? The boy is not wailing, Leo. This is a good sign, ja?" His old face cracked into a pleased smile.

Master Leo shook his head. "Nein, he is not screaming, that is true, but the boy is hearing voices and delusional. Go ahead, try speaking with him. You will see."

Master Claus frowned at that bullshit lie then came to my side looking at me with sternness. "Does your Master Leo tell me the truth, Mad Maxx? You hear illusions or believe in false tales?"

I shook my head. "Nein, most honorable Master. I do not hear voices nor believe in the children's fairy stories as truth. Do understand, I dare not call my Master Leo the fibber though. I think he is merely tired, is all. I beg you to release me of these bonds. I will be most happy to provide for your services in return for that mercy. Allow me to demonstrate my perfect skills for you. You will not be disappointed." I looked away from his gaze to show my submissiveness to his authority.

Master Claus chuckled with much glee. “Ah, our Priceless has returned to us Leo. Untie the boy this minute. Bladrick was right, the madness was only momentary. Thank Gott.”

Master Leo clicked his tongue and snapped his fingers. “Oh, meine Lord. You are going insane yourself, Claus. Did you not fucking listen to word he just said? Perfect skills? That is the delusion of grandiosity.”

Master Claus’s good humor went dark in seconds. “I have been served by this collar a lot fucking longer than you have, Leo. He is not being delusional about it nor bragging. His abilities are the finest in this motherfucking Haus, that I can vouch for. That is why he is leveled Priceless. He is logical, coherent, and shows proper politeness for one in his low station. You untie this boy and let him return to his duties or I will call Jonas in here to do it for you.”

Master Leo crossed his arms with a scoff. “Call Jonas then. He will agree with me. The boy is a danger and should not be freed to engage in whatever horror that is lurking in his shattered mind.”

Master Claus glared at Leo a moment then shouted so loudly it made me wince, “Jonas, get your ass in here this minute.”

He didn’t have to yell twice, thank goodness. That fucker was a loud bastard when he wanted to be, you know. The Vampire came rushing into the room appearing pale with fear. I guess he thought maybe I was causing trouble or said something about his own illegal blood bonding with the boy. Whatever the reason, the Elder Jonas was nearly sweating in a panic when he came to the side of Master Leo's bed.

"I am here Claus. What has happened? Did he threaten you? Never mind whatever he says. The boy babbles. He is not even aware of what he is speaking about," The Vampire spewed out before Master Claus could even get a single word out.

Master Leo nodded. "See, told you, Jonas knows. The boy is not capable of service, Claus. Jonas, Claus wants me to cut Christian loose from his bonds. He thinks the boy is recovered."

Master Jonas shot a look of surprise at me, then back to Master Claus. "Huh? You think he is capable, Claus? You surely must be jesting with Leo, there is no way." Master Claus held up his hand to silence the Vampire.

The Elder pointed at me. "Go ahead. Speak to the boy Jonas. He is lucid. Leo is being overly cautious. I tell you the medication and rest have brought him back to Earth."

Master Jonas furrowed he brow, then leaned down into my face. I kept my gaze from his own as is proper protocol for a submissive with their Dominant. He reached out and grabbed my face demanding I look him in his eyes.

"Are you in there, Christian Axel? Claus says you are conscious of yourself. Tell me, how many people are in this room? Who am I? What day and month is it? Can you say where you are located right this minute?" He narrowed his dark eyes awaiting my answers.

I trembled a bit. "As you wish Master. There are four people that I can see in this room. Three Elder Dominants, and the nothing Mad Maxx. You are my Master and man the Vampire Jonas. I think it must be Wednesday, but I have been asleep a few days, ja? The month, uhm, that I am unclear on. It is maybe the fall or winter. I am in Deutschland and the Das Kaiser Haus, not a hospital like Master Leo says I am. Thank you for the mercy of allowing this worthless boy to serve you Master. I pray I have pleased you well."

Master Jonas let go of my jaw and backed up with a frown on his face. "Christian Axel is not completely lucid Claus, but he is logical enough to untie him, I think. The boy is a schizophrenic. You cannot expect him to ever be without some symptoms of the madness. I realize that we can never be totally assured he is well enough to return to service, but I don't think there will be any difficulties with him demonstrating proper docility as he appears to be."

Master Leo gasped and grabbed his chest dramatically. "You have got to be funning me, Jonas. Do you hear yourself? You of all people know what can happen if you release him and he has another fit. He is only being calm for this minute. You let him go and maybe he rushes for the banister. Better yet, maybe one of us do by his hand."

Master Claus chuckled. "Be still Leo. This boy is too small to harm the gnats flying round a cow's backside. Let him go and let's see if he can behave himself before we start this arguing."

Master Jonas nodded. "I agree with Claus. We untie him and watch to see if he is compliant. He gives us any grief, then we immediately rebind him." The Vampire leaned over me and began untying the ropes holding my wrists above my head.

I lay still waiting with patience and my eyes down caste. I was miffed that Master Leo thought me a danger to any of them, but I forgave his arguing over it. The man was merely misguided. I had no intention of killing him, Master Jonas nor Master Claus. I also was not going to jump from the fucking banister. I had work to do. I simply had no time for dying that day.

When I was free of my ropes, I sat up rubbing my wrists for a moment, then slipped off the bed to a kneel at Master Jonas and Master Claus's feet. I realized at that moment the boy was still naked with a chastity device in place, perverts. I shook off this one with the promise that I would pick the fucking lock the second I got the chance.

Master Claus let out a yelp of happiness. "Ah, see, the boy is subdued Leo. You worry wort. I told you he knows his place again. Jonas, you tell me, is this boy a threat to himself or others? He seems fine to me."

Master Jonas frowned. "We shall see. Christian Axel, you need a shower. Go clean yourself up and get dressed. You have twenty minutes, or you get a thudding. This you understand?"

I nodded, keeping my eyes to the floor. “Ja, Master, I thank you for the mercy of it.”

He backed up. “Then get to it. I will be watching you so no funny business. Move it.” I got up and rushed to Master Leo’s master bathroom and turned on the water to his tub.

I could see the sickness deeply rooted in the flesh, but it was advanced to the stage beyond my aid with a fast shower. I made the mental note that I would slip to the pool water the moment my Masters went into their slumber. For now, I would have to endure this horror without cure. I glanced to see Master Jonas standing at the door watching me. I jumped into the shower and scrubbed the flesh with much speed, wincing at the ineffectiveness of this false cleansing.

The sham shower was quickly finished. When I got out, Master Jonas came forward and handed me a towel. I thanked him, then dropped to my kneel and dried off the flesh. This made the Vampire laugh out loud.

“Overdoing this a bit aren’t you, Christian Axel? I think you need not be on your knees to dry off.” He chuckled with his eyes dancing.

I stopped my task then looked to the floor. “I know better, Master. I am aware you intend to keep me here on the floor in reverence of your magnificent person. If it be your pleasure, I request permission to retrieve my bag for fresh clothing. Otherwise, I wear this towel or whatever you desire I cover myself with. I thank you for the mercy of it.”

Master Jonas appeared startled by my response "What? I do not intend to keep you on your knees, Christian Axel. Where the hell did you get that idea?"

I shook my head, never looking up. "Your cock told me, Master. May I be released for that required task? I beg your forgiveness that I am wasting your time using my mouth in a way that does nothing for your truest desires."

Master Jonas gasped. "You stop this speaking like I only want you for my lust, Christian Axel. That is not fair to assume."

I shrugged. "I assume nothing, Master. May I beg your pardon and ask once again for your release to mind your instructions. I am happy to take punishment for failure if this is your ultimate goal. Your pleasure is always my own."

He growled. "Ja. Go get your fucking bag. I want to say I don't like this attitude you demonstrate to your man, Christian Axel. You better cut that shit out right this minute or I will take you to the chains for insulting me."

I got up and rushed for the door refusing to respond to that. I knew he was trying to start an argument so he would have just cause to re-bond me. I was not being insolent to him, and he knew it. These Dominants are all nuts, you know. You tell them nein and they whip you. You say what, they beat you to and still they bitch. There is no middle ground with them, ja?

I found my bag in Master Leo's room. The two Elders Leo and Claus stood dare whispering quietly while I tore through it seeking my outfitting. Master Jonas joined them as my audience while I dressed in my breeches and blouse fast as possible. The flesh still groaned and complained in agony, but I ignored the pain. I was gonna be damned if I would give Master Jonas cause to hit me for missing his deadline to finish his command. I got my socks and boots on then rushed to kneel at the Vampires feet with one minute to spare.

He grinned then patted my head while flashing an expression of confidence at Master Leo. "See Leo, this boy is capable of service to his Masters. Call Bladrick, Claus. Let's take our breakfast at the Great Hall to celebrate the good news that our Priceless collar has recovered."

Master Leo yelped with horror. "Are you out of your fucking mind Jonas? Bad enough you untie him, now you plan to trot him downstairs like the show pony? The boy needs a quiet, stress-free environment. He just had serious trauma and a fucking psychotic fit over that shit Malfred and his men pulled. If your intention is to kill the boy, then why be so elaborate about it? Just call the fucking Guard and be done with it."

I heard that shit right there. I flashed a look of terror at Master Jonas then quickly looked back to the floor trembling. He wanted to kill me. I knew the man wanted to drink my blood, and certainly to fuck me half to death, but murder me? That was a new plot I had not considered. I looked to Christian and told him to move Master Jonas up on the X list. I would have to watch this nutball close or no doubt he would get me first.

Master Jonas scoffed. "Oh, shut the fuck up, Leo. Those criminals Grisham and Gustov were put to the yard for their foul actions. Malfred will join the brutes soon enough. Christian Axel is fine. That bullshit didn't bother him a bit."

Master Leo's eyes went wide in disbelief. "What? Holy hell. The boy was gang raped and nearly killed, Jonas. That nightmare would bother anyone. Are you stupid or just an asshole?

Master Jonas reached down and snatched my chain leash while I winced at each of Master Leo's words. "Christ, Leo. The boy is the pleasure submissive. You cannot rape one of them. Sex is there fucking job. Malfred had no intentions of killing the Priceless collar fool. He wants the boy for his own. Christian Axel knew that. Tell him my love. You weren't upset by those brutes, were you?" He glared down at me.

I kept my head hung low as I said, "Master Jonas is correct. You cannot rape the professional whore, Master Leo. One, two, three or more, doesn't matter to me. My job is to endure whatever I am told to by my betters. My Masters wisely decided to punish all those involved, including this idiot boy. Those brutes have paid the price for their taking without payment to my Masters. I am grateful I was merely trapped in my collar for allowing the brute Grisham and Gustov the pleasure of tasting my metal.

I thank my honorable Masters for the mercy of not ending my life, as surely it should have been, despite my stupidity." I held my tears back with all my strength at that nasty statement.

Master Jonas grinned with a victorious expression. "See there, Leo. Christian Axel is the indestructible Priceless. He knows he was forgiven and accepts his punishment for his compliance with this crime. I thought him merely a bit better, but I can see he is completely recovered." The Vampire ruffled my hair with pride in his eyes.

Master Leo shook his head. "I don't believe this bullshit, Jonas. You were not there. This boy was anything but subdued when those men attacked him. There were three of them, you fool. Christian Axel didn't just lay there and take it with joy. I don't know anyone who either. Those brutes hurt him. I cannot close my eyes without seeing that horror over and over and I was merely the witness. I refuse to acknowledge that this poor boy is not severely traumatized by these rapes. You all can call it theft if you want but I call it what the fuck it is."

Master Claus put up his hand for silence. "Enough Leo. The boy has been punished as have the criminals. This bullshit is over. That is the way it is done in the Haus. You cannot bring this up anymore. Mad Maxx has accepted his fate of lifetime service to his Masters. You would do well to drop the incident that led to this mess. If his assigned punishment bothers you so fucking much then why do you insist on recalling it. I will give your extra day with him to that foul Malfred. I am sure he won't see the trapped Priceless as the burden you seem to think he is."

Master Leo crossed his arms. "I will drop this only because I see your both hardheaded fucks that hear nothing but the sounds of your arrogant, selfish voices. One day, this boy will rise up and make all of you sorry for ignoring that he is a human being with feelings. You treat someone like a dog, they become one. and this one is the mad canine, you'll see. I warn none of you again. Fucking fools, the lot of you."

Master Claus rolled his eyes at Master Jonas then chuckled. "Well, good. Now that we have that off our chest, I will call brother Bladrick. I think breakfast in the Great Hall is a good idea. I will call Malfred as well to join us."

Master Jonas growled out in anger. "Why? Leave that cocksucker out of this. He has done enough. That motherfucker should be in the yard with his brutes, not breaking bread with us. You dare to embrace him as a brother. I will never accept him as one of us.

Master Claus grinned with wickedness. "Calm down, Jonas. You know I didn't get to be second in command of this entire Haus and hold the spot even in Xavier's time while being the forgiving fool. You should have a little faith in old Claus. The man has been plaguing us for many years. He was willing to murder, manipulate, and even dared the wrath of the Elders to obtain his spot among this brutal wolf pack. When you have an enemy foolish enough to be willing to come to your house, then you invite them. The second they dare to turn their back, you stick your blade in to the hilt. The coverup is much easier when everyone thinks you were their associate not their foe. This Malfred has signed his death warrant, and he knows this. Therefore, we must work together to make him think all is forgotten. Wait and see if he doesn't buy into the bullshit, we sell him. He will be in hell an hour before he realizes we are not demented enough to ever lose the memory of the crimes he has committed against the Elders."

The angered Vampire suddenly smiled with evil. "Ah, I see. This is very clever, Claus. Okay, I will keep my mouth shut and fury in check as best I can. You can count me in on your plan as long as that fucker dies and soon."

Master Claus nodded with a smile, then looked to Master Leo. "And you Leo? What about you? Can the brotherhood count on your aid in this? If not, then can we at least obtain your silence?"

Master Leo glanced at me then frowned. "You can all count on me to do whatever I must to see this cocksucker growing grass from below. I would ask for the pleasure of sending him to his well-deserved reward for Christian Axel's sake. I want meine Hase to know the man paid dearly for what he did to him."

Master Claus shook his head with a huge diabolical smile. "Nein. I must regrettably refuse you request, brother Leo. That honor is not yours to hold. We have the Priceless of legend right here in this room. He is the Hand of the Elders. Mad Maxx will send this Malfred to the Devil when the time comes. Won't you, my love?" He focused on my bowed head.

I looked up at him with a startle. "If this is your pleasure Master, it is most certainly mine." I couldn't believe Master Claus was openly granting me permission to kill the man I hated the most on Earth.

Master Claus laughed while Master Jonas joined him. "Ah, it is more than my pleasure, meine little one. This motherfucker used our Priceless collar to clear his path. Well, we shall shoot him with his own weapon. I will tell you Mad Maxx. You do this successfully and never get caught, I will withdraw the punishment of your life servitude to the Elders."

I shook my head with confusion. "You can do that, Master? I thought if I am trapped in my collar. I assumed I am submissive to this Haus for all time."

The crossdressing Elder nodded. "Ja, it is if you don't end him before collar selection. However, if he is dead, then no crime of theft was ever committed against us. If you can silence his ability to brag of his blood bonding, then it is quite simple, it never happened. Beware though, Mad Maxx, ending this brute will be a challenge. You must make it look natural, and somehow keep your association with it unknown to any but the men in this room. The Haus already expects her Elders to rise up and kill him. He has earned the respect of every fucking degenerate in this place by obtaining the forbidden one of his age and lack of credentials. Malfred never served as a Dungeon Master, you know. They all see him as the hero they wish to be. If we murder him openly, then anarchy will reign among the Dominants, and all of us will be feeding the worms by sunrise of the next day. You will be passed around till you are torn to bits. This bastard Malfred managed to obtain his honorable place by what appears to be legal means. Though this is not true, the others in this place will refuse to believe it because they want to watch one of their own rise. Therefore, he is untouchable to me, Bladrick, Jonas, Leo, and even Cora. We could hire one that is not Elder to do this, but I thought you would want the task since it was you, they most grievously dishonored by this devious plot."

I smiled with demons rising. "I thank you for this mercy, Master."

Master Claus smiled then walked over and stroked my cheek lovingly. "I hope you realize how very difficult this will be on you. You will have to tolerate much torment for this revenge. I know you though. I have not been blind. I watched as you have continually endured what you must. If you were to kill him tomorrow then even Cora cannot prevent the Guard from putting a bullet in your shattered mind. Do you understand this man will hold you in his clutches and force you to take his lust for possibly many months before it is safe to end his life?"

I nodded with a bitter sigh. "Ja, Master, I do realize this. I am prepared to do what I must to see Master Malfred in his grave by my own hands."

Master Leo shook his head. “Claus, you are making a huge mistake sending this disturbed boy to do a man’s job. Christian Axel is too unstable to do this. He will be caught and sent to the yard with Malfred. I cannot just sit back and watch you allow him to do our dirty work. This is exploitation of the worst kind. Hire a fucking black collar brute or one of the blood thirsty Russians. Leave our Priceless out of this foul business.”

Master Claus frowned at Master Leo. “You will be silent, brother. I exploit no one. This right belongs to Mad Maxx, and we all know it. You heard with your own ears he is willing to accept the task and the possible punishment for it. I have no doubt in my mind he will accomplish it. You listen to me closely, Leo. If he cannot defend himself as the submissive, he will not survive long in this Haus as a Dominant. No Priceless has ever broken their metal. I think he will be an even bigger target if he is freed, than he is right this moment. However, I realize this thing I ask will be time consuming and painful for him. Therefore, I will hereby wave the final two sections of the Dominant testing. I replace them with this single proof of his right to face me as my equal. This collar will instead fulfil the dangerous task of ending the legendary Elder Malfred. I add the two conditions that this be done only upon my all-clear command and without committing any further insults that carry a punishment of life service. If he can do this, then he is Dominant, and that silver will be judged false. I swear this on my soul, that of my mother and with both of you fine gentlemen as my witness. Do you accept my offer as I have made it without quarrel, Mad Maxx?”

I smiled with glee and nodded wildly. "I accept this offer Master and offer my eternal gratitude for your generosity and mercy." I fell to my face and kissed the toes of his boots in prostrate feeling new hope surging within the boy.

If Master Claus were being truthful, then I would indeed be finishing the mission as the winner of all we had suffered for. I had no fear that I could fulfil his required task and prove myself a Dominant rather than a fucking submissive. I did understand this would mean playing the role of "grateful submissive" at the feet of my enemy, Malfred, for an undisclosed amount of time. I had already suffered just as badly on the leash of my father Peter. Not to mention the many other horrors I had born ranging from the chains of Xavier to the brutal blood fetish of the Vampire Jonas. I was sure I could handle this one final indignity in my quest for the sacred bolt cutters with ease.

I shot a look of wonder at Taube the "game player." He stood there smiling back at me nodding with an expression of confidence. I suddenly realized Taube couldn't have arrived at a better time. This Mirror shard was exactly what the boy needed to seduce and then gain complacency from that rat fucker Malfred. We were as good as free. I could just feel it within. All we had to do was survive this horror life another seven months, then all our dreams would finally come true.

Master Claus left the room to call his brothers Master Bladrick and Master Malfred for this breakfast gathering. I kept my place kneeling while Master Jonas and Master Leo spoke quietly about the menu and the weather.

I had trouble hearing them over all the damned thoughts of the residents in the Haus. I shook my head then covered my ears with my hands. I then noticed that the boy still wore the leather cuffs of Master Malfred's design. I growled to myself about that humiliation, but the noises bothered me enough I let this bullshit go for now.

Master Leo saw my discomfort. "Meine Hase? You hear the voices, ja? See I told you, Jonas. The boy is still having significant symptoms. You fools will not stop till he is dead."

Master Jonas grimaced. "Christian Axel, you cannot walk around holding your ears, my love. This causes tongues to wag. You heard Master Claus, if you commit another infraction against the Haus, he cannot save you anymore. Insanity is a crime fool. Stop this now, I command it." He lightly kicked me in the side.

Master Leo reached out to grab Master Jonas begging him to let me be. "I apologize Master. The noise, I can hear better than anyone on Earth. I can hear the ones downstairs talking of their gossips and chore lists. I must drown out the sounds of them. It is my burden with these superpowers I have you know." I assumed that my explanation would be accepted as fact, since it is the damned truth.

Master Jonas gasped. "Oh shit. Leo, I see now what you mean. Okay, what the fuck do we do now? If you say send him to the hospital or tie him to the bed, I will beat you to death. I mean it. Claus has offered this boy a deal too good to refuse. Show the boy how much you and I genuinely love him. Or was that mere bullshit you fed him to gain his special services? If you were not faking your feelings, then I must beg you to aid me in this task. If you and I join forces, we might be capable of hiding these psychotic behaviors of his from those that would use it against him.

Master Leo grabbed his chest in surprise. “What? You admit that I love him too and are asking for my help? This cannot be.”

The Vampire spit on the floor growling with much irritation. “I hate that I am in this position, but there is no doubt the boy will listen to you when he minds no other. You have stolen his heart from me, you lucky bastard. I still think I could steal it back, but not if he is put to the fucking yard, Leo. You are going to help me or not. I won’t lower myself to ask you twice motherfucker.”

Master Leo seemed stunned but nodded. “Uhm, ja. If there is no other way, I think maybe together we could frame his madness to appear as eccentricity expected of any Priceless collar. The real problem is that our aid to him must truly curb the symptoms down from its painful levels. The boy is reacting to things you and I cannot see, hear, or sense. Like this minute, he hears voices. My Maus would cover her ears like that. The only thing that helped her was music and, oh wait, I have an idea.” The Elder rushed from the room.

I spoke in whispers to Taube. “Brother, can you see if fucking Evelyn will answer that bell? It is giving me a headache. Send Mad Max to murder that bitch. She was telling Malfred when we were going to the kitchen, you know. That was how Malfred, and the brutes, had the knowledge we were alone. Ja, I hear that fucking song too. I hate that one. Ah, I will get a black car. It will match our heart, ja? I hate the fucking black collars though. They all need to be buried in the…What? Nein, I didn’t say that. Tell Mad Max he can suck my cock if he is missing his Master so bad.” I began to giggle at that insult.

Master Jonas stood there listening to us. “Meine heart. You must stop this speaking to your masks. It is okay in front of me or your Master Leo, but I command you to cease it anywhere else.”

I looked at him in a startle. “Uhm, forgive me Master but I said nothing. You are hearing your radio is all. Those sounds come through the walls like paper. It is not my place to tell my betters of their pleasures, ja? However, I feel it my duty to warn you that listening to your music so loud will make you go deaf one day.” I pushed my hands on my ears harder as the noise rose another notch.

Master Leo came rushing back into the room with a pair of Pioneer SE 305 headphones he pulled off his record player. He stood over me panting from his wild run listening as if he could hear that fucking radio of Master Jonas’s too.

"This is bad, Jonas. He is speaking to the voices. Maybe this will help a bit. Christian Axel, take your hands out of my way. I want you to wear these headphones. They drown out noises of, uhm. loud noises and stereos turned up too loud." He waited till I begrudgingly removed my hand then put the things on my head.

Master Jonas snorted. "He looks a fool in those crazy things Leo. How will this hide him speaking to his shards? You planning to put duct tape on his mouth or maybe a ball gag in everywhere we go?"

Master Leo sneered at Master Jonas. "Give this a second to see if it works will you. Christian Axel, listen to me meine hase. These are special ear bumpers. The material is soundproof. You should notice there are almost no other sounds but those of your Masters voices. They were extremely expensive to buy. I had to go all the way to Rome and only a few existed in the entire world. The experts in espionage created them so they could target single sounds from millions of them through the airwaves. This you understand, ja?"

I did notice the noises were tolerable all the sudden. I smiled then lowered my hands waiting to see if the fancy spy tool would work to keep my superpower hearing under control. When after a few moments the sounds stayed muffled, I nodded and wrung my hands with relief. That shit was driving me insane. Thank Gott Master Leo had those wonderful, cushioned headphones.

Master Jonas smiled upon seeing my keeping my hands off my ears. “Well, sonofabitch. It worked. Damn Leo, you’re the genius.”

Master Leo took up my leash. “Nein, I am sadly the experienced one when it comes to schizophrenia Jonas. My Maus got like this just before she took her own life. I was thinking of your offer. The truth is that I do love Christian Axel more than anything I have ever cared for. I want him to be safe, adored, and comfortable as possible given his disease. Even more than that, I want to be with him for the rest of my worthless life. I realize this is not what the boy wants, nor you either. I am a reasonable man, and I am hoping you are too. I realize you and I can share his attentions as his honest lovers. What I propose is that in return for your helping me watch out for him during this dangerous time in his cycle. I will help you woo him to adore you the way he loves his Leo. Like you Jonas, I only offer this agreement with you this once. I am a more jealous man than you think. Sharing his heart with you is hard for me to stomach but I would rather share this glorious soul’s love with you than lose him for all time. I cannot do this alone, or with you always at my back. Do we have a deal?”

Master Jonas spit on the floor. He always does that, not sure why though to this very day. “Ja brother, I agree to your offer. I have tried everything to gain his true love and failed most miserably. The legend is that if you can gain the true heart of the Priceless, you’re assured a long and peaceful life. I want this prize almost as much as I desire the cure for death that only Christian Axel can find for me. He must live, break his collar, and go out there to seek out his mate of legendary power. Thanks to this alone, you have me at the disadvantage. The Haus is going to see this madness in him if we cannot explain it away. Then, I have almost no time left to await the next forbidden silver to rise. That said, I can see the true love he has for you no matter how much either of you attempt to deny it. I don't think it is possible to love more than one. It would weaken the bond of each involved, but I am willing to try it your way. I swear my allegiance to you and Christian Axel to do whatever it takes to keep his symptoms from getting himself, or anyone other than that fucker Malfred, killed."

Master Leo smiled, pulled my leash lightly and hand motioned me to stand. "Well, that was not exactly the brotherly "hell ja I am with you Leo" I hoped for, but I suppose it will do. Come, meine hase. You follow your Master Leo and leave that headset alone. You may wring your hands or even whisper to yourself, but no loud speaking nor rocking in your seat when at the Great Hall. Answer your Master that you understand these commands." He stared at me with sternness.

I began at once to wring my hands; grateful he didn't forbid that mercy. "Ja, Master, I do whatever you say and thank you for the mercy of it. Will there be enough room at that table for all these people you have invited?" I looked around at the glowing orbs and fleeting shadows of that fast-growing space.

He shot a nervous glance at the Vampire. "You focus on your commands and ignore what the Masters do or do not do. That is not your place to decide who is invited to sit at our table, now is it?"

I nodded. "I apologize for my overstepping my bounds, Master. I beg your forgiveness for my forgetfulness." I shifted a glance at the others and wondered if they would mind Master Leo's commands the way I had to.

He nodded. "You are forgive. Don't let it happen again, or you will be punished. Come now. You will eat your breakfast and behave yourself." I followed Master Leo and Master Jonas out of the bedroom in my proper protocol.

The Elders Claus and Bladrick awaited us in Master Leo's living room. They smiled with joy until they saw me walking behind Master Leo with the headset on. Master Bladrick wanted them removed. Master Jonas told him the music device would help keep my overactive mind still and they should be left alone. The two Elders grumbled but dropped their arguments. Master Leo handed my leash to Master Claus and the five of us took off to the Elders back stairwell.

I barely looked up to notice that Master Malfred was standing at the top step with an evil smile. He was wearing his finest fancy suit, and I could smell his expensive cologne many steps away. I assumed he needed that fake perfume to hide the stink of his foul rodent nature.

The group stopped to offer him polite greetings. That shady bastard puffed up his chest in pride while each Elder smiled and shook his hand calling him "brother Malfred." I wanted to puke at that sight, but I kept my eyes to the floor and wrung my hands like I was told. Then the shithead come forward and kissed me on the top of my head. I closed my eyes and held still as he reached out and lifted my chin examining the headphones on my ears.

“Ah, this Pioneer is a great company. These are excellent headphones the Priceless wears. Smart thinking brothers to calm his hallucinations with such a brilliant cover. He is still hearing the voices to extreme I assume?” I had sung under my breath the song Master Leo taught me by the Moody Blues. Master Malfred couldn’t speak English, you know.

He let my face go with an expression of arrogance. He shot looks at the four Elders as if waiting for one of them to verify his assumption that I was the schizophrenic that heard auditory hallucinations. Well, he was wrong. I have the super hearing is all. Malfred always was the snotty prick.

Master Claus and Master Bladrick shot the Vampire and Master Leo a look of fear. “Nein, the boy was granted this headset as a gift by the Elders, is all. He is just a kid at fourteen. You know how the young can become very caught up in their material things. None of us can get the boy to stop wearing them as if they are a fashion statement,” Master Claus stammered out.

Master Leo nodded then snapped his fingers while rolling his eyes. “Ah, the things we tolerate from these youth. They are such the rebels with their long hair and crazy clothing. And the music, well, actually that is one thing about this new generation I do so enjoy. These kids do have rhythm, ja?" He wiggled around as if dancing.

I let out a loud yell, then laughed at Master Leo's overblown dramatic behavior. I suddenly recalled I was to be silent when Master Claus jerked hard on my leash and shot me an angered look. I covered my mouth with my hands trying to stifle the horrid chuckling. Master Malfred smiled with viciousness in his expression "I see. This is the latest fashion. I had no idea. I will maybe have to get a pair of these fine headphones for myself. What do you think of that Mad Maxx? I can get you another pair if you want me to."

I scoffed. "There aren't anymore, Master. Master Leo gave me the last pair on Earth. It cost him a lot of money to get them too. Thank you for the mercy, but these will have to last me for all time."

Master Malfred gasped then smiled with demons in his eyes. "Oh, the last one on Earth is what your Master told you? Well, I will have to do my best to find something just as fine as these for meine taube then, won't I? You are indeed a true gem. I am the lucky man to have so many honorable brothers and this beautiful boy to serve me for the rest of my life, ja?" He backed up, looked me over a moment then broke his lustful trance and took his place to the right of Master Leo behind me.

I wrung my hands furiously and dropped my gaze singing the Nights in White Satin a bit louder to drown out the sounds of Master Malfred's breathing. I was already sick of him being anywhere near me, that rapist motherfucker. I hated that he was behind me watching my backside.

Master Claus jerked my chain hard again. "You be silent, Mad Maxx. Enough of this chit chat. I am starving. We are off. Follow or go back home boys." The crossdresser took off down the stairs hauling my leash behind him with Master Bladrick to my right and Master Jonas to my left.

We arrived at the packed Great Hall. I felt the terror starting to rise within the boy as the black collar attendant led us to the table. I stood there unable to shake the sinking feeling of dread when the staff pulled out the chairs for the Elders, except for Master Claus. I pulled out his chair as was my duty.

I nearly tripped, unable to take my eyes off the empty chair meant for me. This was the table that I was enforced to endure the painful blood bonding with my Elder Masters only the few days before. The chair for me was the exact spot Master Jonas had forced me to my face for their pleasures. I trembled and wrung my hands faster when Master Jonas demanded I come sit down and join the Elders. I looked around that crowed hall with terror overcoming my good senses.

Everyone was staring at me. I could hear them wondering how they could eat their meal with such a vile creature in their midst. Master Jonas glared and growled a second time demanding I sit down next to him and Master Claus.

I heard the music come across the speakers of the Great Hall. The song was the Animals, "The Haus of the Rising Sun." Before I could stop him, Taube pushed me from the wheel. We easily pulled our leash out of the surprised Master Claus's hands and took off rushing for the large empty spot in the Hall meant for dancing.

The melancholic music filled our flesh and overtook our mind. I began to spin and dance keeping pace with my ghostly dance partners. Ryker led for a moment then spun me. Next, I took the lead with the brute Ben. Geraldine came for her turn, and I bowed to her while she curtseyed. The two of us took off wildly following the changed tune of the Hollies, "Long Cool Woman in a Black Dress."

I giggled, outstretched my arms, and spun with the frau fatale of blond hair and no flesh. I repeated my begging her forgiveness for the thousandth time since I sent her to the orchard. She whispered that she forgave me for ending her life. Ben finally tired of my handling his girl and came to tap me on the shoulder to take her for his own.

I was the gentlemen. I backed away and returned to my Ryker. He snickered and told me that women are always fickle like that. I was lost in the music, the company, and the flashing lights of the tapestry when the next song began, the Rolling Stones, "Sympathy for the Devil."

I closed my eyes and laughed wildly when Ryker told me this song was about my type. I then took off with a graceful spin. I could hear the universe calling me through the bongo drums and screeches of the guitars. I was still spinning without the use of my vision when soft arms reached out and gripped me around my waist.

I opened my lids thinking Geraldine had returned for another go. I stopped dead in my tracks stunned too stupid. There holding me in her embrace with a loving smile on her face was my mother Agnette.

She frowned at my trance and then reached up and softly ran her hand along me dropped jaw. “Ah, meine beautiful boy Christian. How have you been doing, meine little lamb? Do you have nothing loving to say to your mother? It has been too long since they have kept us apart. You are surprised to finally get to be with the one that loves you, ja? Well, I know they will be angry that I snuck over here to speak to you, but you looked so handsome dancing alone. I had to come see if my son would honor me with his company. I have missed you so badly.” She leaned down and kissed my forehead with adoration in her expression.

I shook my head in disbelief. “How dare you touch me, you murderous bitch. Get the fuck off me. Help, someone help me. This woman is trying to molest the Priceless,” I screamed wildly as Agnetta dug her claws into my side and pulled me close to whisper in my ear.

“They made me do it all, meine Christian. I love you, please believe me. I have suffered so watching how day treated my only son. Please hear me. They will come take me from you again. These crooks and monsters tricked me.

I would never have let this happen. That rat Claus promised me you wouldn't be harmed if I did them the favor of letting the Haus have you. They needed a Priceless to end Xavier, meine heart. He promised you would be rewarded for cleaning out the Haus of the cruel bastard and his men. I was only playing a role. I didn't know they would trap you in your metal for life. The Greedy Elders wanted a young boy for their foul pleasures. I am your mother, Christian. Please think about this. What mother would ever abandon her son like you were led to believe I had." I saw Vilber and Olaf come storming toward Agnette and me.

I stood there dumbfounded, confused, and unsure what the hell was going on when the black collar brutes jerked the begging and now weeping Agnette off me. She wailed repeatedly she loved her son and that these criminals stole her family as the door guards dragged her from the Great Hall with much drama.

I was in a trance watching them haul her off when I recalled I was supposed to be with my Masters. I couldn't remember how I had gotten out on the dance floor. I saw Master Jonas and Master Leo rushing my direction. I fell to a kneel trembling in terror at this strange and disturbing situation.

They were fast approaching me but not nearly as fast as Master Malfred was. What the fuck just happened? What did Agnette mean Master Claus promised her I wouldn't be harmed? Was Claus working with Malfred all along? Was she right and the Elders would never let me go? I had to face that anything was possible in this fucking Haus of nightmares. Even that my mother was telling the truth.

Chapter 53: Motherly Love

I trembled there on the dance floor on my knees as my Elder Masters came running my direction. Master Malfred easily beat his older brothers in their wild foot race. He came flying up to the boy, his face wearing a look of concern tinged with a little fear.

"You okay, meine taube? Did that hideous creature injure you? Stand up and let me check you." Master Malfred gave the hand signal for me to face him.

I kept my eyes to the floor hearing my mother's words echoing in the ears of my unconsciousness. "The Mistress did nothing but paw me, Master. She was unable to break the flesh. Thank you for your concern. I am most unworthy of such a fuss."

Master Malfred reached out and patted around my waist where Agnetta had placed her arms looking closely at my white blouse. "You can never be too sure when dealing with vipers like that woman." He pulled my shirt close to his eyes exposing my stomach to the watching eyes of the breakfast crowd.

Master Jonas and Master Leo arrived out of breath. The Vampire slapped Master Malfred's hands off his hold of my clothing.

"What the fuck are you doing with Christian Axel? You keep your fucking filthy hands-off my man," yelled out the furious Vampire.

Master Malfred shot a nervous look at Master Leo, then pointed at the door of the Great Hall, "I was merely checking our man for marks of any needles, Jonas. That bitch maybe shot him up with something. That would be something Agnette would be capable of."

Master Jonas's anger melted to a look of fear. "What? You think she did such a foul thing? Leo, check Christian Axel. Hurry!"

I watched as the three big Masters come at me tearing at my clothing. I let out a loud wail of terror thinking day were trying to gang rape me. I twisted wildly as the Vampire shouted for Master Leo to grab my leash to hold me still. Master Malfred was ripping my blouse buttons open. I dropped to me knees and then crawled till I was free of all them.

I got up and fled that Hall fast as my legs could carry me. I was screaming bloody murder the whole way too. The Elders shouted in panic demanded there Priceless be "captured immediately."

All of a sudden, every Dominant in that room came flying out of their seats trying to snatch me as I rushed past them. I screeched with insane fear when one or another managed to grab a handful of my blouse or hair. My frightening sounds caused every one of my captors to freak for a moment, allowing me to quickly break free of their weak holds.

One large man I knew only as Karl managed to grip my chain leash. I took off Master Leo's earphones when my intense pulling and wail didn't break his hold. I swung them with much strength hitting this man in his face several times before he released me. I fell backward from the force of my tugging against him but didn't completely trip to the floor.

Without another setback I made it out the of that Great Hall. I fled down the hallway headed for the Haus door. I could hear the crowd and my Masters insisting that I stop my running behind me. I ignored all them. I wasn't going to be bent over any more tables and forced to endure the lusts of those monsters.

I heard Agnette's screams of indignation hurled at the brutes Olaf and Vilber off to my left. I turned down the hallway following her voice. I had not gone far when I found the three of them. Agnette was still being dragged by her upper arms. Her voice was full of rage. She was threatening the brutes with the dungeons and lashing. She almost didn't seem me coming toward her until I was near the trio.

Agnette's fury immediately melted into one of joy. "Meine son. Your meine son. You brutes are in trouble now. Meine Christian will make you pay for this insult to his mother. Come, meine heart. You kick these low snakes in their bellies, ja?" She practically dripped honey as I approached.

Olaf and Vilber saw me and shot each other a look of fear as Vilber yelled, "You go back to your Masters, Mad Maxx. This is none of your affair. We are only following orders. We don't wish to start issues with you." The brutes stopped their march but held on to Agnette's upper arms tightly appearing unsure what to do.

I was breathing a bit hard, but I managed to smile at the door guards. "Ah, well you have a problem with me Vilber, you too Olaf. I be seeing the both of you by summertime. The Haus will be a fine sight with your carcasses there to decorate the door. What a fine welcome that will be. Worthy of this place of filth. You let my mother go, or I will redecorate this minute. I will paint this hallway with your blood boys." I began walking toward the three of them and noticed Vilber was trembling.

My mother's face sprung into an arrogant smile. "You tell them, meine lamb. You heard him brutes. Let his honorable mother go or pay with your lives for it." She jerked and the black collars let her free of their hold appearing dumbfounded about what to do.

Agnette glared at them as she smoothed out her dress and patted her hair. "I will deal with your disgraceful manhandling of a Mistress of my level later. You are both dismissed." The door guards staired at each other but neither withdrew as she commanded.

I chuckled. "Mother, come away from that useless rabble. I wish to speak to you." I stood there and outstretched my hand in an offer to take her own.

She giggled then took it. "I knew you could never forget your loving mother, meine lamb." I pulled her into an embrace and took up her right hand holding it to my lips.

"Why Mistress, I think of you all the time. Where would a son be without his mother? Tell me Mistress, is this the hand that signed the check that the Haus gave you for your unworthy son's life? You are right-handed if I recall or nein? I do tend to forget unimportant things such as that. I only recall the real important stuff you know. Like how much a son is loved by his mother. That right there, I could never forget." I kissed her knuckles as she kissed my forehead.

I heard my Masters and many other chasing me round the corner behind me. I looked into Agnetta's eyes in a trance. She frowned as she looked at the long scar down the left side of my face.

"Meine poor, little lamb. These men have ruined the perfect beauty of meine only son. What have these brutes done to you." She sniffed as if about to cry.

I shook my head with a wicked smile crossing my lips as I sang to her, "Rock a bye mother, do not you fear. Never mind mother, your baby is here. Wee little fingers, shut your eyes tight. Now your lack of love brings a monster to light. Why mother, these people only did what you have done to your little lamb Christian. Use, abuse, and fuck me." I forced her right-hand open then put all four of her fingers into my mouth biting down with all my strength.

She screamed out in agony and terror. I withstood her blows as she struggled to get her lily white digits from my teeth. I heard her bones crumbling and could taste her blood. A laughter erupted in my throat just as Master

Malfred reached the boy yelling out a command to let Agnetta go.

The shady Master wrapped his arm around my neck and began applying pressure. Agnetta wailed and wept while I increased my jaw strength, cutting deep into her flesh. I saw Olaf und Vilber turn and run away down the hallway in sheer terror of their mistakenly allowing me a moment to be in contact with the harpy that birthed me. *I have to say, the family reunion went better than I thought it would, ja? Master Maxx and I howled in laughter for several minutes over that statement.*

The strong Dominant's sleeper hold was doing the trick. I felt the boy's knees buckling. I closed my eyes from the dizziness but maintained my hold on Agnette's fingers until the last moment. My weight collapsed as I fell into a momentary unconsciousness. The pursuers were able to free my mother of my toothy trap before I could become alert once more.

Peter came out of the crowd and snuggled the weeping Agnette to his chest. He rushed her away from there to seek medical attention for her mangled fingers. I had managed to break them all with my mouth.

Happily, I was informed later that she suffered much pain. I was even told she gained several deep scars from the little payback move of mine. I believed that was not even close to what she really deserved. Though it did make me sleep a bit better at night.

You know, nothing could chase away the despair like biting the hand that fed me lies to keep me believing this nightmare she sold me into was my fault. The way I saw it, she didn't need her fingers anyway. That bitch never offered even a moment of comfort in my whole shitty life. So, one hand should have been plenty for her to get along just fine.

She thought she could twist my mind into buying her claims that Master Claus was the enemy. I was a little confused back in those days, I admit it. I even had some troubles with stress reactions, but I was not the fool. No matter who set up my life of indignity from within that Haus, Agnette was the real one at fault.

What kind of a mother allows brutes, criminals, and molesters to come into their home in the middle of the night? Agnette opened that door and invited the kidnappers inside. She watched the brutes beating me down and bonding my wrists and ankles from my bedroom door. She never called the police nor even begged them to stop.

When I pleaded with her to help me, she told me that I brought this on myself being the trouble starter and never minding no one. My mother led me to believe if she didn't let the men take me then I was going to prison for all my life. She even helped the Guard hold me down for re-bonding when I managed to undo one of the ropes.

We are not even going to speak again about her foul behavior with Xavier nor her hateful nature when I was seducing Master Claus. I also had not forgotten she was with Peter the day Master Leo commanded the "vengeance" blow job from me in the torture rooms.

She told me the Elders wanted a boy to sate their foul pleasures. She reported that Master Claus was behind the whole thing. Nah. Agnetta gave them what they wanted. Master Claus or Master Malfred wanting and getting are two different things, ja? There was only one real mastermind of all that had happen to me.

My Elder Masters and even Malfred used what they were granted to play their games. It was nothing personal. Could have been any young male that they could snatch. I was just the unlucky bastard chosen is all. The one person that should have cared for me and protected me didn't. A real mother would die to defend her young. Well, unless they are your mother or mine.

If she was being truthful about her being misled and was only playing a role. Then I would have to believe her a moron or a fucking actress of the finest quality. She did a perfect job at her behavior of the cruel, unloving mother. All I can say is, if she was faking, Hollywood missed out. That woman deserved an Oscar.

I wasn't buying her bullshit anymore. Though it did cross my mind Master Claus may have been the actual mastermind behind my fall, it no longer mattered to me. Master Claus didn't rape me and invite all his buddies to have their fill like Master Malfred did. That old crossdresser was a treacherous cuss. Yet, he did offer me a chance to break my metal in a way I would enjoy a great deal.

Whatever his role was in my existence I really couldn't do shit about it as long as I wore his collar. I could only hope this time he was on my side.

Master Malfred eased his tight grip on my neck the second Agnetta had been released. I slowly regained my alertness to find him still holding me from behind. He noticed my spasm and came back to hold my own weight that indicated I was no longer unaware.

He leaned into my ear (I lost my headphones beating that Dominant up in the Hall, shit). "You be still, meine taube. Struggle and I will constrict you to sleep once more. Mind me or be sorry for it. I will not tell you twice," he whispered sounding quite sinister.

I nodded. "I can hear you, Master. No need to shout. Why are we here in the hallway? I thought we were dancing. Is the party over?" I blinked unsure what the hell was with all the staring Dominants and angered looks on my Masters' faces.

I suddenly felt a burst of electricity go through my chest. "Ah, ha-ha-ha-ha, yee-haw," I shouted out, unable to control the outburst of, well, nonsense.

Master Claus came forward and backhanded the snot out of the boy. "Shut up, Mad Maxx. You be quiet or be punished."

I dropped my gaze and felt oddly disconnected. "Ja, Master, blaster, faster, castor, disaster, disaster, disaster. Disaster Master, ah, ha-ha-ha-ha." I began to shake my head feeling the bees singing my face and ears. I hate those fuckers, you know.

Master Malfred let go of my neck. I flapped my hands around my swinging head. I stomped my feet spinning in a circle, then yelled out nonsensically while laughing. The wheel was stuck. Taube looked at me and Christian in horror. We all ran for it trying to break it from the locks that held it in place.

The boy swung his arms, rocked his head, made shouting sounds of joy, and spun wildly. His eyes rolled back into his head. The mouth hung uselessly. Drool poured out while the zombie stormed in the hallway bouncing off the walls. He fell to his knees, then quickly got back up and spun after a bow. All the while he babbled, rambled, and was unable to focus the eyes on anything.

The Masters stood there in horrified shock as their Priceless collar lost his shit. Master Leo came to his senses first. He turned to the audience of other Dominants that had rushed to watch the show from the Great Hall.

He growled out to the few black collars there entranced at my psychotic trance dancing. “Get these people out of here. Mistress Agnette shot up our priceless with psychedelic drugs. Shit, Malfred, call the Haus doctor. We need an antidote. Clear this space, Gott damn it. Our collar is ill. He needs medical aid.” The clever Leo covered my obviously mentally ill behaviors by blaming the hateful Mistress Agnette.

The zombie wailed out, "Get these people out of here. Gott damn it. Our collar is ill. He needs to be killed. Don't worry, Agnette will be billed. Ah, there she blows. There he blows. Rows and rows, o so many woes." It spun once, then turned to the wall, and began to slam its head into the wood with much force.

Master Jonas yelped in terror, "Fuck, Leo, help me. The boy is about to bash his damned head into mush." They came flying at the zombie.

It saw them and let out a blood curdling scream as it fled from the Vampire and Master Leo. It didn't get far. The men leapt on it, knocking it to the floor. It wailed, kicked, bit, and spit at the attackers. It was wailing in incoherent fear, unable to understand what the hell was going on.

The two of them managed to hold the struggling thing to the ground until the Haus doctor came. The old sawbones quickly administered a sedative to the screaming zombie. Within only a few moments the riot was over. The flesh was calmed but not asleep as it had been during previous injections from this quack.

It was at that moment I managed to finally get the wheel unstuck. I sighed a breath of relief as did Taube and Christian. That was a close one. To this day it is unclear what the hell happened there. The wheel does get stuck at times, but usually there is some stickiness prior to a halt like that. Not this time. Everything just sort of stopped working the way it was told to. Oh well, sucks to be me, ja?

Master Leo and Master Jonas got off the boy while Master Claus took up my leash. "Well, doctor, thank you for that antidote. That sneaky Agnette really messed him up."

Th doctor shot a confused look at Master Claus then looked back at me. "Oh, uhm, ja. The antidote will calm that stuff Agnette gave to him." He began to quicky pack his bag to leave with trembling hands.

Master Malfred scoffed. "You are full of shit, all of you. That Priceless is real. You think me a fucking fool? You all know he is not fake. There is neither an antidote nor cure for the forbidden silver. That madness is in his blood. This collar is sublime. The first one of his kind I had ever seen. I read so much about them, but here he is in the flesh. It is magnificent to see for truth." He looked at me with adoration.

Master Jonas glared at him. "Ja, he is a fucking real Priceless, you dumbass. What the hell are you speaking about fakes? You think us Elders would be fooled by one that is not worth the top metal? That said, you should be aware this is not madness for truth. That snake Agnette give him drugs just as you suspected. This bullshit will pass, you'll see."

Master Malfred grinned. "Okay brother, whatever you say. I know fucking symptoms of schizophrenia when I see them. Christian Axel is quiet well advanced in the disease, further than I could have imagined. You are clever fellows to keep him alive and hidden all this time. I do bow in awe of all of your amazing skills to accomplish this in a Haus that can hear every secret. How long has he been onset, oh wait, I apologize brother. I forgot. This is not real madness; it is merely an acid or drug overdose. I am happy to play the games of the Elders since I am now one myself." He chuckled as Master Jonas clicked his tongue glaring at him with rage in his eyes.

I was still laying on my side on the floor. I could hear the Elders talking to each other, but I wasn't interested in their conversations. There were so many others going on to choose from. I looked at my hands then began to wring them. A sense of dread was filling me. I didn't know how much longer the Masters were gonna make me stay on the ground but without a release I had to wait for their pleasures.

Master Claus jerked on my leash. "Get up Mad Maxx. You kneel and mind me. Do you understand what I say to you?"

I stood up and began wringing my hands keeping my eyes to the floor. "Ja, I do whatever you say, whenever you say and however you say Master. Please, Master, I want to go see the lambs. I cleaned up the apartment and my plate. Was this enough to earn the favor? Did you see that fight in the Great Hall? There will be many silvers in the chains over that insolence, ja? Can you find my headset? I think that Karl stole it from me. He told me his brother wanted a pair like them. I tried to stop him from taking them. Will I get punished for that? You know the spies were talking to me in them? I found out some important stuff about them bad guys, but I cannot tell you with everyone listening. Can you ask them to speak more quietly? I don't want any more of that fucking cake. It tastes like blood you know. Mistress Cora keeps running that vacuum. How motherfucking dirty can her apartment be? Ah, she is the party animal, ja?" I wrung my hands and began to hum the tune playing on Master Jonas's radio.

Master Claus shot a look of irritation at the Haus doctor. "He is not any better doctor. You give him something to stop this behavior or I will have your hodensack in a vice."

The doctor flashed an anxious look at Master Malfred then back to Master Claus. "Uhm, the antidote won't calm all the symptoms of this, uhm, drugging. You will have to ride it out. I suggest quiet, calm, and dark. If things get too out of control use a set of sheets in icy water and wrap him tightly in it. That will take the fight from his, uhm, overdose fit."

Master Claus winced. "That is all you have to say? Fuck, you are a useless bastard. Get out of my sight cocksucker. You aren't worth the money you are paid."

The doctor nodded. "In this hopeless situation, I would have to agree with you Claus. You will not allow the boy the rest he needs, you expect more than is humanly possible from him, and continue to ignore my advice to send him to a stellar hospital for the aid he surely needs. This shit you see, well, get ready. This is not even close to as bad as it will get. Good day gentlemen." He grabbed his bag and began to rush away.

I gasped, "Good day to you. Tell your Frau I said thank you for the cake. Good day to you. Tell your Frau I said thank you for the cake." Then I whispered to Claus, "No wonder that doctor is so skinny. That woman of his cannot cook. I barely could eat that horrible shit. Tastes like blood you know. Did you know the spies are listening? Oh hell, I forgot. Don't tell the doctor what I said about his Frau. She loves him, you know? I think they have a dog and two children but that is only the rumor the shadows tell me." I began humming that weird tune on the Vampire's radio again, stifling my giggle at the face Christian was making when he tried a bite of the woman's cake.

Master Claus frowned at me and shook his head. "Jonas, what the fuck should we do? Mad Maxx is babbling over here. I don't know what the fuck he is talking about. The Guard will be here in no time, and we will lose our beautiful boy." He reached out with a sadness in his expression and stroked my cheek softly.

I frowned then dropped to my knees. "As you wish Master. I thank you for the mercy of it." I reached up to undo the buttons on his pants.

He let out a yelp. "What the hell? Get off me Mad Maxx." He pushed me off his crotch and backed away.

This confused me a great deal. I stayed on my knees shaking my head and wringing my hands unsure what he wanted from me. I never could understand these fucking

Dominants. He was touching me like he always did when he wanted special services. I followed his command, and he behaved like I was about to chew his cock off. Weirdo.

Master Leo growled out, “We need to get Christian Axel home. This drama is not good for him nor us. I told you he was not ready for all the stress, but you refused to listen. That doctor is right. He needs rest, quiet and no stress.”

Master Claus nodded. “So, it would seem Leo. I stand corrected. I am not such a big man that I cannot see when I am wrong, nor am I afraid to admit it. We must work together to get him past the nosey residents. Even you, Malfred. I will warn you brother, speak of schizophrenia and Mad Maxx in the same sentence again, and I will throw you from the top floor. I won’t give a fuck what happens after and guess what? Neither will you.”

Master Malfred chuckled evilly. “Well, you can count on my silence, brother. I can even get this collar back to our floor without drawing attention if you will allow it. In fact, I can get that boy to do whatever you tell him without endangering him or us. However, I want something for both my stilled tongue and for my aid in controlling this beastly madness in our Priceless.”

Master Jonas started to take a step to punch Master Malfred, but Master Leo held him back. “I will knock out your teeth and that will shut your mouth, wouldn’t it. If you have some fucking way to save our Priceless collar, then you share it this minute. You have no right to demand payment from your brothers for such knowledge."

Master Malfred nodded, still grinning like a stealthy cat chasing a mouse. "Threatening me isn't going to get you what you want from me Jonas. I offer you a fair deal and you act like a brute. So, be it. I keep my silence anyway, on everything I know, including the way to handle this boy to keep him serving. Good luck with the Guard, you will need it." He began to walk away.

Master Claus shot a look of anger at Master Jonas and Master Leo. "Wait, Malfred. If you really have a way, I want to hear it. What is the price you ask."

Master Malfred stopped in his tracks but didn't turn to face the Elders. "I want three days a week with the collar: Thursdays, Fridays, and Saturdays. You make that happen, and I will take control of this fast-sinking situation to save our collar. Otherwise, figure it out on your own."

Master Leo nearly had to knock Master Jonas into the wall the Vampire struggled his hold so roughly. "Fuck you, Malfred. That is outrageous.

Master Leo barked out, "Pick another price Malfred. That one is unfair to your brothers."

Master Claus sighed. "You are a bastard Malfred. You try to take more than your fair share. I agree with Leo. Jonas, calm your ass down." The Vampire was turning red in the face ready to pummel Master Malfred.

Master Malfred turned around to face them with an arrogant smile on his face. "I take only what I will earn. I could have asked for all four of the extra days and ignored our dear brother Bladrick. However, I only ask for the extra day Jonas and Leo take on this current clock. You keep your two days Claus. This is the price I demand. You can choose to pay it, or I will go home. This is the only thing I will accept as payment for my services to my brothers."

At this time Master Bladrick arrived. He was elderly and very sick. It had taken him a lot of time to walk all the way to the hallway of this drama. He coughed and limped slowly taking a place next to Master Malfred. Master Claus informed him of the situation. The eldest Elder listened quietly then when he had heard everything, he cleared his throat.

He flashed a look of irritation at Master Malfred. "Give this greedy sonofabitch whatever the hell he wants, brothers."

Master Leo and Master Jonas growled out in unison, "Hell no!"

Master Claus looked at the floor. "I understand why you say this Bladrick. Leo, Jonas, you need to be thinking of the boy instead of your own selfish desires for his attentions. If something isn't done, he is good as dead. Then none of us gets any days with him, do we? I am with Bladrick. If Malfred can do what he claims, which I doubt, then I vote to pay him in extra days with the Priceless."

Master Leo snapped his fingers and clicked his tongue. “You pay the rapist with the victim. Shame on you Claus, and you too Bladrick. I vote against it.”

Master Jonas shook off Master Leo’s grip then nodded. “I am with my brother Leo on this one. This motherfucker already nearly tore Christian Axel apart. You hand him over like he is a favored and trusted uncle? I think not. I vote against it.”

Master Malfred grinned even more largely. “Well, that is two votes for and two against. I suppose I must break the tie. I vote yes. Brothers Jonas and Leo are outvoted. I take my three days and you boys work out the remaining four. Not my problem, I do believe today is Wednesday. Come midnight the leash of Mad Maxx belongs to me. However, I will take that from you right this minute Honorable Claus. We need to get him back to Leo’s safely or I have nothing to collect tonight, ja?” He walked past the furious Master Leo and Master Jonas without any sign of fear.

He took my leash from Master Claus. I was still standing there rocking on my feet and humming while wringing my hands. Master Malfred watched me a moment then pulled my leash till he was sure I noticed him.

“You listen to me Mad Maxx. That noise you hear, that is the Guard. You follow me quietly and I sneak you passed them. You must not make a sound, or they will find us. Come, be on your best protocol, and let’s hurry, ja?” Master Malfred said in a near whisper to me.

I snapped my head up looking around in terror. "They are coming. Oh why. I didn't do anything. I swear I am serving without quarrel. I break no rules." I whimpered and wrung my hands faster.

Master Leo growled out in irritation. "Nice going, fool. You scared the piss out of Christian Axel. Hell, Jonas here could have done that." He snapped and crossed his arms while Master Jonas nodded his approval of that statement.

Master Malfred ignored them he leaned in closer. "You did break the rules, meine Taube. You were loud and disturbed dinner. You come with me, be quiet, compliant, and work hard, then maybe they will forgive your insolence ja?"

I nodded. "Ja. Ja. I will not disobey. Help me, Master. I didn't mean to offend them. I swear it." I trembled and tears began to flow down my cheeks.

The Master put his finger to his lips, "I will help you. You must come with me this minute. Make no noise. Do not look up from the floor. Move with stealth and speed." He took off and I rushed after him in full protocol wringing my hands but following his command of silence and keeping my head down.

The other Elders packed up and followed us back to the sixth floor. I kept my silence as requested and never looked up the whole trip. When at last even Master Bladrick had made it safely to the Elders' apartments, Master Malfred stopped our rapid march. He turned around while I dropped to a kneel at his heels still wringing my hands but saying nothing.

Master Claus watched me a moment while the Vampire grumbled into Master Leo's ear. They were observably angered at Master Malfred. I didn't know what had upset them. It stressed me a little that maybe I had done something wrong. I rocked back and forth in my kneel and whispered to Taube and Christian asking them if day had any idea what had set them off like that.

Master Claus shook his head. "Well, I give you credit. You got him through the Haus without any insane behaviors. Everyone saw him walking behind you without throwing fits. I think that should still the wagging tongues about that incident with Mistress Agnette."

Master Malfred nodded with a smile of triumph. "Ah, don't worry brothers. The residents of this Haus will see him many times on my leash acting demure, calm and with all the grace of one of his station. The Priceless is safe as long as Malfred is around."

Master Leo scoffed. "Oh? Could have fooled me a few days ago. I seem to recall this collar was screaming and crying your name, and it was not in pleasure. Was he so safe then?"

Master Jonas bellowed out. "So, you got him to the sixth floor. So, what? I say that the clock stays as it was. I am not giving up my day with my man for nothing."

Master Claus groaned. "Okay that is it. I am tired of the fighting, Jonas. You and Leo were outvoted. Deal with it. Leo, you bring up that punished incident one more fucking time then I will turn both your fucking days over to Malfred. I don't want to hear another word out of either of you. Tonight, at midnight Leo, you turn Mad Maxx over to Malfred. Saturday night when the hand strikes midnight Malfred you bring that leash to me and Bladrick. I will turn the boy over to Jonas Monday night and Jonas you to Leo on Tuesday. Then we begin the cycle all over again. That is my final word. Shit what will we do when the boy no longer has the penetration virginity Bladrick? What if that woman Cora decides she wants her time with the Priceless as well?"

"Then I will bring her hay and carrots, Master. The horses like that, and the sugar cubes. Can I go see my lambs now? I don't like the air in here, it is too loud." I mumbled out with a giggle.

Master Malfred jerked my chain. "Meine taube. You be silent or the Guard will find you."

I shuddered, then hushed my babbling but continued to rock in place. Master Leo came forward and demanded my leash from Master Malfred.

"Well, if my time is nearly up then I want my man Malfred. I cannot do shit about this sorry situation but I for one will be happy to piss on your grave one day. These others may think what you did is forgotten, but Leo will not be so quick to get over it. Come on, meine hase. We are going home." Master Leo jerked my leash from the grinning Master Malfred's hands and motioned me to follow.

Master Leo was pissed off. He stormed to his apartment nearly dragging me behind him. I was afraid but I dared not say anything. I didn't want to upset my Master. I almost let out a yelp of relief when Mad Max and Max came barreling down the hallway and jumped into the boy. Taube, Christian and me were knocked out of the flesh by the force.

I rubbed my head and looked at Mad Max and Max. "Be careful brothers. The Guard is lurking, and Master Leo is angered. You make sure to get that headset back. I never got the entire message from the spies. We cannot proceed without hearing the next part of the mission."

Mad Max nodded. "Ja, I will get them back. You be ready for Claus and Bladrick. Taube you are up at midnight. Look sharp boys. The blade of Damocles is at our chest and that thread is weak, ja?"

We saluted him as Master Leo dragged the boy through his apartment door. Christian nudged me then Taube with a grin of mischief.

"Let's go swimming, try to see up the pretty girls' dresses, and then get a fucking drink. I am beat. Time to let down our hair and have a little fun, ja?" He yawned.

Taube giggled. "Sounds like a plan. You in Maximillian?"

I frowned. “We should stick around and watch Mad Max’s back.”

Christian groaned. “He is with Master Leo, schwuler boy. There is nothing to worry about. Come on. I want to see that red head down in the kitchen a little closer.”

I smiled. “Ja, I know the one you are speaking about. Okay, let’s go. I am sick of all this fucking work and never any play. Come on Taube, I will race you.”

Taube smiled with wickedness. “Ah brother, you should never try to beat Taube. In any competition there can only be one winner, and all the rest are the losers. You must win because I will kill anyone for daring to play games with me.” He winked then took off after the giggling Christian.

I stood dare letting my Mirror shards words sink in. I shuddered with the understanding the Christian would not get a chance at Malfred, or anyone else. Taube was a big a killer as he ever hoped to be. The only difference was the Mirror would strike the enemies first, unlike Christian who only would murder when the flesh was threatened.

Taube would be with Master Malfred for three days. I prayed my brother would be capable of recalling Master Claus’s condition for our release of the metal. I took a deep breath then chased after the two killer shards to get a break from all the damned seriousness of our existence.

I walked right over to Master Leo’s records, sat down, and began thumbing through them. He stood there watching me with a look of worry. I hummed a tune I heard on that radio of Master Jonas's. I heard the DJ man say the band was called Led Zepplin. I was dying to see if Master Leo had these guys. They were good.

I let out a gasp of joy when I found an album marked Led Zepplin III. I was very weak with English still, but I had enough of a grasp to read that. I knew this was a word I heard the announcer say before he played the song called "Immigrant Song." I put the record on his machine and played this marvelous music loudly to block out all the other radios playing around the Haus. E*specially Master Jonas's loud ass one. How that man can still hear anything after years of blasting his stereo is beyond me.*

Master Leo covered his ears and rushed to turn the volume down. I glared at him then turned it back up. He again turned it down and slapped my hand when I tried to fix the level to my desires. I let out a yell of anger but backed away never taking my fury filled eyes off him.

He shook his head and crossed his arms staring at me with shock. "Christian Axel, you are covered in your mother's blood, drool, and grim from rolling on the floor. Your clothes are torn and filthy. Get to the bathroom and take a shower, then change at once. I find it hard to believe I am having to order you to get clean."

I was startled, then looked down at my blouse. Many of the buttons were missing and bloodstains already turning brown pelted the white surface. I shrugged at him. I sat down by the record player and went back to focusing on learning the words to this latest music of my interest.

Master Leo stomped his foot. “I told you to get a shower and change those nasty clothes. What the fuck do you think you are doing? When you finish I will have food and medication for you waiting. This is a horrible mess with Malfred. You and I need to talk about it, meine hase. Now hurry up. Do what you were commanded this minute.”

I shot him a look of irritation but got up and went to his room. I dug in my bag till I found another blouse and pair of breeches that were not dirty, yet. I walked into his bath and shut the door. I looked at the tub and shuddered. There was no fucking way I was getting in there. Master Leo would just come in and want to fuck me.

I instead pulled the blouse on and buttoned it rapidly. I dressed in the fresh breeches and got a drink of water from his sink. I didn’t bother with my toothbrush, nor any other of my hygiene stuff. What was the use anyway? That sickness already ate the flesh alive. There was no curing it anymore. We lost that battle the minute we got trapped in that collar.

I went back into his living room and returned to his stereo digging through the rest of his records. I wanted to hear all the songs he owned, maybe a few twice. Master Leo had been in his kitchenette calling in a food order. He returned to find me examining his equipment with intense focus.

He let out a loud gasp. “What the holy fuck, Christian Axel. I thought I told you to shower and change.”

I didn't bother to look up. "I did what you commanded, Master. I thank you for the mercy of it." I flipped through his albums and marveled at the color and designs on each cover.

Master Leo stormed over and grabbed me by my upper arm, making me yelp in surprise. "You put new clothing over dirty ones, meine heart. I heard no water running. Your face is still disgusting with foulness, meine hase. What is going on with you? Please talk to me. You always have to be watched that you don't showers too often, now I demand you do it and this, what is this." His eyes were wide in fear.

I dropped my gaze trying not to tear up but to be honest I think one may have escaped. "Please don't make me take a shower. The water brings pain, Master. I will be quiet and eat my supper if you grant this mercy. Can I go see the lambs? Are they doing okay? Do they ask you about me?"

Master Leo sighed. "This is because of the pool. What happened there? You think getting in the water will bring brutes to hurt you?"

I wrung my hands and looked at the door. "How is Der Makellos? Can we go see him? Tell Master Jonas to turn down his records I beg of you. I cannot hear anything with all his noise."

Master Leo reached out and grabbed me by my arms pulling me into his embrace. I felt sick to my stomach and terror rose within me. I began panting unable to catch my breath. My Master noticed my distress. He pulled back from his tight hug and tried to look into my eyes.

I couldn't take his gazing at me like that. I felt him pulling my thoughts into his head. I trembled as he continued to search my face doing his best to force my gaze. He leaned in and kissed my forehead. I began to feel hot, sweaty, and full of panic.

Then he leaned in to kiss my lips. My mind filled with the images of Grisham and Gustov's eyes and the sounds of their flesh pounding into my own. I plead with them, but they would not stop. I then could hear Gretta and Cora laughing coming through the walls. I could feel the claw of Master Jonas holding me down to keep me from escaping Master Claus and Master Leo's brutal thrusting.

Master Leo had no time to respond as I wildly struggled to get out of his grip, wailing in pure desperation. I had to get him off me. I cried out in agony as I blindly punched Master Leo in his nose. He let me go and shouted in pain while clutching his bleeding face.

I rushed to the other side of the room backed into a corner and covered my head weeping like a lost soul. I just knew that Master Leo was going to hurt me, and I couldn't take that shit anymore. I was scared beyond imagination. I thought for sure my Master would call the Guard for my refusing to grant him the special services he seemed to be requesting of me.

Master Leo sat there nursing his busted nose for a bit. He didn't attempt to approach me, nor did he say anything. I rocked, cried, and covered my head for at least an hour trapped in a full-blown hell of misery. I didn't know what to do.

It seemed that everywhere I went, no matter what I did, someone was trying to beat me up, fuck me till I begged for death, or threaten to kill me. I couldn't even go to my precious water anymore without a dick being shoved in the boy. Nowhere was safe, and there was no longer a cure to beat back the disease of obscene filth that clung to every inch of the flesh. It had burrowed so deep it had made it to the flesh of my heart.

Master Leo waited until I had calmed from a loud sobbing to a mild shuddering with a sniff. He then kept a safe distance and sat down on the floor across from me. He crossed his legs while keeping silent. I noticed him there.

Initially this made me start weeping harder. I assumed he was going to beat me then take whatever he wished whether I was willing to mind his commands or nein. When he never moved to attack me, I slowly settled down. I heard him sigh loudly and begin humming the song Nights in White Satin.

I quieted my bawling to listen to his pretty voice. The words soothed my troubled soul. *I forgot to mention Max was the one crying hard like that. I was just kind of hauled along against my will. That fucker is strong I tell you.* I peeked through my arm shielding to look at my Master. He saw my eyes. He smiled then began singing the actual words loudly.

This made me feel safe enough to lower my arms. Nothing bad could happen during that song. It was a magic spell for healing inner hurts and frightened away despair. I sat there enjoying his serenade for some time. When he finished, he would start over. It was as if my Master were a record that had a huge scratch on the vinyl. My tears dried and my blubbering ceased by the time he reached his fifth repeat.

Master Leo stopped his siren song at last. He smiled when I managed to talk myself into looking at him. I winced when I saw I had bruised his face with my blow. I just knew my ass was due a thudding. I groaned and leaned my head into the wall.

“I should have checked that stove. The lazy always get there come apace. That is why the cake tastes bad. It was burned, ja? I thought it was the blood pudding, but not in this case. You should never go to the door. There is a hole that goes to the center of the Earth there. The water is silver because it is too deep for the sun to reach it. Can you believe that? It is the secret of the lost you know. There are ghosts without faces, and children without their mothers that haunt that place. I told my lambs to watch out, but I didn’t follow my own advice. Ja, the parents are not always so smart.” I whispered out, feeling a deep depression washing over the boy.

Master Leo looked at the floor seeming very sad. “Meine hase, I know you are trying to tell me something, but I admit I cannot understand you, not anymore. I wish I knew how to help you. I feel so helpless.”

I shook my head. "Did you check the stove? I apologize for Master Jonas's radio. I know he plays it too loud but if you ask him, he will turn it down. Didn't the lambs tell you this? I would have to correct their insolence if they neglected to remind you of their dinner time." I sniffed loudly and wrung my hands feeling extremely nervous, but I couldn't recall why any longer.

Master Leo gasped. "Would you like to go see the lambs meine hase? Is that what you are asking me? We can go right after you eat something."

I nodded. "You didn't get that woman's cake, I hope. Did you know she loves her doctor man? I am going to be a doctor. I wanted to be a doctor. Now I think I will be a plumber."

Master Leo frowned "A plumber? Why not the doctor, Christian Axel?"

I rubbed my legs marveling at the softness of the material my breeches were made of. "I could fix all the leaks and drain the hole in the middle of the worlds. There, you hear that fucking noise. What is that?" I stood up and put my ear to the wall listing to the tapping.

I loud out a shout of joy. "It's Der Hund. He is sending me the morse code. Thank Gott. All is not lost Max. Quick, get the pen. He is sending us his wishes for the mission. Call the boys. This is great news." I rushed past a startled Master Leo nearly falling down before I could get to his bedroom.

I tore through my bag seeking the writing stuff. The tapping was getting louder and louder. I fell to my stomach and began decoding it with speed. I smiled as the answers became clearer. Der Hund was sure we could break the metal. This plan was perfect to make that happen. I giggled with Max full of glee that this nightmare was nearly over.

Master Leo came into the room carrying a tray of food. He put this on the floor but kept his distance. I kept a nervous eye on this rapist. He slid it across the floor. When I continued to work on the codes and ignored the meal, he came a little closer and pushed it within my reach.

“Christian Axel, you need to eat my love. You have refused the food for days. If you don’t have a little something, then you will weaken. You need your strength to deal with Malfred, meine heart.” He said almost in a whisper.

I stared at that tray then looked back at him. “Master, I will not eat this cake. How can I enjoy such kindness when my lambs starve? There is no justice in this brutal world. Can I do something for you? Did you come here to request services? I warn you; I have blood in my mouth. That can be dangerous you know. The water was contaminated. If you try to couple you will get the sickness. Your cock turns to metal like the Dominant’s heart, cold and unfeeling. It is not fun, let me tell you. I want you to understand. It is my duty to protect you from such disasters, Master. Did you say you needed something?”

I went back to my coding, forgetting that Master Leo was there. The man was quiet as a mouse, I tell you. He watched me for another hour. Once in a while he would try to get me to eat that stuff. I wasn't stupid. I knew that food was radioactive.

Der Hund told me they were trying to poison the boy. I was not a fool. I remembered that Malfred already killed us twice. I wondered if my friend Casper ever found his sunglasses. I seemed to recall he left them in that horrible pool room on the floor. I have to say Meine Liebe, the land of the dead is the strangest place. *I have been there many times, and I am not a fan of it let me tell you.*

Master Leo told me a few years later that thanks to my being dead it was difficult for him to communicate with me during those tough last months before I broke my collar. He said the next day after I was murdered in the Great Hall, he bought some books on how to speak the language of the dead. He said that way he could continue to talk with my ghost you know.

Master Max giggled. "Ja, which is what he told me. Don't look so surprised. They have a book on everything Meine Liebe. I told you this man is the drama queen. I knew damned well German is his native tongue. Even dead I was speaking my mother's tongue. I suppose he thought he could use more practice with it. Eventually, I wished all the Masters had studied up on Master Leo's ghost language books. At the very least they should have had their ears checked. For the next year Master Leo was the only one that seemed to understand me. That really is not a surprise though, since no one really cared to listen to anything I had to say anyway the entire time I was in that fucking collar of theirs."

I shook my head feeling very confused by his statements. "Wait if you were dead Master, then how can you be here right now? I thought if you die, you stay dead?"

Master Mad Maxx immediately swatted me with his cane. Shit, I forgot this was Mad Max not the kind Maximillian. I let out a yelp as he chuckled.

"I told you I would get you eventually, big mouth. Well, for your information I am the undead kind of dead. That means I can go back and forth between the living world and the one of the dead. I have never figured out how the fuck I get in or out of there, but it happens from time to time. It is one of my superpowers, but to be honest I do not care much for this one. Though it comes in handy when the boy gets killed. That dumbass Haus doctor called it psychosis from the acute cycle of schizophrenia, but I knew better. That quack would say anything to save his ass. He didn't want to report my murder you know, plus he knew I would figure out how to return from that insane place anyway. That fucker could have helped me out. Yet, he seemed to like giving the flesh a bunch of shots and pills saying there was nothing he could do. That was bullshit. He was like most of the criminals in that place. He made good money fucking me over, you know. I was left in that hellish limbo of the dead for nineteen months. I turned sixteen in the fucking mental hospital. It took forever for Der Hund to get back to

us. When he finally found his way home, he got us the fuck out of that awful world that someone sent us ta. If I ever find out who was the rat that killed us that time, I will return the fucking favor. That you can be assured Meine Liebe." Master Mad Maxx sighed then asked me if I wanted another thud or was I ready to listen to the story.

I shook my head but said nothing. I have to be honest; I was too freaked out with the idea that even had I wanted to; I couldn't kill Master Maxx. He would come back like a damned cat with nine lives. After hearing so much of his story, I didn't doubt that he could indeed do what he claimed. Only someone with magical powers could have survived all that shit, right?

He laughed with a sound of evil in his noise. "Well, you are learning. Too bad for Mad Max. Never mind, I will get you in my chains soon enough. Now on with the story, where was I? Ah, ja, Master Leo was watching us decoding Der Hund's communications."

Master Leo demanded I eat something after I continued to push that nasty stuff away for all that time. He was starting to sound angered with me.

I worked out the latest code from Der Hund and shrugged, never looking up at him. "You think the lambs' grain is full of that fallout from the bomb Master? I think Geraldine and Ryker are getting agitated from all that fucking radiation, you know. That stuff is not good for the growing lambs. That is how little Bo Peep lost her sheep. I heard that news through the electrical grid so you must believe it to be true."

Master Leo sucked in his breath and crossed his arms. He has been sitting on the floor by his bedroom door the whole time. "You won't bath, change your clothing nor eat. Christian Axel, you will die if you don't do these dings. If you don't wish for this food, then tell me what you will eat. I demand you do at least that."

I looked up at him with a startle. "Huh? The dead don't eat Master. They need no clothing, nor do they care about sleeping. You can surely see that we are ghosts. Look around you. Do you recognize anything? Me neither. I am working on finding out who killed me. Thank you very much for not interrupting this important message from the Core. Now I forgot my place. Where the hell is the headset, Master? I cannot hear the spies without it."

Master Leo's eyes went wide. "You think you are dead, meine heart? Oh, meine Gott. A delusion has onset. This is a bad thing. We need to speak to Jonas and Claus about this Christian Axel. You will tell them about your being dead, ja?"

I giggled. "They already know this, Master. I need not say anything. Did the lambs ask about me? I cannot find any letters from them. I guess they forgot to write me, ja?" I dug in my bag to be sure I had not missed any mail from my friends.

Master Leo got up and came toward me. I cowered and covered my head thinking he was gonna hit me for not eating his radioactive meal. I almost felt relieved when he took up my collar and hand motioned me to follow him in silence.

I did as he told me wondering if he was taking me for that thudding, I thought I may deserve. Master Malfred said I had been insolent. I wasn't too worried. A thudding is better than the Guard any day. Master Leo told me to put on my coat. I followed his order wondering why I needed a jacket for my ride in his chains.

To my surprise and relief, he wasn't takin me downstairs. He led me out of the Haus right out the front door. I shot hate filled looks at Olaf and Vilber when they opened the door and allowed us to step outside. They seemed nervous for some reason. Both were looking me up and down with their eyes in shock. I flipped them the bird and giggled about that as I followed Master Leo across the lawn in my protocol.

The sun was setting low. It will be dark soon. I felt more invigorated with the coming of night. I wondered if maybe the reason I was still conscious after dying like I had was because Master Jonas bit me. I shivered at the thought that maybe I was the Vampire from it. I was thinking of ways to undo his vampire virus when I saw that Master Leo was taking me to the barn.

I became extremely excited by this good news. I let out yelps of thrill until Master Leo stopped and demanded I mind his order for silence. I looked at the ground quickly and wrung my hands afraid I was going to get struck for forgetting his command. He stood there watching me a moment, but then turned around continuing our journey to see my friends the lambs.

He barely got the gate opened when I flew past him with an excited shout. My lambs were happy to see me too. I fell to me knees and laughed with joy as they surrounded me and nuzzled my face and chest. I petted and kissed them all many times. Annette fell into my lap and Ryker bullied Milo. It was a great moment to be back home with my family at last. I couldn't recall the last time we had been together.

I was holding my Annette and singing her the new songs by Led Zepplin when Master Leo came into the pen and sat down in the hay. He was holding a sandwich in his hands. I glanced at him wondering where the hell he got that from. I shot a look around the barn to see if maybe Evelyn was lurking about.

He looked to see what I was seeking then said. "The lambs want you to have this sandwich. It is their gift for your coming to see them." He reached out his arm trying to hand me the thing.

I looked at Milo that stood next to me nuzzling my ear. "Did you tell the others about that terrible cake? You are the thoughtful one Milo. I didn't eat it you know. I pretended to spare her feelings, ja? I am the gentlemen like you always told me to be. They are not very nice to me though. Is that normal? To be so mean to those that didn't ask for their blood?"

Master Leo frowned. "Christian Axel, uhm, Geraldine will cry if you don't eat the lambs' present to you. She made this for you with her own uhm hands?"

I flashed a look at Geraldine pushing Ryker around with her head to get a better spot next to me. "You did that for me? Well how can I refuse your love? I know I did that one time, but you were being unfair. I make this up to you now, ja? I will eat all of it. I thank you for the mercy of it Geraldine." I reached out and took the sandwich, eating all of it. *I even licked the wrapper. That Geraldine could make a great sandwich, you know.*

Master Leo smiled with happiness as he watched me kissing my lambs in gratefulness for their gift. "Ah that is meine heart. Maybe the lambs' can make more sandwiches for you if you will eat them?"

I didn't look up at him. "I never deny my lambs their pleasures Master. Did you find that headset? Master Jonas's radio is too loud. I don't mean to complain but it is getting rather annoying."

My Master smiled. "I will find it and bring it to you tomorrow at Malfred's apartment."

I frowned. "I think that he killed me you know. Casper looks just like him. Though Casper has a pair of sunglasses like yours Master. You got yours in Paris. I think his are not as fancy as yours. Can we go to the kitchen? I think that headset is in there."

Master Leo clapped his hand with joy. “Ja, I would be happy to take you to the kitchen. We can go tell Evelyn to fix you some dinner.”

I glared at him. “I think not Master. You never tell her anything. She talks far too much.”

Master Leo nodded with his smile, turning to seriousness. “Okay ja, I will tell her nothing. You come with me. I take you to look for that headset in the kitchen now.” He took up my leash.

I gave my lambs many kisses and hugs then looked back at Master Leo. “Uhm, they will want to write to me Master. Will you make sure to get their letters to me? I will write them every day.”

He nodded. “Ja, meine heart. I will make sure their correspondence gets to you. Maybe though you can visit them in person instead? I am happy to bring you every day if you want?”

I smiled. “Ja, that I would perfect, Master. Thank you for the mercy of it.” I got up and followed him back to the Haus, right to the kitchen.

Master Leo held my leash and walked up to the window to speaking to the horrible woman Evelyn. She smiled and laughed while the two of them chattered. I stood behind him wringing my hands with anxiety. All the silvers and trainees in that place hauled ass the second Master Leo passed them, and they could leave their kneeling.

None of them wanted anything to do with being around an Elder and his Priceless. It may seem cowardly, but I completely understood why they ran away like that. The Elders were known for their easy furies. No silver needed more stress. If they could avoid any, they sure would.

Master Leo turned to me and asked me if I wanted to get something to eat, maybe another sandwich. I was telling him that I would only eat Geraldine's cooking when there was a blood curdling scream ringing out from the hallway outside the entry. Master Leo and I watched Dominants, silver and black collars go running by the door.

My Master yelled out at that hideous Karl when he went rushing by, "What is going on Karl? What is this racket."

Karl stopped his flight and shouted back. "The honorable Stefan has been found dead in his apartment. They are saying he's been gone many weeks, and the scene is gruesome, and perverted. I am on my way to see if the word is true." He took off with haste.

Master Leo shot me a look of fear. "Meine Hase, they say that Stefan is dead. This is terrible, isn't it?" I kept my eyes to the ground nodding.

"We are all dead here, Master. Can you ask Karl to give back that headset?" I wrung my hands.

He nodded. "Ja, I will go this minute. You come with me but no sounds. That is a directive." He pulled my leash and took off for the door.

Evelyn came from around her place behind the kitchen stove area. She ran up next to me in a rush to see this disturbing sight of Master Stefan's decayed flesh. I recalled that weird knife in my hidden pocket. As the round black collar walked next to me, I reached into my jacket and palmed the weapon.

There was a huge crowd gathered outside that cruel Dominant's apartment. Master Leo and Evelyn were prevented from getting too close to the door because of it. Master Leo was distracted by trying to push his way past the many collars and Dominants. Evelyn was busy with looking for an opening through that mass of people herself.

I allowed the swarming group of those residents to push me into the heavy-set black collar cook. With stealth and speed, I pulled the knife and slammed it into her back with all my strength. She let out a loud wail, but it was drowned out by the excited squealing, screams, and shouting of the audience witnessing the Haus doctor pulling out what was left of Master Stefan.

She turned around and stood there with her eyes open wide in shock. "Mad Max?"

I smiled as I dropped the knife back into my hidden pocket. "Ja, I know, you expected Christian. Well surprise. He is not the only one that can backstab a backstabber, Evelyn. You should have minded your own business. I hope you made enough money to pay for those medical bills. Equal service for equal, my love."

Evelyn fell to her knees with that stunned expression. "Julius and Grisham promised they would never tell anyone that I was involved. They lied to me."

I chuckled. "The Dominants didn't tell me, Evelyn. Ryker did. You remember him, ja? The boy you and your boyfriend Felix had put to the yard. He told me that it was you that told Claus he set that fire in the closet. That was a bit ago, but I bet you can recall it. I sure do. He was twelve Evelyn, just a little boy. He wanted me to give you a message, Felix too. They say they will be seeing you, maybe soon." I followed Master Leo as he pulled me away from the injured cook that was slowly collapsing onto the floor unnoticed by anyone.

Master Leo stared in disbelief at the sheet the Haus doctor used to cover the gross sight of Master Stefan. He asked the doctor if day knew how the man died. The doctor shook his head and said the remains were too decomposed to tell anything. He added that the official statement was a heart attack from a mild ticker condition the fellow had since birth.

My Master nodded, then took off with me fast as his feet could carry him. I was dragged along behind him singing under my breath and wringing my hands. He was upset for some reason. I told him I killed that man. I had no idea why he seemed so upset about it now.

When he got me back to his apartment he sat down on his couch and ordered me to kneel before him. I did as commanded but was angered he never asked Karl about that headset.

He looked at my face with a frown. "You were telling me the truth about all those you have sent to their graves around this Haus. I thought maybe only delusions of the schizophrenic, but Stefan was just as you said. I worry that this Malfred and others have used your suggestable mind to do horrible things. What will this beast do with you now that your mind is blown, I wonder? Will he send you to kill Leo next?"

I giggled and rocked in place. "Nay, Master. You're already dead. All of you are. This is hell where each of you belong. I am here too because I was born here. I am sorry to say that, but that is the truth of it. Why didn't you ask Karl for that headset? He will never give it back I bet."

There was a knocking at the door. Master Leo growled and told me to stay still while he answered. I nodded, rocked, and sung to myself. Then I saw Casper come around to look at me with a smile on his face. Master Leo was angered that the bank robber ghost had come to visit.

Chapter 54: Pioneering a Cure

Casper ignored the fuming Master Leo. He reached out and handed me the missing headset. I let out a yell of thrill and snatched them from him. I put them back on my ears, feeling immediately better. The anxiety was always calmed by that wonderful tool of the spies.

Casper knelt with an expression of wonder on his face. He tried to force my eye contact with his own. I dropped my gaze and wrung my hands trying to block him from looking at me. I was quite sure that the bank robber had designs to try to steal my thoughts. That is what the thieves do, take things that do not belong to them.

He glanced up at Master Leo that was still fussing over his visit. "I wish to take Christian Axel this minute. Give me his leash and you can get some rest. I can bet he has been of no use in any kind of service to you Leo. This will be my first time holding him for my own. It is special, and I want to get him settled in properly. He needs rest like the doctor said. This hauling him around at midnight is too stressful. This is a more reasonable hour for a transfer." He reached out to touch my hair, and I backed away from his reach with a hateful glare.

Master Leo snapped his fingers. "You get the fuck out of here Malfred. Christian Axel belongs to me for another four hours. You only want him early to start taking your pleasure. You just cannot kept your cock in your pants, can you? Meine poor little hase has had enough of your type of rest."

Casper nodded. "Ja, his leash is yours for a bit, but I tell you what. I am a reasonable man. Are you? You give him to me this minute and I return the favor by granting you time with him while he is in my care. This will give you four whole hours of such a pleasure. As for my interests in possession, I don't believe that is any of your business. I seriously doubt you keep this gorgeous boy around here to play with your records. However, I bet you give him something to sing about, ja? Never mind, we are wasting time with this petty arguing. No matter what you do, in four hours he will be on his knees to his Master Malfred. You can get a chance to visit him over the next three days or you can uselessly hog him without stopping his fate. Do you wish to take my deal, ja or nein?"

Master Leo paused for a moment. "You will swear to this understanding you offer? I get to see him any time during your holding his leash to reclaim this extra time you desire to take from me?"

Casper grinned. "Well, not in the middle of the night, but ja. All you need to do is call ahead. You give me the mercy of these extra four hours to settle him at an early hour. Then I give my word to grant them back at your discretion. Come on Leo. You have to give him to me shortly anyway. just think this way you can check on him to see I am not injuring the boy."

Master Leo shifted and looked at the floor as if deep in thought. "Okay, you have a deal. You are right. I would rather hand him over to you early and have safety checks with him. I will warn you right this minute Malfred, Christian Axel has been severely traumatized by what you did to him. If he rises up and kills you, I for one will laugh my ass off. You would be smart to give him his space and leave that eager cock of yours in your pants. I think you have done enough damage with it don't you?"

Casper sighed. "Are you done with your lecture, mother hen? If so then order him to gather his things. Before you do that I would like to inquire as to why he is wearing double clothing and not minding his hygiene? He looks worse than when you took his leash earlier today."

Master Leo snorted. "He is ill, Malfred. None of us will be able to get him to do anything. He will barely eat. That is what a marvelous Priceless he is. Are you still enamored with your getting to see the real thing up close? I bet not. Insanity is not pretty Malfred, nor is this boy enjoying his waking nightmare. He is fragile. You would be wise to use patience and gentle care with him. I will come by tomorrow to make sure he gets something in his stomach. I ask you to leave his crumbling hygiene issues alone till I can do some research to see if there is a way to fix this phobia you caused him. He is deathly afraid of the water because of your raping. In fact, you caused this failure in him, Malfred. He is extremely psychotic and nonfunctional thanks to your nasty tricks."

Casper nodded. “Ah well, I seem to recall you didn’t turn down the chance to blood bond this amazing creature when your chance came. I do believe you call the kettle black, Leo. Ah, but you are wasting my time again trying to pull me into this useless argument. I will get him to change and wash. I have my ways. Get him to get his stuff. Time to go, Christian Axel.” He reached out and grabbed my chain leash.

I shook my head and mumbled. “I go with you to haunt this Haus, Casper, if you want. You can take the Great Hall and pool. I don’t like those places. The boogie man lives there, and he blasts his radio. I really hate that guy you know?” I wrung my hands faster, reaching up a few times to tap the headset with my fingers. It kept losing my signal.

Master Leo yelled out in fury. “Christian Axel, this man is Malfred not Casper. Damn it Malfred you correct this misunderstanding, or I go tell Claus you are misleading the Priceless.”

Master Malfred nodded. “Okay Leo calm down. Christian Axel, you can call me Master. Don’t use my name anymore or I will have Master Claus take you to the chains.”

I shrugged. “As you say Master. Can you move? I am getting interference in the transmissions. How can I know the plan without the next codes? This headset is sensitive you know.” I tapped it several more times with a worried brow wondering if that brute Karl broke them.

Master Casper, I mean Malfred, had me gather my bag. He took up my leash and dragged me back to his apartment. Master Leo bitched and gave directions the entire time before we could get out of his house.

I was surprised at how angry my Master was at this ghost over his taking me to his home. I wondered why all the fuss. I had met Casper before. He was a thief and a liar, but Master Leo acted like he was also a killer. That made me anxious. I thought maybe Master Leo knew something I didn't. I decided to tell Taube to be careful with this guy. I no longer trusted Master Leo, but dare was no sense in taking any chances.

I was a little concerned when the Mirror shard still had not shown up to take over as Master Malfred (Casper) locked his door behind us. What the hell was taking that fool so long? I worried maybe he had shattered already. With Der Hund trapped in the tapestry anything was possible.

I paced and wrung my hands with the anxiety at the lateness of Taube. My Master sat in his leather chair and watched me with a large smile as I walked back and forth like a caged animal. I began mumbling to Max about my concerns that Taube wasn't coming at all. I was getting agitated over all this weirdness.

Master Malfred finally tired of being the voyeur, "Meine Taube. Get over here and kneel at my feet boy. You are giving me a headache with all that movement. Do you ever get tired?"

I stopped my pacing and looked around the room. "I cannot afford a car Master. I cannot get those rubber wheels for your pleasure until I get out of this Gott damned Haus. I apologize for my poverty. I can get you a Tylenol dough. A headache is not fun. It is from that fucking radio, or maybe the Mistress's vacuum? I hear that too. I am sick of her constantly moving the furniture. Will someone tell her to go to bed and go to sleep, for fucks sake." I stomped my boot and glared above my head at the Head of the Haus floor.

Master Malfred appeared surprised by my response. He sat forward never takin his snake-like gaze from me. I kept watching the ceiling listening to Mistress Cora slide her couches across the floor. I was trying to remember why I was upset. Something about someone being late for an appointment?

He got up and grabbed my chain leash dragging me behind him without a word. I followed him wringing my hands and singing under my breath. I didn't know where we were going but the man was strong. I had to go or lose my head when the collar ripped it from my shoulders, you know.

The Master entered a room with a blue door. I stood dare while he smiled and pointed at a large bed with a fancy wooden headboard. The place was decorated with matching dressers, bookshelves, lamps, and a velvet chair with a pedestal for reading.

All the furniture was of expensive dark wood. I kept my gaze to the floor and noticed the same fancy carpets as in his living room. This man was wealthy beyond imagination, Meine Liebe. I bet even the lamps were worth more than most cars normal people drive.

He smiled with pride while babbling to me about his paintings by famous artists that hung on the walls. I merely nodded and wrung my hands. I didn't care about any of this crap he was speaking. I wanted to go back to the living room and wait for Taube. I neither liked the way this was going nor the look in that man's eyes.

Master Malfred finished his diatribe about his things. He looked at me and frowned then jerked my chain pulling me toward a door off to the left of his fancy bed. He opened the door and dragged me into his master bathroom. The place was huge. He had a large garden tub in the center of this room with mirrors around it. A stand-up shower was off to the right of it with a door instead of the usual plastic curtain.

He turned to me with a smile. "I am requesting bath service. Only the one you will clean is not your Master. I will not stand for this foulness in my prize. You will clean up this minute, meine taube. There is the tub, get over there and start this service. That is a directive." He jerked my leash harshly.

I looked at that tub, then back to Master Malfred. "That water is contaminated Master. If I get it on me then I will glow. Everyone will see me coming. How can I haunt this Haus with that going on? The ghost is heard not seen."

Master Malfred backhanded me several times with obvious fury. I finally fell to my knees in an attempt to prevent another blow to my cheeks. He was hell bent that I provide myself with bath service, but I would not relent.

He stood there sweating from his working me over. "I told you to run that water and get into the tub. I demand bath service. You deny me again and I will call the fucking Guard."

I winced while covering my ears, feeling like he was throwing rocks instead of saying words. "I swear to you Master. That water is poisoned. I must protect and defend the Master. I would rather you call the Guard then have me break my vows."

The Dominant grew furious. He held my leash tightly and went to the tub. He turned on the facets and put in the plug never letting go his hold on me. I trembled and whimpered as I watched that green glowing water fill up that ceramic monster. He spun around and knocked my ass to the floor.

I tried to get up, but he leapt on me with speed. He was struggling with me, tearing at my clothing. I screamed in terror and tried to claw and punch him.

He stopped his attack long enough to grab my throat and force me to look into his face. "You hold still. Move again, I will cut you up. I would rather have you ripped to pieces than be seen with a smelly, unclean silver. I will not stand for this filth, not ever. You will learn to mind me. I can make your life pure hell, Christian Axel." He let go of my neck and continued ripping off my blouse and breeches.

I didn't dare move another muscle. The Dominant was beyond furious. He told me he intended to cut me up like Gerard had. I closed my eyes and endured his stripping but did weep silently I have to admit, fucking Max, what a crybaby.

When Master Malfred had me naked, he looked at the chastity device with anger. "That is coming off. I will not have fucking Jonas tell me what I can and cannot touch." He got up and rushed out of that room.

I sat up on the floor trembling and wiping my face of the salty wetness. I got up to my knees and looked around for a place to hide before he came back. I spotted a closet door and was about to head for it when the Dominant came storming through the door with a small pair of bolt cutters in his hands. I dropped to my face covering my head with a scream. I thought he had come to uncollar me.

He grabbed my upper arm and flipped me to my back with me begging him not to cut off my collar. Casper ignored my wailing of anguish. He reached down and took my chastity device into his hand roughly. He nearly ripped my manhood out at the root in his rush. I cried out in torment and tried to pull him off me. He turned and backhanded me harshly demanding I be still.

I was dizzy from all his knocking me in my head. I wept with fear thinking he was going to de-sex me. I nearly let out a cry of gratitude when Master Malfred used that tool to cut the padlock from that metal tether. I wasn't glad he removed it, but happy to still have all my parts and collar intact.

He removed the chastity device and threw it across the room with a loud growl of anger. Then without pause he pulled me up from the floor like I was light as a feather. I let out a gasp of horror just as the boy hit that water in his filling tub. I tried to scramble out, terrified out of my mind with the stings and pricking of that contaminated stuff.

Master Malfred pushed me back each time I tried to climb off the tub. He laughed as if he was having a lot of fun. I rushed to the other side and tried escaping from the other side. He ran over and grabbed me just as my feet hit the floor. He tossed me back in like a rag doll. I fell on my back splashing and wailing nearly insane in my desperation. I tried again to get out but no matter which way I went he blocked me from escaping with speed.

I finally gave up this useless game. He was faster than I was, and stronger too. That contaminated stuff had poisoned the flesh beyond repair anyway. I was doomed. I laid my head into my arms on the lip of the tub and began weeping heavily at this horror. Master Malfred chuckled sounding quite humored at my defeat.

After turning off the water he stripped off his fancy suit rapidly. "Calm down, Christian Axel. This is merely a fucking bath. You act like this is torture. I was told by Peter you love the water. Am I to assume you no longer enjoy the swimming? I think you are simply confused. Well, luckily your Master will aid you in rediscovering your joy in this liquid. Or at least I will remind you of your duties to be bringing pleasure to your Master." He grabbed my leash then jumped into the tub with me.

I struggled with much fierceness as he pulled me toward him. He seemed to be thrilled a great deal over my distressed behaviors. Master Malfred's smile melted when I was within striking distance. Without warning he grabbed the back of my head. He held me tightly by my hair and demanded I pleasure him with my mouth in the water the way "he heard I had Master Leo." When I refused to do such a foul thing he forced my head under the water into his lap. I kept my mouth shut tight and refused the special service.

After my continued denying him his pleasure despite three dunks underwater, he backhanded me with much strength busting my mouth open. "Now you can suck cock with a cracked lip. Do you wish to do it without teeth either? You will mind me. If you don't do what you are told I can make your life pure hell. I don't care if you are psychotic. The Schizophrenic bleeds just as quick as any silver does." He yelled into my face, turning red with anger.

I shook my head. "You can drown me, Master. I thank you for the mercy of it. Please tell Jonas to turn down the radio."

He bellowed, "Fucking loon. There is no radio playing. That shit is in your fucking head. Gott dammit. You are going to serve your Master even if I need to restrain you."

He spun me around forcefully bending me over the side of the tub.

I clawed at the ceramic trying to get enough traction to escape. He held my leash taunt as if I were the angry dog. It was effective at keeping me from fleeing from his lustful interest. He got behind the struggling boy.

The sound of him spitting rang in my ears. I pulled away from the wheel running to the other side of the flesh's mind. I dragged the weeping Max with me. I knew what that spitting sound meant. I couldn't take this, not again. I closed my eyes as did Max. The boy went limp immediately in a catatonic trance. Master Malfred had just entered the boy when Max and I were thrown from the boy onto the floor.

I looked up to see Taube smiling with wickedness. "Looks like the party started without me. You boys go rest up. Taube has this." Without another word he jumped into the boy.

Max and I fled that bathroom as fast as we could. We didn't want to be anywhere around that scene when the Mirror shard awoke the flesh. We didn't quite make it out in time. Max and I heard the boy let out a loud gasp as Master Malfred speed up his thrusting. I was so upset by the sounds of the Master enforcing his special services rights I wasn't looking where I was going. Me and Max slammed right into Maximillian. We went to the floor outside the bathroom door as the submissive shard groaned out in pain from our collision.

Maximillian rubbed his head and offered his hand to help us back to our feet. "Evelyn is dead, brother. What the hell have you done? Mad Max. You are not the killer shard. Christian is. Why did you do that? She was not even on our list."

I groaned in terror. "I didn't kill anyone, brother. Max did it. I tried to stop him. Oh Meine Gott. What is going on? What the hell is happening to us?" Max shot an evil smile at both of us but said nothing.

Maximillian shook his head and trembled. "I don't know. Even our fucking soul is killing people. I am lost as you are. What the hell is Taube doing?"

I rubbed my eyes trying to clear the foggy vision that had been plaguing me for hours. "Getting raped in the tub most violently is what the hell he is doing. You don't want to go in there, brother. That scene is ugly trust me. By the way. That Mirror shard of yours left Max and I stranded. He is unstable."

Maximillian nodded. "We all are brothers. Without Der Hund, apparently none of us knows his fucking job. Okay, freaking out isn't going to fix this. Max and you go find Christian. I lost him in the tapestry on my way here. Has anyone seen Mad Maxx? Shit, he is up next. This is a nightmare."

Taube snickered behind us causing us both to startle. "Ja, a real game of chance brothers."

I screamed in horror. "What the fuck, Taube. Who is at the wheel if you are here?"

Taube shrugged. "Christian is, you fool. Did you think I would just leave the flesh catatonic? Nein. I am reliable. I wasn't enjoying that game Malfred was playing with the boy. Brother Christian said he would be happy to take my spot for a bit."

Maximillian and I looked at each other with fear griping our hearts. "Oh shit. Christian, that motherfucker, he will kill Master Malfred before we are ready," we wailed in unison.

We knocked Taube over rushing back into the bathroom just in time to see the boy reaching quietly for his jacket. Master Malfred was too busy violating the boy to notice Christian nearly had his hands on that knife.

I saw Maximillian jump into the boy. I hesitated but Max pushed me from behind forcing both of us to join our submissive brother. The three of us were quickly joined by Taube that thought we were all playing a game of chase. I arrived to find Maximillian in a hand-to-hand combat with our killer shard Christian. He was losing.

I rushed over and pried Christian off Maximillian. He turned to see me and let out a wild screech. Taube grabbed Maximillian that was coming in to shatter the subdued Christian. For that moment, the four of us were in a stalemate. Then Christian saw Max glaring with that goofy smile of his.

"Get that motherfucker away from me," he howled, then wiggled out of my grip, fleeing the flesh as if the boy were on fire.

The five of us stood there unsure what to do. The wheel was unsharded and rolling limply. None of us wanted to handle Master Malfred's intercourse. A verbal argument broke out. Taube refused to endure this humiliation. Maximillian reported he already suffered the five-blood bonding rapes. Max and I already tolerated Grisham and Julius. No one was strong enough to take this stress.

Then out of nowhere we saw Mad Maxx come from the shadows rubbing his eyes and yawning. He stood there next to the angered Christian.

He stretched. "What did I miss?"

Christian growled out, his eyes glowing red. "Nothing brother. These fools let this rapist do what he pleases. Well good riddance. I will be no part of this dishonor." The killer shard slipped into the shadows.

Mad Maxx looked at the five of us. "Why is everyone in the boy? Why the fuck is that criminal Malfred doing the boy too? Fuck! He suddenly noticed the tranced flesh was being held down and screwed by the foul Dominant.

He jumped into the wheel room with us demanding answers. Another several moments passed while everyone tried to catch up the masochistic shard up on the horrors of the last many days. Mad Maxx's eyes bugged the second he heard Der Hund was lost to us.

"Motherfucker, and we are trapped in the fucking metal? Nein, this must be fixed at once. I am not going to spend my life dealing with this shit." He grabbed the wheel, but it was too late.

Master Malfred had finally noticed the boy was not responding to his sexual assault. He had uncoupled unsatiated. He started to shake the boy hard demanding he wake up. The ground shook and the walls caved. All five of us spilled across the floor, smacking into each odder. Mad Maxx was thrown from the wheel onto the mind's floor.

All us Max boys and Taube yelled in terror. None of us could navigate the seizing flesh to take hold of the wheel to end the spasms. Master Malfred struck the boy's face several times. He had an expression of fear. He realized too late the catatonic fit had onset. He had to figure out how to re-awake the Priceless quickly or it would be days or even months before we could return from the statue like state of living death.

Master Malfred looked down at his knees into the water. Without another moment's hesitation he dunked the flesh deep and flipped on the cold tap. He pulled the boy up rapidly then forced his head under the freezing stream. Electricity rolled past us striking the wheel. The outflow hit each Max brother and Taube, holding us captive in its heated bolts.

Maximillian and Mad Maxx fought against our electric restraints. They reached the wheel together. The boys took it in their hands despite the excruciating shock of that lightening flashing in every corner of their minds. We all wailed in pain, terror, and despair in unison. The flesh opened its mouth and joined our screams of trauma.

Master Malfred pulled the boy from the drink the second he heard that gurgling cry coming from him. He held him tightly into an embrace, panting and speaking gently, telling the Priceless he was okay and to calm down. The boy wept loudly and clung to the Dominant unable to gain his bearings or location.

Mad Maxx and Maximillian fell to their knees never releasing the wheel as they gasped and shuddered from that horrifying experience. Taube, Max, and I leaned into the mind wall trying to catch our breath, groaning from the agony of the electrical strike.

Master Malfred pulled the boy from the tub. Mad Maxx didn't let go hanging on like a kid would his mother. The Master found a towel and began drying the two of them off, still speaking softly to the confused and frightened boy.

Maximillian looked at Taube. "This is your game Taube. Your take the wheel for this motherfucker. You are not allowed to leave your post until relieved by the proper brother shard. Fuck, you nearly got Malfred killed and us by proxy."

Taube looked at his feet appearing ashamed. "I apologize brothers. I know better. I don't know how Christian talked me into letting him do my job. I couldn't seem to resist him. That game Malfred was playing hurt. I guess I let it get to me."

Mad Maxx nodded. "Taube there is not a shard here that doesn't understand the desire to escape their duties when the special services get called or the rapes happen. However, you must do your job. Each of us shoulders this burden in his turn. Are you one of us or are you Christian? If Christian, you need to stop riding the flesh. We are in a lot of trouble, maybe for good. We have a small sliver of a chance. That means we must work together and do our tasks no matter how foul. You understand?"

Taube sniffed back his tears. "Ja. I understand. I take the wheel now. No matter what Malfred does, I will handle it like the pleasure submissive we were trained to be without quarrel."

I looked at Taube and scoffed. "This motherfucker cannot even get that radio turned down. What good are any of you? I swear to Gott someone needs to shut that fucking Mistress Cora up. I cannot take all this noise." I was getting really annoyed with that shit by then, you know.

Maximillian, Mad Maxx, and Taube all shot confused looks at each other, then Maximillian spoke up. "Mad Max, you and Max need a rest brother. You are, uhm, tired it seems, ja?"

I growled out. "I am not fucking tired. I am Mad Max the sadist. Stop calling me names, motherfucker. Can someone get that headset? Fuck, this noise is killing my head, said, red, Fred, lead, Ted, shit. Where are the codes? Codes! I need the codes." I covered my ears and paced back and forth trying to drown out the noise. That fucking noise.

Mad Maxx shuddered. "Oh, shit. The madness is affecting our brother. Maximillian and Taube, push Mad Max and Max out. Get him out of here." Taube came flying at me and Max.

Max began to laugh wildly. "I knew you sonofabitches are against us. You are the ones poisoning our food. I heard it over the radio waves. The fucking Russians are behind this, you know. Mad Max, shatter the enemies. They are going to tell all our secrets." He ran and hid behind me acting afraid and suspicious of his brother shards.

I nodded, took my hands off my ears then immediately punched Taube in the face knocking him to the ground. I returned to my attempts to stifle that racket that was making me deaf.

Taube grabbed his jaw, near shattering when he hit the floor. "Oh, meine Gott. Who am I? I can't remember. I did know, right? Can one of you tell me who the fuck I am?" Taube got up staggering as if he were blind and drunk, unable to figure out which way to go.

Mad Maxx shot a look of terror at Maximillian. "It is spreading, brother. We have to get out of here. Hurry before we are infected with the madness." He took off to jump from the boy.

Maximillian stood dare with a diabolical smile spreading across his face. "I am not Maximillian. I am Mad Maxx the Brutal. I do not run from anything you pussies do. I have the powers of the universe at my fingertips. I will kill them all and burn this Gott damned Haus right to the ground." He began laughing maniacally his eyes glowing blue as the hottest part of a fire.

Mad Maxx screamed when he tried to jump and bounced back right onto his ass. He got up trying to escape the boy a second time. He once again was thrown to the floor. The masochistic shard recovered then hit the wall, biting, scratching, and kicking, begging to be released from schizophrenic hell.

He fell to his bottom crying and babbling. "The door is the floor, but there is more. Oh, the poor man never ins. Woe be it to the tiny feet that scatter to the four winds that blow in the trees. Could you get me that cup over there, love? I think I heard Gott calling. This is the thing about knowing and seeing there is no reason for any of it. Are you listening to me whoever the hell you are."

Max put his finger to his lips. "Hush, do you boys hear that. They are coming. The Guard is coming. Hurry, cover your heads. If they cannot see us, then they cannot shoot us."

I growled in irritation. "What? I cannot hear shit over that fucking radio. What did you say?" I dropped to my knees, holding my head, moaning in agony from the noise.

Taube tripped and fell to his face. "Hug? What is the Guard? Who are you again? Shit, did I leave on the stove? Wait, what was I talking about?" He looked around the mind appearing lost and unable to focus on anything.

Mad Maxx babbled. “This is the thing of horses. They have the biggest eyes in the universal too. Did you read that book? I left it here somewhere in her hair. Over there? It is the stallion not the mare. If you have the cake, I will ask you to share. Of course, to see anyone do that would be rare.”

Maximillian grinned with evil. “I got the wheel boys. You all just keep your Frau asses away from me. I don’t want any of that insane shit rubbing off. Now where were we, ah, Karl. He stole the headset. I kill him next. If you are hungry brother Maxx, give me a moment to hunt down Agnette. We will eat her for our dinner. She tastes great, ja.” He walked over and grabbed the wheel spinning it with a wild look in his glowing eyes.

The boy stopped weeping as Master Malfred carried him out of the bathroom. He took him to his bed and laid down with him in his embrace. Maximillian opened his eyes and took the mind. He smiled wickedly at Master Malfred. The Dominant was startled by this odd expression. He jerked back his head looking hard into the boy’s eyes.

“Meine taube? You are alert, ja?” Master Malfred narrowed his eyes appearing unsure of what he was looking at.

I grinned even wider. “More than you know, Master. Can I get you anything? Your pleasure is my own.”

Master Malfred frowned. “Is it? Didn’t seem that way a moment ago, meine taube. I requested bath and special services and was treated like a rapist.”

I shrugged. "You behaved like one, Master. I assumed this was your fetish. You need not beat me to get what you want. Equal service for equal service, you know."

He chuckled. "Is that so? Well, what is the service I need to provide to get what I asked for without quarrel?"

I looked around the room, not seeing what I was seeking. "I will need my headset and I want to see my lambs every morning to feed them their breakfast, Master."

Master Malfred blew out his breath still smiling with glee. "Well, you drive a hard bargain, but I think that can be arranged." He moved toward me to try to engage a kiss.

I pulled back. "I wasn't done Master. I also require a pair of sunglasses, no more baths, and I want two hours a morning to be left the fuck alone. I will do as I please and go where I want, no questions asked."

He scoffed. "The sunglasses are not a problem, but you will bath and no fucking way I am allowing a schizophrenic to have the run of this Haus. Besides, you're too valuable to let wander. Others will be looking to have a taste of that which is mine."

I sat up and glared at him with hate dripping from my eyes. "Then you get your ropes, Master. You will have to beat me to the ground and rape me every time. I will make you sorry if you ever met me. I can and will make sure you lose your two days the Elders gave you to keep me in line. You all think I am retarded. I can hear you when you plot in front of me motherfucker. I need those two hours to practice for my Dominant testing. As for the bathing, fuck you. I never bath again. That is final."

Master Malfred reached out and slapped me hard. "You insolent little prick. You will not tell me what to do. I am the Master here."

I laughed with insanity. "I am a corpse, Master. You cannot control the dead, fool. You provide me my demands and I make your darkest dreams come true. You fuck with me; you will find a grave next to my own."

He glared with fury. "Are you threatening me, Christian Axel?"

I giggled with a nod. "I am saying I am a reasonable man, but are you? Hahaha. You meet my demands or find you are without hands. I will never give you what you really want."

Master Malfred growled. "Oh? And what do you think it is I desire, meine taube?"

"To be envied, aspired to, and the head of Father Christmas on a platter. I even give you the horse he rode in on for free, Master. You going to take my deal, or will you attempt to steal? I warn you, I am a fighter, lighter, biter, pull the ropes tighter." I wrung my hands and rocked a little to calm my nerves, just a bit you know, long day.

Master Malfred snorted. "You are mad as a hatter, Christian Axel. I do not deal with silvers and especially the insane Priceless ones."

I shook my head. "Too bad, Master. You have me trapped here in a nasty hole in the center of the Earth. Well, you could have had a delicious cake, but you insist upon eating that woman's cooking. I tell you she is dead now. You shall starve without her feeding you the codes, won't you? Ah, that is bad for you. All your good friends keep dying. It is the winter you know. The cold long days make you wish for the old ways. That is the problem. The son will always chase away the darkness, and make the shadows flee. wonder what will be found in the light? Ignite. That's right. Maybe my headset, your sunglasses, the rocks in the world, which are silver but stained red?"

Master Malfred shook his head and blew out his breath. "Well, the conversation with you has been interesting, but I tire of this babbling. You will grant me the special services without quarrel, or I will send you down to the chains for a tune up. I seem to recall you were a hard one to break but break you did, apparently a bit further than expected. You waste my time. Get to it, I will not repeat myself again."

I shook my head. "Go fuck yourself, Master. I say that with respect." Master Malfred let out a loud howl of anger and grabbed my throat.

He pushed me to my back, blocking off my air. I was turning blue and thinking I would pass out soon. Master Malfred had definitely lost his temper.

He got into my bulging eyes, looking deep into my mind with a victorious grin. "You ready to mind your Master and grant me the Priceless special service I have dreamt of since the first rumor of them crossed my threshold?”

I forced a smile while gasping and held up a trembling hand. I lifted my middle finger and gurgled in an attempt to laugh when he let out a loud shout of indignation. I began to see the tunnel of the void closing on me. I closed my eyes relieved to be finally able to shut off this noise, chaos, pain, confusion, and never-ending despair at last.

Just as I was losing consciousness the Master let me go and threw me from his bed. I landed on the floor too groggy to attempt to break my fall. He jumped off after me and dragged me by my arms to his living room. There he locked my chain to the foot of his huge leather sofa. I was still recovering when he bonded my arms behind my back with those cuffs that I could not break out of yet.

He stood over me glaring, “You can stay here for the night out of my sight. If I were you, I would be thinking of a way to curb my anger before I get my first cup of coffee in me. If not, then I am taking you down to the chains, and maybe the cutters, or sharps. I will make you mind or at least make you wish the fucking Guard ended you when this disease came for you.”

I coughed and giggled. “I wish the Guard would come for me the second I was born Master. I thank you for the mercy of allowing me sleep where I need not smell your stink. You are indeed a gracious host. Ja, ja, hey, hey, ha, ha, I am naked. You know what? You know what, Master? Hello darkness my old friend. I’ve come to talk with you again. And in n the naked light I saw ten thousand people, maybe more. People talking without speaking. People hear without listening. People write songs that voices never share. and no one dared disturb the sound of silence. Fools, said I, you do not know Silence like a cancer grows. Hear my words that I might teach you. Take my arms that I might reach you. But my words, like silent raindrops fell. And echoed in the wells of silence. In the wells of silence where the silvers weep and sleep." I sung out parroting one of Master Leo's songs by them fellows Simon and Garfunkel. *Good song too, you know. A little elderly for your time though ja?*

Master Malfred was not impressed with my singing to him like that *(some people are just not the music lovers, ja?)* He growled out and kicked me in my backside telling me to shut the fuck up. To my relief he then stormed off to his room to sleep alone. I looked at my ailing brothers with a smile of triumph. We had managed to leave the Master with blue balls and stuck cuddling his pillow. That was something worth celebrating, ja?

I got up and danced – well the best I could give my restrictions with that fucking chain leash and those cuffs – while singing the songs I had learned from Master Leo's records. Throughout the night I enjoyed the freedom of not having some hairy old fucker holding me to their chest while snoring in my ears. I was not sleepy anyway.

There was no doubt all the problems with this odd madness that gripped the other shards interfered a bit with my partying. I didn't let it get me down. Mad Max told me to shut up most of the night. Max continued to believe I was giving away our secrets in my words. I only could parrot the English songs as I had no idea what I was actually saying. Mad Maxx made absolutely no sense at all but wouldn't stop speaking his crazy thoughts. Taube, well he partied with me, but I had to continually tell him what the fuck we were doing and re-introducing myself to him.

Otherwise, I think my revelry went rather well. It was about time we stopped being so damned serious. Not everything had to be about survival. I had informed Master Malfred what it would take to get my compliance with his demands. He would either meet them or end my pathetic life.

You see, Meine Liebe, it had become clear to me the Master Claus intended to keep me trapped in my metal. I was looking for another doorway out. This greasy bastard was just the cure for my deadly case of the silver I was seeking.

After all those years doing everything solo, I had decided it was time to get myself a partner. Master Malfred fit the job description perfectly. He was cutthroat, full of himself, evil to the core, and has a personal vendetta against the Head of the Haus Horse face Mistress Cora and second in command clever Master Claus.

We even shared some of the same enemies, Master Jonas, and Mistress Agnette. I was not too keen on his interest in Master Peter, but hey, I needed my old man for that big medical school bill. A poor boy like me could not afford to turn down that financial aid that old sonofabitch was offering, ja?

Now I know you are thinking, Maximillian, how could you even consider teaming up with Mastermind Malfred after all he had done to you? Well, Meine Liebe, understand this, all these motherfuckers were rapists and exploiters, even Master Leo. I was maybe the angriest with him. I expected Master Jonas, Master Claus, or even Master Malfred to be snakes that would look for any chance to fuck me over.

Master Leo though, he hurt me in a way none of them ever could. I trusted him, and even loved him. For that, he was the one that actually sealed my metal around my throat. His blood bonding assured I could never escape without crossing a river so fucking wide I would need a damned ship with a crew to transverse it.

He told me he did it to save me from becoming blood bonded by another that may be looking to use me to rise to Elder. Oh? With all the slots filled, it would have been real fucking hard to do it the way Malfred had, wouldn't it?

I was not a fool. Master Leo took his turn because he wanted to be my man. He feared being blocked out of my special services. He cared nothing for what it would do to my psychology, or my physical being once stuck on my knees for life.

The way I saw it, he kind of hoped I would never find my freedom. Then his place as my lover was assured. It was a fucking selfish move that he made a weak excuse to justify. He may have enforced his right to call himself my man, but he lost my heart, almost for good. I would eventually get over it, but not for a few years. That is a long way off so we will speak of that on a future day, ja?

With all that in mind, I realized I had been betrayed by the Vampire through forced blood bonding and lying to my Master Peter to steal my collar. Master Claus was going to betray me. No one can go to the vote without passing the testing, which was Haus law, and he thought me too insane to know it took a full Elder vote with Gretta approval to change the law. He was lying to me. I just told you about Master Leo. Even my mother and father had been nothing but sleezy rats.

This Malfred, well he had obviously made his way to the top using wet work but do remember it was nothing personal like with all the others I listed. Believe it or not, he had never personally met me until that day in the pool room when he taught me to swim. All the dirty shit he had pulled were with others and they were the ones that set me on my course to end another's life.

It was even questionable if he directly told his men and women to actually use me or simply to get the fucking job done. I do believe at least with Felix, he did intend to get me directly involved, but other than having to kill Geraldine I was more than happy to end the horrible Felix. He had that coming for what he did to little Ryker.

As for his raping me like he had done, well let's face it. If I were to kill everyone that was guilty of that, I would have to bury the whole sixth floor, the door guards, and my parents. Not that I wasn't planning on doing all that in time, but I had to be realistic. If I wanted to get my revenge, first I needed to get back my right to call myself a free man.

That brings me back to this plot of mine. I intended to secretly work on passing the two Dominant test sections I had left. I would bypass Master Claus's attempts to trip me up. Then if that went as planned, I intended to send that crossdresser, the Head of the Haus, the Head of the Voters, and Malfred right to hell. My breaking of my metal would be no problem since there would be no one left to block me.

I wasn't concerned with Master Jonas, the terminal Master Bladrick, Master Leo, or my parents. They would be the only ones left when I was done cleaning that Haus. I had the goods on Peter and Agnette. If they dared to vote nein, I had every intention of proving my birthright. That would send all three of us to the yard.

I had realized neither of them wanted that. What's a little blackmail among family? Hell, fucking your own seemed to be the letter of the day with those two skunks. It runs in the bloodline, you know. Besides with Gretta gone, Peter would be the Head Voter. No doubt, he wasn't interested in standing in the way of my blade.

The second part of my plan was tricky. I had to get Master Malfred to aid me in moving all his men toward getting Mistress Cora, Mistress Gretta, and Master Claus in the crosshairs of well-planned accidents. That would take getting Master Malfred to trust he had a tight alliance with me, and seduction was the key.

The man, for whatever reason, saw me as his Golden Calf. That was good for adoration, but I wanted more. I wanted his associates, his loyalty, and his fucking head on a pike. I knew a fellow like this one only valued something when it cost him dearly. He liked expensive things. If the price tag proved worthy, then my affections would have to go to the limit of his ability to pay.

I did realize there was a chance he could turn the tables and make me foot a hefty bill of my own to deny him what he already thought he had stolen for free. Oh well, sucks to be me, ja? Like it or not, I may have to endure rapes in bondage and even torture before this dumbass realized it was as easy as giving me all the I had requested.

The morning came like it always does. I was still stomping and singing under my breath having a grand old time when the grouchy Dominant come into the living room. He glared at me, and I ignored him continuing with my wild movements.

He cleared his throat, thinking I didn't see him. "You kept me up half the night with all that racket. Do you ever fucking sleep?"

I snickered. "Counting sheep will bring the sleep, Master. I think you need to get your coffee. I will slumber later when you leave all the marks for the other Masters to enjoy. Though maybe they will not appreciate that art. I believe they paid a great deal for the blank canvas, ha-ha.

You said what? Liar, get that drunk bastard off the wheel. Mad Max, quite marking up the mind. That is not codes from Der Hund you dumb bastard. It is our stomach growling, fool." I kicked at Mad Max that was trying to write his stupid morse code everywhere.

Master Malfred walked over and sat down rubbing his forehead harshly. "Gott dammit. I don't know what the hell I am going to do with you. This is a fucking nightmare. I was sure I could reach you through threats and manhandling. Peter told me you always gave in when he beat you enough, but this is not working this time."

I nodded. "I am the monster these days, Master. You could end this pain, but none of you will. I ask you for my fucking headset. You give me nothing but ask much. Call the fucking Guard. Tell them I want my headset, my sunglasses, and some time away from all of you. I am sick of this dusty old Haus. I need to stretch my eyes and open my muscles. This is not good for the gardens, you know. Weeds grow when you don't watch out for all the nasty rodents." I kicked at Mad Max again when he tried to sneak past me to write on the wheel.

Master Malfred groaned then got up and rushed from the room. I shouted at the ceiling demanding Mistress Cora stop running that fucking vacuum of hers. My Master returned with the headset. He walked over and put it on my head. I held still till he adjusted it to cover both my ears. I smiled, feeling instantly relieved.

The Dominant noticed my sudden calming. "These really work. I thought them only a ploy. So, getting those sunglasses would calm you even more?"

I nodded with a smirk. "Ja, Master. Nein to the baths, see my lambs and two hours away from your hold. You give me those things and I will show you why they level me priceless."

He frowned. "I already fucking see why they level you the forbidden silver. I cannot miss it in fact. Shit, I cannot let you go without hygiene nor cut you lose for two hours unsupervised, Christian Axel. You are mad. You would jump from the banister or kill the fucking cook."

I laughed maniacally. "Nein, not me Master. I didn't kill the cook. That backstabber was lain low by the soul. She was the surprised one though, ja, Max? Did you see that look of shock? She didn't know we were talking with the dead. I can hear them too. All of us can. Tap, tap, tap, tap, trapped like a rat. She stood up when she should have sat. and all the king's horse and all the king's men cannot put the dumpty cook together again. She fell off that wall. Ja, get the glue boys. We have much work to do. Did anyone see if we left the stove on? Can I have my clothes now?"

Master Malfred shook his head. "Nein, not jet. Okay, let me think about your offer for a moment. What if I were to allow you to bypass the bathing when on my leash and I take you wherever you want to go for two hours a day and I promise not to interfere with your business? Will that be agreeable?"

I paced and pulled my leash to its limits. "Ah, ja. There is a trouble in the bushes. Catch him quickly. He will bring us luck, ha-ha. You think you are so clever. Nein. The colors don't match Gott damnit. Put that down Mad Maxx. What the fuck is wrong with all of you? Do we need to see Geraldine? The flesh is getting weak, but she has the cure."

Master Malfred sat down staring at me appearing confused. "I don't understand a fucking thing you are saying to me. Are you even aware? How can I fix this."

I stopped my frantic pacing and looked at him with curiosity. "You are Casper. Find the glasses. You left them in the pool room, remember? I see the light is bothering you. The boogie man doesn't like the son, ja? Can you call Geraldine? That cake you got from that fucking woman was tainted with blood. Oh shit. You know what? I need to be checked for fleas. Taube, find the flea collar. We will never recover the next time if we get all our blood sucked out. They carry the plague, you know. Well, the rats carry the bugs, and the bugs the bacteria. Master, can you please give me my clothes now? I don't like the air in here. It has fleas in it. I need protection."

Master Malfred groaned. "I will not give you anything of comfort until you grant me my services. I may not be able to cut you or beat you anymore, but I can keep you uncomfortable as hell. I hope you don't like being naked. I happen to enjoy it a great deal. I at least can look at what I cannot have this way."

There was a knocking at the door. Master Malfred glared at me and demanded I be still. He went to see who was visiting. Master Leo came charging in without an invite carrying a book in his hand. It was that ghost language book I told you about.

He looked at me, then let out a loud yell pulling his hand to his chest. The queen had arrived, ja. "What the fuck, Malfred. His face is bruised to shit. What the hell did you do to his neck? He is naked and purple and black. You beat him up. Did you rape him too? You fucking animal. Why?" He glared at Master Malfred with hate in his eyes.

Master Malfred let out his breath then sat back down in his easy chair. "I didn't rape the boy. Okay maybe I started to, but he is so fucking far gone it wasn't any fun. He is naked, beaten, and restrained because I cannot get him to do anything he is told nor understand a fucking word he is saying. He doesn't bath, sleep, eat, or fuck. What that hell good is having a Priceless if you cannot do anything but battle them." He sighed and looked at me with fatigue in his expression.

Master Leo growled. "You are supposed to care for your silver collars Malfred. There is more to them than sex. You serve them as much as they serve you, fool."

Master Malfred's head sprung up. "Wait. what did you say?"

Master Leo snapped his fingers and clicked his tongue. “Equal service for equal service when you get to this level of silver, Malfred. This boy doesn’t work for free you know. If you have to beat him and still get nothing, then you are to blame. Christian Axel is the finest pleasure submissive in this Haus. He is well trained, affectionate, and compliant if you can earn that right. Otherwise, you end up like Jonas and the boy will make you fight him for everything.”

Master Malfred nodded and smiled with sudden understanding. “Ah, I think you are on to something. He said that last night, this equal for his service stuff. I must say though his requests for giving me his favors are too much, Leo. I cannot give him what he wants. It will endanger him.”

Master Leo sat down in the chair next to Master Malfred appearing curious all at once. “Oh? and what did he ask you for, I am not being nosey for the sake of gossip. What does he want that you cannot give him without risking his life?”

The Dominant shook his head. “The boy wants no bathing and two hours without supervision, to be let loose to run. I cannot do that, Leo. I think he sets these limits too high to make me look a fool. I am about ready to give back my days and call the fucking Guard on him myself.”

Master Leo gasped in horror. “Nein, don’t do that. Settle down. I came here this morning to speak to Christian Axel. Let me see if I can help. I shouldn’t help you but to keep your tongue still from calling for his uncollaring I will. I want something for my aid though. You don't work for free and neither does Leo."

Master Malfred frowned. "I will call the Guard before I give you back your day, Leo. I warn you."

He scoffed. "I think I already got that loud and clear Malfred. Nein, I want to have regular visits with him during your three days to make sure he is doing well. And I better never see any more bruises like this, or I will throw you from the banister and call the Guard on myself."

Master Malfred sighed. "Okay, I will accept your offer and aid with joy, but I want to add one condition. You call first before you barge in here," he growled out in irritation.

Master Leo giggled. "I apologize for my rudeness this morning. I was just so excited to see if this will work to curb this communication issue with Christian Axel. I came right to your place the second I got back from town. If we have the deal, then let me see if I can find out what is going on inside his head."

Master Malfred laughed with bitterness. "Nothing from what I can tell. The boy has been speaking nonsense since he arrived. He just sticks words together, sings, shouts, and rhymes. He is gone, I tell you. No one is home inside his head."

Master Leo snorted. "We shall see about that. Christian Axel, come kneel for me and wish me a good morning. We go to see the lambs if you are good and mind me. They are asking for you."

I had been pacing and singing but I heard that. I rushed over as far as my leash would allow and knelt immediately before Master Leo. Master Malfred gasped in surprise.

Master Leo opened his book then asked me to tell him if I was feeling alright.

I looked at the floor and said, "Fine, Master." He nodded then looked in his book for a moment.

He looked at Master Malfred then back to me with sternness. "Is the radio too loud? Have you heard from Der Hund this morning? Did you eat any of the cake, or is the blood still bothering you?"

Master Malfred scoffed. "Shit Leo, you sound as insane as the boy. What the fuck."

Master Leo glared at him. "Do you want my help or nein? If so, then I would politely ask you to keep your mouth closed. I am speaking his language, but I am not fluent in it. I need quiet."

I rocked a bit. "The air in here is foul, Master. I don't have any cake. That woman stopped cooking. She broke her stove, I think. Mad Max says Der Hund is doing well but lost. Did you speak to Master Jonas? His radio is less loud for the moment, but he needs to change the station. It is interfering with my messages from the spies. Did Geraldine ask about me? I haven't got her letters yet. Did you bring them with you? Never mind, can I see the lambs now? I will need to borrow their coats for this autumn's evening onset."

Master Leo smiled. "Ah. He is telling us he is cold, hungry, and confused. He was thinking someone was slipping things in his food, but apparently, he no longer fears her. She is not cooking anymore because she no longer works there, wait, how did you know Evelyn was found dead Christian Axel?" His eyes went wide.

I smiled and shot a look at a suddenly stunned appearing Master Malfred. "The dead talk to me, Master. She ate her own cake. It was tainted with blood. Not good for the system. That contamination made her a ghost, but it took a few years to dig in deep enough. Can you call Geraldine? I think I need to see if she misses me." I looked back at the floor.

Master Leo appeared nervous but nodded. "Ja, we go to see the lambs the minute your Master Malfred releases you. I am to understand you refuse him service. This is unbecoming of one of your station. He is complaining, meine hase. How can I help you receive the service return you want for his own pleasures?"

I shook my head. "I told the king already, Master. I need not resort to hiring a messenger. They kill those guys, you know. With large rocks from the well. Can you get me my coat? I think I have a pen to record these tapings in it. How is Der Makellos? Do you think he will have much difficult with the pattycakes and snoozing? Ah, Gott verdammt. Mad Max, get off my toes. I was still using that, you fucking horse's ass. I am working here, there, here, mirror, dear, rear."

Master Malfred groaned. "What the fuck was that nonsense. Leo this is hopeless."

Master Leo put up his hand and shot him a hateful look. "I know you are frightened, meine hase. This trouble inside your head is a brain disease. You must try to trust your Masters to protect you. You are right Der Makellos will help look after you. Malfred is not going to kill me. If he does, then Jonas and Claus would string him up. You must try to calm down. I will speak to Jonas about his brutal behavior to you as of late. He is not so dense he is not aware he must tone down his abuses or you will never be able to serve him properly. I will also speak to him about that damned blood fetish if that will make you feel safer around him. Now, Malfred says you wish to be let loose unattended two hours a day and no more hygiene. Christian Axel, that is too much to ask any Master. You make provisions and I am sure that Malfred can come to an agreement with you that you both will benefit from."

I groaned and shook my head. "The needle is never a fair price. I need a lawyer; can you call one? Did you know they rape young boys in this Haus? I hear them screaming through the walls."

Master Leo looked at the floor and Master Malfred sat forward. "Well? What did that crazy shit mean, Doctor Freud?"

My Master glanced up at Master Malfred with a deep breath. “Uhm, he said he doesn’t want to be used as a pleasure submissive anymore. The intercourse bothers him a great deal.”

Master Malfred scoffed. “Well, too fucking bad for him. How the fuck are you getting anything out of this drivel he spouts is beyond me. Never mind, if it works, fine. Here is the deal Christian Axel. You may have the two hours to work on your projects, but you will be escorted by me to the destination and handed over to the trainers. You will not wander unsupervised period. As for the bathing, okay I will agree to it, but you will only be granted a pair of clean breeches and your boots while in this Haus. That way I can wipe you down with a rag when you get foul or smell without having to rip every fucking blouse you own off you. You will be permitted to wear a headset and sunglasses anytime you want them. Take this deal or I call the fucking Guard. That is final.”

Master Leo put up his hand. “Malfred, you must never threaten the schizophrenic, strike them in anger, or crowd them when agitated. It will make matters worse. Speak softly, keep your distance, and let them calm unless they are hurting themselves. You must allow them to believe they are in control, or it will get ugly.”

Master Malfred growled, “Well, nevertheless, he is not the one in control here. Even if he wasn’t wearing my collar he cannot be trusted without aid. This you surely don’t argue with me about. I am waiting, Christian Axel. You takin my deal or what?”

I nodded. "The ocean looks like smooth sailing this season. Do you like the band the Rolling Stones? They have this song called "Paint it Black." I think that is my favorite color. Der Makellos is without a single mark and completely midnight. Don't bother to take him to the pond though. The water is full of radiation from that bomb. There is fallout everywhere. You can even see it in the mirrors. It is staining the tapestry. Barnim stuck those hooks in the boy that night, you know. I think it got into him that way. Did you say you had a letter for me?"

Master Malfred looked at Master Leo with a quizzical expression. "Well? What the fuck did he say? Did he agree to my service offer for his minding my commands?"

Master Leo sighed. "Ja, he did. He is still very upset over the water. He associates it with pain and death. I forgot to mention he is delusional that he is dead. You likely had something to do with that too, I bet. No matter. That is going to be a big problem. I will need to do some more research to see how to fix this. In the meantime, we work together to keep him clean and hygienic as possible. No more traumatizing him in bathtub like you did last night Malfred.

Master Malfred looked startled. "What? He told you I gave him a bath last night. When? I didn't hear that in his babbling."

Master Leo glared at him. "He said it just now, but you were not listening. He said you put him in a tub of the water he fears and then penetrated him. I fear I may be a bit responsible for this phobia upon reflection. I have to ask you for Christian Axel's sake, if you must have your special services with him, avoid the water at all costs. You will only deepen his fear of showering and the pool at this point. I only pray this damage can be undone. Now, can I have this boy dressed? I need to take him to see his lambs."

Master Malfred scoffed. "Hell no. I want to get what I am paying for first. Come back in an hour."

Master Leo snorted. "He needs to eat and take his meds first. Your cock can wait, Malfred."

He shook his head. "I thought you said you are taking him to see these lambs he keeps prattling about."

Master Leo smiled. "I am. They made him breakfast this morning. This boy is malnourished and weak. I wouldn't fuck with me if I were you Malfred or I will go tell Jonas you have removed his chastity device off the boy. He will kick your ass, and I will giggle while playing voyeur."

Master Malfred growled out. "This is bullshit. I am the Master in this Haus."

Master Leo chuckled. "You may be, but I still outrank you. Go get his fucking clothing. I need to get going before Geraldine's pancakes get cold."

I yelled in joy. "Ah, she did that for me, Master. She is the sweetest lamb. I hope she is not too bothered cooking for me like she does. Wait, did Ryker lick the pancakes?

Oh, hurry up. He will eat the breakfast before I can. Geraldine will be upset and cry. I hate that when she cries."

Master Malfred sneered but got up and headed for his room. He returned quickly carrying my clothing in a bundle. He threw them on the floor next to me and leaned down to undo my wrist cuffs. He was still grumbling when he noticed the look on Master Leo's face. He was staring into the floor then shooting frightened looks back at me. He turned his head to see what was causing the Dominant to stir like that.

Next to my coat was that weird knife. It had been thrown from my jacket when Master Malfred tossed my things down. It was covered in blood. I smiled with wickedness keeping my eyes to the floor. I sang out "Felix sprat could eat nein fat, his wife could eat nein lean, betwixt them both the Priceless killed them clean."

Chapter 55: Wisdom of the Lamb

"Christian Axel, what the fuck. Where did you get that knife? Why is there blood on it," yelled out Master Malfred.

Master Leo shot a look of terror at him. "Nein, hush. I told you don't show excitement nor yell at Christian Axel, Malfred. It agitates the schizophrenic. Let me speak to him to determine what has happened here. Don't make assumptions that is really blood, not yet anyway."

I wrung my hand and giggled. "I cut that cake with the knife. The sweets tasted bad, but I realized that the problem was that the food was tainted. You can see there was blood in the cake. I told you this already. I finally shut off that fucking stove. I had to or it would have burned down the Haus. Did you say that Geraldine made me pancakes? I worry that Ryker will eat them. Can we please go now?" I whined like a bitch but damn it I was hungry, you know.

Master Malfred's face was wearing an expression of terror. "What the fuck is he talking about? He shut off the stove? Blood in the cake? Leo, I swear to Gott I cannot take this. He is babbling nonsense and probably killed Evelyn. That is what he is telling us, isn't it? Could he have killed her? You said she was found dead in the hallway. From what did she die?"

Master Leo looked back at the knife. "Uhm, I heard it rumored she was stabbed in the back and found dead in the hallway in front of Stefan's apartment."

Master Malfred gasped. “He did kill her. He killed Stefan too.”

Master Leo frowned. “Now you just wait a minute. You must have heard Stefan died of a heart condition. The Haus doctor told me this himself. As for Evelyn, no way he did that either Malfred. He was with me the whole time. I would have seen it if he stabbed the woman to death. There were people everywhere. He couldn’t have done it.”

Master Malfred shook his head. “I don’t care what that fucking doctor told you Leo. I know he killed Stefan. I also know Claus sent him to do it. As for Evelyn, maybe he got her when your back was turned. This boy is violent. I have seen it with my own eyes.”

The schwuler Elder frowned at that “You have seen his violence When? You don’t know he killed Stefan. Whoever told you that is the fucking liar.”

Master Malfred shot a look of nervousness at me. “I suppose it don’t matter anymore but it was Stefan’s death that set off this whole business with the blood bonding Leo. For all these years I have been using that man as my voice to the others. That way if my plotting and schemes were ever discovered, well everyone would believe it was him. He kept Claus, and the others like Xavier, from looking in my direction. It had worked perfectly for all that time, then one day I saw this Priceless leaving Stefan’s apartment. I went to ask that bastard what the hell he thought he was doing fucking around with something he knew I intended to take for myself. I had assumed Christian Axel come to grant him services. When I went to his door, there was no answer. I let myself in thinking he was in the shower or worn out. Oh, he was indeed taken to another world by this boy here. Stefan was stone cold dead, still warm in fact. Holding a picture of his mother in one hand, his cock in the odder. I thought for sure Claus had finally figured out my game. It set off the plan months too early. It was only after that scene in the Great Hall that I realized the forbidden silver killed my figurehead without any cause nor order from that motherfucker Claus. You can tell anyone you like Leo what I just told you, but if you do so you implicate this precious treasure. He killed Stefan and another. I rather not say the name of the other but let me tell you this. This Priceless made one hell of a bloody mess of that big fellow without even trying. If he has gone mad dog and is now killing black collar cooks of no worth, then who is next Leo? You? Me? Any of us? I am sure he would feel justified to kill every Dominant. You and I need to discuss the probability he needs to be taken below and kept in a cell, for good, or we are all at risk."

I heard that shit. I wrung my hands with vigor and shook my head frantically. I did my best to speak to these bastards, but Mad Maxx kept babbling. His constant random thoughts were interrupting my thinking. I looked at Mad Max with fear in my expression. That idiot was trying to decipher taps and codes that were not there.

"Mad Max. Gott dammit. Do something about Mad Maxx. Gag that sonofabitch before we get our asses taken below. Hurry the fuck up. I cannot hear myself think with all the mindless chattering of his. Taube, get the fuck away from the wheel. You are confusing me with your constant questions." I pushed that shard toward the wall while Mad Max and Max rushed and covered Mad Maxx's mouth rapidly.

I cleared my throat. "Uhm, I must apologize for my insolence at speaking without recognition Masters, but I fear you misjudge me harshly. I killed no one, Master Malfred. Master Leo was with me the whole time yesterday. Evelyn was fine the last I time saw her. As for Stefan, you are correct I had left his apartment in a rush that morning of which you speak. He was already dead when I arrived, like he was for you. Master Jonas sent me down to pay for the trainee he had called Annette. He wanted her painted black, you know. You can call and ask him if you wish. I panicked when I find this man dead on his sofa. I should have said something, but they would assume I did this horror. He looked like he had a heart attack to me but what the fuck do I know? I ran away is all. The blood on that knife is my own. I was removing the infected flesh again. Master Leo has to punish me for disobeying his directive I know, but better a thudding then locked up as the insane, which I am not. I say that with respect." I lowered my head staring at the floor hoping this excuse would work. If not fuck I was ready to grab that knife and add two more to my X list.

Master Malfred and Master Leo stared at me appearing shocked. Then Master Leo sat back in his chair rubbing his forehead while Master Malfred smiled with a wicked grin.

Master Leo groaned. "Christian Axel, you tell me, are you hearing voices? What is the day and year?"

I smiled at the floor. "I hear you, Master. I never hear voices. Today is Thursday and it is still 1972, just like the last time you asked me, I say that with respect." I recalled Master Malfred had asked for my leash Thursday until midnight Saturday. This was my first day with him, therefore Thursday.

Master Malfred gasped. "He is back. Oh, thank Gott. I must say though he is a terrible liar. No matter. If he has his mind about him, what the fuck do I care if he killed Stefan, or that stupid black collar cook? I got where I was going, and I never liked that bitch's cooking. Good riddance to them both. Now, you come with me and let's see if you are ready to do your duties to your Master without further delays." He reached down to grab my leash, but Master Leo snatched it up before he could.

"What the fuck, Malfred. The psychotic can focus when threatened with eradication. Christian Axel is blown. He is only holding it together long enough to keep you from hauling him off in chains, fool. In an hour, maybe two, he will be using that knife on someone or himself because a voice told him to do it. The heavier the stress the faster he will collapse into madness again. You take him back to your bed and I will be scraping one of you off the sheets into a doggie bag. I am taking him to see his lambs and to eat something." Master Leo jerked my leash away as Master Malfred tried to snatch it from him once again.

Master Malfred growled in irritation. "Fine, take the motherfucker. I am sick of this stalling. You be back here in a fucking hour. Christian Axel, be ready to give me my rights or so help me I will shoot you my fucking self." He picked up the knife then stormed off down his hallway with it grumbling under his breath.

I giggled at Master Malfred pissy fit. "Peter, Peter, the Priceless eater, had a snitch but couldn't keep her. He hid her in the kitchen hell, but you can tell a rat by the smell. Can I see that Geraldine yet? How much longer till I get those pancakes, Master? She tends to eat things she shouldn't. Hex wrenches are fucking hard to come by you know."

Master Leo looked sad. "Ja, the lambs do have an appetite. You need to get dressed, meine Hase. Then we can go." He pointed at my clothing.

I rushed over and started pulling on my clothing as fast as I could. I was grateful to finally have something to warm me up. That bastard kept his apartment like the north pole, I tell you. Master Leo watched me, but I noticed he kept a baleful eye on Master Malfred's hallway. I stopped a few times in my task to shoot a look to see what he was seeking. That Master Leo was the paranoid one. I knew that man would not come back if he wasn't getting to fuck me.

That is all any of them want, you know. Ryker and Vilhelm told me that the first day I met them. They were right. Without the special services, no Dominant keeps a silver around long. I knew when I came back, I would have no choice but to tolerate this Master Malfred's lustful interests. I was not in a hurry to go there, but if he was willing to pay my price, then at least I got something other than bad dreams from the affair. Though no matter what they give you for your dignity it will fall short of what they take from your flesh and soul. Oh well, sucks to be us Meine Liebe, ja?

We left Master Malfred's apartment headed for the lambs after what seemed like forever. I hummed and wrung my hands but kept my protocol behind Master Leo. I noticed that the walls of the Haus seemed to be moving as if they were breathing.

I wondered if Master Malfred maybe snuck something into the boy to cause this latest acid tripping. I kept my eyes to the ground and my breathing shallow. The whole scene was making me feel a little panicky, I admit it. *I never can stand those drug hallucinations when people sneak stuff into my meals.* Master Leo kept his eyes on me but said nothing the whole trip to the barn.

When we got there he let me into the pen. My lambs came running. They seemed to be growing by the hour. I held and kissed them while Master Leo went to get the pancakes Geraldine cooked for me. I was glad he kept them away from Ryker. That boy ate anything, you know.

I was hugging Geraldine and thanking her for all her hard labors making sure I got uncontaminated food when she shocked me near to death.

She leaned into my ear and whispered. "You need to be seeking out the black collars from the dungeons. They have your secrets, meine heart. Kill them and that sour Haus doctor too. If you let them live, one day they will tell of what they know, and you will be finished."

I was so startled that she could speak I could do nothing but stare at her for a moment. She batted her eyes at me and went back to her natural "lamb speak." I sat there unsure if I could trust her judgement. Though I had to confess she was correct. The black collars that worked with Hemmel for the eight months Master Jonas was drugging me, they were a threat.

If they ever opened their mouths about that bullshit diagnosis, I would never get to be a doctor. I may not even live long enough to be one. If the Guard heard the rumor, I was worm food. I already knew from Olaf's big mouth and that Evelyn I couldn't have faith they would be silent about the things they saw or heard down in the bowls of that Haus.

Then there was that doctor. He wanted to put me away into an institution. He was likely the one that was slipping me the tainted medications too. He had told me once he wanted to smother me with my pillow and put me out of my misery. Ja, I had to face it. Geraldine was right. These men all needed to be kept quiet for all time.

It was not like any of them were innocent blood. Those black collar thugs were known helpers of the Guard. They killed more than their fair share of the silver children. That doctor worked for money helping to keep the poor souls wearing metal collars alive so that the criminals of that place could abuse them long as possible. He was an outsider that never called the authorities to report the horrors he knew occurred in that hell hole. I am not justifying my decision to end their existence but merely stating the facts.

I will not lie and say if they had all been saints, I would rethink my attempts to weed them out. I was dedicated to breaking my collar at any cost to my soul. My flesh was already being badly misused. Another sin would not matter that much to me by this point. To be completely honest my soul, Max, was with me in our choice to send these evil men to hell.

I leaned over and whispered back in to Geraldines ear. "I hear you, meine beauty. I will attend to this immediately. Thank you for the mercy of your wisdom."

She nodded her approval then said, "Kill them, Mad Maxx, kill them all. You come back here without their blood on your hands, I will stop feeding you. I don't feed the loser. They all helped murder you fool. Kill them. There is a silver pool of the forgotten in the woods. Make them become the memory of rumors in the walls of the Haus. No one will miss them if they are never found."

I smiled with wickedness at Geraldine. "Ah, ja. The well, I put them in with the silver children. The souls there will guard my secrets for all time." I clapped in glee at this most perfect place to hide the flesh of those that helped send me to the land of the dead. *Where even the lambs can speak Deutsch. Ja, Meine Liebe, see I told you the realm of the dead is very strange, didn't I?*

I looked at him in shock. "The animals can really talk, Master? Wait, if you are already dead, aren't those black collars and that doctor dead too?"

He shook his head giggling. "Nein, I was the ghost at that time. They live still. I can reach into the world of the living and end them. There you can see everything clearly. You never want to go there, but if you ever do, ask the lambs. They can tell you who put you there or who could harm you when you find your way back."

I frowned. "But if you can come back couldn't the ones you kill do it too, Master?"

Master Maxx smiled with evil. "Nein, I put them in the silver water. There is no escaping that rock hell. They cannot climb out you know."

I nodded. "Can we put Debbie, Russell, and Peter in there, Master?"

He hugged me tight and let out a yip. "A, you are my perfect treasure. Of course, we will put them in that well. They cannot get out if you encase them in stone. One day, we will laugh and watch them fall, then splash. No more problems, ja?"

I smiled brightly. "Yeah, I can't wait Master."

Master Maxx (Maximillian) ruffled my hair. "Now back to the story little one. We can play later, but for this minute I give you the recipe for freedom."

I nodded and leaned back into his lap while he stroked my arms lovingly as he began his tale once more.

Master Leo returned with the pancakes Geraldine made for me. I stuffed them down and licked the plate. I patted her on the head for her efforts. She wasn't cooking enough to sate my terrible hunger, but she was at least trying. I loved her for bothering with a nothing like me.

I spent some time loving my family until Master Leo told me we had to return to Master Malfred's apartment. I grimaced at the memory that I would have to serve this motherfucker. I didn't give my Master any trouble. I followed him from the pen at his command. There was no escaping my job as the Priceless pleasure submissive of the Elders. Like it or not I had to endure the good and the bad, but to be honest the awful tasks far exceeded the few kindnesses they offered in trade for my dignity.

Master Leo stopped at Master Malfred's door then turned to me without knocking. "Meine hase, I don't think I can leave you here with this monster. He is going to attack you. How can I justify leaving my love behind to suffer such horrors?"

I sneered at him. "You need not worry, Master, I will attend your needs when your turn comes. This man will do nothing that you haven't already done and will do again. That is my function in the world of the Dominants. If you need me to make you feel better by hating this Master more than you or the others, I am happy to lie to you. Your pleasure is surely my own. Isn't that what I am told?

Mirror, mirror on the wall, who is the foulest Dominant of them all? Ah, Christian Axel, you cannot stand because the Master makes you crawl. Ah, dd you just hear that sound? Tap. Tap. Set the trap. There you can do your nap. I thank you for the mercy of it." I giggled into my hand over his stunned look at my calling him out like that. *He is a self-righteous rapist bastard.*

Master Leo shook his head still staring at me in disbelief. "Christian Axel, meine heart, why do you say such a terrible thing to your lover Leo? I thought you and I had something special between us."

I laughed loudly. "Ah, that we do. A cock is between us and there has been no bigger dick in my whole life than you. Malfred will give me the headset, sunglasses, the two hours, and no baths for my pain. You give me lambs and Der Makellos and a belly full of contaminated rain. Malfred will only hurt me with a cane. You and he are the sadists all the same. You, Master Leo, decided to take so much more. You injured me deeply with that contamination you pour. Well, I will not drink that deadly water anymore. There is radiation in it you know. It will kill the flesh and twist the soul. It is blue but may as well be the silver of that rock crypt. Strip, chip, tiny snip. Take a little, take a lot. You would take it all if I don't make it stop." I wrung my hands and snickered at this foolish Dominant that pretends to be the fairy of kindness. He was nothing more than just a mythical creature period.

Master Leo shook his head. "Nein, Christian Axel, you misunderstand. I didn't trick you into loving me, I swear it.

I think that is what you are saying to me. Is this what you believe? That I lied to you to have my way with you?"

I nodded. "Ah, that is okay. There is a fool born every day, ja. Can you move please, you are blocking my transmissions from the spies? They watch this place for the criminal behaviors. You are already the guilty as charged. I need to discover the rats nest, and they are helping me." I tapped on my headphones trying to get the reception to stop that static noise that had started to interrupt my information that was coming through them.

Then suddenly I heard the signal loud and clear from the spies. "The black collars are available for purchase at your local dungeon. Slashed prices, everything must go in this going out of business sale."

I giggled. "Ah, ja I understand this message from my sponsor. Thank you for the mercy of it." I bowed to the spies and did a twirl of joy.

Master Leo frowned. "Shit. Malfred will call the guard for sure. You are worse than ever, meine heart. I almost went against my own good judgement. I shouldn't take anything the mad say for the truth. You love me and I love you. You are just not yourself is all."

I narrowed my eyes at that. "Huh? Then who am I Master if I am not me? Are you saying I am possessed with a demon? Oh, meine Gott. That is, it. I am not me. Holy shit. Where have I gone? Please Master, tell me, where have I gone?" I fell to my knees and threw myself at his feet clinging to his ankles weeping at the idea that someone had hijacked me.

My Master seemed upset. “Oh hell. I didn’t mean it like that. I need to watch my words. Get up, Christian Axel. You are you; I was meaning you are not thinking straight is all.”

I moaned. “Not straight? Ah, nein. When did that happen? Oh, I am so confused. Please stop drugging me. I am frightened, Master. Nothing makes sense. I am lost. Help me. Help,” I began to scream begging for aid at the top of my lungs.

Master Leo panicked and banged hard on Master Malfred’s door. The Dominant answered quickly to find me on the floor yelling into Master Leo’s shoes and the Master freaking out that someone would hear my wailing like that. He rushed forward and grabbed my upper arms and dragged me into his apartment with Master Leo following rapidly.

Master Malfred pulled me onto his lap on his couch, then into his chest making soft cooing noises. I wept and cried for help nonstop while the man rocked us back and forth trying to calm me. Master Leo stood there, his eyes wide in terror at my latest fit throwing.

I wrapped my arms around his waist. “Please help me, Master. I am possessed. The demons have taken control of the boy. I think they want to kill me.” I sobbed into his chest.

Master Malfred stroked my back. "There is no reason to fear, Christian Axel. I won't let them get you. They are afraid of me. I will beat them back. You'll see."

I nodded, trying to quell my tears. "Thank you for the mercy, Master."

Master Leo clicked his tongue. "You shouldn't play into a delusion, Malfred. This boy is not possessed. He is mentally ill. There are no demons fueling his pains."

Master Malfred growled. "Oh, I beg to differ with you there, Leo. The demons are in this room with him right now. Didn't you tell me this yourself? I would like you to leave now. I am asking nicely. You ignore my politeness then I show you just how much of a bastard I can truly be. Thank you for feeding, Christian Axel, but I have this boy now. This is my Priceless until Sunday morning. You know where the door is."

Master Leo stood there another moment, appearing unsure what to do, then he turned and stormed from the apartment. He slammed the door behind him. I flinched at that loud noise and began weeping louder. I was just so fucked up from the drugs, you know. Everything was scaring the shit out of me.

Master Malfred held me there on his lap another few moments. Then he got up and picked me up like a kid. He told me to hold him around his neck as he walked over and locked his door. I sobbed but did as commanded. He then walked down the hallway to his room. I closed my eyes realizing what he was about to do.

I was not disappointed. Once in his room he crawled into his bed with me still held tightly in his grip. He leaned back into his headboard, then pulled me up to look at him in his face.

"You owe me service, Christian Axel. I have been patient with you this far, but you fail to please me this time, I will send you to that cell in the dungeons. I have agreed to your price, and I will not beat you anymore if you mind my commands. I don't desire to ruin your good looks by bruises and more scars. We understand each other?" He looked at me hard to see if I understood him.

I sobbed but nodded, "Ja. I understand you, Master. I don't wish to be put into the dungeons."

He smiled bitterly then reached out to wipe my wet cheeks. "You will make your Master very happy. In return I will give you a gentle life compared to the one you are accustomed to. I will kill Claus, Jonas, and Leo, then you will be mine exclusively. I don't share my things. You mind me boy and I will make you the luckiest pleasure submissive in this Haus."

I shuddered and sniffed. "If I don't pleasure you, then what, Master?"

Master Malfred chuckled with humor. "Ah, I already have tasted you, meine taube. I already know you will pleasure me a great deal. I gave up my Tamina, and even sacrificed my best men Gustov and Grisham, to have you here this minute. When you finish giving me all that I have suffered to have, I will take you somewhere very special to demonstrate how much you truly mean to me. I request your Priceless special services and do not skimp. I am also not going to wait another minute." He grabbed the back of my head and forced me into his mouth embrace.

I had to endure the full deployment of special services from the lustful kissing with heavy petting to the oral full services. Then, much to my dismay he insisted on a long drawn-out intercourse with many shifts in positions. I did my best to endure this horror without tears, but in the end, I did cry a great deal in silence as always.

Master Malfred on the other hand apparently enjoyed his power over me a great deal. He ignored my discomfort, sorrow, and lack of lustful response in return to his constant grabbing of my sexual organ. He was quite aware I was only granting him whatever he asked for without any joy or pleasure in it. That didn't bother him a bit. He loudly reported at each service his thrill and satisfaction that I was "a well-trained artist in the sexual ways of same gendered coupling."

I swallowed the humiliation of being the pincushion for this cruel man. There was no reason to feel worse about being his whore than any of the others. At least Master Malfred didn't suck my blood, make me drink his piss, take off his panty hose with my teeth, nor lie about being in love with him as his brother Elders did. He treated me like his sexual plaything, and for what it was worth, at least he was being honest and without insane fetishes.

When he was reaching his climax – finally, shit he was taking forever – he enforced me to take his orgasm in my mouth. He moaned out while in his ecstasy that as long as I was refusing to take a bath, he would not be "avoiding making a mess of his treasure" in this fashion. I tolerated this final indignity with as much honor as I could muster.

To be brutally honest, I agreed with his decision. I thought it was better to have to swallow his seed than have him ejaculate it within the body with no water available to cleanse. *Ja, I know it is gross but there it is. You shouldn't look at me that way Meine Liebe. You know Gott damned well if given the choice you would always choose to dispatch that foul shit without having to go scrubbing for it. I dropped my gaze and nodded. He sure had me dead to rights on that one.*

He fell to the bed next to me spent at last and panting with a smile of satisfaction. I laid there hoping that he was pleased enough to prevent his sending me to a fucking cell. Master Malfred rolled over to look at me. He ran his hand down my left chest muscle frowning when he noticed the large healing cut wound there.

"Did one of my men do this during the rapes," he asked while he got closer to look at the injury.

I shook my head. "Nein Master. The Vampire last fed there. He cuts in different places. I don't know his reasoning for any one area or another. I think eventually I will become a bat like him. That is why I am not completely dead Casper. Is that why you are alive too? You had a

Vampire Master in your youth?" I looked at him with curiosity.

He chuckled. "Ja, you got me. Only mine was the female kind of Vampire, and she gave birth to me the natural way. Fucking harpy sucked me near dry before I got the hell out of her haus. Well, meine Taube, you are a true Priceless in every way. You beat my Tamina all to hell in the oral services. While she had some physical attributes that I will miss, I can be much more satisfied with you in my bed. I don't even have to pay back the pleasure services like I did with her, nor cuddle after getting my thrills. It is wonderful that I no longer have to listen to her bitching that I can't make children. Best of all, you're much better looking and younger. My cock can tell no difference in the intercourse like I thought it would. Shit, if I had known this sooner, I would only have had the beautiful boys and left the moody females where there lay."

I narrowed my eyes. "Wait Master, you surely slept with your male silvers before this moment, didn't you?"

He scoffed. "Hell no. I had Tamina. I kept them around for decorations. I never had an interest in them for anything other than art for the eyes. That day in the pool room was my first time to couple with one of my own gender. I never found a male silver worthy of my attentions. The legendary Priceless Mad Maxx the Brutal, he is the only one leveled high enough for me to consider. Now that I have tasted the full prowess, I am converted. Only you shall be blessed by my carnal attentions." W*ell lucky me, ja? Yuck!*

It took all I had not to roll my eyes and groan at those words. “Thank you for your affection, Master. Can I do anything else for you? If not, then I ask for the mercy of that headset you removed and those sunglasses you promised.”

Master Malfred laughed. “Ja, sure thing. You certainly earned them and will earn even more before I let you leave me on Saturday night. Come, dress me, then put back on your breeches and boots. I wish to take you for that reward I promised.” He slid to the side of the bed pushing me out in front of him to await his dressing service.

I did as ordered after he allowed me to put back on my headset. I hummed to myself and dressed him. He chuckled at my constant noise but said nothing about it. Then he watched me rapidly put on my breeches, socks, and boots. I looked at my blouse and coat then went to put them on as well. I was stopped in my actions when he put up a hand signal to halt.

He shook his head. “Nein, no shirts, remember? You will remain bare chested, or you will go back to showers. That was the agreement Christian Axel. As it is you kneel and wait for me.” I did as commanded while he left the room for his bathroom.

Master Malfred returned with a rag and a bottle of rubbing alcohol. He poured some of the liquid on the cloth with me watching him. Then he came at me and rubbed the entire upper part of the boy down with the stinging stuff. I said nothing keeping my head down as he performed this disinfecting process. He told me that at night I was to rub all my flesh in this way until I was over my water phobia. I was informed that if I didn't smell of the antiseptic when called to his bed, he would whip me in the torture rooms for the insolence.

I nodded that I understood while he showed me where to find this substance so that I could obey his orders. He then handed me the pair of sunglasses he was wearing the first day I met him at the playground. I put them on and felt much better with the horrid glare out of my eyes.

He smiled with joy. "Well, I worried you would look silly wearing that headset and the sunglasses but to be honest you are more handsome than ever. Come meine gorgeous boy. Follow your man. We are going somewhere special. You keep your mouth shut unless I speak to you until we return. I warn you one more time in case you forgot. Displease me, and I send you to the cells below. Make me smile, and I reward your loyalty." He took up my leash and hand signaled me to rise and follow.

He took off with speed down the hallway to the back stairs. I rushed behind him in my protocol wringing my hands and singing under my breath. The sunglasses kept the walls from moving and the headset directed my thoughts. For the moment, I had managed to hold that demon possessing me at bay. Things seemed clearer and I felt surer of my location.

When we got to the fifth floor I nearly groaned in agony when Peter came out of his apartment and rushed up to join us. I would have rather been tossed over the banister by Master Malfred. My father yelled for my Master to wait up. He stopped our fast journey and shot me a wicked smile. I dropped my gaze and fell to a kneel waiting till he told me to follow once more.

Master Peter walked by me shooting a hateful look at the boy. “Well, I see you have Maximillian at last Malfred. Took you long enough to retake our prize.” He sneered.

Master Malfred chuckled. “No thanks to you, fool. You lost him to Jonas in the first place. I must say he is a real gem, Peter. I am most thrilled to have such an exceptional quality silver. I hate to admit that it was worth the wait, but it was and is.”

Master Peter snorted. “Don’t get too used to him, Malfred. When he breaks that collar, I will be taking him back from you.” I looked up with fear at Peter wondering what the hell was wrong with that pervert.

Master Malfred must have read my mind. “Seriously Peter? The boy is your, you know. I already thought it fucked up that you insisted on training him yourself. Fantastic job by the way, but I would have thought it a hardship. You must be truly messed up in the head to desire resuming that which is no longer required or natural.” His eyes were wide in horror at Peter.

Master Peter scoffed. “You are right about only one thing, Malfred. I did take on the hardship of breaking this boy into the Priceless pleasure submissive you so adore this minute. I will remind you that I did this to meet my interests. Since that time, I have been incapable of finding full satisfaction from any other. That is the trouble with raising your own lover, after you had the tailored suit, the off the rack shit doesn't fit right anymore." He looked at me with lust in his eyes. That made me shiver down to my toes. Fucking yuck, Peter is a sicko.

Master Malfred rolled his eyes. "I am not even going to comment on this perverted discussion, Peter. This Haus is mother to the misfits of society, but you, never mind. I have no time for insulting you. I will say you are not getting the boy back though. Claus has made sure he never breaks that collar. He is blood bonded to the hilt brother. His metal unbreakable."

Master Peter let out a gasp. "Nein, that cannot be. Fucking Jonas would never allow that. How will he accomplish his mythical Goddess? How do you know this to be the case?

My Master sighed. "I saw it with my own eyes. Don't believe me? Go to the hall of records and check. The boy is blood bonded times four. It was his punishment for the theft I had to commit to undo the damage you caused by tossing his collar in the first Gott damned place. You may as well get over this thinking you will ever touch my treasure again. I will kill Claus and the others in time, but there is no way I can do it in time to give this boy a chance at the sacred bolt cutters. He is stuck and that means so are you. Seems fair considering your stupidity. I intend to keep him all for myself anyway. You would have to kill me to get him back in your nasty grip and you try that shit, I will see you torn to bits by the Haus dogs, Peter. Now that we got our greetings out of the way, what the fuck did you want? I am a busy man."

Peter seemed so stunned by the news my Master shared he just stood there a moment, then said, "Oh, uhm, Karl wants to speak to you. He wants to be raised to Voter and I thought I would speak to you first. Is this a correct match? Do you owe him any favors? He lays claim you do."

Master Malfred thought a moment. "Uhm, ja, raise him for Gustov and raise Alexie for Grisham. Then for my spot I think you raise Mila. She is my closest associate and a valuable information gatherer. That will refill the Council and keep Gretta on a leash, ja."

Peter nodded. "Okay if you think this is the right group. I wanted to suggest Anna instead of Alexie maybe?"

Master Malfred frowned then shook his head. "Nein. She is Jonas's creature, fool. Quit thinking with your dick will you. That bitch is likely the one that set you up in the dungeon. She was fucking Hemmel you know. She is interested in that Vampire freak and has been for years. Her big problem is she is too much of a rodent for even that blood sucker to fall for her wiles. That won't stop her from fucking anyone over she dinks would please that motherfucker though. I suggest you stick to that crazy bitch Agnette. The worst she will do to you is make you chase her around a room. Anna will cut your hodensack off and feed it to you, brother."

I giggled. “Old mother Hubbard went to her cupboard after getting Peter’s bone. Much to her despair her wallet was bare, even though she sold off her own.” Master Malfred jerked my leash hard.

“I told you to be still Mad Maxx. You wish to be taken below,” he growled out.

I dropped my head lower and wrung my hands. “Nein. Thank you for the mercy, Master.”

Peter glared at me a moment. “He is worse than ever Malfred. Did Jonas drug him again to sabotage his service to you perhaps?” I nodded my head, even dough I hated to agree with that rat bastard. I thought he was likely right.

Master Malfred blew out his breath. “Uhm, ja. Doesn’t matter though. The boy is so well trained he can do his job even flying higher than a kite. Are we done here? You are getting on my nerves Peter.”

Peter nodded. “Ja. I see you later then.”

Master Malfred growled out while hand signaling me to rise and follow. “Nein. You keep your distance fool. I am an Elder now. If I want you for any reason I will say so. Otherwise, stay the fuck away from me and especially my Christian Axel. Pervert.” He took off with speed while I shot a smile of wickedness at the steamed Peter fast disappearing in the distance.

I was starting to like this Master Malfred a bit. The man was a total arrogant asshole of the worst kind. He thought himself Gott of the Universe, and cared not that he insulted the ones that got him where he wanted to be.

With that attitude I thought him an even better partner in my quest to break my collar than I had hoped. Mainly because when I finished using him, he would never expect me to kill him. I liked it when they didn't make me chase them. I am lazy that way, you know. *Master Maxx laughed and so did I. I wasn't sure why I was laughing since his idea of killing all the Dominants and some of the black collars in the Haus was kind of creepy. Then again, even that far back, I had found I liked it creepy.*

I became a bit nervous when Master Malfred took the turn and headed down the steps to the torture rooms. I craned my neck all around in worry. I thought I had pleased him with the special services. I recalled I did speak out of turn on the steps with Peter around, but I didn't realize I had earned a thudding for that moment of indiscretion. I whimpered when he pulled me down the hallway to the "burn" door. I felt my heart speed up and I wrung my hands faster as he knocked and waited to see if anyone was in there.

When no one answered, he opened it and hauled me inside with him. He turned on the lights. I was immediately ready to scream. There was a table with bindings for arms and legs in the center. There were white lockers all around the walls and in one corner a sink, with a table that held a Bunsen burner. I had never been in this room and was most unhappy to be introduced to it that day, or any day to be quite honest.

I flinched and whimpered when Master Malfred dragged me along to one of the lockers and opened it. He turned to hear my noises of stress.

He chuckled then began digging in the locker. "Calm down Christian Axel. This is an honor I am bestowing on you. I see the marks left on you by Jonas and that criminal Gerard trying to mark you up as their own. Well fuck them. I, Malfred, will show these amateurs the proper way to mark the Priceless to claim him as exclusive property. Ah, I wondered if my iron was still here. I haven't seen this since my Tamina was fifteen." He took up a branding iron that had a large M with a circle around it. *Just like they brand the cattle and herd animals, ja*?

I trembled at the sight of that torture device. I realized too late this fucker was intending to burn his mark into the boys flesh. I shook my head and tapped my headset as he tried dragging me to the branding table to restrain.

"Master, I feel it my duty to warn you there is an agreement with the Elders. No piercing, scars tattoos nor branding of the Priceless collar they share. If you breach the agreement, they will kick you from the cycle rotation." I let out a sigh that Master Jonas had thought of this protection device. *Neither Barnim nor Drexel paid it any mind. Of course, where are they now, ha-ha-ha.*

Master Malfred stopped and turned to me with a look of anger. "Oh? Is that so? Well, meine taube, they never asked me to vow or to sign such a contract with them. I am sure after this day they will demand I do that, but then it will be too late. I agree I don't want you pierced, scared, branded nor tattooed by those creeps because I will be marking you exclusively. Get on the table for my binding now. If I have to force you up there, you know what happens to schizophrenic silvers, Priceless or not, they don't get mercy from the Guard do they?"

I shivered and dropped my gaze with anxiety building within. "Master, I beg mercy. I wish you to reconsider this marking. I have enough scars to choose from."

Master Malfred glared with a stone-cold expression on his face. "Did you say something other than thank you for the honor of granting you the right to wear my brand? I sure hope not, Christian Axel. However, I don't see you on that table. Do you wish to refuse this gift I offer?"

I felt the tears welling up. "Nein, Master. I will mind your command and thank you for the mercy of it." I felt my feet taking me to the table to be marked up like a farmer's prize bull.

Master Malfred tied my arms and ankles up tightly telling me this was to prevent me from moving too much during the branding. He was worried if I struggled reflexively it would mar up his perfect mark. I closed my eyes while he lit the burner. I took slow deep breaths and told the boys to brace for hell on Earth. I had not been burned since the days of Xavier, but I couldn't forget the nightmare of such a wound.

He brought the cherry red M on his iron pole at me then to my horror set it to my chest just above Master

Jonas's feeding mark. I wailed out in pure agony as my tissues cooked then dissolved under the intruding heated iron. Smoke rose from my flesh and the smell of burned skin filled the air. Even Master Malfred covered his nose, the scent was so disturbing.

He pulled the brander off his selected spot and quickly applied a cooling gel. I wailed even louder each time he rubbed on my screaming injury. The agony nearly made me piss my pants. He had accidentally, or on purpose, overheated his tool. The burn was deeper than he expected.

I laid there weeping, silently sucking in my breath in torment while he gave apologies for his being rusty at the branding process. The heat from the iron seemed to still be hanging in my flesh despite his attempts to cool it off. I couldn't even speak for fear I would scream and lose my shit.

He worked with the burn for a full thirty minutes before I felt any calming of the torturous charred nerves. When he had done all he could to fix his error, he finally unbound my arms and legs. I sat up with a cry out the second I tried to move my left arm. The pain was sublime and sent my mind right to the pits of hell. I decided right there and then when I killed this bastard I would light him up like a forest fire for this horror. That motherfucker was toast.

He took up my leash with an embarrassed smile. "Well, a little deeper than I should have gone but it looks wonderful. Perfect just like my Priceless. Now you belong to me for truth, and everyone can see that. You wear my mark. You should dry your tears, meine taube. Are you not pleased with my gift to you?"

I glared at him with hate then said through clenched teeth. "I am most grateful for your honoring me so Master. I am most unworthy to wear such a glorious mark though I am thankful for the mercy of it." I wanted to take that iron and shove it up his ass, I swear to Gott Meine Liebe. He is a bastard.

Master Malfred chuckled. "Ah, you speak the high protocol beautifully, meine taube. I am so thrilled I want to show you off to all the rabble of this Haus. Come, let's go to the Great Hall. I feel like a little supper and a dance with my Christian Axel. Let them all be jealous of my treasure." He motioned me to follow him.

I winced and did as commanded keeping my thoughts to myself. Then as we approached the steps I saw Egon standing near the "Showers" door. He shot me a confused smile and looked at my half naked flesh with a bit of humor.

I cleared my throat then called out, wincing at the biting burn in my chest "Master. I need to speak to that black collar. It is about my training. May I have a moment? I beg this mercy."

Master Malfred stopped then turned around appearing surprised. "I told you to be silent."

I dropped to a kneel. "I beg your punishment for such insolence, but I need to speak to that man as part of our agreed upon price with you regarding services." I hoped he wasn't planning to rip me off though, if he did I knew how to take away his pleasure of his couple with me, trust me.

He narrowed his eyes. "Okay, fine. You have five minutes. You go over there, say what you need to say, then return here, and kneel. Punishment denied this time. However, you interrupt me like this again I will do worse than burn a little deep, ja?"

I nodded eagerly. "Thank you for the mercy." I took off and nearly scared the loitering Egon with my rush at him like that.

He began to take off into the Shower room. "Hey, Egon. Wait, I need to speak to you," I yelled out in desperation.

Egon stopped then turned with a nervous smile breaking out on his face. "Ja, what can I do for you, Mad Maxx?"

I shot a look at Master Malfred that was standing there watching me. "Uhm, I need to meet with you a few hours in the morning for training. I have the thudding test to pass. Can you be of service?" I whispered to him.

He nodded and gave a baleful look at Master Malfred. "Ja, I have nine till eleven free if you want the time. I can find subjects for the training if you give me a couple days."

I nodded then leaned closer. "Can I offer a trade for a service from you, breath not a word."

Egon narrowed his eyes and leaned in. "You know my price already. What can I do in return for Mad Maxx."

I smiled with evil. "Contact Gunter from the dungeon and see if he would like to meet with me privately for a taste of the forbidden. If he says ja, then tell him to meet me at the playground in the yard tonight at one in the morning."

Egon paused as if smacked with a two by four. "Huh? You are offering to sleep with the lowly black collar Gunter? What the fuck, Mad Maxx? Have you lost your mind."

I nodded. "Ja, you bet I have, or that is what Gunter will think. Look you do this and forget I asked it then I pay your price. Otherwise, we never speak of anything else from this point forward, ja?"

Egon sighed. "Okay, you know me. I ask nothing and hear nothing. You can consider it done. I will relay this message and forget it. I see you tomorrow at nine for thudding. I have a feeling I don't wish to know what this is about."

I smiled with insane humor. "Bye-bye baby Gunting, father's gone a hunting. Mother's gone a milking. Sister's gone a silking but brother is going a fishing, for silver water to throw the black in."

Egon furrowed his brow. "Uhm, okay I never did understand poetry. That is a nice one though. I like the ones that rhyme the best. Oh hey, that brand is too deep you know. You better have the Haus doctor treat that, or you will get a nasty infection."

I nodded. "I intend to brother, you need not worry about that. That doctor is on Geraldine's list as well. The order of the lambs makes everything in the universe go in the right direction. I see you soon Egon." I took off back to Master Malfred leaving a very confused Egon standing there scratching his head.

Master Malfred dragged me to the Great Hall demanding I remain silent. I wrung my hands and kept my head down even when he ordered me to sit in a chair practically in his lap. He ordered us both a meal, then bitched and threatened me till I picked at the plate pretending to eat that crap.

The other Dominants in the Hall whispered and shot adoring looks at him and me. He puffed up his chest then dropped his head down covering his mouth.

"They all wish they were me, meine taube. The youngest Elder ever with the legendary Priceless at his side. Ah, the dark fantasies that will ride in their brains tonight when they are in the darkness and privacy of their bedrooms. They can only dream, but Malfred will be enjoying the reality." He grabbed the back of my head and pulled me into a deep kiss with his tongue.

I closed my eyes with my ears heating up in embarrassment. I thought of Edgar and his boys at the basketball court. No wonder they said the nasty things about me that they did. With public blood bonding couples, the deadly rape in Xavier's chains, and shit like this, I was surely viewed as the wanton sex pot. I was most unhappy over this forced misuse of my truthful nature. There was nothing I could do about it but endure the humiliation like I always do.

When he was sure every eye in that place, and all of them in the spirit world, had seen his lustful rights attended he pulled away at last. I took a shuddering breath and looked at my uneaten dinner. I thought for a moment of taking all of it and swallowing. If I could just give up my struggle to survive I could end this torture once and for all. I wondered if poisoning hurt much.

Master Malfred stood up and dragged me to the dance floor. I was forced to endure his embrace in a few slow dances. I wanted to die again when the bastard started to openly paw at me. Several other couples came out to the floor to get a better look at this outrageous display. I reminded myself he would not be so fucking proud of himself soon enough. I closed my eyes again and imagined the screams that he would make when at last he felt my flames of passion in return for this most unwanted service he was providing me.

I was forced to follow him off the floor. He made his rounds by stopping at most of the tables to pretend to be engaging in small talk. I had to kneel each time he stopped. I wrung my hands while he bragged loudly of his sexual conquests with me, and of his clever hijacking of Barnum's apartment on the Elder's floor.

I noticed; besides the universal lustful expressions each gave, most of their eyes settled on his bright red and black brand. I could hear the green-eyed monster of envy in their voices as they asked him many questions about his rise, and his precautions regarding my legendary status as being a dangerous sex partner. He would laugh, then offer outlandish and untruthful things he did to protect himself from being killed during intercourse with me. He told them everything from lighting a black candle to spreading salt around his bed. Pure insanity I tell you.

However, the fools bought his stories. They were hanging on his every word as if he were a Gott dropped from Heaven. A few got so excited by his descriptions they offered to pay him unimaginable sums just to watch any sexual act with his Priceless that he would be willing to demonstrate.

I felt sweat breaking out on my brow that if he kept tempting these perverts, I would have another rapist in no time. He was laying it on thick and they were eating it up like starving dogs. I had been through this bullshit with Peter before him. Master Malfred was overselling just as my idiot father had done. These foul creatures were already sold long before this overstuffed shirt ever entered my life. There was no need for more myths to be spread.

I was so grateful when at last he tired of his showing me off that I was nearly happy to head back to his apartment. I quickly was sorry for that momentary thought of relief. The second we got back he demanded special services again. I was to learn rapidly that Master Malfred was still a relatively young man. Father time had not robbed him of his passions yet. He had much more stamina and a higher sex drive than my Elderly Masters. To my horror and dismay, he spent most of that afternoon and early part of the night being the glutton for my adorations, nonstop, yuck.

When he finally had his fill, for now, I was full of discomfort. My throat was sore, my backside nearly ready to fall off and I was scratched to hell from his constant pawing. I wondered how Tamina had ever put up with this nymphomaniac. I supposed she didn't mind his constant lustful aggressions as much as I did. After all, he told me she got a return. Christian Axel was not so lucky. I got nothing but reminded that I was a couple of holes in the flesh for this Dominant to find his orgasm with.

He wiped me down with his alcohol bath then treated his brand before the motherfucker was finally ready for his slumber. My Master insisted I lay there in his cuddle as he drifted off into sleep. I laid there wishing that lightning would come from the Heavens and strike us both dead.

It took almost an hour for his breathing to get deep enough for me to be relatively certain he was asleep deeply. I shook off my despair at my place as the pincushion pleasure device, and very carefully escaped his hold. I went to my breeches and boots. With the stealth of my years as the pleasure submissive I dressed in the dark. I put on my long coat but not a blouse.

Master Malfred's brand was aching with the fires of hell once again. I didn't want anything touching the damaged area by this time. The jacket I had to wear to hide my weapon, or I would have left it off too despite the cold. I went to the Master's kitchenette and grabbed a large kitchen knife. I slipped it into my hidden pocket then went to the door and picked his locks.

Within moments I was free of the apartment. I moved in the shadows, with an ever-vigilant eye out to avoid being spotted by any late night staff or black collar wandering the Haus hallways. I went down the deserted torture room steps, then stepped out the side door. I stood in the darkness waiting to be attacked by Haus dogs or have a bullet ring out.

When neither happened, I took off like a rocket in a straight line headed for that playground. I prayed Egon relayed my message. If I was risking my life, I hoped to take the black collar Gunter with me to the place beyond the land of the dead.

I arrived at the swing set to find it as deserted as the Haus had been. I sighed with the realization this was going to be harder than I hoped. I turned to head back when I saw a dark spot moving toward me with speed. I backed up with a moment of anxiety unsure who was coming, Gunter or the Guard.

Gunter saw my apprehension and yelled in a whisper. "Nein. Stay put. It's me Gunter, Mad Maxx. I got your message."

I smiled with my demons rising. "Ah, shit. I thought for sure the Guard spotted me."

The heavy set black collar came within sight distance, shooting a smile back at me. "I bet. I thought Egon was funning me when he told me you wished to see me? What the hell is this about, Mad Maxx? Surely, he got his wires crossed. I find it hard to believe you would be willing to be with me."

I shook my head with a coy expression. "I remembered you from the cell. You were nice to me. I couldn't get you out of my head. I thought the only way to end my pain would be to see you and find out if you are as good as my fantasies."

He looked at the ground bashfully. "You are being cruel, Mad Maxx. I did try to be kind, which is true. I never liked that order Hemmel gave to beat you like that. I thought a legend like yourself should be adored not stomped near to death. I hope you understand it was nothing personal. Around here you do what you are told, or you remain the poor man."

I nodded,. "Oh, I understand completely. You forgot my station, my friend. I have no choice but to do what I am told. If I deny them, I am killed for it. You, of course, need the money. Jobs in the world outside this place are hard to come by, ja?"

He sniffed, then spit on the ground. "Well, ones that pay like this one does, ja. I want to retire to the sweet cottages, fuck, and drink till they put me to the grave. That is my dream, but hey if I can make extra cash, Gunter will take the job." He chuckled.

I narrowed my eyes. “Well, can I trust you to keep your mouth shut about this tryst? If so then follow me. We need to get out of the open. If not, then it has been nice reminiscing. You are free to be on your way.”

He looked around. “I am the straight man Mad Maxx, but for you, well the rumors I hear about the things you can do. Hell, no one will ever know right? I come with you and then I can wear a smile like your Masters do without anyone being the wiser.”

I chuckled,. “Oh, I assure you this thing we do will remain unsaid for all time. Come with me then and I show you why they level me Priceless.”

Gunter spit on the ground behind me but followed. “I already know why they do. You have that insanity in you. It is good to see you in your senses though. I admit I expected you to be rhyming and saying crazy shit.”

I said nothing as he prattled on about my schizophrenic behaviors in the cell. I carefully traveled along till we arrived at the rock “silver well.” I stopped then turned to face my lover.

“Here should be safe I think. Only the eyes of the Gott that does not exist can see you now Gunter.” I giggled and wrung my hands as he approached looking at the well with concern.

“I never knew this was here, Mad Maxx. How the hell did you find this place?” He walked over to investigate the hole.

I shrugged. "An ex-lover of mine brought me here not that long ago. Do not worry, that affair ended. He was the hardheaded kind. It did take a few times to get it into his head it was over, you know. I admit it was quite a blow, but he has not complained about my lack of affections since."

Gunter grinned. "Well, I intend to wreck you, Mad Maxx. I guess I should tell you I expected you to be calling me out to take out a bit of revenge for my harsh treatment. I will warn you if you are up to no good, then I have a weapon. I will throw you in this well. No one would ever find you. You would do well to do what you are told and keep that pretty mouth shut except when my cock is in it." He pulled out a small handgun and showed it to me.

I pretended to be horrified. "Nein. I pull no tricks, Gunter. I am offended that I offer you a taste of my metal and you come out here to bully me. Maybe I go home and forget this shit." I began to storm off feigning indignation.

Gunter yelled out. "Oh no you don't, Maxx. Get back over here or I will shoot you. I came out here to fuck you and fuck you I shall. Willing or not matters not to me. Turn around and get on your knees, Priceless." I turned to find him aiming the gun at me with a large smile on his face.

I pretended to be afraid. I put up my hands and came back while he chuckled under his breath. He waited till I was near, then demanded I drop to a knee once more. I did as he commanded. Gunter kept the gun pointed at my head and clumsily undid his jeans. I reached around my waist into my hidden pocket as he approached me with his manhood exposed.

He grabbed the back of my head and forced my face onto him. He let out a loud groan as I began my oral services. Gunter kept the gun on me for that moment. I watched it as he became more enthralled, and his lust began to rise.

Gunter looked down to watch my talents. "You know I was going to blackmail you for money when you broke that collar. All the Dominants are eventually rich. However, this is amazing. I think I will keep doing this. You will meet me here every week for the special services or I will tell everyone of your madness. How would that be? Oh, you have your mouthful don't you? I apologize, a nod will work." He chuckled and lowered the gun.

I pulled back with a wicked smile. "Why only once a week, lover boy? Why not let this moment last forever?" I slipped the knife out and stabbed him in the belly with speed before he could even answer.

He let out a scream and dropped the gun grabbing wildly for his spewing belly. Blood poured from the wound as he fell to his knees gurgling in agony. I stood up and walked behind the sputtering black collar. I grabbed the back of his hair lifted his head then slit his throat in a single cold move without expression. He kicked and spasmed in his death throws. I walked over and picked up his gun. I realized it was not loaded. I chuckled while Gunter went still, and his eyes fixed into oblivion.

I knelt next to the cooling corpse with a grin. "Ah, you know you talk too much Gunter. I think maybe I should have cut out your tongue instead of your throat. You know Christian always called me the schwuler pussy shard. Guess he was wrong, ja? I am just as capable of slaying a monster as he ever was. I am Maximillian the Brutal, motherfucker. You can tell all your friends that too. I am going to send you to serve Julius and the others. Hope you enjoyed the blow job. I am told my oral services are to die for. Too bad you can never verify this is not the rumor but a truth, ja?" I took the knife and shoved it into his eyes with a wild laugh.

It took me almost an hour to lift that big brute to the edge of the well. I cleaned off my knife on his clothing then stuck it back in my pocket. I got him over the side then let his flesh fall. I stood there until I heard the faint splash. I giggled while I grabbed all the blood drenched leaves throwing them in after Gunter. Then I kicked up the earth to hide all I could not pick up.

With much care, I checked the entire area for signs of struggle. At last, I was satisfied I had cleaned up all I could see of his death in the pale moon light. I threw in the gun as well then took off running like the wind to return to Master Malfred's bed before I was discovered missing.

As I had done to get there, I stuck to the shadows. I managed to make it back to the apartment without being seen. I snuck inside, replaced the knife, and rushed to the bedroom. I slipped through the door quiet as the mouse. I slowly slipped into the bed holding my breath.

I closed my eyes feeling fatigue coming over the flesh when suddenly Master Malfred come up out of the bed and grabbed me around the throat slamming me into the pillow with an insane look in his eyes.

"Where the fuck did you go? Don't you lie, Christian Axel. You have been gone over two hours. You have a lover? You tell me or I will snap your neck you bastard." He applied pressure to demonstrate he wasn't kidding.

I smiled at him then sang out, "he used to love pussy, but he found my coat warm. He tried to hurt me, so I had to do harm. He wanted to pull my tail, so I threw him away. He is down with the silvers, where day are used to rough play."

Master Malfred let me go and sat back with a look of terror. "You killed someone else, that is what you are saying to me isn't it? Someone tried to rape you. Meine taube, you must speak to me. If they find this man like they did Stefan, they will take you away from me. They kill the Priceless's when they begin to kill."

I laughed out loud. "Ah, there is no need for such worry. I kill no one. I went for a stroll in the hallways and haunted the pool. I am a ghost like you are, Casper. Calm down. Do you hear that? It is Der Hund. He speaks to Geraldine. I need to go. I have to break this code. There is the mission to consider." I jumped from the bed and grabbed my bag taking out my pen and paper.

Master Malfred watched me with a look of fear in his eyes as I began writing down Der Hund's correspondence from Geraldine. She had told him Ivar was next.

I winced when I felt the burn in my chest. I needed that brand of Master Malfred's looked at. This time I think I would be the one making the Haus call.

Chapter 56: Branded Insanity

I was working on the codes while Master Malfred sat up in his bed watching me. I had already forgotten he was in that room. Something was wrong with my memory around that time. Must have been all those seizures, you know? I heard him cough and it caused me to flinch, and anxiety filled the boy.

"Shut up. I cannot think with all the Gott damned noise around here. What the fuck is wrong with all of you? Can I get a motherfucking moment of peace or what," I yelled out and covered my headset ears with my hands.

Maximillian was taking a break from the wheel at that moment. Max and I decided to take that time to see what Der Hund found out from Geraldine. It was deafening with all the thoughts of everyone in the Haus begging for my attention. I never realized how much people think. Shit, I always wondered what another person wonders about. Well, not anymore. I wish I didn't know.

Anyway, that coughing was like being punched in the fucking face you know. I glared at Master Malfred. I was ready to kill that sonofabitch if he dared to make one more tiny noise. Maximillian served that greedy bastard to the hilt. He was the hog if he expected to be taking anymore liberties with the boy. I told Max to get ready to grab that kitchen knife. I was not in a hurry to head back to the well, but hell, I was ready to do anything to get some Gott damned peace and quiet.

Master Malfred was the clever one. He didn't say a word. We stared at each other a few more minutes, then I went back to my codes. I was satisfied he heard my warning to shut the fuck up loud and clear. Good thing for him, bad for Mad Max. I was aching to have a valid excuse to break the directive of not killing a Master. I hated this guy Casper. I told Christian to add him to the list some time ago. I had no idea what the fuck Maximillian was doing fooling around with him. I wondered why we were not with Master Leo. That is where the boy belonged.

I let out a gasp when I saw Taube wandering around the room. I thought we were all trapped inside the flesh, but there was that dumb shard staggering around on the outside.

I turned to Maximillian. "Do you see that shit, brother? The Mirror got out." I pointed at the wandering Taube.

Maximillian was relaxing against the mind's all. "You are hallucinating, fool. Taube is right here." He pointed next to him to Taube sitting there wide eyed and confused.

I let out another big gasp. "What the fuck. This is not possible. Shit, call the exorcist. We are being haunted by ghosts of shards." I jumped up and ran from the room to the living area terrified out of my mind.

I started pacing and wringing my hands, freaking out. There was a rumbling in the distance, and I swore a storm was coming. I saw the lights flashing. The tapestry lit up with green gases and the sound of the winds picked up to near tempest levels. I rubbed my eyes, stomped my feet, and tapped the headset trying to gain my location from the spies.

It was no use. That electrical interference was scrambling all the incoming transmissions. I began to panic at the loss of my pilots. I took short, shallow breaths, while my heart sped up. I saw a shadow flitter by, then another and another. I whimpered. They were gathering their forces.

I shot a horrified look at Maximillian. “You better get over here brother. This doesn’t look good. I have never seen anything like this. Of fuck, we’re super screwed this time.” Maximillian rolled his eyes and came to the wheel to join the dumbstruck Max and me.

His eyes went as wide as Max’s as he was frozen in his spot by fear at the sight. “Oh, meine Gott. What the fuck is happening,” he wailed into my over sensitive ear, causing me instant agony.

“Holy shit, Maximillian. Shut the fuck up. You are making me deaf. Help, someone help us. They are coming. Oh Gott,” I screamed out in terror while backing up into the wall unable to tear the boy’s sight off the group of demonic shadows with blood red eyes that surrounded us.

Taube stood up and rushed for the wheel. “Move, move, I know what to do, Mad Max. They are after the information. Destroy the evidence and they will go away.” He knocked me, Max and Maximillian from the controls then turned the boy around.

We all screamed in terror together, even the babbling Mad Maxx, as Taube ran for the wall headfirst. The second his forehead made the direct hit, flashes of electricity shot from the wheel striking Maximillian and Mad Maxx.

I ducked and pulled Max down with me. “Get down, fool. Taube, Jesus Christ, asshole. What the fuck are you doing. You’ll kill the boy.”

Taube let out an insane sounding laugh. “Nein, I knocked the crazy out of us. Watch this.” He ran for the wall again and struck it so hard this time the drywall cracked from the impact.

Lightening filled the wheel room making direct hits into almost every inch of the place. I screamed in pain as the white, hot agony filled me and Max through our chain connection. Taube fell over knocked out by a blow. Maximillian dropped to the floor seizing up in an epileptic fit. Mad Maxx immediately went catatonic, staring like a statue without expression. I turned to check on Max and almost died when I saw him fading in and out as if about to shatter.

“Hang in there, brothers. Everyone needs to calm down. Someone help me, Gott damn it. I cannot do this alone. You cocksucker, why did you do that? Where the hell is, what the fuck is that noise? What is happening? I cannot get out. Holy shit, I am stuck. Call Master Leo. Please find Master Leo. I need help,” I wailed out in terror as I took the wheel and my hands melted to it.

I pulled with all my might, but I couldn't get myself free of the wheel. The flesh had fallen to his backside. He shook his head as I struggled. Then got up and ran for the wall smashing his head a third time into the crumbling barrier.

Blood flowed down into my eyes making it impossible to see, not that it mattered. I was too busy trying to break away from the controls to pay any mind to what the boy was up to. Every shard was out cold, except Max and myself. Max was weakening from the shock of the misfiring brain. I had to find a way to stop the flesh from bashing his own skull into smithereens.

Master Malfred had followed the boy into the living area. He heard all of us screaming for aid, about that attack from the shadowland, and to his horror watched the flesh mindlessly pounding its head through the wall. He had rushed and called for Master Leo's aid upon hearing me yell for him. Thank Gott he hung up the phone then tackled the boy before he could slam himself into oblivion.

Master Malfred pinned me to the floor on my face. "Christian Axel, meine taube. Stop this. Please listen to me. You are killing yourself." He sounded as if he were near tears. What a weirdo.

I tried not to struggle in his hold, but I couldn't pull off the wheel. It continued to shake and shudder in my grip. I wailed out again for help. I was more than a little panicked at this point. The other Max boys and Taube were still not stirring from their differing states of unconsciousness. Max moaned loudly on the floor at my feet still shimmering as if he may blow out at any moment. I broke down sobbing at the hopelessness of this nightmare come to life. There was no way out. I was trapped.

A loud knocking began at the door. Master Malfred yelled out to kick the fucker in. Master Leo did just that. With a crash he came barreling through that entry, his hair sticking up, and eyes red with sleep. He took one look at Master Malfred holding me down on the floor. Ha-ha, he was naked, and I only had my breeches on, and Leo assumed he crashed a rape scene.

He came flying at Master Malfred and punched him in the face with vigor. I didn't know he had that in him, you know. "Get the fuck off, Christian Axel. What have you done to him, you animal? I will fucking kill you, rapist." He reared back and punched Master Malfred for a second time right in his face.

My Master groaned and fell forward but did not release his hold. "Stop hitting me Leo. Help me with the boy. He is trying to bash his brains out on the wall. Look over there, motherfucker." He motioned with his own head to the cracked and bloody wall.

Master Leo took a glance at it and let out a loud yelp. "Holy hell. Christian Axel did that? With his head?" He looked down at my busted forehead then dropped to his knees to aid Master Malfred in restraining the boy from further damage to himself.

Master Malfred let out a loud breath. “This boy is way fucking stronger than I recalled.”

Master Leo grunted as the flesh pushed hard trying to knock them off his back. “Well, you had three thugs with you the last time you held Christian Axel down I seem to recall. What the hell did you do to set this fit off? Did you get rough in special services? Or try something kinky, you pervert.”

Master Malfred growled out. “Oh, go fuck yourself Leo. I didn’t do anything. The boy disappeared for two fucking hours. When I asked him where he went, he started talking to himself using both Mad Max and Maximillian as if they were two different people. Next thing I know, he took off in here and started beating his brains out into the wall. He was calling out to himself as if there were many of him and referring to an attack from shadows. Leo, we have to take him down below. I am afraid he is beyond our help.”

Master Leo gasped. “Nein. I will not let you lock him up like a monster. Tell me where did he go? Maybe that is the key to the fit.” He groaned when the flesh tried rolling to escape and he had to grab its neck and hold tightly.

Master Malfred sighed loudly. “Well, I thought at first he was out fucking around, but that was silly. I doubt the boy could barely walk much less service another.”

Master Leo scoffed. “Enough of the bragging, Malfred. We all have heard what a big stud you are. I for one could care less. This is important, Gott dammit. Where the fuck did he go?”

Master Malfred stayed silent several moments then he mumbled out. "I must be honest. I t think he went out to kill someone Leo. We must lock him away. He will kill one of us soon. He is fucking mad."

Master Leo shook his head wildly. "I told you nein. We get wet sheets like the doctor said. Wrap him up and this fit will pass, ja. That is what we do."

"What the fuck is going on," bellowed out the Vampire Jonas.

The Masters let out yells of surprise as Master Jonas came rushing into the apartment. Master Malfred's door was busted open by Master Leo, so it was wide open, you know. He knocked both Master Malfred and Master Leo off the boy then grabbed me by my upper arms and lifted me to my feet.

I panted and shuddered looking wildly around the room. "Help, they are coming. Where is Master Leo? Call the police. Did you hear that? Oh Gott, make it stop."

Master Jonas stared into my face with a look of fury. "Which one of you motherfuckers punched Christian Axel to stupid. What the, Malfred you cocksucker. You branded him, I will fucking kill you for this mark on my man." The Vampire slung me around and gripped my upper arms holding the flesh still from behind.

He forced me to face the stunned Malfred laying on the floor. "Answer me you sonofabitch or I will call the fucking

Guard. You branded my collar, Malfred. Did you hit him like this too? Leo, did you do it?"

Master Malfred looked frightened. He pointed at the wall behind Master Jonas but said nothing. Master Leo began to rise from where the Vampire had knocked him.

"Jonas, Christian Axel did the injury to himself. We were restraining him from head banging further. Malfred, go get those sheets. Make sure they are soaked and bring them back. Hurry, we need them now," Master Leo growled out.

Master Malfred got up and took off to his bedroom. Master Jonas turned his head and saw the damaged wall then turned back to Master Leo with a gasp.

"Holy hell, what is going on Leo. Christian Axel, stop this screaming and fighting this minute or I will haul you to the dungeon. You mind me, damn you." He shook the boy harshly.

Master Leo came rushing for the Vampire. "Nein. Don't do that, Jonas. You will upset him further. Hush, lower your voice, be calm. He needs to have silence. He is confused and agitated. Don't threaten him right now. He is scared enough. Look at him, Jonas. The boy is hallucinating and whatever it is, you can bet it is more frightening than even you are." He stood in front of me trying to block me from the shadows coming for the boy.

I was sobbing uncontrollably. "LEO, call the police. They are trying to kill me. Help me. I cannot get out. I am trapped. They found me and want me dead," I vailed.

Master Leo nodded. "Ja, calm down Christian Axel. The police are on the way. Jonas, Malfred and I are here. We won't let them get you, will we Jonas. Remember speak in a calm, soft voice." He shot a look of caution at Master Jonas.

Master Jonas cleared his throat. "Uhm, ja, we got you Christian Axel. No one is going to hurt you. They have to get through us first."

I wailed out, "Kill me please. It hurts. I don't know what is happening anymore. I cannot take this. Tell Geraldine I am sorry. I am the loser. You can call the Guard. I want to go with them." I wept even harder and collapsed in Master Jonas's grip.

Master Leo came forward to attempt a look at my wounded forehead. Master Jonas growled and pulled me away from him. He used his shoulders to block the Dominant from getting too close. Master Leo halted his actions and stood there glaring with fury at the Vampire in silence.

Master Malfred returned to the living room to find the two of them squaring up against each other. He was dragging a set of fancy Egyptian cotton sheets he had soaked in the tub. He stopped his wild run to look from Master Jonas to Master Leo with an expression of confusion on his face.

"I have the sheets like you asked for Leo. What has happened? How did you get Christian Axel to stop wailing?" He started to approach me and Master Jonas.

The Vampire snorted, then shot an agitated look at the man. "Put on a fucking robe or something will you Malfred. I am not able to even form a reasonable thought with your naked ass running around here like that. Leo, help me get the boy wrapped up in the sheet. Malfred, you can keep your bloody hands off man."

Master Malfred's concerned expression melted into one of fury. "He is my man, too, and Leo's. We have as many rights to him as you do. Just who the fuck do you think you are barging into my haus and telling me what I can and cannot do on my Gott damned clock. I should call the Guard and have you removed."

Master Jonas's eyes lit with the fires of hell. "Why you rapist, thieving, perverted, cocksucking, sonofabitch, I should have murdered you the second I found out you attacked my man. This is bullshit sharing my collar with the likes of you. As it is, the second I have him stabilized I am going to kill you. You dared to put your brand on him. I will see you devoured by the buzzards for that alone."

Master Malfred narrowed his eyes and doubled up his fists and began to come at Master Jonas. "That is it. I am sick to death of you Jonas. I was going to kill you later but now is as good a time as any other. Let Leo hold Christian and let's see who the better man is. We settle this once and for all." Master Jonas started pushing me toward a startled Master Leo.

Master Leo let out a yelp of fear. "Enough, both of you cool off. This is no time for cock measuring boys. You need to grow the fuck up. We all must get along for Christian Axel's sake. Or should I call the fucking Guard and have him put out of his misery as he claims he desires. Make up your minds right fucking now. We work together or we will have nothing to tie us together any longer." He stepped between the dueling Dominants.

I was sobbing like a kid feeling damned helpless to even swallow. Rivets of drool poured from my mouth dripping down my bare chest onto the floor. The world was moving too fast. I could hear my Master's rumbling with each other, but it no longer mattered. I stared at Max with despair as he blinked on and off like a strobe light. I was almost certain he was a goner.

Oddly, I had hated him all that time, but in those moments of chaos, I realized I couldn't live without him anymore. It pissed me off to realize this goofy grinning motherfucker was so important to me but there it is.

I just wanted it to go back to the way it used to be. We used to know who our enemies were, but not anymore. It seemed to me these days we were more deadly to ourselves than any of the Dominants or Masters in that Haus ever had been to us.

I was about to give up when to my joy Maximillian began to stir, moaning out in pain. He sat up slowly holding his head with his eyes closed. Taube, as if he were taking a cue from the Seductive shard began to twitch and whimper. I shot a look at Mad Maxx. He sat there staring into the nothing. He was still trapped in that hellish living death state of catatonia.

Maximillian yelled out. “What the fuck was that shit. My head is killing me.”

Taube groaned. “Ah, I think I broke my legs. I cannot stand up. Help me Mad Max.”

I shook my head,. “I cannot help you Taube. My hands are melted to the wheel. I am stuck.”

Maximillian opened his eyes in a startle at my words. “Huh? You are what? Holy shit. Oh, this is not good.” He stood up and swooned for a moment before he could steady himself and approach me.

I looked at Max as Maximillian came towards me to examine the damage. He had stopped blinking but was seeing through with wispy boarders. He shot me a look of fatigue and a bitter smile. Max then laid his head down and closed his eyes to rest for a bit.

Maximillian stared at the weakened Max laying at my feet. “Oh, shit, our soul is tired and injured Mad Max. You should have protected him better. Why did you grab the wheel? You are stuck in the worst spot available during these troubled times. I was doing my best to keep you and Max from suffering this horror. Now our most precious shard is vulnerable. What the hell were you thinking? As soul bearer you are the only thing between us and the nightmare of reality. Fuck this horror. What are we going to do?"

I trembled and wept. "I didn't mean for it to happen. Everyone else was out cold. Please help me get off this wheel. Cut off my hands if you must but get me out of here Maximillian. I cannot handle this boy alone."

Maximillian nodded and looked sympathetic, "It is okay brother. I apologize for blowing up like that. Bitching and blaming aren't going to fix this disaster. Taube, get up. We need your help. We need to protect Max at all costs. This drugging that doctor or whoever is doing to the boy has made us all weak. I have an idea. Come with me Taube, follow me to Mad Maxx." He helped his mirror shard off the floor.

I watched helplessly as the two of them approached the catatonic Mad Maxx. Maximillian told Taube to focus. Maximillian knelt and had his mirror mimic his behaviors.

"I apologize for this my brother, but dare is no other way. If Max fades or shatters there will be nothing left for you to return to someday. I will owe you one if we survive. If we don't, then let me say it was a pleasure working with you." Maximillian took a deep breath and laid his hands on Mad Maxx's forehead while Taube did the same.

I gasped in terror when I saw all three of them light up like ghosts. Then to my shock the glow of Maximillian and Taube began to feed into Mad Maxx making him shine until you would almost go blind looking at him.

The Seductive and Mirror shard lost their shimmer completely having emptied most of their symptoms from the drugging into Mad Maxx. They dropped their hold on him and backed away. Mad Maxx didn't move nor blink. He sat there unable to move, fight, or speak as the glowing began to fade away leaving him full of the madness trapped in his statue state of being.

Maximillian looked at the wheel floor sighing with the sound of much sadness. "I feel like an ass, the nightmare we just dumped on our brother Mad Maxx. Taube, I pray one day he can forgive me for it. We must all protect him and Max with all we have. They are helpless now to defend themselves. It is up to us three to run this ship. We in together or die trying. Now come with me and we join Mad Max in his predicament." Taube nodded and wiped his eyes from the tears that had started to fall.

"I am with you brothers. No matter what happens, I am ready," Taube said as he sniffed loudly.

I watched the two of them coming toward me. Maximillian stood on one side and Taube the other. They smiled at me while they took the wheel and allowed it to melt there to it. Now, all three of us were trapped, unable to escape or take a rest from the experiences of the flesh.

I suddenly understood why Maximillian and Taube did this. The three of us had formed a protective barrier designed to protect our weakened soul and ailing masochistic shard as he endured most of the growing madness. This was our last stand. Shattering of any of us would at this point mean death.

Maximillian smiled with wickedness on my left. “Well, boys, I am ready for anything. I always loved a party.”

Taube giggled to my right. “Ah the best news is that if this fails then we won’t have to clean up after the revelry is through.”

I chuckled with bitterness. “As long as there is a pinata to smack with my cane, I am a happy boy. I can live without having to serve next to you dogs, but I must request the boy start brushing his teeth again. Maximillian your breath is putrid.”

Maximillian’s eyes went wide in shock. “Bitch to Master Malfred if it bothers you brother. You know, if you would allow the boy a fucking bath, my breath wouldn’t smell like the whore Haus after payday. That man is the sex fiend. He won’t soil his sheets with his fluids, but he throws them into the water and wraps the boy in them. What the fuck is wrong with that madman?”

I scoffed. “He is like Taube. He doesn’t want to clean up after the revelry either.”

We all began to laugh maniacally at our crass discussion of Maximillian’s foul breath. This caused the Masters to briefly pause their actions that had been taking place during our drama inside the wheel room. The three of them had stopped arguing long enough to work together to restrain the boy in the fancy wet sheets.

Master Jonas pinned the boy while Master Leo worked with the naked Master Malfred to restrain him tightly in the soaked silk. The boy laughed, babbled, and drooled while the Dominants did their best to get him bound up.

The three of us could do nothing but watch helplessly. None of us could budge the wheel until the mind reset. It had been most grievously stunned to stupid when it got stuck in the tapestry. Taube's plan to knock the shit out of the boy didn't help that situation either, let me tell you.

When the Masters finished their job the boy looked like a human enchilada. He couldn't move except to roll. I breathed a sigh of relief that at least there was no chance the flesh could injure itself in this state. *I have to be honest; it was quite uncomfortable. Being stuck like that was similar to being in that damned strait jacket we had been locked in for months, yuck.*

The three Masters Malfred, Jonas and Leo stood over me staring, each wearing an expression of worry on their faces. I struggled by rolling around a bit but eventually gave that fruitless behavior. It was clear I wasn't going anywhere until someone unwrapped me. I broke out into laughter without humor that I was lying in a puddle of drool flowing by the bucket load.

Master Malfred left for a moment to finally get something on while Master Jonas and Master Leo glared at each other. They appeared ready to begin their arguing anew. Neither said a word as they sat down on Master

Malfred's couch and recliner as far as possible from each other.

When the Dominant returned wearing a sweatsuit he wore an angrier look on his face than the two already filled with rage in his living room. He stood there in the hallway entry crossing his arms and narrowing his eyes, shooting both of them his disgusted looks.

"Well,? The boy is secured, ja? Why the fuck are you still here gentlemen? I think you can leave now. I got this from here," he growled out.

Master Jonas shook his head. "Nein, I am not leaving till this shit is settled."

Master Malfred scoffed. "I have nothing more to say to you, Jonas. This is my clock, and I already tolerated you as far as I am willing to go."

Master Leo groaned. "Oh hell. I for one am not going to sit through another argument boys. Sit down Malfred. We are going to fix this fighting among us right this second. Christian Axel is in a lot of trouble. Jonas, you want the boy to break that collar. I desire to see him freed like you do. Well, I have got news for you. If we don't work with Malfred, then we will indeed get that bat collar back broken by the Guard."

Master Jonas chuckled with evil. "You are wrong there, Leo. This stupid motherfucker said he could keep the Priceless in line. Look at him lying dare out of his mind. It took him, you, and me to get this boy calmed. He is not able to command a fucking dog. I will call Claus to report his boasts were nothing more than hot air."

Master Malfred dropped his arms and shook his fist at Master Jonas. "Fichen Dich, Jonas. This bullshit was under control. You came in here without my asking for you aid. You try to bring Claus into this I will see you at the bottom of the stairs, you sonofabitch."

Master Leo sighed. "Here we go again. Enough already. Okay, come sit down Malfred and join your brothers. This can be peacefully worked out. If you two brutes would be willing to listen to Leo for a minute instead of your own overblown threats."

Master Malfred looked at the ceiling, then blew out his breath and came over to take the recliner next to Master Leo. He still glared at the Vampire with anger but kept his quiet. Master Jonas sat back on the couch crossing his arms returning the irritated stares.

Master Leo looked at them both then sat forward. "Okay, it is pretty evident that Christian Axel is off into the acute part of his cycle. Jonas and Malfred, I have unwelcome news for you. The schizophrenics do not get better just because you threaten them or pump them full of medications. This shit will last for more than six months. Jonas, you of all of us should be aware of this nightmare. You were there at the onset ja?"

Master Jonas looked at the floor and nodded,. "Ja. It was eight months the last time, I confess. He was worse than this, but many of these behaviors I have seen in him before. If it gets that bad again, I fear dare will be no breaking that metal." He took a deep breath then shot me a look of worry.

Master Malfred narrowed his eyes. "You mean he can get worse than this?"

Master Leo nodded as did Master Jonas. "Ja, Malfred. This is relatively mild compared to how bad it could get. That is why I say we need to work together or be prepared to lose this treasure forever. I for one love the boy. I am even willing to work with you bastards to keep him from a grave in the orchard. I will do whatever it takes. I pray you both feel the same."

Master Jonas's expression of fury broke into one of resignation. "Leo is right though; I hate to admit it. Okay, I am listening carefully Leo. You have my oath to work with you in any way necessary to save the boy. That said, the second he is back to himself, I won't swear to not kill your ass."

Master Leo scoffed. "Uhm, well I suppose that is a better response than I expected of you Jonas. Malfred? What do you say? Are you in or out?"

Master Malfred shook his head "Why should I help? I have this boy most of the time. It seems to me I don't need either of you. He is not that big. I can handle a fourteen year old without your old asses."

Master Jonas growled while Master Leo put up his hand for silence. "Ah, you have him the majority until

Jonas, and I go to Claus to report Christian Axel is throwing fits, been branded, and sneaking out at night under your leash. You either work with us Malfred, or I will help Jonas make sure you are thrown from the schedule for good. I should do that anyway after that shit you pulled to get onto our floor in the first place. However, you are here now. Better to have you as an ally then an enemy, I say, for the sake of the Priceless."

Master Malfred's eyes went wide. "You cannot get me thrown from the cycle."

Master Jonas smiled with hate. "Do you want to test that, you cocksucker?"

Master Malfred looked at Master Leo that was also smiling with dark thrill. "Ja, Malfred we can. Surely the boy told you about that contract agreement among the Elders that bans branding or breaking his flesh? You are in violation. The punishment is withdrawal of privileges with the Elders silver." Master Leo chuckled at that.

Master Malfred shook his head,. "I never agreed to such. I only just now hear of this bullshit."

Master Jonas laughed out loud. "You are so full of shit Malfred. I know Christian Axel told you. He didn't just get hot and bothered to wear you mark, fool. Even Claus will know better. Even if he had not warned you, there is no excuse to place your mark of exclusivity on a piece of property that is shared by four others equally. You will have no excuse and I for one will vote you out of the rotation. Leo will too and so will Bladrick. You will never enjoy our collar's favor again. You know what Leo? I changed my mind. Fuck this working with Malfred. I say we go wake up Claus and complain. I would love to see my man out of his slimy clutches." The Vampire stood up ready to head for the crossdresser's door.

Master Malfred let out a gasp. "Sit down, Jonas. I thought we were speaking like men here. No need to get your feathers in a ruffle. I am willing to hear what Leo proposes to fix this disagreement between us."

Master Leo laughed "Ah, there we go. Sit down Jonas. Malfred is willing to work with us. Better to have him inside the tent pissing out then outside pissing in ja?"

Master Jonas sat back down with a look of irritation. "This better be good Leo. I think murdering Malfred is the best route. Then I need not worry about him pissing anywhere."

Master Leo took a deep breath. "Okay the way I see it, Claus and Bladrick get the two days of the rotation no matter what the rest of us do. They are satisfied with that arrangement so that leave five days for the three of us. Christian Axel is very ill and none of us have the skill to attend to all his symptoms exclusively. Jonas you seem to have an ability to make him mind when it comes to stopping his fit throwing. Malfred, you appear capable of keeping him calm during public appearances. However, neither of you can get him to eat, take his meds or bath. Nor can you understand his language. In those areas I am the best. Do you gentlemen agree with my assessment of this situation?"

The two of them shot each other a spiteful look but then nodded that Master Leo was correct.

Master Leo sighed. "Good that you both can see the problem. What we need is to have all these skills in one Dominant. I don't think that is possible given the relationship each has with the boy is private between him and Christian Axel. So, I think what should be done is we all take our one day exclusive with the Priceless in the rotation, then we all three shares equally the two remaining."

The two Dominants began to yell and complain loudly at that statement then Master Jonas growled out, "How the fuck can we share two fucking days equally, Leo? You sound as fucking insane as Christian Axel."

Master Malfred nodded. "I agree with Jonas. The only way that we could share the boy equal is if we moved in together. This plan of yours is the stupidest thing I have ever heard."

Master Leo groaned,. "Ja, I am suggesting that two days a week we share an apartment and this boy as roommates. It will take all three of us to handle him. I think for his sake five days a week of full sharing would be smarter than the two."

Master Jonas stood up his veins popping out on his forehead. "Oh, meine Gott. I wouldn't share the plague with you two much less my fucking home and bed."

Master Malfred shouted out. "I hate to agree with this bloodsucker, but he is right. I don't want either of you near me even at the fucking Elders' table in the Great Hall. Your stink makes me sick."

Master Leo glared at them both with fury. "Sit down, Jonas you pervert. Shut up Malfred, you rapist. Do you think I want to be around your nasty asses? Hell, nein, yet for my Christian Axel I would make a deal with any devil. I love the boy. You claim the same Jonas. Do you, Malfred? I heard tale you said the same, Malfred. Prove it to both of us. Do what we must to save him, or I will call the fucking Guard to report he murdered that black collar Evelyn. I would rather end this pain for him and for us than keep arguing." He shook his fist at them to make it clear he was serious.

Master Jonas sat down suddenly dumbfounded "He killed Evelyn? You know this for truth?"

Master Leo nodded while dropping his gaze to the floor, then Master Malfred moaned. "Ja, Jonas. He did. He also killed Stefan. I fear he may have killed another tonight that we have no knowledge of as well. The boy has gone mad dog."

Master Jonas shot me a look of horror. "Oh shit. This is bad. He has become a true Priceless then. You really think this plan will stop the nature of his silver?"

Master Leo shrugged. “I really don’t know Jonas. All I can say is we can try it. As you both are aware, the Priceless collars are sent to the yard when they start the killing. It is only a matter of time before he is discovered doing these foul deeds. His mind is too cracked to hide the evidence as he has done in the past. You saw him kill Drexel, Jonas. You are aware of how capable the boy is of murder. Worse, he has every reason to want to end everyone in this Haus. So, again, I say to you brothers, do we work together as a united team, or do we take our chances he gets each of us separately?”

Master Malfred sighed deeply. “Fuck, I hate to admit it Jonas, but Leo has a point. The boy will kill you, me, him, all of us eventually. He is mad. I know he will return from the place of insanity at some point and be worth the sacrifices we make now. Okay, I have made up my mind. I am in Leo. You come up with a living arrangement for the five days, and I will do my best to endure the bullshit.”

Master Jonas growled. “Well, I am also in, but I will say I am only willing to stay in a single apartment during the dark hours. I intend to keep to my Haus as much as possible to avoid you both.”

Master Leo chuckled. “Jonas I am not suggesting we all become roomies motherfucker. I am saying that we will need to share the burdens and the joys equally. I think the best plan is to rotate among the three of us. This week we are staying with Malfred. Next time, we will stay with Jonas and then my place. If we do this together, it will only be hard at first. Over time, we will all get used to it.”

Master Jonas looked at the busted door. "Guess I better fix that fucking door if we are to stay here then. I wouldn't want Christian Axel escaping nor either of you when I murder you in your sleep."

Master Malfred chuckled, "Ah, well this will work better than I thought. I think like Jonas. I was just planning how I was going to kill you in your slumber."

Master Leo clicked his tongue. "See we already are getting along like family. Enough of this threatening. We should agree right this minute if any of us feel irritated and need a break, he is to leave immediately and take a break at home before fighting among us starts. If we do this, Christian Axel must see us fully united. Any weakness in our team, he will likely use to manipulate and destroy us all."

All three of the Dominants swore oaths of loyalty to each other. Master Jonas and Master Malfred then left Master Leo to keep an eye on me while they fixed the apartment door.

I shot looks of fear at Maximillian and Taube. They stood there staring back at me with the same look of horror. We all heard and saw that unbelievable nightmare unfold. The three monstrous Dominants had ganged their forces against us. We were so fucked, and I mean that literally and figuratively. This was bad news for the boy. I began to struggle to let loose the wheel again. No way was I sticking around for this bullshit.

Maximillian dropped his gaze and sighed. "Let it go brother. There is no escape other than breaking that collar. You, me, Taube, we will endure this like we always have. Only another seven months, then it is over. We either walk out that door on our feet with our collar removed or be carried out by the Guard. Try to remember nothing can go on forever. Not even the pain of our existence. We can do this together. Have faith Mad Max."

I dropped to my knees. "Oh, shit I wish I could believe that Maximillian. I was not designed for this life like you were. I cannot take them coming at the boy. I beg of you to cut off my hands and set me free."

Taube shook his head. "Brother Max, you can do this. Just remember you are not alone this time. Maximillian and I are here to help. Scream if you must. Cry all you like. We will not judge you for it. In the end, we all will share the nightmares and the thrill of their blood running in rivers through the hallways. Let them try to beat us. We are unstoppable. They only make their end more painful and our joy at it higher."

Maximillian smiled with evil. "That is a truth brother. We kill them all for everything they have done and will do. Then in the darkness when the boys shudders and vails from the horrible memories he can find peace knowing they suck the Devil's crooked cock for what they did to us."

I closed my eyes and trembled. "Ja, ja, we got this. I can try to handle the horror. Seven months will fly, right?"

Ma brother shards nodded. “As smooth and quickly as Barnim and Drexel did brother. Stand tall. We have work to do,” said Maximillian with urgency in his voice.

The rest of that night the three Elders took turns watching me. Master Malfred took the first shift after Master Leo and Master Jonas returned with things to make them more comfortable for an overnight stay in my Masters apartment.

The Vampire and Master Leo went to Master Malfred’s bed to resume their slumber with Master Leo selected to take the next shift in four hours. The Dominant sat there on the couch reading while the boy giggled and rolled. The three of us shards still had no control of the flesh. It was one long night for sure.

When Master Leo’s turn came, the boy finally found peace in slumber at last. He didn’t even awaken when the Vampire came up for his watch duty. The night had long passed, and the new day well began before my eyes opened once more.

The sheets had begun to dry. I found them loosened and the three Masters staring at me from the living room furniture. I shuddered as I recalled their dark discussions of working together as a unit of Masters against me. I didn’t attempt to bust out of the sheet nor say a word out of pure terror of this most disturbing situation.

There was a sudden knocking at the door. Master Malfred got up and answered. The Elders Claus and Bladrick entered. Both took a seat on the couch next to the

Vampire. I felt very small and scared as they all focused their eyes on me laying there like the sausage. Ha, a piece of meat is a good analogy, ja?

Master Claus cleared his throat. "Leo explained this unusual situation to me. I have relayed it to Bladrick. We are willing to work with you fellows any way you desire. I personally find the idea quite clever. However, I don't give it a week. You boys are still too full of fire to ever stop fighting over something you already won. None of you are known for your generous nature, nor do Bladrick and I think for a second you can curb the personality of this Priceless collar. That said, you have your full five days in consecutive order. You can have him from Thursday to Tuesday nights. Bladrick and I will settle for Wednesday and Thursday till midnight. We will no longer change this schedule. You will work out the five between you and never bring it up to us again or so help me, we will take the full seven and throw all of you off the banister. Now, as for this branding business, Malfred you have to be punished for that."

Master Malfred growled "Bullshit. I didn't know there was a ban on it."

Master Claus held up his hand while Master Leo and Master Jonas groaned. "Be that truth or lie matters not anymore, does it? The boy will carry that scar for life won't he? Well, I thought it over and decided that since we cannot undo the damage, I offer every Master here the same right to brand the Priceless."

I closed my eyes and moaned with despair. The Dominants all shot their heads at me for a moment. They stared until sure I wasn't going to dare interrupt them in this horrid discussion.

Master Claus nodded. "As I was saying, all of you have the right to put your mark on the boy. You wish to do this thing, say so right this moment. Otherwise, you can shut your mouth and deal with what cannot be changed. Malfred, you will keep your silence, or I will have you whipped for putting us in this position in the first fucking place."

Master Jonas spoke up. "I hereby take this offer and claim the boy's right pectoral muscle for my brand."

Master Claus nodded. "Fair enough. Leo what do you say?"

Master Leo scoffed. "I refuse this and add punishing Malfred is what you should be doing. Adding more burns to the boy is punishing him nor the guilty party."

Master Claus snorted. "Be that as it may Leo if you are done with your say, then I want you to know I withdraw your right to brand the collar forever."

Master Leo nodded. "Good. You are all a bunch of animals." He crossed his arms and pouted. *Though he certainly earned my respect, and I forgave him, a little, for the betrayal at the Great Hall. He still had a long way to go to unbreak my heart, but this was a great start.*

Master Claus looked at Master Bladrick. "What say you brother? You want to dust off your old iron?"

Master Bladrick shook his head. “Nein, I see no reason to markup that beautiful boy with my ugly iron. He will live a long time after my bones are dust. I will be burning in hell for all my evils, but I will not have to endure an eternity of damnation with the addition of his hatred for such a petty vanity.”

Master Claus chuckled. “I hear you brother. I, however, do not share your view. I will take my right to brand him with my mark. I claim his left shoulder blade which is my custom. If everyone is satisfied all the hurts have been settled, I believe my brother and I will be headed to breakfast in the Great Hall. Prepare the boy for the brands so he can heal evenly. We meet in the torture chamber tonight at nine Jonas to complete your pleasure. Gag the boy if he is railing, and make sure he is secure. Come brother Bladrick. I am starving.” The Elders got up to leave still watching me with a baleful eye.

I looked away feeling tears welling up in my eyes. I couldn’t believe Master Claus was going to allow this branding bullshit to happen. It made me even more aware he never intended for me to break my metal. No Dominant would dare to put their brand on a collar they expected to be their equal one day soon. I tried to swallow my hurt that the crossdresser thought so little of my happiness, but I admit, it was pure agony. I had thought he liked me, at least a little.

I know it was childish of me to think in such a fantastical way, I mean the London bridge said it all, but I had not completely grown up yet. Try to remember Meine Liebe, just because they use you to keep their cock warm doesn't mean they really care a thing about you. Love is not equal to sex, nor is saying the words an indication of the true emotion.

If they treat you like a whore, then that is all you are to them, like it or not. That doesn't make you one, but it sure does make them a liar. Never ever trust someone that tells you untruths, even if they think they do it to spare your feelings. One lie leads to many, and a glorious lie will injure you when the bitter reality comes a knocking. *I nodded at that most wise advice.*

The rest of the day I stayed quiet and subdued. I will confess I was too depressed to bother with anything but laying dare in my drool. The Masters took turns forcing in food, pills and re-wetting the sheets that bound me. I didn't bother to struggle against them nor say anything.

Only Master Leo seemed concerned by my lack of responses to their rough handling of me. He kept asking me to converse with him. I would close my eyes and pretend to sleep each time he attempted to communicate. I no longer believed any of them genuinely cared about anything I had to say. Why bother wasting my breath?

When eight thirty came along Master Jonas became loud, seeming in great spirits. I wanted to kill him more than ever as I realized he was happy that Master Malfred had opened the door to allow for his marking me as his property. I should have known that, but again, I cannot predict everything, ja?

He and Master Malfred came for me shortly after to begin their unraveling of the sheets. Master Leo refused to aid them stating he thought them worse than barbarians for branding a human being. They laughed and ignored his passive protests. I endured the big men as they pulled and rolled me along the floor to free the boy.

Once out of the restraint Master Jonas took up my leash. I sat up but kept my eyes to the floor as he examined my forehead by pushing my hair back. He grumbled that I was cut and needed to be looked at by the Haus doctor.

Master Malfred nodded; then told him he would make arrangements for that to happen the next morning. The Vampire looked at the irritated brand already in place.

"You burned too deep, Malfred. We need the doctor to treat this wound as well. Maybe you should come with me to see Claus downstairs. We will show you how to do this correctly," the Elder growled out.

Master Malfred nodded. "Oh, I am coming with you Jonas, but not to watch your techniques. I want to be sure you don't try to cover my own mark. There will be no more branding for Malfred. I have the Priceless at last. No other silver will do. I don't foresee another of his caliber rising in my lifetime. This boy will do for the remainder of my days."

Master Jonas's eyes went wide. "Oh? Well, you will be a lonely man, Malfred. This boy will break my collar in a short time. I don't think for a second as the Dominant he will grace your bed ever again."

Master Malfred chuckled. “He won’t break that collar Jonas. You are deluded. He is blood bonded times four. One of us will have to die to free him from that metal. You plan to kill me brother? Or Leo perhaps?”

Master Jonas narrowed his eyes. “You forgot one, Malfred. You can join that motherfucker in the grave as far as I am concerned if you dare to breath another word.”

Master Malfred gasped then grinned with great joy. “You know what, Jonas? I have judged you far too fast. I am beginning to think you are not as much a dumb brute as I thought. I think this may be the start of a fantastic friendship.”

Master Jonas shot a perturbed look at Master Malfred. “Well, strange things have happened, I suppose. You coming? I am headed downstairs. Oh, you may want to keep your distance. If I get the chance I am going to trip you on the stairs. Christian Axel you come with your man without quarrel or suffer for it.” He chuckled as he motioned me to stand and follow in silence.

I shuddered and began to wring my hands but did as commanded. Master Malfred followed at a safe distance which made the Vampire chuckle under his breath. I looked at Maximillian and Taube. They took deep breaths and motioned me to join them in this calming behavior.

Master Claus and Master Bladrick were already in the branding room waiting. I was ordered to get on the table for restraining. Master Jonas dug for his branding iron in the lockers while Master Malfred lit the burner. Master Claus and Master Bladrick restrained me on my back to the table.

Master Jonas found his J with a circle iron and went to heat it up. Master Malfred stood dare examining his mark while the eldest Elders reminisced about their younger years and other silvers they had branded.

Maximillian nudged me and whispered in my ear, "Let the heat fuel your hate brother. That is the key to survival as the submissive. Fed your beast till he is full of blood lust." I nodded and braced for the pain with my brother shards.

Master Jonas didn't hesitate to burn his mark into my chest opposite the side of Master Malfred's M. I screamed out in agony despite my best efforts. The flesh shook and I gritted my teeth nearly breaking them in half as the white hot pain lit me up with the flames of hate.

I was not even permitted a moment before I was unrestrained and told to flip over. Master Jonas aided Malfred in retying me down. The cool tabletop aided the fresh burning and sent me into fresh torment from the original brand. It was sore as hell by now, you know.

Master Claus, like the Vampire before him, didn't fool around. I wailed out in pure torture as his C with a circle sheered into my left shoulder blade. Master Claus chuckled at my moaning in pain.

"Shit, I am getting turned on hearing all this panting you're doing Mad Maxx. You will give this old man something to dream of tonight. Ah, there boys. Isn't that pretty? Nothing like a fresh brand. I think that it is too bad they cool off to pink from the beautiful bright red in time," said the crossdresser to his brothers.

Master Malfred nodded. "Well, I don't disagree with that. You know, I will have to start scouring mine tonight to get it to set. You wish me to attend yours too, brother?" I winced when I heard Master Claus grant him permission.

I swear to Gott, I wanted to get that Bunson burner and burn that fucking place to the ground. I decided that if I could ever get such a chance at that pleasure, I would not allow them to die right away. First I would burn them and scour the wounds for a bit before dispatching them to the afterlife.

I nodded as I thought of the three scars on his chest and shoulder blades shaped like letters. I had noticed them all that time but never questioned why he had an M, J, and C, and a P. I turned to look at him with wonder. He apparently read my mind.

"That is another story Meine Liebe. You will let me tell this story, or do you want the cane?" I looked down to see his wrist twitching.

I nodded and turned around in silence wondering if I was going to end up branded as badly as he had been at some point. I shuddered but said nothing.

The Elders untied me, then applied cooling gels to my burns. I sat there trembling, silently weeping, feeling so low I didn't bother to even look up from the floor. The four of them chattered happily, ignoring my obvious despondency. Master Claus even had the audacity to brag to the others I was "the bravest" silver he ever branded. He based that on my silence and lack of struggle to get me on the table.

I ignored them. I thought only of my next target on the X list. The pain of the brands focused my resolve to work my way on gaining my revenge. Far as I saw it they were only assuring that at some point I would rise up and brutally kill all of them. Master Bladrick was the only one I had no plans to send to his grave. Mother nature had already attended to him mercifully. There was no need to do anything but wait to see him dead.

When they were satisfied I was triaged enough to return to Master Malfred's apartment, Master Jonas took up my leash and motioned me to follow in silence. I did as commanded with my cheeks wet with tears, and chin wet with uncontrollable drool. I wrung my hands and kept my head down following the group of Elders. They all laughed and spoke loudly appearing to be in high spirits.

I had wanted to unite the brothers. I had been successful. There was no doubt the Elder brothers were getting along famously at last, at my expense of course. Who knew a couple of gang rapes and community branding could heal their deep discords. It sucks to be me, you know.

As we traveled down the hallway the black collar staff for the Great Hall were being released for the day. I saw several of them bowing as they put their backs to the wall in proper protocol to let the Dominants pass. It was then I noticed one of them I had never seen before.

A beautiful blond girl of maybe twenty took to the wall and bowed as we walked by. I near fell down from my gawking in sheer awe at this amazing female. An older black collar woman had to push her back further to the wall because she was not far enough back to be minding the rules for her level. She was obviously new to the Haus due to her being unaware of such common knowledge. I craned my neck staring at her openly my eyes feasting on every inch of this Goddess. She glanced up to see me brazenly lusting after her. She blushed with a cat smile, then dropped her sight down coyly as if returning my interest.

I immediately wanted this girl with all my being. I tripped over my own feet nearly stupid from desire. Master Jonas noticed the slack in my leash. He jerked it hard and turned around breaking from his loud conversation with Master Malfred about history.

"What the fuck, Christian Axel. You have two left feet or something? Keep up or so help me." He growled out as the other Dominants stopped and turned to stare at me as well.

I dropped to a kneel mainly so I could stay there longer near that gorgeous black collar girl. "I apologize Master. It won't happen again. Thank you for the mercy." I mumbled through my drool.

Master Jonas scoffed. “Get the fuck up. What the hell is wrong with you? When you beat your head into the wall, did you knock out all your training in protocol?”

I shrugged. “That must be the problem, Master. Twinkle, twinkle little retard, don’t you wonder who you are? Christian Axel never was that bright. His screws were not very tight.” I began wringing my hands faster while dropping my gaze to the floor.

Master Jonas stared at me for a moment in disbelief, then suddenly broke out in deep laughter. “Oh, meine Gott. You clever bastard. Now that was funny shit. Did you hear that Malfred? Shit. A real comedian this one. Get up Christian Axel. You mind your manners, and the sheets will be under you. Your Master’s arms will be wrapped around you instead.”

I caste a look at the door thinking of running for them but dropped my sight back to the floor in defeat “Master, if wishes were horses, then Christian Axel would ride. If turnips were swords, I would put one in your side. If ‘ifs’ and ‘ands’ were pots and pans, then I would touch that pretty server instead of you with my hands.”

Master Jonas frowned. “Well, wishes are not horses, nor turnips swords. I think you better watch your mouth Christian Axel. I do not care for your tone.”

I nodded. “Ah, watching that is your pleasure Master I seem to recall. You will care for it just fine soon enough I believe or make me sorry for it.” I stood up ready to follow him without getting the beating I was about to talk myself into.

He nodded. "That is correct little man. You come along and stop this rambling and rhyming shit. Save it for Leo. He likes that type of poetry." He and Master Malfred laughed at that as they took off back toward the apartment.

I looked behind me seeking that lovely girl. She was standing there still glancing back and covering her mouth with wickedness in her eyes. I smiled with thrill that she seemed to be flirting. I turned and walked backward for a moment drinking in every bit of her. I was going to need that wonderful vision to get me through the horror the surely awaited me the second the lusty Masters got me behind closed doors.

Then to me joy, she blew a kiss at me. I nearly fell again but managed to catch myself before setting off the Vampire. I turned around begrudgingly, but this time with a new spring in my step. Maximillian and Taube smiled at me. We decided unanimously we now had a side mission. Find out who this girl was and make her ours.

When we arrived back at the apartment Master Claus and Master Bladrick bid us good night. The Vampire and Master Malfred took me inside to find Master Leo on the couch reading one of his romance novels with a look of irritation. He bitched at the two grinning Dominants as they had me stand there to demonstrate the dishonor of their brands.

They ignored Leo and laughed a great deal at his dramatic movements of disdain over this horrid affair. Then to my horror Master Malfred informed the two of them he intended to call in his rights for special services. That was bad enough but to double my nightmare he offered to allow the other two to join him in his pleasures.

I held my breath near in panic while Master Leo loudly protested such evil even being discussed, much less accepted. Master Jonas on the other hand was most pleased to partner up with Master Malfred.

Master Leo jumped to his feet and, for effect, threw down his novel. “Are you both stupid? The boy just nearly knocked his brains onto the floor. You burned him like cattle. Now you plan to tag team him. You know he is straight, fools. You cannot keep mistreating him like this. No wonder he is insane. Hell, I would be too. You both are fucking monsters.”

Master Malfred chuckled. “Look Leo, you are the one that suggested this arrangement. I am trying to be accommodating to my brothers. Shit, you go acting all high and mighty if you want but I don’t see you innocent of fucking the boy. This is a pleasure submissive idiot. What the hell did you think that means? If I wanted my Haus cleaned I call for the black collar. If I want my cock sucked I call on the services of the silver. You see that collar on this boy, what color is it? Do you see that brand? I do believe that means whatever I do with him in my bed it is his job to comply. If I choose to invite my brothers, then maybe they will recall my generosity when their turn comes up, ja?"

Master Jonas laughed. "Ja, generosity goes a long way, Malfred. Leo here should remember that. Besides, if I am with you when you call your rights I can keep my eyes on your behavior."

Master Malfred shrugged. "Whatever Jonas. I do nothing as gross as you do, that I can promise. If Leo doesn't want to enjoy this treasure with us, I say fine. Let him sleep alone tonight. Christian Axel, you come along, meine taube. Your services are requested. Time to earn your place in my Haus boy." He pulled me along with my leash as Master Jonas followed behind me.

I kept my eyes to the floor and sucked back my tears of despair. I was no stranger to the threesome, but this match up was the most heinous. Maximillian and Taube reminded me to recall enduring this humiliation by feeding my hate. I closed my eyes and pulled the image of the beauty in the hallway. I would do my best to keep my mind on that vision and ignore the disgraceful unfolding in Master Malfred's bedroom.

I was told to keep my silence or find myself spider gagged before the two of them used me for their pleasures that night. I would like to say I took it like the professional I am, but that would be a lie.

Despite my long history of special services, this first experience with Master Malfred and the Vampire was almost too much for me to bear. I got through it with many tears, and a few cries of pain. They were neither gentle nor conscientious lovers. The two of them did their damnest to outdo the other in a contest over their conquest.

When at last day were both sated (and it took several times each, yuck and double yuck) I was held down and rubbed with alcohol most viciously by the Vampire to clean up the mess day had made of the boy with dare lusts.

Master Malfred then took a wire pad and scrubbed the dead flesh from his brand mark on my chest. Master Jonas had to hold me down while he did this. The pain was terrible. I openly sobbed and wailed during the whole process. Neither of them paid me any mind nor did they offer any words of kindness.

To complete this horrific experience, Master Jonas cuffed my arms behind me then hauled me into the bed forced to lay between him and Master Malfred. This was their answer to guarding me so they could slumber without fear of my fit throwing.

I laid there in the dark with the two vile creatures snuggling the bonded boy imagining the fantasy love affair with the girl in the black collar. I admit I broke down weeping several times over this latest indignity.

I did manage to stay focused on that girl's pretty heart shaped lips and ample bosom enough to make it till daylight without losing my shit too badly. Thank Gott I saw her when I did, or I really think that night would have been the final one for Christian Axel.

That morning Master Malfred called for the Haus doctor to come check on my brands to make sure there were no signs of infection. Master Leo come into the room and demanded they let me free of my bonds before that man came for the examination. Master Malfred and Master Jonas finally relented though they argued quite a bit that it was safer to keep me restrained.

The doctor came by in record time. He lived on the first floor in a fancy apartment granted him by the Dominants of the Haus. My Masters had decided to wait in the next room to allow the doctor to work uninterrupted. I was looking for signs of disgust, pity, anything that may suggest I had misjudged this poisoning, enabling motherfucker.

He finished his task, then began to put up his things. I cleared my throat to catch his attention. When he was distracted I reached out and carefully palmed the thermometer he laid on the bedside table next to me.

I narrowed my eyes and glared at him with disgust. “Uhm, Sir, does it bother you much to treat the ailments of children that are being held hostage, raped, and eventually killed by the rich adults of this Haus?”

The old doctor chuckled. “That is none of your business, Maxx. I do my job like you do for your Masters.”

I shook my head and looked down. “There was no other job outside this Haus you could have acquired. Or at least you could call the authorities and tell them what happens in this place, ja?”

He laughed even harder at that. "Nein, I could get other jobs. I am a doctor after all. I chose this job because I like the perks. I get the finest boys and girls trained in the art of sex for my bed as gifts from their grateful Dominants. Then I have a fine apartment and the pay is marvelous. My only real pain in the ass has always been you Maxx. I never had to deal with insanity in this job. All the rest of your kind were mercifully put to the yard before they caused me issues. I don't know what you have, but these idiots keep protecting you and having me sew you up. I personally would shoot you full of an overdose and end your life if I thought I wouldn't be fined for it. I look forward to the day you are finally taken to the yard. My life will be full of peace and quiet once more. I don't care much for you Maxx, but I seem to recall you already knew that. My advice to you is to jump from the banister and end this bullshit. You are hopelessly schizophrenic, and let's face it soon enough they will tie you down for good to take the only thing you ever been good for."

I nodded. "Ah, you are right. I am good for nothing but warming a cock. I will certainly consider your advice. Thank you for the mercy of it."

He scoffed. "I told you many times, Maxx, there is no mercy in this Haus. You haven't learned that yet, then you are not only crazy you are stupid too. Good day to you." He turned around and left in a huff.

I grinned while I got off the bed and put on my breeches with speed. I rushed down the hall but stopped to listen to the doctor tell my Masters of his latest findings.

When day thanked him I waited until he had left before emerging appearing demure.

Master Malfred laughed "Ah, Christian Axel. There you are, meine Taube. Your doctor says you are good to go. Isn't that wonderful news?"

I nodded never looking up from the floor. "Ja, it is great Master. Uhm, I need to catch the doctor. He left his tool behind. May I call him back to give it to him?"

Master Leo frowned. "Malfred, don't allow this. I will go yell for the doctor."

Master Malfred growled. "You don't tell me what to do Leo. Ja, meine Taube, go to the door and yell for him to return this minute. He is within hearing distance if you hurry."

I ran to the door, threw it open then took off running at full speed without hesitation. I heard Master Malfred and Master Leo yelling for me to stop. I rushed right for the retreating doctor. I caught him just at the top step.

He saw me heading for him holding up his thermometer in my hand, "Ah, Maxx. Thank you. I would have been lost without that." He reached out to take it from me.

I stopped my flight and walked over slowly with my hand outstretched ignoring my screaming Masters quickly running my way. The doctor noticed them and looked past me with his brows raised.

"What the hell? Maxx. What are they yelling about?" He shot me a look of concern.

I turned around and shot a wicked smile at my nearing pursuers then turned back to the doctor. "One is for all the sorrows, two is for your perverted joys. Three is for all the lost girls, and four is for every dead boy. Five is for your fixing the silver, and six that brought you much gold. Seven is the punishment for the secrets you never told." I then pushed the startled doctor with all my strength.

He was surprised by the sudden weight shift. He tripped and was unable to recapture his balance. With a loud scream he went headfirst right down the stairs. Master Jonas, Master Malfred and Master Leo all arrived just in time to hear the doctors neck snap. He traveled the rest of the way to his apartment in silence, just the way he had lived his life he found his death. My Masters looked at me with fear in dare eyes.

Master Leo wailed out. "Christian Axel, what the fuck have you done?."

I giggled and sang out with a spin, "Ring around the roses. A pocket full of posies, ashes…ashes…the doctor fell down…"

Chapter 57: Family Ties

Master Malfred grabbed my leash and yelled out in a panic. "We have to get back inside the apartment before someone sees us. We must hurry." He dragged me with much strength toward his house, Master Jonas and Master Leo following at full speed behind us.

Once inside, the frightened Elder Malfred slammed his door shut and locked it tightly. The other Masters stood there panting and sweating, shooting looks of terror at me. I giggled and twirled with glee. I got that rat bastard at last. I had waited a long time to send that motherfucker to hell. This was a happy day for Mad Maxx.

Master Malfred turned around to face his brothers still out of breath from the wild running. "Okay, I don't think anyone saw Christian Axel do that but us in this room. Bladrick and Claus will find his corpse when they come home from their breakfast in the Great Hall. He is on the back step so unless Gretta, Peter or Agnette come by sooner, the man will be cold as the winter before anyone even knows he has expired. We need only play dumb and agree that all of us were here in this apartment when the good doctor fell to his death. He must have tripped, ja?"

Master Leo and Master Jonas nodded their heads in agreement. I watched them walk to the couch and sit down together with expressions of disbelief. Master Malfred looked at me and then to the floor.

He took a deep breath. “Why did you do that, Christian Axel? You must realize we should call the Guard to have you put to the yard or sent below to be locked away in a cell for what you just did.”

I giggled at that. “Ja, you should but you won’t. I cannot suck your cock from the grave, and you throw out your back in the stone cell when you fuck me, ha-ha. Call them. Send me. I don’t fucking care. I wish you would. I dare you to call. I double dog dare you.”

He reared back and backhanded me with force sending me to my knees. “You insolent little bastard. I am sick of this insanity. Stop this now or I will kill you with my bare hands.” Master Leo and Master Jonas jumped up from their seats protesting loudly at his loss of temper at me.

“You hit that boy again, I will murder you Malfred,” shouted Master Jonas.

“Hitting him and your threats is what caused this nightmare in the first place, dumbass. Keep your hands off him,” cried out Master Leo.

I laughed then sung out loudly, “Cross your hearts, I hope you all die. I will stick a needle in your eyes.” I rubbed my burning cheek and rocked in place drooling like the mad dog I had become.

Master Malfred glared at me. “Are you motherfuckers listening to this? Do you not hear him threatening to kill us? Am I the only sane one around here? We have to do something. He is going to rise up and murder us all. The legend of the Priceless is not all hype. These mad ones are able to override their directives, you know."

Master Jonas growled. "The boy is barely big enough to injure a fly Malfred. That stupid doctor was in a precarious position is all. Did you think he has a leash for decorations? Nein, it is to keep him in line, fool. There is a reasonable way to fix this attitude of his. We restrain those arms, then he cannot push anyone down the stairs. Nor be sticking needles anywhere."

Master Leo clicked his tongue then snapped, "How about this, you stop abusing the boy. He is killing out of frustration. You never listen to him. So, he has found a way to get you to hear him. You and Malfred use him like the plaything and burn him like a cow. Well, he was merciful enough to grant you a warning. Keep fucking with him and you will end up like the doctor. Leo for one will not end up on this boy's shit list. Christian Axel, you listen to me, your Master Leo. whatever it is that I done to offend you, I offer my apologies and demand punishment for it right this minute."

I shook my head and giggled. "Leo is the crooked man, who went the crooked mile. He has the crooked sixpence and lives a crooked style. He is a crooked rat that lied to the crooked Maus. He betrayed Christian Axel within the crooked Haus. Ah, ha-ha-ha." I wrung my hands and tapped on my forehead to try to get better reception from the transmissions you know.

Master Leo's eyes went wide as he led himself fall back to his bottom on the couch. "Oh shit. I didn't think, Oh meine Gott, what will I do?"

Master Malfred gasped. "You understood that nonsense? What the fuck did he just say?"

Master Jonas glared at Master Malfred. "He said nothing. The boy has blown his fucking gaskets. I for one will not entertain the rantings of this mad boy. You are both fools to even bother speaking to him. Get the ball gag and this shit will stop."

Master Leo groaned and put up his hand demanding silence. "Nein, Jonas. Christian Axel is angry with me for the blood bonding. I was so busy trying to keep Gretta from punishing him by sending him to the yard, I didn't consider that he would find offense in my trapping him in the metal. I listened to you Jonas and Claus and forgot to hear the voice of the one I love. I deserve his anger, maybe more than any of you do. He trusted me and I let him down, like my Maus." He sighed then looked at the floor. *He finally got it. Leo was now on his way to redemption with me, but he still had a journey ahead of him. I wasn't going to just forgive his selfishness because he recognized it.*

Master Jonas shook his head. "You are the biggest pussy I ever met, Leo. You are going to let the desires of this disturbed boy dictate your moves as his Dominant? Really? You are his better. It is his function to do what he is told. His will belongs to his Masters. He has no right to question them for any decision we make regarding his best interests."

Master Malfred nodded. "Jonas is correct Leo. You give this boy rights that are not his to receive. He is our property and should be fucking grateful for our kindness. Others that have done less found their graves."

Master Leo scoffed. "Equal service means exactly that, fellas. You take more than you give Christian Axel, or you grant him hell, then he is going to level that out, or return the favor."

Master Jonas shot a look of anger at me. "You listen to your man and Master Jonas, Christian Axel. You dare to attack me, or if you think to send me to the bottom of the stairs, you better rethink it this minute. I will make you sorry you were ever born. I for one will not be intimidated by this little kid."

I covered my mouth and giggled while singing. "Three blind mice. Three deaf mice. See how day run. It will be so much fun. Day all chased after their Priceless blood bonded wife. He will cut their tails off with his kitchen knife. Have you ever seen the corpse when it is drained of life? Three dead mice."

Master Malfred reached out and backhanded me harder than the first time right in the mouth. "Shut the fuck up, Christian Axel. Enough of this rhyming. I am getting the gag." He stormed to his bedroom to retrieve the restraining object.

I rubbed the blood that poured from my busted lips and laughed without humor singing the rhyme under my breath. I never rose from my kneeling nor stopped my gentle swaying. The madness was erupting like the volcano from Mad Maxx's catatonic form. The wheel room began to fill with the random strikes of the lightning of an electrical storm within.

I glanced above my head to see the vortex cyclone growing in strength. I shrugged and giggled harder. There was nothing I could do about this strange world of the dead. I was trapped there until I found my way home. I shot a look at the saddened Master Leo and shuddered.

"Master Leo. Did you say I could see the lambs? I need to see them. They will make the confusion go away." I looked back above me to see the cyclone dropping down closer every moment.

Master Jonas looked at Master Leo in bewilderment. "Lambs? What the hell is he rambling about now?"

Master Leo smiled with glee. "Ah, that's it. Come Jonas. Grab Malfred too. We will take Christian Axel to see his lambs I bought for him. We will take the main stairs. When the doctor is found none of us will be home. They are in the barn Jonas, don't you see? No one will suspect our involvement in his fall. Come hurry." He dashed at me and grabbed my leash headed for the door rapidly unlocking it.

Master Malfred came into the room carrying the spider gag demanding to know what was going on. Master Jonas shrugged and told him there was a plan to hide the murder but to do it they had to go with the schwuler. The Dominant threw the gag onto his couch without another question and took off to follow Master Leo, Master Jonas, and me out of his apartment.

The four of us moved with much speed to the Haus door. I glared at the door guards for a moment. Then I saw the pretty blond from the hallway come through the door with another black collar female. I immediately melted in a swoon as she and the other woman backed up into the door and bowed to us as our group walked out.

She glanced up and flashed a coy smile at me. I nearly broke my neck trying to keep my eyes on that girl. I didn't even consider that it was strange her flirting so openly with me. One must understand, I was topless, scarred beyond reason, freshly burned to shit, drooling and filthy as hell.

All I cared about was a beautiful female seemed interested in this worthless boy. I wanted nothing more than to make this woman my frau and start my family with her. This was truly insane since I didn't even know her name.

Master Jonas and Master Malfred were following behind me. They noticed my constant turning and craning to look at this girl. They turned around to see what had caught my interest. The two of them saw the object of my sudden attraction. Master Malfred narrowed his eyes at Master Jonas. The Vampire shrugged and rolled his as if he found my attention to the female silly.

Master Jonas then said, "Keep your eyes to the ground, Christian Axel. You stop ogling things that are forbidden to you this minute or I blindfold you for good." I groaned but did as told not willing to incite him to carry out his threat.

The weather was cold, and as I said I was topless thanks to Master Malfred's directive that I wear no shirt until I was willing to bathe. I shivered in the cruel winter wind. Master Leo rushed even faster toward the warmth of the barn when he realized the error of not at least grabbing my jacket. I nearly had to run to keep up with him.

Thankfully, we made it to the lambs in record time. I rushed into the pen into the awaiting affections of my family. The three Masters stood at the doorway watching me and casting baleful looks around the place. They appeared anxious that the doctor had not been discovered yet. I could sense none of them wanted to be hanging out in a cool, smelly barn, but this was their best hope to keep safe from scrutiny.

In a short time, the two made small talk with Master Leo inquiring about the reasons behind his odd purchase for the Priceless. As my Master told the story of how he came to own five lambs, I pulled Geraldine close to me for our own private discussion.

I whispered into her ear. "I got Gunter and the doctor. Ivar will fall next, meine liebe. Is this enough for your happiness?"

Geraldine chewed for a moment then leaned forward and said, "Beware Peter. He raises Karl, Alexie, and Mila. You must also consider Anna for the X list. All of Peter's brothers and sisters must die. There must be nothing between you and that Haus door. Kill them. Destroy the Voting Council and unblock the door. You are a man of your word. Olaf and Vilber will line the yard. You will destroy Malfred and Claus the moment the metal is gone. Then in order, Gretta, Cora, Agnette, Peter, Jonas, and Leo last. You will leave alive no one that rules this place of lawlessness. You must burn this Haus to the ground and avenge the murdered silvers. That is your mission."

I nodded, "I understand Geraldine. I thank you for your wise counsel and mercy." I kissed her cheek, and she licked my face in return making me giggle.

Master Malfred bellowed out, "Are you speaking to the lamb, Christian Axel? What is this you say to it?"

I looked at the ground and wrung my hands in a startle "I ask if she likes her oats. I wondered what they would taste like in case I wanted to try some of it," I lied.

Master Jonas rolled his eyes. "Damn boy. You won't even eat your own food. Leave the lambs' dinner alone."

Master Malfred put up his hand demanding silence. "Nein. The boy lies. I heard him speaking of killing you and me. I swear it, the Priceless is taking orders from a Gott damned lamb."

Master Leo gasped. "Surely you are being paranoid Malfred. Lambs cannot speak, fool."

Master Malfred nodded. "Not to us maybe, but to the schizophrenic anything is possible. Answer me, Christian

Axel. Did you hear that lamb order my death and your Master Jonas's too?"

I shrugged as I hugged Ryker by the neck singing out. "Baa-baa black sheep do you know a fool? Ja, sir. Ja, sir, he is the one that drools. He will kill the Masters. He will ravish the maids. Watch out for the little boy, which knows only pain."

Master Jonas growled out in fury. "That is, it. Get your ass out here Christian Axel. I have had it. I will not entertain this underhanded threatening you keep doing." I got up and walked to the gate as the Vampire reached inside snatching my leash with a harsh jerk nearly pulling me face first to the ground.

Master Leo came forward trying to speak some sense into Master Jonas, but he would hear nothing. He took off storming for the Haus dragging me behind him. Master Leo and Master Malfred had to run to keep up with the fuming Vampire.

He practically kicked in the Haus door then marched me right down the stairs to the torture chambers below. I wrung my hands, giggled, and sung nasty little nursery rhymes under my breath the whole way.

I was not frightened of his thudding. I no longer cared about anything the monsters did to me. I hoped that maybe a bit of pain would focus my shattering mind, but in reality I thought I was too high to feel much. That fucking doctor had shot me up with something before I ended his poisoning me.

When we arrived in the crowded torture rooms the place began to clear. Frightened, black and silver collars fell to dare knees till we passed them. I watched them scatter running fast as day could to get the fuck away from the observably angered Vampire and frightened looking Elders following his path.

Curious Dominants took to the walls allowing Master Jonas to get by them without difficulty. I smiled and giggled at all the hubbub this false tough guy was causing. It doesn't make you a bad ass to beat up a little kid. It makes you a bully without a hodensack. You know, like that Russell and Debbie, speaking of which.

There was one Dominant that didn't scurry away when day saw Master Jonas on his rampage. Master Peter stood at the branding room door with a strange woman standing on his left. That idiot father of mine yelled out at the furious Vampire that he wanted him to meet this female.

Master Jonas bellowed out, "Fuck off, Peter. I have discipline to do. I meet your worthless friends another time."

Master Peter shot a look of embarrassment at this heavy set, and super ugly female, then stepped in front of Master Jonas. "Jonas. I must insist you take a moment to be polite. This is an American. She has the streak of the Priceless in her mate and she has a daughter born last March for sale. The year, pedigree and gender are correct. This may be the myth you seek."

Master Jonas's mouth about hit the floor and he stopped dead in his tracks. "Huh? You say she has the markings of the female priceless in her blood?"

Master Peter shook his head. "Nein, her mate, the kid's father does. The kid could be the one of legend. This woman is vile, brother. The environment is already violent, and she is looking to sell."

Master Jonas turned to shoot me a look of wonder. "Ah, did she bring the kid? I wish to see this creature."

Master Peter nodded. "Ja, she did. The kid is in my apartment with Agnette. She desired to see this setup in the Haus. I was contacted by a mutual friend of ours, he is her lover and teaching her the ways of D/s. He told me of this possible match."

Master Jonas nodded. "Ah ja, Karl. Malfred told me this man has been repaid for a favor but didn't say the nature of it."

Master Peter laughed. "Uhm, ja the favor was Karl claims paternity. His mother is the schizophrenic. He cannot prove this kid his own, but the woman has a man in the States. She is here on holiday. The man is off in Turkey enlisted in that dreadful war with Vietnam. Ah, but we are wasting time. Do you dare to ignore this opportunity? Come meet this beast and bring the Priceless with you. She would like a demonstration of correction methods. Perhaps you would allow me the honor of proving our methods worthy?" Master Peter looked at me with an evil grin.

I looked at the woman of whom he was speaking. She was foul looking and had beady cruel eyes. I saw her looking me over with disgust. I immediately disliked her and wondered how any mother, other than my own worthless one, could be so brutal to offer to sell a baby to this Haus of monsters.

Master Jonas shot a look of worry at Master Leo then whispered to Master Peter. "Uhm, tell you what, I agree to allow you punish Christian Axel in my stead. I will take Leo and Malfred to view this kid in your apartment to keep them busy. Beware, he is in the acute phase of his cycle. Make fucking sure you restrain him tight, or he will get you, not that I would miss you much."

Master Peter scoffed but reached out and snatched my leash from Master Jonas's grip. "I know how to handle Maximillian, Jonas. You go see the item and let me know what you think. That fucking Karl is riding my ass for his favor and Malfred told me that it took much convincing him to fuck this foul woman to begin with. I think you can see why, ja?" He shot a look at that chunky female with disgust.

Master Jonas laughed. "Ja, I bet. Get going. I will handle the dogs." He turned around to deal with his railing Dominant brothers while Master Peter dragged me behind him to rejoin that evil looking female.

The American woman stood there eyeing me while Master Peter spoke to her in English. I didn't understand enough of the language at the time to know what he was saying. She smiled then walked around me eyeing my flesh.

It made me shiver to have that nasty creature examining me like a piece of beef. Then she walked back to Master Peter's side and pointed at the branding door. Master Peter laughed then shot a nervous look to see if Master Jonas, Leo and Malfred had left the torture rooms.

Master Jonas had successfully pushed the two of them up the stairs headed for the fifth floor to see this woman's female kid that she wished to sell to Master Jonas. I then suddenly realized Peter and the Vampire were attempting to purchase a female Priceless for my mate.

I shot a look of horror at this woman. I could not even fathom making children with a kid from this woman's loins, yuck. Master Peter opened the branding door and dragged me inside. I thought he was giving this female a tour until he ordered me to get on the table.

I stood there feeling confused by his order. "Nein. You cannot burn me, Master Peter. It is forbidden. You do not hold my silver any longer."

He jerked my leash harshly. "You will do what the fuck I tell you. Your man and Master Jonas gave me permission to punish you anyway I see fit. Debbie here wants a demonstration of a branding. Well guess what, you are it Maximillian."

I spun in Master Maxx's lap so fast I nearly fell to the floor. "What did you just say? You said Debbie, Master. My mother Debbie? No, wait, you said that baby was for sale and that the father was Karl. That is not my daddy, but..." I trailed off nearly coming to tears as I recalled my father was in Turkey in January 1973, and my mother did visit Germany with me before I turned a year old.

Master Maxx reached out and grabbed my chin looking into my eyes with pity. "Ja, Meine Liebe. I told you I met your mother a long time ago. Well, I knew your father too, the one that claims you for his own. To be honest, no one really knows if Karl was truthfully your father or if the American is the honest one. She was cuckolding him with that vicious bastard from the Haus. To this day it is unsure. Karl was a Dane and German, my heart. Your American father was of a Danish line too. Only a blood test would tell, and I don't think I would want to know if I were you. Either way, here I am and here you are too."

I stared at the floor breaking out into a full-on crying jag. "You already knew you would buy me when you came here didn't you Master. You lied to me. This was a set up. You fucked with my head. I never had a choice."

He shook his head and pulled me into a tight hug. "Nein, Meine Liebe, I swear to you I never thought in a million years I would choose you nor you would choose me in return. I only came here because of Peter and Jonas's continuing to pressure me to at least look at you. Thanks to my meeting and knowing your mother from so long ago I refused for eight years. I intended only to take a quick look to shut them up, then move on. I was going to call the authorities to have you removed from this horror life, but when I saw you I knew it was always meant to be. The authorities never did come to save you in all this time she has been abusing you. I knew it was hopeless, besides you are the Priceless mate that I waited all my life to find. We are the same Meine Liebe; our hearts are intertwined by the same brutal fate."

I sobbed. "I have been in that horrible Haus. Oh Master, you said if you go through the doors they never let you go free. They are going to come after me even if I break my collar. That is what you are telling me, isn't it."

Master Maxx sighed loudly, "Ja, which is what I am telling you. The Haus will never let you go free once you enter her doors. Meine Liebe, if I had not chosen you, Debbie would have killed you by now. Please listen to me. This is not the life we wanted; it is the life we got. Please let me continue this story. I can explain everything if you allow me to. This was not a set up, but it surely was destiny. You and I were meant to be together for all our lives. I have to believe that and meine heart, I think you do too. If not, then I assure you time will tell the truth of it. I want to be free of Das Kaiser Haus, and I am taking meine Demonseed Frau with me when I go."

I looked up into his eyes. "You swear that, Master? You and I will not raise our children in that horrible place? We will escape from it forever?"

He nodded with an expression of sureness on his face. "Ja, I swear this Meine Liebe. My children will never set foot in the Haus. I will protect you with my life and one day we will both have that home with the sheep and the hund. Have faith in me. I have it in you." He kissed my lips gently.

I sniffed loudly. "I do believe in you, Master. I apologize for being upset. It won't happen again."

Master Maxx chuckled bitterly. "I wish that were true, Meine Liebe. However, that is one apology I will not accept nor believe. You and I will shed many tears, but we shall do it together. Nothing worth having is easy, meine heart. We were born to demons in the bowels of Hell. Crawling up from that inferno pit will cause much pain and even losses we never expected. That said, do understand we will get to the top. Now I continue this horror story, ja?"

I nodded. "Thank you for the mercy of it, Master." He nodded and hugged me for a few more moments before turning me back around and beginning his tale once more.

"Master Peter grabbed my collar and lifted me with much strength to the table before I could protest further. The American woman couldn't understand my cries of terror as my father began to restrain me to the table. I attempted to get up and he smacked me down, nearly knocking me unconscious from his blow.

I had only barely recovered from his strike when he lit the Bunsen burner. The woman leaned up against the wall with an arrogant smile on her face. I called her many foul names in my language, but she didn't understand my insults. Master Peter told me to shut my mouth. I glared at him full of fury.

"I will kill you for this Master. You just wait. You sign your death warrant this day with that branding iron." I struggled against my bounds.

He chuckled then began heating up his P iron. "Ah, you will do no such a thing, Maximillian. I am your ticket to medical school. You will do whatever I tell you to do or find yourself in a world of monsters without any aid. Do you think you have it bad in this Haus? Wait till you see what awaits you outside it. Like this Frau here, this is the normal, feast your eyes on the real devil, my boy. The Americans are the power of the world, and they will eat ignorant little German boys for their breakfast." He pressed his branding iron to my right shoulder sending me into shrieks of agony.

Debbie began laughing with thrill at my screams of pain. I shot her a look of anger then recalled the only English curse words I knew.

"Fucking bitch," I yelled at her.

That shut the fat harpy up. She glared at me with her rat eyes. I sucked in my wails by focusing my mind on hating her with all my being. I decided right then and there, I wanted nothing to do with anything that came from her world. That baby she brought was never to be my frau.

Master Maxx chuckled. "So much for that. Never say never, ja? I was way off on that idea. Thank Gott too. I never been happier with any choice I ever made than I have been with choosing you Meine Liebe." He hugged me tightly from behind while I hugged his big arms back.

Well, that said, it would be eight years before I re-thought that plan, so on with the story in the right order, ja?

Master Jonas, Malfred and Leo come barging through the door too fucking late to stop that branding business just as Master Peter began to untie me. Master Leo let out a loud angry jell. Master Jonas growled, and Master Malfred fell into the wall in disbelief at what he was witness to.

“What the fuck, Peter,” Master Jonas bellowed in a fury.

Master Peter chuckled with evil “You said to punish the Priceless. Well, he is punished and won’t soon forget it.”

Master Leo groaned,. “You motherfucker. You took advantage. Jonas. Call Claus, have this fucker exiled.”

Master Jonas nodded. “I need not call Claus. Peter, I demand retribution. You will receive lashes and time in the dungeon along with a fine for marking up our Priceless.”

Master Peter smiled. “Sure thing, Jonas. Do your worst. No matter what you do, the boy wears my mark. You all look at it closely. It is the future. Enjoy it while you can. Soon enough he will belong to me again. Enough of this bullshit. What did you think Jonas? Is this the one?”

Master Jonas glared at Master Peter. “Get the price. This is the legend’s mate. The stars are right for her day of birth and the omens of this day say, ja. The myth is a reality at long last. Even the eyes are the right color. Do not let this creature leave with that prize no matter the price she wants, pay it.”

I glared at Debbie, who couldn't understand the discussion, over to Master Jonas. "I refuse this match. Go to hell, all of you," I growled out.

Master Malfred shook his head still appearing confused. "You say that today, but that baby will be a woman soon enough. You will change your mind Christian Axel. I agree with Jonas. Pay this beast, then send her the fuck away. She stinks of cheap wine and is foul on the eyes."

Master Peter sighed. "There is a problem. She desires to have membership with the Haus along with a cash payment for this kid."

The Masters immediately shot her looks of disbelief then Master Jonas bellowed out, "Thief, she is a greed monster."

Master Peter smiled. "Wait, I know. We put her through the submissive program to gain entry. She will be told all have to do it. That will end her desire to enter this Haus as a member, ja? Let me handle the details. You need to take the boy for treatment. I may have burned a bit too deep; I am rusty, ja?" He giggled.

Master Jonas shot a look of hate at Master Malfred as he dropped his head feigning shame. "Seems everyone around here needs a refresher course in branding lately. You handle the details with this monstrosity, then you meet with me in the thud room in two hours for your punishment. Take the baby to our contact black collar for holding till we find a proper place to keep her till the Guard can take her into custody at her eighth year. Make sure the American authorities will not miss the kid. We want no questions nor snoopers."

Master Leo snapped, "Are you serious? You are going to buy this little treasure I just held for this horrible Haus to tear apart? Fuck, you are bloodthirsty, Jonas. She is tiny. What the hell is wrong with all of you?"

Master Jonas glared at Master Leo. "Mind your business, Leo. In fact, you take Christian Axel back home and see he is treated. I have decided to stay here with Malfred and Peter to make sure this transaction goes smoothly. I trust neither of them. Get going, you two. Oh, beware the stairs. It would be terrible if you were tripped, I mean fell down them." He chuckled with diabolical humor.

Master Leo grabbed my leash. "Oh, I am fucking leaving with Christian Axel. I am taking this nightmare shit right to Gretta too. You cannot just go buying little baby girls to save and fuck in your perverted fantasies. She will put a stop to this." He pulled me toward the door.

Master Malfred laughed loudly. "Ah, fool. Who the fuck do you think chose Karl to be the daddy? Tell Gretta all you like. She is in on it as is Cora. See you later, brother." Master Leo gasped, then tore out of there hauling me behind him to the sounds of the room breaking out in laughter behind us.

Master Leo appeared distracted to the point of panic. He rushed through the crowded room muttering under his breath that the Haus was nothing but a rat's nest. I moaned in pain from that latest burn. My chest, back and arm were on fire from the brutal treatment of them. I was as upset as Master Leo about this discovery of the Vampire and Master Malfred trying to buy a female to play my Priceless mate.

This could only mean that even Master Jonas intended to keep me in my metal. Why else try to bring my mate to me rather than allow me to seek her out. I reeled inside with the final understanding the collar had always been a trap, and the promise of the bolt cutters a fantasy. I wanted to break down in a crying jag but somehow none of it mattered.

I understood that I never had believed any of them anyway. I had assumed from the beginning they had no reason to want to see me free. If I were going to break my collar it would be by outfoxing them or murdering anyone that stood in my way. If I kept quiet and pretended to still be buying their bullshit, then it was possible to sneak through their barriers.

It was risky to play this game so close to my hip, but I was sure it could be done. I would wait until the last possible moment, then kill the entire Voting Council but Peter, Agnette and Gretta. There would be no time to rise anyone to replace the missing members. Cora, Claus, Malfred and Jonas would assume that with their men and woman in place to prevent my rise, there would be no need to push them to vote nein for me to be Dominant.

Master Peter and Master Leo were the only ones that wanted to see me bust my metal for truth. It suddenly occurred to me that my twisted father's lust was my salvation and my lover Leo's caring soul my vehicle for escape. I would have no choice but to team up in a plot with both of them or face a lifetime of servitude on my knees sucking these bastards' cocks.

I shook my head in pure disbelief at the horror of having to sell myself back into my father's bed to find my freedom. To make things worse, I knew if I failed to raise my future Frau as per my agreement with him, then I would be trapped providing him the special services. This was a rock and a hard place either way I went.

At least with Peter, I had a chance to be shut of the nightmare life. If I tried to do this without his and Leo's aid I would be as good as dead. The conspiracy of the Priceless was much deeper than I could have ever imagined. Almost everyone in power was in on it in some way or another.

I had to pray Peter was willing to work out a private deal behind everyone's back. I had to wonder if he wanted me to break that collar so badly why he continued to work with the shady Master Malfred. I finally decided he expected me to come to my senses and contact him.

I knew my father. He was arrogant in his statements despite doing the opposite, hoping I would catch his hint. He was saying to me that he no longer wanted to ride with the liars that left him behind. With my aid he could eventually rise to claim Elder or even Head of the Haus when he came of age.

However, to do that, he needed Cora moved out of the way. It wouldn't do him harm to remove Jonas, Malfred and Claus. He was right about one thing. He had trained me well. Peter knew there was one person in that Haus close enough to his enemies, who had the skills to clear his path right to the top. Like it or not. I was ready to bury the hatchet with my father at long last.

Well, at least for a bit. I assumed I had waited this long to kill the bastard what was a few more years? Besides, I had already been fucked by him hundreds of times before I knew who he was to me. What was a few hundred more? With all I had already endured, this twisted shit was normal for the Mad Maxx by this point. You cannot do worse when you already have.

Master Leo took me right to his apartment and locked all his devices with shallow breaths appearing to be hyperventilating. I stood there wringing my hands and staring at the floor while he panted and wiped his forehead of sweat.

Then I cleared my throat without looking up. "Master Leo, we must speak to Peter. He will help us."

Master Leo gasped. "Oh, meine Gott. Not now Christian Axel. We don't have time for another psychotic fit."

I chuckled at that. "Uhm, nein, I am not talking of hallucinations nor delusions Master. Peter is the key to my breaking my metal. You asked for my forgiveness for trapping me in my collar? I give you the punishment this minute. You must arrange for me to meet with my father and join me in a side plot to beat Jonas, Claus, Gretta, Cora and Malfred. They have all fooled us. Peter knows how to fool them back."

My Master shook his head. "Christian Axel, meine hase, listen to yourself. The man is an incestuous child molester. He will, I cannot even say it. If you make a deal with him who is to say he won't hand you over to the conspirators anyway? The man is a slimy two-faced rat."

I nodded. "I certainly hope he is, Master. If so then he will choose the side that grants him everything he desires. He wants to be the Power, and he wants to have his son back in his possession. I can give him both if he will aid me in breaking my collar. Peter is out for Peter. He won't hand over his secret weapon, trust me on this."

Master Leo walked over and dropped down onto his couch. "If I do this thing, meine hase, you will forgive me my transgressions against you, but I may be handing you over to be killed or hijacked. You ask much of me."

I sighed. "And you took much from me, Master. You cannot undo the hurt you caused me. I am not one to forgive so easily. I have thought of killing you and still think it would be for the best. However, you do this for me, I will forget that you handed me over for raping, then raped me into unbreakable metal for daring to love and trust you."

Master Leo looked at the floor. "Is that how you see it? That I used your love and trust against you to trap you in your collar?"

I nodded. “It is the only way to see it because it is the truth of what you did. You can lie to yourself, but not to me. You knew you were sending me to flush out the enemies of Cora and Claus. You also knew if you blood bonded me I was trapped in my metal. You knew I would not question the one I loved. You betrayed me, and I should not trust you ever again, but I have no choice as usual. You do it this time, then I will murder slow and painfully no matter how long it takes me to do it.”

Master Leo sniffed back his tears. “Okay, I will stop playing the innocent fool. I think you are right, Christian Axel. I wanted to have you for my own so much I never stopped to think about your feelings in the matter. I thought I was doing you a service by stepping up as your guardian. I admit I didn’t desire to see you break that metal. It was wrong and selfish of me, but there it is.”

I looked at him with fury in my eyes,. “Ah, you see I already knew that Leo. You helping me or not? I ask only this once. You deny me then I wouldn’t want to be you.”

He nodded. “Ja. I will do as you ask and take what comes as my punishment. I must ask, is there any chance that I could earn your love and trust once more?”

I kept my hateful glare on him. “I doubt it, but stranger things have happened, ja? You will do well to recall you threw away that so called treasure you found in my heart. I didn’t steal it back from you. You must first earn my forgiveness, then help me earn my freedom from the metal you trapped me in. Then, and only then, can we revisit this trust and love bullshit."

Master Leo nodded while looking at the floor. "I understand Christian Axel. I will do both of those things and prove my honesty to you in time. I will vow to never touch you any longer as well."

I laughed with sarcasm. "Cut the bullshit, Leo. You are still my Master and man. I do what I am fucking told. You want your special services rights, then so be it. Do you think I give two shits anymore what any of you do to me? Nein, stop playing the martyr. It is unfashionable around this Haus of criminals. You wanted to fuck me so bad you raped your way into keeping all others from disputing your rights to do it. You fucking knew I was straight and admitted I would never be the raging homosexual. Despite that you used me for your pleasures like all the others do, because that is all I am good for around here. You proved that the second you cut that member of your and broke my heart with it. You want your services, so take them, but don't you ever tell me you love me again or I will bite your motherfucking cock off the next time I blow you."

Master Leo pulled his hand to his chest and gasped dramatically. "You are going too far. I never used you. I did respect your space. I never took without your coming on to me first."

I roared with laughter. "Oh? I thought I was going swimming in the blue water. Instead, I ended up being told we were there for your rights, or did I hallucinate that lover boy? I don't believe I did, but let's call Gretta in here and see what she recalls of that incident?"

Master Leo growled out angrily. "I did that because you thought I would leave you if I didn't call my rights. You are brainwashed into thinking you are only worth what others can take from you."

I could barely breathe; I was laughing so hard at this point. "Ah, so clever Leo. You thought the best way to undo the evil of these men around me is to do the same thing, only a bit more gently? That is fucking genius. You allowed my fears to incite you to create a phobia. Brilliant. Bravo. I say give this man a medal. I believed in your bullshit Leo. I really fell for it. You were no better than Ryker. He told me he loved me for truth too. He also saw nothing wrong with guilting me into laying there for his penetration, though he also knew I was straight. He tried to give me the orgasm, but I couldn't find interest in him like that. You lucked out and got me a few times, but luckily that madness has passed. I no longer find you desirable Master. I find you to be the least burdensome of my sorry lot in life, nothing more and nothing less. You wish to end me because I will be truthful, unlike you, then call the fucking Guard. I am done with this game you play with me."

Master Leo teared up. "You are cruel, Christian Axel. I have never been so hurt in my life as I am this minute. I swear you are breaking my heart."

I nodded with a brutal smile. "Equal service for equal service motherfucker. Welcome to the hell I have no choice but to endure at your hands."

There was a loud knocking at the door. Master Leo looked at me with a startle. I wrung my hands and giggled. The knocking came again, louder this time.

I flashed a look of bitter humor at him. "Ding-dong bell. Christian Axel is in hell. Who put him in? Everyone in this Haus of sin. Who will pull him out? Leo, if he doesn't sit there and pout. What a naughty Master was that who lied about love, that rat. I never asked him for all this harm. The only ones that care live in the barn."

Master Leo sniffed back his tears then rushed to his door and cracked it. "What the hell do you want Jonas?"

I heard the Vampire growl out, "Let Malfred and me in, Leo. We come to call our rights with the boy."

Master Leo sneered. "I am busy with him for my own desires. You can come back in a few hours. You already had him for yourselves. It is my turn."

They pushed the door open, knocking Master Leo out of their way. Master Jonas smiled with evil as he glanced at me standing there drooling and wringing my hands quietly.

"Well, if you are taking your rights, it seems like you have forgotten.

how Leo. The boy is mostly dressed and seems to be open for business." He came over and took up my leash.

Master Leo pushed past Master Malfred and snatched the leash out of his grip. “Fichen Dich, Jonas. I only just got started. Get out. I want my privacy with him. I am not an exhibitionist like you two. I want no audience participation.”

Master Malfred went and sat down on Master Leo’s couch. “Fine by me. Take him to your room then. Me and Jonas will find other things to entertain ourselves until you’re finished. Then we take him for our pleasure. Get to it, Leo. I don’t want to wait all night you know.” He picked up Master Leo’s romance novel and began to read the back cover.

Master Jonas crossed his arms with a grin. “Well? You heard Malfred. Get going. We will wait our turn like proper gentlemen.”

Master Leo nodded then turned to drag me down his hallway but stopped just as we got to the entry. “Uhm, what about that poor little female? Did you purchase her?”

Master Malfred scoffed. “Shit we tried. Those Americans are the most arrogant shitheads on Earth. We had to agree to let her come do the training first. When the bitch found out we wouldn’t pay for the kid until she turned eight, that harpy said, ‘you can collect that little twat in eight years then.’ can you believe that snotty cunt?”

Master Jonas snorted. “So what? We get that female in eight years and this Debbie has to put up with the bills to feed and clothe it. What the fuck do we care? She will return in six years for her so called training in this Haus.

When we get done with her she will be sorry she ever fucked with us. You be nice to Christian Axel in there, he has children to make for me. Oh shit, wait, before you go I need to put a cage back on the boy. Idiot Malfred removed my guard I noticed." He shot a hateful look at Master Malfred, that giggled at his angry glare.

I spoke out. "That won't be necessary, Master. I will find no pleasure from Master Leo. Thank you for the mercy."

Master Jonas's eyes went wide. "That is bullshit. You come here and let me put back on the device. I went to my apartment and got a fresh one." Master Leo let go of my leash while I endured the Vampire putting on a new chastity device.

Master Jonas then swatted my backside while I pulled back up my breeches, "Just leave them off Christian Axel. What is the point of putting them back on when old Leo here is about to rip them off?" He and Master Malfred laughed hard at that.

Master Leo came forward and took up my leash. "Enough, I don't care for this tormenting the boy for doing his job without quarrel. Keep your filthy hands-off my records Malfred. Come on meine hase." He pulled me behind him to his bedroom.

Master Leo dropped my leash then walked to his bed and sat down on the edge of it ordering me to shut the door. "Meine hase, the bastards will not listen to me about leaving you alone. What do you wish for me to do? Just tell me and I will do it."

I dropped my gaze to the floor. "Request your special services or leave and send them to take your place."

He scoffed. "You don't mean that Christian Axel. They intend to…" I interrupted him.

"They intend to call in their rights with me Master. You're stalling them won't make them change their minds. You either call your own or leave and let me get this out of the way. It is my job like it or not. If I refuse them or you then I get beaten to shit or worse, sent to the orchard. You do me no favors holding them off so that I can stress and worry about how bad this will hurt or make me feel. Better to just do it and end my pain quickly as possible. I asked you a bit ago to take me from this place and let me go. You didn't want to do that. I begged you to help me break my metal. You instead helped them trap me in it. I told you to call the Guard and end your games. That would not do either. Now you do me the favor of calling your privileges so I can get this bullshit out of the way or let them come take their own. Up to you. If I recall correctly, you are the Master, and I am the whore that serves him." I dropped to the floor and began removing my boots and breeches to prepare for work.

Once I was disrobed I looked back at Master Leo still holding his forehead as if in pain. "Well,? What will it be Master? Make the choice that I don't have the right to make. Sitting there wishing it were different doesn't change anything. If it did, I would be in the arms of a most beautiful frau right this minute instead of at your feet."

Master Leo looked up and sighed. "If I leave you be then the others will not hurt you as much."

I chuckled at that. "If you stay or go they will do what they do Master. Don't even try to justify this nightmare. If you wish for the special services then call them. Makes no difference to me, this I already told you. It stopped mattering a long time ago when I thought I still had a chance at a real life. That dumb boy grew the fuck up."

Master Leo shook his head. "You are ill and wounded. It is not right to ask such things of you at this time."

I nodded. "Ah, there is the truth, but I don't think Master Malfred nor Master Jonas will see it that way, will they? You will abstain but those two would fuck me if I were a week old corpse."

He chuckled at that with much bitterness in his tone. "You got that right. I hear you, meine hase. I want to be with you but maybe I only hold you and kiss you a bit."

I shrugged. "Whatever you want, however you want, and wherever you want, I do it Master. That is the way of the pleasure submissive."

He held out his arms "Then come to me, meine hase. I have missed having you in my embrace. I will make those brutes wait while I re-bond with my lover." I got up and allowed him to pull me to him.

Master Leo kissed me deeply and hauled me to his cuddle in his bed. I responded the way I was trained to do. As he kissed and hugged he became more heated with passion. It didn't take long for him to signal he was indeed calling his special services rights in full. I said nothing as I dropped to his lap to prepare him for his couple with the boy.

In the end I was right. Master Leo enjoyed his privileges to his apex with me. There are three things I will say about this particular sexual experience with him. First, this was the first time he engaged me in penetration intercourse that was not in the water. Second, he was gentle and careful with his actions during the carnal act. Third, he never again pulled the whole "I respect your right to say nein" bullshit after this single honest taking advantage of his place as my man and Master.

When he was fully satisfied he pulled me back into a spooning with him and sighed while running his hands through my hair. "I suppose you hate me for good now that I took services from you without your willingness."

I laughed. "Uhm, Leo, I hate to tell you, but I have never been willing to let you fuck me. I was always doing my job and nothing more. I am straight. That didn't change because I loved you. It only made it a little easier to endure your lust that I find unnatural. I must be honest since you will not. I always thought of a beautiful woman when you used your hand or mouth on me. I have never found my interest in the man, but I was able to believe I was enjoying the touching of someone that loved me. You were neither the man nor the frau. It was that amazing thing that brought me to my orgasm with you, not the actions. It was your heart, not your part, that I found thrill width."

Master Leo took a deep breath. "And just now? Do you still feel that way? If Jonas's nasty contraption had been gone could you have found your release with me?"

I shook my head. "Nein. I see you for what you are, Leo. You are just another man that cannot face his own truthful reflection in the mirror. I will love you again the day you can see yourself as clearly as I can. There is nothing wrong with being imperfect, Master. Where you failed is your constant making excuses for it. Now, if you are sated with my services I would kindly ask you to send in the other two. I wish to have this nightmarish part of my existence over as soon as possible. Thank you in advance for the mercy of it."

He gasped. "You don't mean that, Christian Axel. They will tear you apart. You just finished with me."

I sat up and glared at him. "Get some fucking empathy, will you? If you were me and me you, would you want to wait in a falsely kind cuddle fearing what is coming no matter what you do? Nein, you would want it over and done. When you leave Leo, glance in your mirror will you? Notice you have no silver collar, nor black either. Stop pretending you are better than the Vampire or Malfred when you are the Gott damned master by choice."

Master Leo nodded. "I hear you, meine hase. I will do as you ask. For what it is worth, believe it or not, I do love you." He got out of his bed while I attended his redressing task.

Once clothed again he began to leave but stopped at the door to look back at me waiting in my kneel next to the bed. "I know you said not to say this, but I do love you Christian Axel. I am going to prove it. I will contact Peter and help you break my hold on your collar and be free to choose to say nein." He then left and closed the door behind him.

I braced for my next workload. The Vampire and Malfred arrived within moments of Master Leo's exit. The smile on their faces told me, this would be a long night.

As usual I was not wrong about that. The Vampire and Master Malfred were the tag team from hell. I really hoped that after their bullshit the night before, some steam would have been knocked out of them, but I was not the lucky one.

The only thing that saved me, not that there was much saving to it, was that the appointment with Master Peter in the dungeons came up just as the two of them were going in for thirds. Master Leo came banging on the door informing Master Jonas that Egon from below was on the phone asking for him.

Apparently my father was in the thudding room, angered that the Vampire had gotten so caught up, uhm, in me, that he forgot he had told Peter to be there for his punishment. I was breathing a sigh of relief until Master Malfred bid Master Jonas goodbye then went back to using me for his pleasures. I managed to get through it, but I must say I was worn the hell out before that bastard finished his thrills.

Then to finish my terror of that afternoon, he demanded bath service. I winced and groaned but turned on the water to Master Leo's tub. The Dominant stood dare watching me attempt to keep my hands and other parts out of that contaminated stuff.

He chuckled with much humor while getting in. "Give it up, Christian Axel. You are already wet from the bath. May as well be ready to get in here with me."

I pulled away from the side with a tremble. "You made a deal with me Master. Nein. You would break your promise after I gave you proper service. That is not equal."

Master Malfred laughed harder. "Foolish boy. I fuck you nine ways to Sunday and all you get in return is sunglasses, a headset and release from taking a fucking bath. That is far from equal already. I am sick of seeing you filthy, and those burns need the rest of your flesh to be clean. You killed the fucking doctor. You know Claus nearly had a heart attack when he and Bladrick found him stiff and cold. I would have rewarded you had Claus actually died, but that old fart lives still. Therefore, you will get into this bathtub tonight or I will beat the living hell out of you till you do. Oh, do give me a threatening rhyme about what you are going to do to me for making you bathe. I am waiting." He smiled then splashed water on me.

I led out a howl of terror and rushed to the towel trying to get that green glowing stuff of me. Master Leo heard my wails and came running to find me in the floor rubbing my naked flesh with vigor and Master Malfred chuckling with much glee.

"Gott dammit, Malfred. Stop torturing Christian Axel. You know he fears the water. Fuck. You are asking for a push down the damned stairs." Master Leo clicked his tongue and snapped.

Master Malfred rolled his eyes. "Oh, shut the fuck up Leo. I was merely having some fun with our little man."

Master Leo snorted. "From his yells of torment for the last two hours I think you and Jonas have had enough fun with him for the rest of the night. Let him rest and do your own bath service."

I finished wiping away the radiation and looked at the floor. "I beg of you, Master Malfred. Ask another task other than the bath service. I cannot get that poison on me. It will make me sick and then I die."

"Oh, Christ, Christian Axel. You sound like my fucking mother with all your insane complaints. Next you will be telling me about the tapestry or the electricity that flows all around your head. Damned schizophrenics make the sane go mad with all their bullshit." Master Malfred groaned and laid his head back onto the tub.

Master Leo looked at the floor. "I forgot your mother was touched by the illness, Malfred. I don't know why that had slipped my memory."

Master Malfred closed his eyes. "That she was Leo. Stark raving mad. A fucking lunatic if there was ever one born. I never could understand the woman. She nearly killed Karl and me before we could reach our manhood and run away from her nightmarish world. Now here I am again in love with another one. Thank Gott this one is under me instead of over me."

Master Leo gasped. "Oh, meine Gott. That is why Gretta picked your brother Karl to father this kid you and Jonas tried to purchase today. You two hoped to pass on, wait, is that what you and Tamina were up to as well?"

Master Malfred let out a long sigh "Ja, if only I could have sired the Priceless female with my Tamina. However, that was never meant to be. I left this up to my brother. We both knew he could father children plus he lost his only kid more than a year ago. Dreadful thing too. I miss that boy to this day. I cannot imagine the pain he must have suffered having to uncollar him, then watch the Guard take him to the yard."

I let out a gasp of horror. "Nein, nein, this cannot be."

I also let out a gasp of terror then turned around and looked at Master Maxx. "Ryker was his son."

He nodded. "Ja, Karl is Master Malfred's brother, and Ryker's father. He was the man that I watched uncollaring the boy that night."

My eyes when wider. "Master that means, oh no."

Mad Maxx brushed the hair from my face with a sad smile. "You have his eyes. Ja, Meine Liebe. Ryker is your half-brother."

I looked at my hands and whimpered. "That means Malfred created me just like he created you."

Mad Maxx nodded then held my face up to look into his own. "I can only say that Malfred may be the greatest genius to ever live. He managed to create the perfect Priceless pair from four of the foulest people that have ever walked this Earth. Debbie and Karl plus Agnette and Peter. There is a special place in hell for all of us Meine Liebe. I bet we even manage to get a whole floor to ourself right next to old Scratch himself."

I nodded with huge tears forming in my eyes just as Master Maxx handed me a photo of a boy standing next to the twelve year old Maximillian wearing a smile. He was a spitting reverse gender image of the girl I saw every time I looked in the mirror. There was no longer any doubt this was the brother I had always wanted but lost before I ever knew him, Ryker.

Chapter 58: My Enemy, My Savior

I stared at the floor realizing this baby the American woman was trying to sell was my Ryker's little sister. The irony, disgust, and terror of such an unholy attempt to match me with Master Malfred's niece was not lost to me even in my disturbed state.

I flashed a look at Master Malfred laying there in the bathtub appearing to be at peace. He was without any sign of remorse nor repentance for the obscenity he was attempting to create. How could anyone be so heartless I wondered? Ryker was his damned favorite nephew and Karl's only son. They already lost him to the Guard, now they were bringing another helpless kid into this hell hole. All for what?

Ah, you see then I realized, the men planned to create a dynasty on the backs of their youngest generation. This little girl was their ticket to becoming the most powerful and famous Dominants in the Haus. If they could get me to pair with her, then our children would be the pure Priceless of legends.

Malfred and Karl would be the full-blooded relatives of the myths. It was clear to me at last. Master Malfred didn't intend to take over as Head of the Haus. He wanted more. He desired to be the Gott on Earth. Shit. I couldn't believe the audacity of this motherfucker. The understanding of this latest plot meant several things for the Mad Maxx.

For starters, Malfred would do his damnest to keep me from escaping my metal. If I managed to obtain Dominant status, he couldn't force me to couple with his creation, nor could he even be sure I wouldn't choose another Priceless female mate on my own.

This also explained why Master Malfred was in such a hurry to get me into his claws as my only Dominant. It was one thing to own the female but to gain full power you would need control of the pair of Priceless pleasure submissives.

His blood bonding and the branding me were all part of his plan to do this. He either hoped to brainwash me into following only his voice or this was his way of trying to gain a bigger piece of the Mad Maxx pie than any of the other Masters holding my leash.

It also occurred to me they had chosen an American woman to have his brother's kid for a specific purpose. Master Peter had already told me in the branding room earlier before he put his mark on me. The Americans were the power of the world. A half American, female Priceless, would be exotic and a silver no one in the Haus would not covet with all their heart.

To add to her worth, this kid was High Born with her uncle on the Elder's floor and father a Voting Council member. Her pedigree was impressive with a direct line to many high ranking Dominants with a long history of descendants in this horror Haus.

To top this all off, she had the schizophrenia in her blood. Ryker had tried to tell me. He had every right to believe himself Priceless. He likely was but never lived to prove it. This girl was the poster child for everything the legend said she should be.

I cleared my throat full of curiosity. “Uhm, Master, may I inquire as to the name of this baby of your brother Master Karl?”

He didn’t open his eyes but smiled with joy. “Ah, Karl named this little beauty of ours Rachel Lady Krause. Isn’t that a lovely name for your future Frau?”

I didn’t look up nor demonstrate a change in my demeanor “What if this Rachel is not the correct match? Is it not the legend that only I can know my Priceless mate? What if were are not compatible or she is of a hateful nature?”

Master Malfred opened his eyes and glared at me with anger. “This girl is your Priceless match, Christian Axel. Rachel was named after our late sister; Gott rest her soul. She was cursed with the mother of madness just as you are, just as this kid will be. The girl will be trained to attend your sexual interest’s with great skill without quarrel. She has the correct parts for bearing your children. That is all you require for either of you to do your duty to your Masters. What the fuck do you care if she even likes you? Long as the bitch can bend over and your dick works, then this match is sound. Besides, she is of my family’s bloodline. This girl will be a beauty that will bring down the planets. I have seen the girl. She is not even a year old and already rivals Aphrodite in beauty. I am almost sorry that this is my own kin. I cannot enjoy what you the unworthy Christian Axel will thrill at for all your days. Not like either of you have a choice anyway. You drop this nonsense about choosing your own mate. It is foolishness. You do as you are told and so will she."

I felt the tears welling up in my eyes for both this little baby girl and myself. "May I ask, what happened to your sister, the one struck down with the Priceless curse?"

He scoffed. "Hitler is what happened to my beloved sister Rachel, meine taube. The war came and those with mental illness were a drain on our country according to that despotic madman. She was sent away to a concentration camp and disposed of with our mother. That horrible government took all those away that were marked as having the disease. I was still a young man of only fourteen when the SS came and hauled our family members away. I hear Rachel and my mother's screams in my nightmares to this day. I was lucky that Karl was of the age of eighteen or I would have been in the orphanage. My sister was only a sixteen year old girl but they took her for the purging anyway. You will remember that if you had been struck down less than thirty years before today, Hitler's dogs would have taken you away too. Those evil men wanted to cleanse our blood lines of what they called weakness and imperfections. You were lucky to come down Priceless in 1972 instead of 1942. That idiot had it all wrong. There is plenty of use for the insane. Look at you for example. You bring a smile to my face and serve a purpose just fine as long as you behave yourself, that will continue to be the way it is for all your life. However, you keep killing, well you will be culled, just like all of those that come before you. You hear me, meine taube?"

I sniffed loudly and kept my eyes to the floor. "Ja, I am listening Master. I know my place and will mind my betters without further quarrels."

He smiled with happiness. "Ah, now see that, Leo. You merely speak to those under you with authority. Christian Axel had not considered how lucky he is that we don't send him to a grave like they usually do his kind. You need only remind him of his place and then he remembers. It is a pain I know, but the memories of the schizophrenics don't hold for long, ja?"

Master Leo stood there with his jaw on the floor in disbelief. "I cannot even find the words to respond to that horrid shit you just said to this, your fellow, human being. Malfred, the boy is in enough pain from his brain disease, and you tell him all he is good for is your penetration and making children abused in the same way as he is? You are aware my sister Maus also had this illness. She was a better person than most anyone I have ever known. You admit your own sister Rachel and mother utter were afflicted. Were they all not any good for anything but fucking to you?"

Master Malfred narrowed his eyes. "Ma sister was but a kid. Of course, she wasn't doing such a thing yet. My mother, well to be honest I am surprised anyone ever made children with that harpy. I don't agree with what Hitler and his men did, but I will also say that Rachel nor my mother should have ever been allowed to run free. Christian Axel has a function that makes him useful, but I think we all grant him too much room to move. If I had it my way, he would be bonded in more than a fucking flimsy leash. You cannot trust these crazy people Leo. They will hurt you, whether they mean it or not, they will. There is no reasoning with them when they get violent. You surely admit to that at least."

Master Leo shook his head and crossed his arms in fury. "I will not admit such bullshit. My Maus never hurt a soul. I happen to know your sister Rachel never did either. Christian Axel acts out because we all abuse him. Anyone schizophrenic or not would strike out when being burned, raped, tortured, and worse. You are a Gott damned ignorant fool Malfred. I thought Jonas was delusional. You both are the insane ones in this horror story the way I can see it. If you are quite done upsetting the boy, I am taking him with me for a walk around the Haus. I think I need some air and I know he could use it after enduring your stink for the last couple hours."

Master Malfred sat up in the tub. "Nein, I am not done with him Leo. I told the boy I want bath service. Get your ass over here and do your job Christian Axel or be punished."

I stayed in my kneel, wringing my hands. "Please mercy Master. I fear the water. You and I had an agreement there would be no making me get near that stuff."

Master Malfred chuckled with fury driven laughter. “Ah, nein. That is not what we agreed to. I said I would not enforce bathing, meine taube. There was not an arrangement made about granting me my bath services. Do you wish that I get out of this bathtub and take your back downstairs? I bet Jonas is still down there with Peter. Maybe there is room in the chains next to him. Want to go see?”

I closed my eyes sobbing openly. “Nein. I do not wish that Master.”

Master Leo walked up to me and laid his hand on my shoulder. “The water is not contaminated, meine heart. This is a delusion of your illness. If you touch it there will be no radiation sickness. Your hydrophobia is because of my stupidity. You listen to me. I swear to you I will never take special services from you in the shower or pool again. The bath is safe for you once more, Christian Axel. I realized now this was how you found comfort. It was your only way to deal with the foul things you are forced to endure. It was wrong of me to try to ease your burden by enforcing such horrors in the only place you ever had to wash free of them.”

I shook my head. “I can see the poison, Master. It is green and glowing.”

Master Malfred snorted. “Give this up, Leo. I get out and take him to the chains. The only way to get through to the insane is to beat them down. In time, Christian Axel will stop this crap and do what he is told without further quarrel.

I thought him better trained then this." Malfred started to get out of the tub.

Master Leo held up his hand. "Wait a moment. Let me try one more thing, Malfred."

He leaned down into my ear and whispered. "I have an antidote for the radiation. Do what this Master tells you and I will give it to you in trade for an unusual special services request to be called when I want. Then we can go see Peter down in the dungeons like you requested for yet another favor I call in later. Do you agree to these trades?"

I thought about this for a moment. I didn't know if I could trust Master Leo after all he had done, but he wasn't offering me this antidote for free. I winced at the thought of what weird thing he would want in his special services. I had not known him to be odd in his sexual interests before. That never matters. You can never be sure of anyone no matter how long you have been sleeping with them. Master Leo was new to me still, so I assumed in time I would have found out his proclivities anyway.

I nodded. "Ja, I agree to this Master." I said while wiping my eyes of their tears.

I decided it was better to suffer some horrid situation in Master Leo's bedroom then to die of radiation poisoning or be thudded to near death in the chains. Besides, after hearing the situation with Malfred's niece and his thoughts on the Priceless nature, I had decided that selling myself back to my father wasn't the worst thing in the world. I needed to speak to Peter immediately, and Master Leo was my best chance to make that happen.

Master Leo smiled. “Then you attend to this task without further quarrel. I will see you for our own arrangement when you finish.” He turned to leave the bathroom, but Master Malfred furrowed his brow and called out to him.

“What the hell? Just what did you say to the boy? An arrangement? What is it?” He looked at me with curiosity.

Master Leo snapped his fingers and flounced. “What me and my man discuss regarding my services from him is none of your business. Christian Axel, move your pretty little bottom. I will be seeking my interest’s with you soon. Do not anger me or I will make what Malfred threatened look like a pleasure in comparison.” He snorted then left with speed trying at appear arrogant in his orders to me.

Master Malfred shot me a look of surprise as I approached and went right to work with his bathing. “Are you afraid of Master Leo or did he merely promise something such as seeing those lambs?”

I shrugged. “You don’t know Master Leo as I do Master. The man can be quite brutal when he wishes to be. I dare not incite his anger. Do not allow his gentle words to fool you. When that door closes and he has no eyes to judge him, he becomes the beast. I do what he tells me, or I suffer unimaginable torments for it. I cannot discuss this in detail due to the rule against sharing what happens in my Master’s beds. I thank you for not asking anything further of this private matter." I lied and worked hard not to snicker at that most untrue statement.

He let out his breath in shock. "Really? Wow, I never would have guessed it of that queen. Well, they say it is the ones you least expect it from, ja? I guess that is why he will not join me and Jonas in our pleasures. Too perverted and fears our scrutiny." He shot another look at the door to make sure we were alone.

I shrugged again. "Forgive me Master but I cannot speak for his choices. That is not my place. Master Leo is my better and I do what I am told or find myself in dire straits for such."

Master Malfred smiled. "Ja, you are back from that dark world of madness. I hear the sounds of the perfect submissive you are rumored to be coming from your skilled mouth. This is good for you. You be mindful and watch your behaviors or you will find yourself bonded to the bedpost. I for one am tired of your psychotic antics and rambles. It gives me a headache. When Leo finishes whatever obscene shit he has planned for you, return to me for your branding scouring, alcohol bath, and bed."

I nodded. "As you wish Master. I will respectfully request you allow my two hours in the morning and the feeding of my lambs as we agreed."

He growled. "I do not like you speaking to the lambs, meine taube. As for those two hours we shall see about that."

I shot a look of irritation at him. “I do everything you request without hesitation, Master. I have earned my privileges.”

He reached out and struck my face rapidly. “You do not tell me what you do or do not earn, Christian Axel. You take what I give you and thank me for the mercy of it. I will consider letting you feed the lambs, but as for those two hours, I don’t think you need them. You are not getting out of that collar boy. There is no reason to train for your final section testing.”

I held my cheek. I kept my gaze and anger to the ground. “You would know best, Master. Thank you for your mercy.”

Master Malfred’s stern look softened, and he reached out and ruffled my hair which caused me to flinch thinking he would hit me again. “There you go. We are going to get along famously, meine taube. You keep your head down, mind me completely, and attend to my urges with vigor, then good things will come to you in time. You’ll see I am a most generous Master when my collar remembers their place.”

I nodded but said nothing. I finished his bath service with grace and speed as I had been trained to do. I dried him off and dressed him in his robe never causing him another reason to backhand me. I wanted to kill the man when he demanded I attend his oral hygiene and shave him as well.

However, I did these things again without quarrel or any sign of my irritation over it. He was testing me to see if he could incite me to fury. Master Malfred was pleased to find me quiet, compliant, and mindless in my attending to his toothbrush and razor service.

When he was unable to shake me up or find any other bullshit service to request that dealt with that contaminated water, he left me to attend to my clean up service of the bathroom. I was scrubbing down the bathtub when Master Leo came rushing in with a spray bottle. He had me get into the tub while he sprayed me down with an oily liquid.

It smelled odd and shimmered. “What is this Master?” I held my slick hand to my nose trying to place the scent of it.

He shook his head. “This is an oil based decontaminate. You see the water cannot penetrate the layers of it and it will block your pores from soaking in the poisons. I leave the bottle under the sink in every apartment in case you get called to deal with water. You spray this stuff on and most of the radiation will be thwarted. You need not believe me. In a few days you’ll notice you are not sick nor dead.”

I nodded my head. “I believe you Master. I have no choice anyway. If you lie, then it won’t matter soon when I die of that contamination. Then you will have to find another to suck your cock. So, nothing to lose the way I see it.”

Master Leo frowned. “That is an extremely negative attitude, but I suppose you have no reason to view it any other way. Now, you hurry and get dressed. We are headed below. Jonas just got back. Peter is alone in the dungeon. This is the best time to speak to him. He will be ready to hear any deal with his back in agony and hours of nothing to do."

I rushed to his bedroom and put back on my breeches, socks, and boots. Master Leo frowned when I knelt and waited without putting on a blouse.

"You are half naked, Christian Axel. Put on a at least a t-shirt. Those ugly brands stand out like sore thumbs." He crossed his arms.

I shook my head. "I beg your forgiveness, but Master Malfred forbids my wearing a shirt. If I dare to then I have to bathe. I will not purposely get into that contaminated shit no matter an antidote or nein."

Master Leo rolled his eyes. "This is such a nightmare. I swear I could kick myself for causing this mess. Oh, never mind. What is done is done, ja? We start right now with a clean slate. Let's go take the first steps to undoing all the idiotic moves your Master made." He took up my leash and tore from the room.

We rushed through the living room. He ignored Master Jonas and Master Malfred when they bitched about his leaving the apartment with me in tow. They warned him that I would push him from the stairs. He laughed and said he surely had that coming if I did. The two Dominants scoffed at his careless ignoring of warnings.

Despite their best efforts he managed to extract me from the apartment without the two of them following. He told them he was going to gossip with the girls and stop by the Great Hall for a quick dinner. Neither the Vampire nor Master Malfred desired to listen to Master Leo hen peck with other old biddies.

Master Leo chuckled all the way down to the first floor about his clever covering up our real destination. I listened to him but didn't share his mirth. I wrung my hands and took deep breaths. I was not happy to be headed to visit with my father. Making any deal with him was only second to being burned for all eternity in hell as things I would least like to do.

As usual Master Leo was oblivious to the seriousness of this trip. He had not considered I would not be in a celebratory mood to be promising Gott knows what to a child molesting, incestuous father. I forgave him for his being dense like that. Master Leo is a good man at heart, but sometimes his head is full of the hot air. I believe in the USA they call his kind the "space cadet," ja?

We arrived at the dungeons in record time. I groaned when I saw the Ivar was the man left in charge of the cell block that held Peter for his punishment. I glared at the smiling man with heated anger burning my ears.

He looked me up and down with humor as Master Leo asked him to take us to visit the shamed Dominant. "Ah, sure thing sir. I see you have Mad Maxx with you. I guess he did something special to get this chance to kick his old Dominant in the hodensack. Well, cannot say I wouldn't do the same after all that vile man did to him. Of course, he likely doesn't recall being daft and all. I see he looks the part of the insane thing he is for sure. I have heard tales he is something else in the sack though. Keeps you smiling, I bet."

Master Leo flashed a look of fury at Ivar. "You will silence such speak in my presence worm. I do not take kindly to such an allegation. I need neither justify nor explain my desire to see my old companion to the likes of you. You forget your place, again, you will join him in the cell as his fucking neighbor. As it is, I may report you to the dungeon Master for such foul discussions."

Ivar dropped his gaze immediately appearing fearful. "Oh, I beg your forgiveness honorable Elder. I wasn't thinking. You name your price to forget this uncalled rudeness and Ivar will pay it."

Master Leo frowned. "I tell you already. I want to see Peter. Take us to him and shut your fucking mouth, Ivar. Is that a price you can pay, or do I need to take the payment from your flesh?"

I smiled with my demons rising then sung under my breath. "Little Ivar go blow your horn. I feed the sheep in the morning, and the by night you wish you were never born. Where is that Gunter that looks after this keep? He is in the silver well fast asleep. Oh, you cannot wake him. I stabbed him in the eyes. What I have planned for you will make your mother cry."

Master Leo heard my song and jerked my leash harshly. "Enough, Christian Axel. Don't you dare breath another sound, I mean it." His eyes were wide with fear.

I nodded. “As you wish Master. I will be as quiet as Gunter and Ivar.” I grinned even wider.

Ivar didn’t hear my words. He was too busy nervously digging through his keys, sure that Master Leo would beat him for his indiscretion. The black collar brute found what he was seeking then motioned us to follow him down the cell hallway.

When he unlocked the door, Master Leo reached out and grabbed the key from his grip. “Leave us. You don’t come back here. I will lock this up when we finish. Oh, and where is your partner, Gunter is it?”

Ivar shrugged as he began to haul ass away. “Beats me. The man has been missing since the other night. Likely off drunk in some whore’s bed. Thank you for the mercy Honorable Leo.” He left the hallway.

Master Leo shot me a look of terror. “Christian Axel, did you do something to Gunter? Answer me. Is that where you were when Malfred found you missing?”

I smiled. “They make sausage from dog, and they make them from horses. I guess they make them from Gunter as well.”

Master Leo reached out and grabbed my upper arm pulling me into his face. “You must stop killing people, Christian Axel. If you get caught, they will put you in the yard. Peter is a rat, if he were to find out, oh meine Gott. What the fuck am I doing here? I am leading you to your death.”

I shook my head. “You save yourself, meine heart. You step aside and stay out here to guard this door. You need not worry about Christian Axel. The boy was built for this shit. I am going now to meet my maker and receive the reprograming. The mission is clear. If you get in my way, then you will be the sausage yourself Master. Thank you for the mercy of it.”

He backed away with a groan. “Then go. I did swear to do whatever it takes to free you. I know if anyone is slimy enough to see a way out of this dreadful Haus for you, then it is the monster behind this door. I will do as you ask. I must have faith that with this act I start to earn your trust back, and eventually you love too.”

I chuckled. “You can teach a monkey, Master. I see you shortly. No matter what you hear, leave me be. I will knock three times when I am ready to leave.” He nodded then opened the door to let me walk inside alone.

Peter was laying on the cot with his hand covering his face as if in much pain. He didn’t look up when I walked inside.

He scoffed then said loudly, “What the fuck do you want Ivar? I told you I am not hungry. Get the fuck out of my sight before I beat you half to death motherfucker.”

I looked at the floor and cleared my throat. “Master Peter? I have come to speak to you about a matter you may find of interest to both of us.”

Peter flinched upon hearing my voice. He dropped his hand and turned his head staring at me wide eyed.

"Maximillian? What the fuck? How did you get in here? Is this a joke?" He winced while sitting up on the cot.

I shook my head. "Nein, this is no joke Master. I was brought here by Master Leo. I requested to see you."

He snarled. "Oh? By Leo, you say? To laugh and poke fun I suppose. Well get your licks in Maximillian. You have a lot of nerve daring to come here to get any revenge on me. You forget who I am. That fucking collar you wear is a false one. It should be my Gott damned silver. I was tricked and you know it, you little bastard. I will be out of here in a few days. Maybe next time I do worse than brand your flesh."

I sighed. "I think maybe you were indeed tricked Master. I apologize for any part I played in it. I realized too late the Master Jonas may have been slipping me drugs to cause my loss of logical thinking."

Peter was startled. "Huh? You are admitting I was fooled into tossing your collar?"

I shrugged. "I don't know Master. I merely say it is possible. However, I add I was also the fool, if this is the fact. Does any of that matter anymore? I do wear the bats collar, and you sit in this cell suffering from the lash of the very same Vampire."

He crossed his arms. “Okay Maximillian, I agree with that. What is done is done. So, again I demand to know why you are here if not to mock me?”

I knelt down on the floor which caused him to gasp in surprise. “I come in peace to speak with you Master. The Elder Masters, except Master Leo, have trapped me in my collar. They intend to keep me in it. You already know they chase a Female Priceless of the Krause lineage. You helped Master Malfred and Master Karl obtain the kid.”

Peter scoffed then spat on the floor. “Ja I admit that I intercepted this plot only today. The kid is real and has the markings of the Female Priceless. I was told by Malfred your metal is unbreakable as well. You were there, I seem to recall when I got the news. What the fuck does that have to do with me, Maximillian? Why should I even care? You are not my property anymore. I do believe I was reminded of that most soundly only an hour ago, and here I sit in case I didn’t hear Jonas when he whipped me over it.”

I took a deep breath and closed my eyes. “I know better, Master. You want my collar back. This will not happen if I don’t break Master Jonas’s first. I am here to uhm, I am here to.” I could not bring myself to say the words.

Peter chuckled with evil humor. “You are here to beg me to take you back and help you break that collar I believe is what you are trying to say.”

I felt the tears starting to well up as I nodded, never feeling more broken than at that moment. “Ja, which is why

I am here Master. I need your help, or I am trapped for good and the Krauses win the Haus. I will be a stallion to their mare and a plaything for their pleasures till the yard claims my worthless bones."

He nodded and smiled. "You got that right, my boy. If someone doesn't step in pretty quick you can forget that doctor business. Oh, and Frau? Ja, more like whore. You and this baby will be the breed animals in a cell just like this one. Well, the good news Maximillian is you will finally get all the pussy you ever wanted along with plenty of cock too. Lucky you." He giggled with much humor at my shitty predicament.

I groaned. "Are you able to help me or not Master? Otherwise, I will not debase myself any further in your presence. I thank you for the mercy of it."

Peter stopped laughing and became stern, "The question is not if I am able, but if I am willing, Maximillian. What the fuck do you have to offer me that I cannot get by stepping aside and watching you swing? Malfred is in power and soon he will own it all. In order to save you from this fate worse than death, I have to put myself in his path. I would do well to keep out of his way and even better to aid him in his takeover."

I looked up at him with confusion. "You already have that contract with me, Master. This will never happen if I am trapped in my metal. Is that not enough to gain your aid?"

He shook his head. "What the hell, Maximillian? I get your special services rights till you finish school and make a kid with your blood bonded or until you're forty-two. I also get to pay for that fancy medical school you want to attend. That is if you can break that collar. You ask me to risk my fucking life going against that insane Malfred and terror Jonas for a kiss and a promise with a huge bill attached to your ass."

I began to cry openly. "If this was not important to you then why the fuck did you trick me into it in the first place."

He snorted. "Well, back then you were my Priceless collar. I was going to be the power, not Malfred nor Jonas. Now, that is all a pipe dream. Jonas stole my silver ticket. Malfred gave my position to Gretta, and again I got stuck with watching everyone else enjoy the fruits of my training you, and worse, Malfred will raise his bloody brother Karl, and that fucking bitch Mila when Claus and Bladrick expire. If he kills Leo then he will raise Alexie. I am finished, Maximillian. I was robbed not once but twice. You can suffer in this cell sucking cock and fucking your Priceless whore while your old lover, Master Peter languishes away in a weak position on the voting Council never to rise any further for all his days. And he can sleep alone too without his Maximillian to keep the bed warm. Get out of here boy. It is cruel to make me look upon something that I can no longer hold. I still think of you fondly but if you persist in this hateful game I will not shortly feel so tenderly."

I gasped and coughed almost unable to speak, I was so overwhelmed with terror that he was not going to aid me. “Please Master. You must help me. I can give you all that you desire back. I swear it.”

Peter laughed then rolled his eyes. “Oh? You know what? I wasn’t fooled you are schizophrenic, Maximillian. Only the insane would say something so stupid to me.”

I nodded. “Ja, I can do it. I can clear the path for your rise in this Haus. I am close to your enemies. If you come up with the plan I will do whatever it takes to see you become Head of the Haus. I can remove Cora, like I did Xavier. I can end Malfred and Jonas like I did Drexel and Barnim. Consider Karl, Alexie and Mila worm food. Please Master, you must help me escape my metal. I will do anything you ask.”

Master Peter’s eyes narrowed. “Wait, is this a set up? Did Malfred or Jonas send you to tempt me, Maximillian? If so, then I swear to Gott, I will find a way to end you boy.”

I shook my head. “Nein, I mean this. I will do anything if you help me. Please Master, I don’t have much time. The Masters will recognize my plot if I mess around down here too long with you.”

Master Peter sat back and stared at me for a moment as if deep in thought while I trembled and wept in desperation. “Well, you seem sincere, but if I fall for your tricks again, this time I may end up worse than whipped. I want to believe you are honest Maximillian, I do. Yet, I simply cannot chance it. Be on your way. For what it is worth, I will enjoy this memory for many years to come even if it was only a fake. You are a wonderful actor and more beautiful than even before. Get out." He motioned me to leave him.

I got up and rushed toward him causing him to nearly crawl up the wall as I felt to my knees at his feet then into prostrate position. "Nein, don't deny me, Master. I beg of you. Tell me what I must do to prove my loyalty to you, and I will do it." Master Peter reached down pulling me up to face him.

He looked deep into my tear filled eyes then sighed. "Shit, you are not running a scam. This is for real. You are offering yourself to me for my aid in breaking your collar? Even though you realize I will own you even after that metal is gone?"

I nodded while looking away with shame. "Ja, I am Master. Help me please. I do whatever you ask to prove my seriousness. I cannot do this without your aid. If you send me away, I am finished."

He nodded. "Ja, you are damned right, Maximillian. Well, you will first swear your loyalty and will to me. Then you will consummate it here and now with me. I want a mock collaring ceremony, or you get up, leave then don't you ever come back again. You already betrayed me once; I won't allow it to happen twice. The next time you go behind my back, I will kill you with my bare hands. You agree to this, ja or nein?"

I shuddered but nodded. “I swear my loyalty and will to you, Master. I do this willingly and without regret for the price of my freedom of the silver collar of the Elders.”

He nodded. “I swear to you Maximillian the silver bolt cutters will be yours by my own hands. You can count on my loyalty and aid until your collar is broken. I do this willingly without regret for the price of your services as per our contract agreed upon during the first submission collaring with the addition you will raise me to the Head of the Haus by my fifty-fifth birthday.”

I whimpered as he grabbed the back of my head with a smile. “There is not enough time for this consummation Master. I must get back or they will come looking for me.”

Peter laughed. “You better hurry up and make me cum then boy. You know the rules. No collaring is legit until the lock is sealed properly.”

I groaned. “I am asking to break a collar not lock another on Master.”

He pulled me into a deep kiss then said, “Like it or not, you get rid of the one all can see and replace it with the invisible leash to your Master Peter, Mad Maxx. Get to it the way I trained you.” He pushed my head down toward his lap.

I was forced to endure preparing him for our collaring coupling. I will not even say I took his intercourse with stoic manliness. Hell no. I cried like a little bitch the entire time, just like the first time the man raped me and taught me what special services are.

I admit it near broke my will having to endure the lust of my own fucking father all over again. I did what I had to do without apologies. It was my only chance at avoiding a fate that was far worse awaiting me without his assistance.

The thing I have to say about the price Peter's made me pay and makes me pay is this, the dishonor is all his. I was a lowly submissive without a voice or choice in that Haus. My father was on the voting Council with the ear of the one that could free me in his grasp. He could have aided me and accepted my offer to help him rise by clearing his path but that was not enough for the pervert.

Peter has no need to demand my special service, not then and not now, but he does it anyway. I have spent many years trying to understand his reasoning for it. The man has lovers lined up begging for his affections but to this day any chance he gets he calls his rights to me.

I have no choice but to endure it or be in forfeit of our agreement. He made sure to put in a safety clause that if I dared to deny him then he can demand I be recollared. If that were to happen, then I would be returned to the Elders clutches immediately.

I shot him a look of horror at that news.

Don't look so surprised, meine Frau. I told you my father is one slippery sonofabitch. Meine Liebe, you watch yourself with him. He is not too happy with your lineage. I suspect he would like to see you disappear forever and Jonas forced to send me to seek another. We stick together and you mind my good advice, then he cannot get through our united forces. That said, never make a deal with that monster, ever. On with the story. We will get back to this discussion of my dishonorable water later, ja?

I nodded and he returned to his story.

Master Peter didn't waste time. He bent me over his cot then forced his penetration sex with rapid smoothness. I closed my eyes and wept enduring the horror of my pathetic existence. He didn't take long to reach his orgasm and he didn't bother to hide the evidence of his "theft of services."

I gasped in terror as I heard him moan out in ecstasy deep within the boy. I realized with much disgust I would have to engage in at least a whore bath as quickly as possible or risk Malfred or Jonas discovery of this betrayal.

You see the Elders had all agreed to refrain from emptying their seed within me until I had stopped refusing hygiene rituals. I knew I could ask Master Leo to take the credit for breaching this understanding between them. He would do it for me. Master Leo was not dumb enough to not be aware Master Peter would abuse his position over me.

To be brutally honest, I didn't want to ask him for such a favor. I was not willing to risk opening the door for the tag teaming Master Jonas and Master Malfred to decide they too could just not grant the mercy of keeping me unsoiled by their constant intercourse. It was bad enough enduring the disgusting dispensing of the lustful fluids of those men without adding more humiliation.

I realized I would have to be aware that Master Peter could call on my special services at any time from this point forward. To deny him could result in his withdrawing his aid, and to be caught consorting would result in severe punishment from my Elder Masters, in particular the Vampire and Malfred.

This was a dangerous possibility until that silver of mine was gone. I decided I had better be carrying around something to clean up after him the second he was done or find myself in deeper trouble than I already was.

When Master Peter was sated and felt he had humiliated me to the hilt, he let me up to readjust and wipe away my tears. He smiled while returning to his seat on the cot with an expression of joy on his face. He closed his eyes and took several deep breaths calming down his panting.

"I must admit to you Mad Maxx, I am truly surprised you returned to me willingly. I thought I had lost you for all time when Malfred said you were trapped in that collar. I know that man well. There is no way he will let you out of his clutches now that he has you." He opened his lids as I returned to my kneeling at his feet doing my best to shake off the latest indignity of my nightmare existence.

I shook my head and began to wring my hands in anxiousness at his words "Then I give my loyalty to you for nothing? I am doomed is what you say?"

Master Peter scoffed. “Nein, Malfred only thinks he is unbeatable, Mad Maxx. He is like everyone else. He has many several weak places in his plans. I have been involved in all he has done from the beginning. There is no one on Earth that is more aware of how to shatter the collar of yours. You made a perfect choice coming to me as you have done. Together we can slip you past even his vigilant watch. First though, we need to end Gunter, Ivar, and the Haus doctor. Those assholes know of what happened and are dangerous to our plan. They could compromise us. Then I have a list of others that must go, and the timing is critical.”

I interrupted him. “I already shut the doctor and Gunter the hell up for all time. I am after Ivar now. Then I do believe I need to destroy Karl, Alexie, and Mila, but the timing as you say is critical. Too soon they are replaced, too late they have Mistress Gretta’s ear.”

Master Peter’s eyes went wide, then a wicked smile broke out on his face. “You are indeed a treasure, Mad Maxx. I trained you better than I ever thought. Ivar is guarding the dungeons tonight. If only I had the means I would take this man to hell this very night. However, I cannot have him found lying around with his throat slit.”

I nodded as I whispered, “I am going to kill him, then take his flesh to dump in the well with Julius and his brother Gunter.”

Master Peter gasped. “Ah, perfect. I had never considered the old well. You rid this Haus of Julius too? Good, I hated that prick. Glad he is gone. I had noticed he was missing and Malfred was in a hurry to raise that idiot Gustov. Wait, he knows you took the man out, doesn't he."

I looked at the floor. "Ja, he and Grisham were there when I defended myself. Julius intended to murder me. I had to kill the man. Gunter too but no one has knowledge of his accident."

He sighed. "Killing the low black collars and even that quack doctor is one thing, but killing a high ranking Dominant is a dangerous thing, my boy. You make sure to keep your hands off all of them without my instructions in the future. For now, I must ask, you have Leo with you. Are you a fool? That man will betray you, meine love. I think you need to send him away immediately."

I glared at him. "I will do what you ask in all things but leave Master Leo behind. He owes me this and if he does stray I will put him with Julius, Master. He is my only way to communicate with you. He stays or I will fail. You must work with him, or I walk away this minute."

Master Peter snorted. "I disagree with your decision, but it is yours to make. Okay, enough of the chatter. We test Leo's resolve to be of aid. Have him come in here." He crossed his arms and motioned for the door.

I nodded. "As you wish Master." I got up and knocked on the steel entry three times as agreed.

Master Leo opened the door pale as a ghost. "You alright, meine hase? Did Peter hurt you? I have been worried to death. It was taking too long to work this out with him." He looked me up and down with anxiety in his expression.

I keep my gaze down from shame. "You know better, Master. This is Master Peter we are making deals with. He doesn't work for free. He desires to visit with you," I whispered back.

Master Leo looked disgusted. "Really? Christian Axel, that man is the beast. I had nothing to say to him before now, but the man demands to fuck his own son before he will agree to save him. That is sick," he growled back.

I shot him a look of caution. "Cut out the bullshit, Master. You knew damned well, as I did, Master Peter would demand special services when I came to ask his aid. He wants to test your loyalty thanks to your tendency to change sides. I agree with him on this one. You have betrayed him, and me too, I say the with respect."

He clicked his tongue then snapped. "I don't like that you say that, but I am committed to change your mind about me. I will see Peter, but I do it for you, not him."

I nodded. "I thank you for the mercy of it Master." I moved aside so he could enter the cell.

Master Peter crossed his arms then scoffed. "Well, if it isn't my old friend Leo. Mad Maxx tells me you desire to help him bust that bat collar old Jonas has him trapped in. However, I heard tale it was your blood bond that made the metal unbreakable in the first place. I would like to know your motivation to change your position when only a few days ago you were willing to fuck the boy over, literally."

Master Leo shot me a look of shock. "I will not deny that his lock is tight over my rash behaviors. I admit I wasn't thinking of the seriousness of my actions. I have since come to my senses. Look Peter, I won't stand here wasting time with excuses. I made a mistake. Christian Axel deserves better than I gave him. I wish to make this up to him. You need not believe me. I don't really care. If you are willing to help him gain the sacred bolt cutters than you can count on Leo to do what needs to be done to see that happen for truth. You have my word and oath of loyalty. If that is not enough, then so be it. I leave but still keep my silence in this matter for the sake of this boy that I love with all my heart."

Master Peter chuckled. "Ah, I should have seen that coming. You have been seduced by this gorgeous Priceless. His metal has blinded you to his true nature. Never mind. We waste time. Do you have any sharps on you? Even just a penknife?"

Master Leo narrowed his eyes. "I have a pocketknife like most Dominants do. Why?"

He sat up holding out his hands. "They confiscated all the things that could be used as a weapon when they brought me in this cell. Get your knife out where I can see it, Leo."

I giggled but covered my mouth quickly.

I watched Master Leo pull out his knife but then hesitated. “Wait, what do you need this for? I hope you don’t plan to use it for any foul reasons, Peter. If you or Christian Axel are planning to kill me, then better think again. I won’t go without a hell of a fight.” He shot a look of fear at the both of us.

Master Peter laughed hard. “Nein Leo. I never kill my partners. That knife you will need for Ivar. The man is a threat to Mad Maxx and me. I intend to make him disappear. I want you to cut that idiot’s throat while I keep him distracted. Only then will I trust you. Do you understand me? Call that motherfucker back here. I warn you this minute. You refuse this task then you can be assured when I get out of here, I will come looking to tie up loose ends for good.”

Master Leo’s eyes went wide at that. “Huh? What is this you say? I must kill Ivar to prove I am with you and Christian Axel in the plot to break his collar. That is madness Peter. If the man is an issue for you, then do the dirty work yourself. I will say though you cannot just go around murdering people, not even low black collars. No one is going to believe the man used a knife to kill himself like that.”

Master Peter nodded. “Ja, exactly as I thought. See Mad Maxx, I told you this Leo is a two-faced sonofabitch. You better wise up or you are good as dead yourself boy. Get the fuck out of here both of you.”

I gasped. "Nein, I cannot do this without your help Master Peter. Master Leo, he is truthful. The man must die. You need to do this. You should not worry about getting caught. There is a place to hide the corpse where no one will ever be the wiser. Everyone will believe he ran off. You leave him alive, then he will come for me and for Master Peter. If you will not kill Ivar, then I am most happy to do it. Give me the fucking knife." I stuck out my hand to take the weapon.

Master Leo shot a look of irritation at Master Peter. "For your information I am not a backstabber, Peter. Christian Axel, there is no way we have time to bury this man and where the hell would we even do such a thing without everyone seeing us."

Master Peter snorted. "The boy and I do have a way to cover this murder up Leo. You want to be a part of this arrangement then you should learn to trust I know what is best. Mad Maxx has granted me his total loyalty in this matter and offered payment for my services. You brother are only asked to prove you are with us by getting involved too deeply to tell the secrets without implicating yourself. You are either with us or against us, the way I see it. Give the knife to the Priceless and fucking leave or call that black collar guard back. Hurry up and make up your mind. The shift change happens in less than two hours. We miss this chance; it will make disposing of this asshole much more difficult than need be."

Master Leo looked at me for a moment then back to Master Peter. "Okay. anything for Christian Axel. I am a man of my word. I will go hail Ivar." He left the cell in a rush while I stood there slipping looks of victory at my Master Peter.

Within only a few moments, the black collar Ivar came into the cell followed by Master Leo. Master Peter leaned back on his cot while I retreated to the back wall and kept my head down. Ivar didn't even bother to look behind him. Master Leo took his blade from his pocket and took a ready stance. I noticed he was not even trembling. The man had nerves of steel no doubt.

Master Peter kept Ivar distracted as the schwuler crept up on him. I had to stifle my giggling at Master Peter's bitching that he was not being treated in a manner that was expected for one of his rank.

Like a panther jumping down from a tree on an unsuspecting antelope, Master Leo reached around Ivar's jaw. He turned the shocked black collars head slightly while he opened the man's throat with his knife. blood poured from the wound as Ivar gurgled and attempted to pull Master Leo off his back. He couldn't do anything but flail wildly as Master Peter and I watched in silence while his life flowed out onto the concrete floor.

When Ivar's strength began to leave and his movements slowed, Master Leo let him loose. The man dropped to his knees holding his neck almost in a trance for a moment, then fell to his side. His breathing slowed. Within only a few more moments it stopped for all time.

The last person besides my Masters that had any evidence of my alleged mental illness had been silenced for good.

Master Peter chuckled then stood up flashing a look of triumph at Master Leo. “Well, I didn’t think you had it in you, brother. Amazing job. That fucker never saw you coming. Clean cut too. Ah, you are a cold bastard indeed. Warms my heart to call you partner once more. Come, I will wrap his head in the cot blanket, and we will slip him out the back door. You follow my lead, and we throw out this trash, ja? Mad Maxx, you go to the storage closet down the hallway and get the mop and clean this mess up. Leo and I will be back within an hour or so. You do not go until we come back. Keep this door closed until we come for you. That is a directive.”

I rushed to get the mop bucket and cleaning supplies. I returned to find Master Leo and Master Peter had already left with the dead Ivar. I cleaned up the rivers of crimson flushing all of it down the drain hole in the center of that cell. I left no inch unscrubbed while nervously awaiting the return of my Dominants.

My anxiety was threatening to cut me in half before at last the two of them returned. They were sweaty and both had tossed their shirts into the well after the corpse to assure no blood spots could be spotted on them. Master Leo had zipped up his jacket to hide his bare chest, but Master Peter didn’t have a coat to hide his naked upper half.

I saw the welts of Master Jonas’s whip across his back, purple with angry raised red tops. He didn’t appear to mind them a bit. That one thing I could say about that sonofabitch father of mine is he can take pain like few others can.

Master Peter examined my clean up job. He nodded his approval with a smile that I had gotten every sign of the killing removed. He then looked at his watch and shot a look of worry at Master Leo who was wiping the sweat off his forehead with his kerchief.

“The next shift will be here in another fifteen minutes. You and Mad Maxx need to get out of here before they see you. Leo, you remember what I told you. I need that draft with the four signatures of the Elders done by the end of next week if I am to put it before Gretta for approval. It will effectively end Malfred and Claus’s hold over the boy but do recall they must not know of its existence until the time is right. I cannot have them undoing it.” Master Peter sat down on the cot.

Master Leo nodded his head with a smile. “I hate to say it, but you are a fucking genius Peter. I never would have thought of it. Are you sure that you can get Gretta to sign the Law change though? What if she says nein?”

I shot a confused look at Master Peter, unsure what the hell this was all about. “She will do anything to fuck you, Claus and Malfred over brother. She is a vicious bitch, you know that. Besides if you can get Cora’s signature as I told you to, Gretta will agree without quarrel. I think you also should know it is in the Femdom’s favor if you add that extra line as I dictated it to you. It is time for the change, this is no longer the fucking dark ages, ja?”

Master Leo chuckled. “Well, I agree it is only fair that the FemDoms have the same rights as their male counterparts. I would have been most happy to do this thing without the magnificent underlying reason, Peter. I wish I had thought of it on my own in fact.”

Master Peter scoffed. “Shut up Leo. I don’t care a fig about the fair or unfair practices of this fucking Haus. I only care that I get what I am owed. Mad Maxx, I will be seeing you soon boy. You better not forget your oath to me. It will cost me a great deal to hold you for my own. I expect you to make it worth my while.”

I winced but nodded. “As you wish Master. Thank you for the mercy of it.”

He laughed then motioned me to come to him. I did as commanded then endured his pulling me into a deep passionate kiss with Master Leo watching.

He let me go and smiled. “This has been the best day I have had in a long time. I have everything I thought I had lost back in my grip. One day when these dark days are a memory, we will cover up those foul marks of the fake Masters on your flesh. That is a promise.”

I frowned. “I wish to have all of them gone, including yours Master.”

Master Peter shook his head. “Nein, that P will stay. You always will belong to me boy. Now, get going.” He pushed me backward and Master Leo grabbed my leash rushing us from the cell.

I stood quietly while Master Leo locked the door and tore off dragging me behind him. He stopped only briefly to drop the keys on the Dungeon Masters desk. Then fast as lightening we slipped away into the darkened hallways and back up to the main floor.

Once free of the stone stairwell Master Leo pulled me to the side and crowded me to the wall. He pulled me into a lover embrace with his back to the Haus members moving back and forth all around us. I was confused by his openly forward behavior.

He leaned into my ear and whispered, "You did well Christian Axel. Peter was the right choice to save yourself from that collar. His plan will work. I want to tell you that very soon all the damage I have done to you will be undone. I have proved to you this night that I do love you, and I will not stop until you love Leo back once more. I wish to go to the Great Hall for dinner with you on my arm. When we return to the apartment I am calling that special service I traded for the radiation antidote."

Master Leo kissed my lips briefly then allowed me to move my adoration to his ear. "As you wish Master, but may I ask what this fetish you call for may be? I will not deny your right to it, but I wish to be prepared."

He giggled then dropped back to my neck and whispered, "I want to sleep with you snuggled in my arms tonight, Christian Axel. That is the special service I am demanding in return for saving you from the father."

I closed my eyes and let out a sigh of relief. "Thank you for the mercy, Master."

Master Leo pulled away and took back up my leash. I followed behind him in high protocol to the Great Hall feeling torn emotionally within. On the one hand I never felt surer I was going to make it to the sacred bolt cutters. That made the silver around my throat a bit less heavy for the first time since the Dungeon Master locked the shiny metal on me.

Yet, the darkness of my soul seemed more pitch black than ever. I had sold myself to my own father's foul lusting and covered my hands in the blood of others. All that just so I could walk out the Haus door a mostly free man. I wondered if maybe it would not have been more honorable to end my pathetic life before anyone else got hurt, including me.

I was deep in thought when we arrived at the nearly empty Great Hall. It was after ten that night and most of the Dominants had left for their apartments. The cooks would only be working another hour and Master Leo was in a rush to get his dinner. I almost missed the pretty blond as she rushed past me to hail down another server on their way to the kitchen.

Seeing that the beautiful girl of my dreams was still working the floor snapped me out of my depressive self-introspection. I tracked her with my eyes and found my face break into a goofy smile while I watched her.

Master Leo and I were sat at a table in the back. Thankfully not that one I had been blood bonded on. I went to take my chair next to him when I suddenly recalled Master Peter's indiscretion with me earlier. I winced then shot a look at Master Leo realizing I couldn't chance waiting around to attend to that pressing clean up matter. I have not been having a string of good luck lately. I decided it better to fix the situation before I forgot.

"Master. I need to be excused to the washroom please." I recalled there was a half bathroom in the very back of the Hall.

He nodded. "Hurry up, meine hase. You don't mess around long in there. Come right back. I want you to eat something." I took off with speed to the small room.

I found the place unoccupied and attended my cleansing with rapid skill. I was unhappy about having to deal with the contaminated water but decided to use some of Master Leo's antidote the second I got back to his apartment. I was trying to decide how to hide items for future mobile hygiene needs when I exited the bathroom. I was so deep in thought that I smacked right into the female black collar that I had been fawning over for days.

She and I both let out a yelp. Neither of us fell but we did reflexively grab the other to steady our own flesh from the collision. She looked into my face with her cheeks turning red as her lips with embarrassment as she noticed her hands around my waist.

I chuckled that her soft skin and huge breasts were rubbing into my arms and chest from our accidental embrace. “Uhm, hello…beautiful.” *Hey, I didn’t know the girls name. Cut me some slack.*

Da girl dropped her gaze coyly. “I do apologize Mad Maxx. I didn’t mean to uhm, I didn’t see you coming out.” She let go of me and backed up quickly still blushing with a smile.

I looked to make sure Master Leo was busy, he was yapping with a FemDom buddy of his, and wasn’t watching me. “You know my name?”

She nodded. “Who doesn’t know the legendary Mad Maxx in this Haus?”

I shrugged. “Actually, that is untrue. No one knows me in this place, they only think they do. I would like you to know me though. Do you have a name?”

She giggled and turned even redder. “My name is Elsa.”

I smiled brightly. “That name is gorgeous. It is truly worthy of the girl that comes when called by it.”

Elsa covered her mouth and shot me a wicked glance. “I would come to any name you called me by Mad Maxx.”

I swear I nearly tore out my beeches with excitement when she said that. “Uhm, can I call you then, Elsa? I swear my intentions are pure. I would like to know you better.” I of course was lying through my teeth. *I wanted to fuck that girl. I was like all fourteen year old boys, the hard on without a brain.*

The girl looked around her to make sure no one was listening then leaned in and whispered, "I would like to get to know you intimately, Mad Maxx. If you call me, then I will share with you all my secrets. Do you think you will be willing to hear what it is I tell only you?"

I went dumb immediately, like I always did around the girls, nodding in a trance. "Ja, I would listen harder to you than I ever had to anyone in my whole life if you would share such a treasure with me."

Elsa smiled seductively then breathed out. "When do you think you can find the time to spend with this unworthy girl for a deep conversation?"

I took a deep breath. "I could perhaps clear my schedule two nights from this one around midnight. Do you think you could wait to speak to me in depth until then?"

She nodded. "Ja, I am able to hold my own counsel until then. We can meet for discussion in the storage shed of the main hall. I believe that would offer a quiet place to talk."

I nearly panted in thrill. "I will be there, Elsa."

She giggled and said, "Good, I will be talking to you real soon, Mad Maxx." Then she leaned in and kissed me with speed on my lips.

I nearly swooned and hit the floor as she slipped past me, disappearing into the restroom. I wanted to stand there to see if I could get another kiss before having to head back to Master Leo's table, but it was too risky. I wouldn't dare lose my chance to sleep with this beautiful girl by getting myself caught in superficial teasing.

I walked back to my Master with a dreamy look on my face, and a fast pace in my heartbeat. This girl was hot. She wanted me. The worthless Mad Maxx. I could barely believe my good luck. I never had been any good at catching the eyes of the females. Wait a minute.

This black collar woman of rare beauty was in a hurry to give herself to the schwuler Priceless. Maybe I better be suspicious of that. Everyone seemed to be looking to fuck me over in some way or the other. But not the way this one was offering. This was simply too good to be true, wasn't it?

Where had I heard that name Elsa before? It was right on the tip of my tongue.

To Be Continued in Book 7: Priceless Lost

About Author: Alexandria May Ausman

Alexandria May Ausman in her 16th year was diagnosed with Schizophrenia. She was quickly abandoned by her foster parents. While still only a teen, she was forced to battle this devastating illness alone.

Alexandria has struggled with lack of a support system, numerous psychotic episodes, exploitation, homelessness, and an uncaring mental health system.

Alexandria raised two healthy children. After obtaining her bachelor's degree in psychology she worked as a child abuse investigator and became a diagnostic psychologist while acquiring her Master's in psychology. Alexandria never forgot the experience of 'slipping through the cracks.'

Her life's goal is to help people suffering abuse and/or mental illness have access to necessary services. By accident, she became a model of 'gothic attire' and the World Goth Queen.

She began writing a fictionalized account of her life experiences after a catastrophic return of psychotic symptoms. Today, Alexandria is retired, and homebound due to crippling symptoms of Schizophrenia. She currently lives in Tallahassee, Florida, with her loving husband and a loyal support dog

www.ingramcontent.com/pod-product-compliance
Lightning Source LLC
LaVergne TN
LVHW020654110826
845149LV00012B/1993

* 9 7 8 1 9 6 3 3 3 5 0 0 2 *